The Song Seekers

The Song Seekers

SASWATI SENGUPTA

zubaan

Zubaan
an imprint of Kali for Women
128B Shahpur Jat
1st floor
New Delhi 110 049
Email: contact@zubaanbooks.com
www.zubaanbooks.com

First published by Zubaan, 2011

10 9 8 7 6 5 4 3 2

ISBN: 978 93 81017 03 6
Ebook ISBN: 978-93-81017-48-7

Grateful acknowledgement is made for permission to use the extract on page 327 which appeared in Eric Hobsbawm: *Interesting Times* (Allen Lane, 2002).

Zubaan is an independent feminist publishing house based in New Delhi, India, with a strong academic and general list. It was set up as an imprint of the well-known feminist house Kali for Women and carries forward Kali´s tradition publishing world quality books to high editiorial and production standards. "Zubaan" means tongue, voice, language, speech in Hindustani. Zubaan is a non-profit publisher, working in the areas of the humanities social sciences, as well as in fiction, general non-fiction, and books for young adults that celebrate difference, diversity and equality, especially for and about the children of India and South Asia under its imprint Young Zubaan.

Typeset by: Jojy Philip
Printed at Raj Press, R-3 Inderpuri, New Delhi 110 012

❀

For
Ma and Baba
who told us stories

❀

*A*LL THAT THE CHILD COULD *see were her sister's feet. Across the width of the darkened room. Through the half opened slats. And her saree. A riot of colour on the white bed. The small feet thrashing and thrashing as though in agony.*

Terror made her hold her small frame tight. Instinctively. But that could not stop the tremors. The pillow must be hurting Di. Stuffing her nose. Blocking the air. Was this that dark secret about marriage that older women always talked about?

She had not liked this marriage. It was no fun from the beginning.

She remembered her cousin's wedding. Her grandfather's big house had come alive with laughter and music. A rich and heavy smell of flowers and food had hung in the air. And Didi had led the pack of children allowed to run wild for those few heady, chaotic days.

This hurried affair with strangers while they were on a holiday – pilgrimage Ma called it – was so very different. "All that will happen later, once we go back home," Ma had looked askance at father and then sniffed into her saree. Baba had nodded, "Yes it will. And our village will have a temple too. The Devi temple of Kynsa Mati." The temple bells of the holy Sita kunda of Chandranath in Chittagong had clanged at just that point.

"Will this groom come too?" She had wrinkled her nose.

"Of course. And don't say groom. He is your brother-in-law now." Ma had looked at her with red-rimmed eyes. "I will be the patron of the temple and he the priest." Her father had smiled.

Her tongue was bloating up in her mouth. Thick and heavy and dry. So dry that it could not let slide a word. Leave alone the scream stuck in her throat.

"Ma. Ma."

The thudding inside her bony chest was beginning to hurt.

Her captive breath escaped. In a long wheeze. Despite her.

The man inside the shadowy room pricked up his ears. Alert and taut. But he did not seem to be loosening his hold on the pillow pressed upon Di's face.

Was there a smell? Coming from the room? Dark and wet?

Her small hands, sweating, threatened to slide off the latticed slat of the window.

And make a noise. She knew that she should not have been there. Ma had told her so.

But Di had looked at her. So appealingly.

She could not even remember when Di had looked at her thus last. Older siblings are naturally arrogant and Di was seven to her five. Moreover marriage had plucked Di straight into an adult womanly space a few days ago. Di had turned up her nose at the mention of games. All games. Even those you play sitting in one corner of a room.

Traitor. Wait till we get back home, she had thought.

But resentment and rancour melted away when Di tugged at her saree and said, "Don't go." She was not used to it. Di never pleaded, she always gave orders.

Shut up. Do what I say. Fetch. Carry. Not like this. Not here. Not now. Go away.

"Don't go." "Don't go." The pleading words rendered Di a stranger.

"I have to. I am not supposed to be here. Ma said so when she left this room." But she could not get up and leave.

And so the two sisters had sat there on the bed. Still and quiet. And Di held her saree. She would remember this all her life: the small fist holding her saree tight. Reversing their relationship in a minute.

"I must go," she said again, "Ma will twist my ears, if she gets to know."

Di did not say anything this time. But her lips trembled and her eyes filled with tears. The old fatithful maid peeped in and called her in rasping tones. "So there you are. Come away now, come downstairs. Let *your sister be." The sunken eyes of the old woman measured Di from the doorway. The voice softened, "Don't be scared baby. The night will be over soon. I will wake you up and take you away in the morning." But before Di could say anything the old faithful went away. Wiping her eyes. Muttering about women. And fate.*

The wicks burnt shorter. Something crackled in the lamp's oil. The flame quivered.

They heard the voices first. Male.

There was leashed anger in two. In the other a pleading conciliation which rendered it unfamiliar, not the voice of the father that they knew. And he did not seem to be having the last word either.

Then footsteps.

Di tightening her clutch.

Footsteps drawing closer and closer.

It was she who prised open the fist from her saree then.

"Don't go." Di tried to grab her as she slid off the bed. Di's saree slipped off too from her head where Ma had so carefully drawn it.

"Don't go." Di said again.

Strange she did not like it. This tear-laced pleading from the superior sibling she thought she would never humble. "I will be nearby," she hissed and melted out of the room and into the long verandah. It was then she noticed that two of the wooden slats of the louvered window were askew. It offered her a view of the room. And she paused there.

A lifetime ago.

The thrashing on the bed had been reduced to an occasional tremor. A convulsion. A twitch. The man sat by Di's side now. Calm and quiet. But holding the pillow over Di's face still. And doing something else to her.

Gradually Di's feet slowed down too. Defeated. Tamed silent.

Her own vision was blurring.

Her hands slackened their hold on the window. She felt death, though she had never been this close to it. She felt too the liquid trace of her tremors. Warm. It trickled down her thighs to form a dark puddle at her feet. And moved down her cheek too. But even as she lifted one fist to wipe her eyes the man got up.

In her mind the male voices growled again.

"You lied! Your blood is tainted. You are no Kulin! You tricked us into this marriage."

"Don't be angry."

"Kulin or not?"

"There must be a way out. Trust me. And the temple? I will be generous...."

"Trust you?" The voice rose.

She fled then. Even as her wet saree caught at her feet and the tears coursed down her cheek.

The angry voices throbbed the fatal chant in her head.

"Your blood is tainted."

She tried to run ahead of it.

"You tricked us into this marriage."

Choking on her sobs she almost fell and then picked herself up. She must tell what she had seen and known. She must. She must.

Along the verandah she ran. Down the stairs. Towards the rooms below.

Into what she thought was sanctuary.

❋ One ❋

IT WAS A BALMY SUMMER evening in the month of May in 1962 when Uma stepped out of a taxi and gazed at Kailash for the first time. Arguably the house was at its best then. It was the magic hour of dusk. Godhuli lagna they called it – the time when the cows come home, raising dust. The soft glow of the setting sun lent a rare refulgence to the old building, smoothening the peeling paint and turning the aged white to the pure magic of orange, yellow and pink. A black cursive hand etched in a simple slab of white marble proclaimed, 'Kailash'.

The big wrought iron gates were open and the pebbles along the driveway were contoured soft in the light. The taxis came to a halt between the two pillars in the porch formed by the curve of the first floor verandah. Three wide steps, chequered black and white, led into the house. The panelled doors were a rich mahogany. Palm fronds swayed gently in the evening breeze that is peculiar to the city of Calcutta.

Uma stepped out of the taxi as though in a dream. She had not expected a house like this. Kailash was old but gracious and firm still. Yet the half-shuttered windows and the soft silence hinted concealments. In Uma's fancy the house whispered and to her alone: "Where have you been all these years Uma, while I have been waiting for you, my being steeped in stories, waiting, waiting for you?" Uma gazed in wonder at Kailash and fell in love instantly.

Love is of course easily induced when the material prospects are bright. The house signalled the wealth of a bygone era as well as the comfortable prosperity of the present. Evidently the wealth had also translated into culture covering the gross brambles which often litter the path to prosperity. The present owner Ashutosh Chattopadhyay had already manifested his liberal modernity through the invitation to the prospective bride's family, including the bride herself, to visit Kailash in an iconoclastic reversal of norms.

"Of course they must see each other," Ashutosh Chattopadhyay had said in a rich baritone that suited to perfection his tall, patrician looks, "You are visitors to the city. We live here and if something comes of the proposal so will your daughter. Let her know what she will be getting into. Come to Kailash, all of you, for tea. I insist."

"Very progressive," said Uma's uncle a little uncertainly.

"A bit excessive," his wife admonished.

"Is the son like the father?" asked Uma's mother somewhat anxiously.

The son, the prospective groom, had been to the La Martiniere School and in keeping with family traditions, Presidency College, Calcutta and then the School of Printing, London. The family owned the well-known printing house, The Ganges Press, which was doing well and would hopefully continue to do so given the qualifications, and connections, of the owners. Also, there was no mother-in-law. The good lady had died when the son was only five. Undeniably the gift and the packaging were made for marriage. And perhaps love too. No wonder a quiver of excitement ran through Uma as she saw Kailash for the first time.

It also helped that nothing of the inside was visible and the foundation of Kailash was well camouflaged. But even if it had been open to view, would it have made a difference? Can the writhing of a small seven year old girl's body in death agony fracture the promise of a cushioned future? And this death, the thrash of terror and sweat, the holding in of the warm breath to let the body grow cold, was in another era and another place. Surely such instances of female death are not peculiar to Kailash? Don't whispers run that there are many houses of greater worth in this very region of North Calcutta that have also muffled female lives and tears?

Yes. Calcutta rests on a clay bed made of sandy layers that hold a vast amount of water deposited by the rivers of the Gangetic delta.

But the city appears impervious to this immense water reservoir. The houses belonging to the city, likewise, pay no heed to tears coursing through their inner chambers. Moreover, in Kailash's case the unfortunate incident was not even in this house, though undeniably it helped found it. And the girl anyhow may have died in a couple of years of other causes: malaria, cholera, childbirth or snake bite. Why remember it then and dredge up unrequited tears?

In the magical hour of that summer evening, the tears, macabre or maudlin, did not touch Kailash. Certainly there was no stink of death about it. Kailash invited Uma, in the manner of its gracious and self-assured host, to step inside, stay there and explore it for stories which lay layer upon layer. Uma was more than willing, comfortable in the knowledge that the rest would be taken care of too.

How could she have known that water finds its level naturally?

※ ※

Ma had always warned that Uma's passion for losing herself in stories would be her undoing. But then Uma had been brought up on a rich and varied diet of stories from the very beginning. Uma's grandfather, Dadu, had told her tales of travels, discoveries and inventions. Uma had listened obediently enough but was quick to turn to Thakma, her grandmother, to take her to the more enthralling land of gods, demons and fairies.

"How can a child enjoy your dry tales from school books?" Thakma, who had never seen the inside of a school, would reprimand Dadu with some glee.

"Don't fill the child's head with a pack of fantasy." Dadu would say mildly. He had a gentle voice that never rose, not even while discussing politics. The family said that Uma's soft cadence came from him though she looked more like her mother with large, liquid eyes overwhelming a slightly long face.

"Tell me a story." Uma would intervene.

"Once upon a time…" Thakma would begin, pointedly ignoring Dadu.

Uma's mother had told her stories too when she had the child to herself and the time to spare in a family that consisted not only of her parents-in-law but also a younger brother-in-law and his wife – Uma's Kaku and Kaki. Ma's stories, whether of a woodcutter's family or a king's, were replete with danger lurking everywhere and forlorn girls waiting to be rescued. "Once upon a time…"

"Tell me a story…." was Uma's constant plea.

"What kind?"

"Any. Please…. "

"Ummm….The little girl's name was…."

"No, no, no. Not like this. Begin from the beginning. Say once upon a time…."

No one realized that listening to a story also provoked for little Uma a great deal of anxiety. What if it did not draw to a neat and happy conclusion? The magic words, "Once upon a time," reassured her. Dimly she could perceive that the story was, and yet was not, a part of the world that she inhabited. Its pain and grief were only illusions of reality.

"Once upon a time …."

Uma loved this incantatory beginning.

But houses of course cannot tell stories. Except as a metaphor. Or in that genre called fantasy whose status rises and falls in tandem with the worth of vulgar realism. But just imagine if this house, named Kailash after the mythical abode of Shiva, could tell a story, what could it reveal?

"I am born…"

But who can tell after all these years when Kailash was born for its foundation goes deep, very very deep, and is shaped out of myriad intentions and desires.

❀ ❀

Kailash germinated from a matrix: part geographic genetic, part a historical seizing of opportunities.

The silted clay from the Ganga shaped the village Kolkata, before memory began, in the area that came to be known as

Bengal. Thus a fabled future was set in motion for a metropolis to be mutated out of mud. Later, many centuries later, Job Charnock, a junior member of the Council of Kashimbazar of the East India Company saw its potential as a good landing place even as Captain Heath failed to establish the Company's new Bengal headquarter at Chittagong. The English defeated Siraj, the Nawab of Bengal, in the Battle of Plassey on the 23rd of June, 1757. Eight years later Shah Alam I granted the Dewani of the province to the British. So rose Kolkata.

And so too the foundation of Kailash, the buniyad, that shaped its claim to a status as the city elite, grew from strength to strength as the various depressions of a low lying city got gradually filled by its own trash.

Kailash stands on a strip of land, Dalimbagan, that lies between two areas of great renown – Jorabagan and Jorasanko in Kolkata or Calcutta now in her anglicized avatar. Forresti and Olifres's map of 1742 marks Jorabagan near the present Rabindra Kanan (Beadon Street). It was here that Captain Commandant William Holcomb proposed to build a defence against the invading Marathas. By the next century, Jorabagan could boast of housing the Hindu elites of society such as the Thakurs of Pathuriaghata, the Singhabahini Malliks, the descendents of successful Dewans like Badyanath Mukherji, Radhamadhav Banerji and Sukhamoy Ray of Posta. The area adjoining Jorabagan is Jorasanko. It is named after the twin (jora) Sankos which could be either the two wooden bridges or the two temples devoted to Shankar or Shiva. No one really knows now for certain. But what is known, and remembered, is that Jorasanko boasted of eminent 'native' residents such as the Tagores and Kaliprasanna Sinha who translated the Sanskrit epic *Mahabharata* into Bengali and satirized the city in the guise of a screech owl.

Kailash may have been one of the many houses built by the Sheth family who owned a 'garden' somewhere between Jorabagan and Jorasanko. Throughout the latter half of the 19th century the garden shrank and the houses grew. These belonged to the nouveau riche who still craved the identity of a 'babu' in Calcutta unaware that the real elite had moved on to become the western educated, professional urban bhadralok. The Dalimbagan houses, including Kailash, of mixed stucco, baroque and rococo, though less modest than the mansions in Jorabagan or Jorasanko, remained a material mark of the desired social claim.

No one remembers who built Kailash or lived there initially. But it was bought again in 1885 by Dukari Mukhopadhyay. He himself however continued to live in Kumortuli, an area named after the potters who had settled there but where also had lived some of the most famous 'black' zamindars of the eighteenth century such as Nandaram Sen and Govindaram Mitra – the native deputies to the English Collectors. Dukari Mukhopadhyay's family had made its fortune by hanging on to the coat tails, well, the dhoti really, of men such as these. It had helped too that the Mukhopadhyays were Brahmans so that on religious occasions, somewhat different from conducting business, they could enhance the rituals of their Bengali Kayastha, and later Marwari, benefactors.

Dukari bestowed Kailash to a young student of Presidency College, Shashishekhar Chattopadhyay, along with a printing press and a daughter as the 19th century was drawing to a close. Both the press and the girl were ten years old when the marriage deal was struck. Both seemed to have served Shashishekhar well as can be evinced from Ashutosh's presence in Kailash – Shashishekhar's only son and the current proprietor of The Ganges Press. Ashutosh's son Rudrashekhar was now to be married. Ashutosh's sister was a neighbour of Uma's uncle at Ballygunge Place, South Calcutta. Uma and her family from Delhi were the houseguests of her maternal uncle as part of a one-month-in-every-year summer ritual when the proposal of marriage was suggested.

✿✿

In Ballygunge Place, the family was still lingering over breakfast avidly discussing the public and private lives of Suchitra Sen who had lit up the Bengali cine screen and had even worked in a Hindi film, *Bambai ka Babu* with the charismatic Dev Anand. Uma's

Calcutta cousins, who had not been allowed to see the film, wanted to know yet again if Suchitra's Hindi was really as atrocious as a section of the press had made it out to be.

"Uma reminds me of her," said her fond aunt and then turned towards the kitchen and called out to the maid, "Didn't I tell you that our niece looks like Suchitra Sen?" The maid came out of the kitchen with dripping hands, glad to be part of the jollity for a moment, "Hmmm. All we need now is an Uttam Kumar for her."

The room was still echoing with laughter when Uma's uncle suddenly said, "I have a proposal for Uma's marriage. Rudrashekhar Chattopadhyay. Son of Ashutosh Chattopadhyay. Great grandson of the famous poet Neelkantha. The Chattopadhyays of Dalimbagan who own The Ganges Press. Both father and son studied in London after graduating from Presidency."

"Does he look like Uttam Kumar?" A cheeky cousin intervened.

"Are you serious?" Uma's father edged forward in his chair.

"Why would they..." asked Uma's mother who believed that greeting a happy turn of events with suspicion paradoxically helped them materialize.

"The Chattopadhyas want an educated bride from a decent and cultured Brahman family. They want a girl who can converse in English and is interested in literature but one who knows Bengali too. Thank god you have taught our language to your children. Otherwise in Calcutta..." Mamu paused.

Uma lowered her eyes. The dining table dully shone back a misshapen face amidst its whorls and grains. Calcutta? She thought, a little flustered, get married to someone from Calcutta?

Calcutta had been the British capital of India prior to Delhi until 1911. The transfer of power naturally precluded friendly ties between the two cities. Uma and her brother, Delhi loyalists, were quite used to having their city slighted by Calcutta relatives: that Calcutta had culture and Delhi agriculture, that the Hindu college of Calcutta, which later became the Presidency College, had already been established in 1817 and by 1820 nearly 10,000 Bengalis knew some sort of English and Delhi's most prestigious St. Stephen's college was not only born much later but also was initially attached to Calcutta's Presidency College or that Delhi could only provide Tinda in summer while in Calcutta, only goats condescended to eat that gourd. Seared, Uma and her brother had felt terribly betrayed when their parents too joined the raucous laughter at the last comment made by an elderly realtive. The partisan view had not changed much, even in 1962 when Calcutta was beginning to gasp with its increasing dependents and decreasing income.

Calcutta? Uma's heart fluttered though she said nothing naturally. She had not expected to be married in that summer of 1962 though she knew that the search for the groom would start now that she had finished her B.A Honours in English Literature from Miranda House, Delhi University. Uma would join M.A. of course but it would in effect be the period of anticipation and gestation. Marriage was an inevitable. But Uma had never seen herself as settling after marriage in Calcutta. And certainly not in Dalimbagan, North Calcutta.

Uma's family had been living in Kashmere Gate, Delhi, for two generations. They did continue to have ties with Calcutta but most of their Calcutta relatives stayed in the up and pushing southern section of the city that claimed modernity to cover its evident lack of history and derisively called the North Calcuttan Syambazarer Sasibabu with the dental 's' markedly pronounced as in 'hiss'. This peculiar intonation of the 's' was south Calcutta's mocking stereotype of the older quarter of the metropolis that had once been the habitat of the rich babus when the city was the nerve center of imperial Britain and like all stereotypes this too was not entirely false. The older northern quarter of the metropolis had had its day when Calcutta was the second city of the Empire, outranked only by London. The march of time was now edging it towards the gathering dusk of genteel poverty though it still had its moments.

The two degrees from London across two generations, though not quite like tripos from Cambridge, worked their magic on Uma. They catapulted Dalimbagan into a realm at least worth consideration. The area, though in North Calcutta, was after all sandwiched between Jorasanko and Jorabagan. And Uma was curious too. It was not quite the usual norm, this invitation after the first round of talks when families are vetted and prospects measured, that the prospective bride accompany her parents, her two uncles and one aunt, to the Chattopadhyay residence Kailash, rather than the other way round, in order to be 'seen'.

※ ※

Kailash naturally featured in that evening's conversation. It must be admitted that it was a worthy conversation piece too. The Mughal, the Anglo Indian, the Jews, the Armenian, the Marwari had all contributed to its inception and growth. But the past that was sought for it by Rudra's aunt who was Uma's uncle's neighbour and the chief negotiator for the marriage was unequivocally caste Hindu. She pegged it on a divine realm which was a measure of the success of the meeting. Uma was addressed in a manner both jocular and jaded: "I hope that Shakespeare and Byron have not made you forget your own culture? I trust you know who lives in Kailash? Rudra of course but who with him?" The florid tittering signalled an imminent marriage. Uma did not answer but a blush rose, hot and visible, from her neck upwards. It was rather charming.

Of course Uma did know who lived in Kailash. She had known it in fact ever since she was born. Kailash was the abode of the divine couple, Shiva and Sati. Uma's grandmother, Thakma, had brought home the gods and the goddesses every afternoon for her granddaughter. She had told Uma that Shiva was a carefree and powerful god. His wife Sati was careworn but chaste and devoted. But Shiva loved his wife and they lived happily enough in their mountain home, Kailash.

"In the mountains?"

"Yes, Kailash is in the Himalayas. The god stays there with his wife."

Little Uma, twirling an end of Thakma's soft cotton saree tried to visualise a big house perched safely on top of a triangle. But it kept swaying precariously. Thakma carried on, unaware of the child's anxiety.

"One day the wealthy father of the goddess Sati organized a yagna and invited all the gods but Sati's husband Shiva to it."

"Why?"

"Daksa, Sati's father did not like his son-in-law who had no sense of discrimination and mixed with the low and the outcastes of society, even sitting down to have a smoke with them."

"And Sati? Didn't she want to go?"

"Shiva did not want his wife, Sati, to go uninvited to her parents even though everyone else was going. But Sati insisted."

"Why? She missed her mother?"

"Hmm?"

"Did Sati want to meet her mother?"

"That is female fate," gently Thakma smoothed the child's hair and grew quiet.

"And then? Thakma. What happened?"

"Sati really should have listened to her husband. Sati's father Daksa abused and taunted his son-in-law Shiva in front of all the honoured and divine guests who had come for the occasion. It was too much for the chaste wife to bear. Sati protested against her father's public humiliation of her husband by giving up her own life."

"Sati died?"

"Imagine! All because she could not bear to hear her husband thus insulted."

"And Shiva?"

"When the news reached Shiva in Kailash, he charged over to Daksa's house. He saw his dear wife Sati dead. The usually carefree Shiva transformed into the terrifying deity of wrath and destruction. In a mad frenzy he danced and danced, clasping his dead wife. Daksa and the other deities cowered in fear. The heavens shook and with them the world."

"Did everyone else die then?"

"No. Shiva was restored to his senses by the severing of Sati's body by Narayan. Narayan's discus cut Sati's body into fragments till Shiva had nothing to hold onto. Thus ended the mad dance of destruction."

Uma could see the hands, the legs, the head, the torso, the fingers of Sati slowly falling through space trailing blood. Briefly she shut her eyes but the limbs continued to rain from the sky staining the earth red.

Uma twisted Thakma's saree with a greater degree of agitation this time. "What happenned to the pieces?"

"Pieces?"

"Of Sati's body?"

"The severed parts of the body of Sati scattered over the world. The places where they fell became holy pilgrimages and came to be known as Pithasthan. The world was thus saved."

Uma willed the limbs to disappear into an array of temples. It was not easy. The trails of blood would not go away. She changed track.

"And Shiva? He lived in Kailash all alone?"

"Shiva sank into deep mourning. He retreated within himself to cope with his loss. Clearly the world could not allow him to carry on thus, mourning a wife."

"Why?"

"Really! He is a man. He has to work."

Uma mulled over it for a while, thinking of Baba and Kaku. "And then?"

A smile played on Thakma's face. She bent and kissed the soft face of the child, "The chaste and devoted wife Sati was reborn as Uma to shake Shiva out of his grief stricken asceticism. And so dear Uma, much loved Uma, was born to be Shiva's wife. She observed such severe penance to marry Shiva that even the despondent god was forced to take note. He then took Uma to Kailash to help forget his grief."

Uma nestled deep into the folds of Thakma's saree.

Of course Uma knew who lived in Kailash.

Kailash was where Uma was meant to be. She knew that

tradition, as preserved, had ordained her for Shiva. If he would have her.

And was not Rudra but another name for Shiva?

☙ ☙

Rudra Chattopadhyay's tall frame was slack upon the sofa. Like his father, he too was rather striking to look at. Indeed the relationship between the father and the son was unmistakable as also the hint of an alloy. It was as though someone had gently stroked the perfect Chattopadhyay features with her own imprint. Shadowy but there in Rudra.

Rudra's long legs stretched out a little. His posture suggested ease rather than indifference. Nobody could have said looking at the unruffled surface that there were strong undercurrents buffeting his being.

"A girl from Delhi." His aunt had thus mentioned her neighbour's niece on a visit to Kailash and then much else too about Uma but that is what had struck Rudra. 'A girl from Delhi' is what he had seized upon. "Why don't you meet her?" his aunt had asked somewhat archly having finished the catalogue of Uma's suitability for Kailash.

"Why not?" Rudra had said surprising himself and his father too.

That was then.

But now with 'the girl from Delhi' sitting with her family across him, Rudra wondered at his move. It was not so easy to checkmate Kailash. He had been rash and a retreat would have to be maneuvered. It was always possible to retreat. Rudra knew that, had learnt that, in Kailash. He leaned slightly to his right and placed the cup on the table, his calm movements at odds with the growing restlessness within him. He was good at such camouflage too, having learnt from a very young age, since he was five practically, to hide the eddies and swirls within him from Kailash.

It had not been easy at first. His throat would hurt, his eyes prick, his muscles would quiver and shiver. But Rudra, even though a child, had learnt to discipline his body. Lying quiet between his sleeping grandparents the five year old Rudra would focus away from himself, stare into the depths of the bedroom and try to dispel the thick dark. As the night yielded its shapes to him, he would slowly grow calm. Later, when he started sleeping alongside his father he would sometimes press his fingertips together as he measured the dark, feeling the gentle vibration of his body course through his fingers till he drifted into sleep.

Once upon a time he had tried other methods like talking. But that did not help. He could not quite say what he wished to though what he wanted to say seemed to be plain enough. Plain enough for him at any rate.

"She fell down the stairs."

The five year old Rudra put an arm around his father's leg stopping him as they were going downstairs for breakfast.

"Who?"

The child stood still on the landing. Ashutosh felt the small hand tighten its clutch on his trousers. He knelt down besides his son, disentangled the soft hand and asked gently, "Who fell down?"

The soft lips quivered a bit. The child leaned into his father. His whisper caressed Ashutosh's shoulder and his cheek felt damp. Rudra's hair was wet from the bath but even so a few strands had spiked up from the crown as though in rebellion. Ashutosh smoothened his son's hair, picked him up and then cradling him safe in his arms went down the stairs of Kailash.

Rudra did not remember this conversation though.

The conversation that he remembered took place a couple of nights later though it was not the matter but the mood that stayed with him.

His father was telling him the story of Tarzan. There were just the two of them in bed. The night was quiet outside. The bedside lamp was on. A gentle sense of well being, the precursor to sleep, was beginning to soften Rudra's small body. It made him think of his mother. His mother who was not there, who had always told him stories but not of Tarzan, who probably did not know the

story and would never hear Baba say it either. In a moment the
child was wide awake. His chest felt heavy, his throat hurt and his
eyes pricked and threatened to fill with hot tears. He wanted to
scream and shout but when he spoke it was in a voice that only
quivered.

"Baba."

Ashutosh paused.

"We were there in the afternoon. We were in her room when
she... grandmother... came in."

"Where?"

"The room on one and a half storey. The day Ma fell."

Ashutosh grew quiet. Rudra felt the tears beginning to escape
from his eyes. His small legs started to jiggle as though of their own
volition. He wished Baba would say something. His own throat
was beginning to hurt very much. Then Baba turned and put an
arm around him to drew him up close against his big, warm body
and told him that his mother had died of a violent and raging fever.
"It happens."

Gradually Rudra's body grew quiet in his father's arms.

Ashutosh spoke again. "We have to cope Rudra. You and I." And
then it seemed as though Baba's throat was hurting too as he said,
"Sometimes I can't believe that I will never see her again. Or hear
her voice."

Rudra lay listening to his father's heart beat beneath his ears.
Suddenly he asked, "Can we go away from Kailash?"

The room grew still.

And then Baba talked of his own father Shashishekhar who
had come from a village in Chittagong to Kailash in Calcutta. And
about his grandfather, the poet Neelkantha who had ordained that
the men in the family be named after Shiva. And Kailash was the
abode of the god.

Neelkantha, Shashishekhar, Ashutosh, Rudrashekhar.

Kailash chanted in soft threatening whispers, rising to claim the
child.

Little Rudra shivered.

It took Rudra a long while to fall asleep that night. But his father held him.

The fading intensity of Rudra's memory created less and less ripples in his body and mind but he did still try to break Kailash's hold on him.

The hall in Kailash was resounding with animated conversation about India's victory over England in the fourth test at Eden Gardens earlier in the year. Voices rose discussing the relative merits of Pataudi (whom Ashutosh called Pataudi, Jr.), Borde, Durani and Jaisimha. The soft chink of teacups was drowned entirely. Suddenly impatient, Rudra longed for a cigarette and stretched his legs again. Uma looked up from where she sat holding a cup of tea. Their gaze caught and held for the briefest of moments in the room full of people.

What a fine pair of eyes, Rudra thought in sudden wonder.

⁂

"Was it enough?" asked Uma's parents of each other, as the train sped through the night, away from Calcutta and Uma who had been with them for twenty summers.

It was a month since that first visit to Kailash. A month of flurried activities. Cards, furniture, utensils, gifts, lights, priest, flautists, flowers, feasts…. The Chattopadhyays had of course asked for nothing. But it was an alliance between two educated and cultured bhadra families who would know what to give and how to receive. And Uma was a good girl. She too asked for nothing for her wedding. In fact, a couple of times Uma did ask her Baba was not this or that too expensive? Each time his heart swelled with pride at her gentle consideration and was then followed by a clutching pain that this was all that he could buy for her, no bed of gold, no foot stool of silver. "I have enough," he reassured her and indeed he did for had he not saved for this occasion since the day a daughter was born to him?

Uma had accepted, like a good girl, her parent's role in shaping her future; paying for it was a part of it. Her virtue lay in accepting their wisdom and the gifts. So she had been taught, so she did.

Would it not have shattered her parents otherwise? Besides, she had never been allowed to indulge her senses like this on grounds primarily of principles. The family took pride in that.

Jewellery, glistening gold, the pale of pearl amidst a shining cascade of ruby, emerald and topaz – most of the twinkling haul emerged from her mother's collection, some from Thakma's and one from Kaki's. Sarees, silk and cotton, palest pink, fiery red, azure blue, a new-born green, a richer verdant, sunny yellow and a dramatic black to suit the westernized modern taste, were bought. "Good grief!" Thakma exclaimed, "the price! It would have been enough to buy a thick gold chain in my days." Her old hands lingered on the smooth silk though.

Uma glowed in red and gold during the wedding.

"He is better than Uttam Kumar," the cheeky cousin whispered in her ears.

As instructed, Rudra's arms encircled Uma and her soft hands were placed in his larger ones. It was a very public moment.

The priest chanted in Sanskrit.

Uma's parents, in the dark of the train speeding towards Delhi, realized together that the most important phase of their life was over. They had married and nourished two lives, as was the purpose of their marriage, indeed of their lives. Their son was on his way to becoming an engineer from one of the premier institutions of independent India. He would soon be on his feet. Their daughter was married. She would be taken care of. They had done their bit. Their bit was over.

Over, over, over, over.

The train surged faster and faster into the dark of the night.

Uma's parents did not voice the pain of the void. They belonged to a generation that had been brought up to believe that physical gestures of intimacy between married couples were not just coarse and crude but immoral too. They did not hold each other. Unable to sleep they just sat. Next to each other, without touching.

The others slept.

✿✿

Uma sat in a new crisp yellow cotton saree, surrounded by the female clan of the Chattopadhyays. She had been married for a little over a week now. She had sat thus everyday. Kailash was loud with voices, a blur of faces and names. But now the festivities appeared to be drawing to an end. The guests from outside Calcutta were departing one by one. Those from the city itself who had been coming over regularly after breakfast, to stay on till dinner, were on the wane too. The monsoon seemed late that year. The heat was oppressive and sultry.

Virtually every guest told Uma that she was a very fortunate girl. They repeated for her the family history, the fame and fortune of the Chattopadhyays who had chosen her. She learnt of Neelkantha, the famed ancestral poet who had composed the *Chandimangal*. The poem was written in Chittagong but it acquired a cult status all over Bengal much later, during the turbulent days of the anti-colonial Swadeshi movement of the years between 1903 and 1908 following the partition of the province. Neelkantha's *Chandimangal* had almost rivalled Bankimchandra Chattopadhyay's novel *Anandamath* in those days. The guests talked with reverence of Neelkantha's ascetic lifestyle and his divine poetry. They mentioned the integrity and industry of his only son, Shashishekhar, who came to Calcutta from Chittagong to study in Presidency College and then set up the printing press. Yet, for all his exposure to western culture – Presidency College had real white men on the faculty those days – Shashishekhar remained a devout Hindu Brahman. He was the one who printed his father's *Chandimangal*, thus preserving a part of Bengal's rich tradition. Apparently he got the printing machine washed with the holy water of the Ganga for this work and shaped the book like a punthi, the traditional hand-written manuscripts. His masculine public enterprise was matched by the piety of his home presided over by Haimanti, his wife. Their son, Ashutosh was mentioned with pride. His dignity and decorum were evident in the way in which he had carried on after losing his wife at such a young age. Most men would have rushed to a second wedding straight from the funeral but look at him! Ashutosh went to London in the '30s and was a connoisseur of Western art, literature and music but he still wore a perfect dhoti when required. With a lineage such as this Rudra no doubt would be a saint too. Did any girl ever have such luck in marriage?

There is a belief in some quarters that there are only three basic plots for stories: birth, marriage and death. The world over, these archetypal plots are being constantly hashed and rehashed. Telling is all. Uma loved stories. But this, this family history of the Chattopadhyays, she heard without variation every day. Day in and day out. The endless repetition crusted the story, making it as coarse as the food was rich – fish drowned in mustard paste or in a thick curry of ginger, garlic and onion. Uma longed for a light lentil.

A fat and lugubrious elderly lady entered the bedroom puffing. She had not been able to attend the wedding. Uma got up, touched her feet, received a cylindrical packet that must contain yet another *Tangail* saree of dubious taste and was chucked under the chin.

"Take a good look at our bride. You are the one who had said that every body looks fair in photographs." Rudra's aunt preened.

"She is fair, but our Rudra is much, much fairer," said the fat lady staring intently at Uma.

It was nothing like the last straw. But through that week Uma had been drowned by implied comparisons. Why do they always negate her family? Why did they talk as though she could hear, see or feel nothing? Why did they make her feel like a scarecrow on the Chattopadhyay landscape?

"Uma studied English in Lady Miranda college," Rudra's aunt continued with the fat lady .

The new saree with its heavy starch bit Uma's waist and the sweat trickled down just there to burn it. Her throat felt constricted by the unaccustomed weight of heavy gold.

"Miranda House," Uma said, startling even herself.

"What?"

"Miranda House. Not Lady Miranda."

Out of the corner of her eyes, Uma saw a white form enter the room with a glass of lemonade and a plate of sweets. Rudra's aunt bristled at the correction. Her eldest grand daughter was a first year student of Lady Brabourne College in Calcutta and she was keen to forge a friendship between her and Uma. Acknowledging Lady Miranda was a token of her recognition of this permissible possibility.

The fat lady looked triumphant. Uma was suddenly aware of having spoken out of turn, of being with strangers. Strangers who told her every day how lucky, and by implications unworthy, she was. She felt her eyes smart. Embarrassed, Uma turned to the white form who was now handing the plate to the fat lady. As she willed her tears away the shimmering form took a shape quite old, perhaps seventy or even more. And fair. The old lady was very, very fair. Rudra's aunt, however modern, had lost her composure for a brief while at being corrected by the new bride and stammered out an introduction.

"This is ….Pishi. You must have seen her about."

The pause before the claim of relationship was infinitesimal. The finely calibrated nuance was a disclaimer of equality. But precisely for that reason it drew Uma to the silent and waiting figure at that moment, as two strangers to a family. Partly to hide her tears and partly to prove some point she bent down and touched the old woman's feet.

Hands, gnarled but surprisingly firm, grasped her. The fingers under her chin raising her face were cool and steady though rough in texture. Uma looked up into a pair of eyes that held her gaze.

Steady and a startling green.

❧ Two ❧

THE SUN HAD TILTED NORTHWARD. The winds of summer from the Indian Ocean and the South China Sea blew into the heated continent bringing rain . The monsoon had arrived. The sky remained a variegated grey: now fleeting light, now heavy dark.

Tiptip, tuptup, tapurtupur, jhirjhir, jharjhar, jhamjham....

The Bengali devised a word to echo each fluid motion of rain.

Droplets, drizzle, downpour....

The trees tossed their freshly washed green cover even as sodden filth gathered around their stems. A damp smell hung over Calcutta, the ancient drainage of the city was soon waterlogged, the public transport was strained, rickshaws cautiously negotiated hidden craters in the slushy gullies, sneezing children splashed rebelliously into puddles and gastro-enteritis made its annual appearance. Yet Calcutta sang and ate. This was the favourite season of Bengal's special poet Rabindranath Tagore and the city hummed with his rain songs from the radio to the bathroom. Men returned from work, limp or irascible, and were soothed by steaming khichuri for dinner: red Musoor or golden yellow Mung in a duet with rice, fragrant with bay leaf, full bodied with onions and garlic or without in a purer avatar, daubed with ghee or butter and accompanied by fritters of vegetables, eggs or fish.

The less fortunate were grateful for whatever they got and ate it huddled to avoid the water dripping from their roofs.

Many did not even have the roof to bother about.

Outside Calcutta, peasants toiled with bare backs bent, dawn to dusk, day after day, in mud and water. The monsoon was called the 'badantor' or the back breaker in peasant vocabulary for this was the season when the fragile saplings of paddy had to be torn up from where they were formerly sown and transplanted in fields flooded with rain.

Bend and uproot. Bend and replant. In the rain. In the mud. From dawn to dusk.

But only thus a new lease of life could be given to the stalk. Only thus could one look forward to a golden harvest in autumn.

Yes, the monsoon had arrived with all its threats, pleasures and promises.

Uma woke up to the moving strains of Raga Malhar in the mornings that recalled the viraha of Radha separated from Krishna in another world, by the banks of another river. The music flowing from room to room melded with the pregnant grey of the sky and the rhythm of the rain.

The arrangement of the rooms in Kailash was typical and simple: a single row of rooms built around a central court. The rooms in front and back were large, those at the sides somewhat smaller. The ground floor housed the hall for formal visits, the library, the dining room, storerooms, the kitchen and the servants' quarters. But the family traditionally spent most of its time upstairs where a smaller hall was flanked by the main bedrooms. The family shrine was on the second floor that led out to a covered area and then to a large open terrace. The model signalled an opulent ambition but the proportions were much smaller as the ground to accommodate the original model was never available to Dalimbagan residents. Certainly it was not on the scale of their neighbours in Jorasanko and Jorabagan. The old houses of the really rich and famous Hindu elite were always marked by two features: the thakur dalan facing south and the nach ghar. The former enshrined the family deities of the upper caste Hindu pantheon and assured spiritual salvation. The latter, the dance hall, part Nawabi legacy, part facilitated by trading alliance with the English, signalled more naked aspirations of the flesh. The two portions were often linked.

Kailash had neither. When Shashishekar received it in marriage and built upon the basic structure, his father was still alive in the village. The status of his Calcutta house had to be that of a 'basha', a temporary residence as opposed to 'bari', the permanent home in the Chittagong village. It suited Shashishekar to remember that with deference and not build a thakur dalan. The deities were thus accommodated in the room on the terrace. Ironically though it was the basha that remained, the bari spiralling away over time, first to another province, East Bengal and later to another country, East Pakistan which would metamorphose in the unknown future into a new nation, Bangladesh.

The nach ghar Shashishekhar eschewed being the son of an ascetic Brahman poet.

The verandah in Kailash did not go all around the house but came to an end somewhere at the side with an intricate jaffrey work. But it was generous and impressive from the front with wooden jilmils. This generous front of the verandah now caught the southern breeze and brought in the sight and smell of rain but no water.

Uma lay in bed and thought with compassion of all those who had to go out in the rain to work or stay at home only to worry about damp walls, mildews, wet clothes and coal. The higher reaches of Hindustani classical music washed over her in waves as though drawn by the wild, wet wind. She had been told by her father-in-law that this music was brought by Nawab Wajid Ali Shah of Lucknow and his entourage when they came to Calcutta as the prisoners of the English in 1857. Ashutosh, who loved western classical always played Indian music during the monsoon – sometimes Tagore and sometimes the classical Hindustani Malhar. "The monsoon is peculiarly ours. There is nothing in the western world like this," Ashutosh said.

Uma stretched in bed.

Ma had repeatedly told Uma to be the first one up, to serve the morning tea to her father-in-law and husband no matter how many servants were around. "Uma get up. Do. What will you do Uma, if you don't get up early enough once you are married?" Ma had worried, like a dog with a bone, about Uma's inability to get up on her own in the morning. Kaki had suggested that they buy her a small alarm clock, one that could be slipped under the pillow if required. "Here," Kaku had surprised them with the gift wrapped clock the very next day, "The grandfather-clock of the Chattopadhyay's will stop once you enter the household. Make do with this one then."

"Must you say the inauspicious all the time?" an angry Thakma had reprimanded Kaku who had not looked in the least chastened.

But actually Uma did not really need the clock. Rudra was not only an early riser, but also liked to be by himself in the morning, driving to the club where he swam or played squash according to the weather. Considerate and courteous, he explained to Uma that he needed this oxygen to last him through the day at the Press housed in an area which had become one of Calcutta's most congested over the years. Twice a week Rudra lectured at the Jadavpore College of Printing and three times a week went to the National Tobacco Company at Agarpara to give an expert's suggestion on the running of their in-house printing work before reaching The Ganges Press by lunch time. He did not need or welcome wifely ministrations at the crack of dawn which broke rather early in the eastern city of Calcutta. He hinted, very gently, that his father may not welcome it either. Uma was a little awed for she thought of solitude, silence, squash and swimming in the morning as the prerogatives of an unfamiliar world of privileges. When a particularly heavy downpour forced Rudra to give his games a miss, he sat by the window reading the papers. The tea arrived, in a pot kept warm by a tea cosy, with thin arrowroot biscuits on a tray. Clearly the kitchen did not need Uma early in the mornings either.

Uma found a self-sufficient man in her husband. He had friends whom he met regularly at 'boy's dos'. One group was from his school and the other from college. Many overlapped. Rudra loved sports, poetry, Sherlock Holmes and Perry Mason. He also loved Calcutta. His passion for the former was evident, the latter he hid, sometimes even from himself. Uma loved going out with him, initially in response to invitations to lunches and dinners by relatives and friends and later by themselves. She luxuriated in being alone with a visibly relaxed Rudra. Inevitably he took the longer route back home. It must have been nice for him too, this companionship after the protracted solitude of his childhood and youth, despite everything.

Driving past the shanty slums being pelted with rain and already deep in slush and garbage, Rudra showed her the city. They saw the Royal Calcutta Turf Club with its glistening wet tracks, the green spaces of the Maidan speckled with umbrellas, the rampart of Fort William still white despite the downpour and the classical edifice of the Victoria Memorial under a rainbow. One morning on their way to Magnolia, Rudra took Uma to the South Park Cemetery and showed her a great granddaughter of Charles II, Fanny Burney's half brother, the sons of Captain Cook and Charles Dickens. Clearly, of the imperial rulers, one in three didn't make it through their first monsoon. And by 1830 the cemetery was full.

They walked in silence for a while. The sky rumbled.

Rudra looked at the sky, "It was a grey afternoon when I disembarked in London and certainly Tilbury Docks seemed most unlike any imperial port of my imagination."

"We read that by the early 18th century the East India Company was already England's greatest business. SK, who taught us Dickens, used to say that the profit may have spurred the industrial revolution there." Uma spoke very carefully, self-conscious of her companion, half amazed at herself for being able to engage a man such as Rudra in conversation. Her man. It was a novel experience and exhilarating too, almost sexual in its excitement.

"And here? By the second half of the 18th century the traditional trade and industry were already on the decline thanks to imperial policies." Rudra took Uma's elbow and helped her get in the car. The raindrops splashed silver on its black body. Rudra revved the Ambassador, confident behind the wheels.

The restaurant hummed gently. The road gleamed dark and wet in the lights of the moving vehicles outside. The yellow and the red lights rendered a fluorescent glow to the wet atmosphere.

"Why did you return to Calcutta, I mean were you not tempted to stay on in London?" Uma picked up the thread of an earlier conversation, "After all many Bengali men are settling in England, or even America, with fair memsahib brides." It was a gentle probing of her husband's past. Flirtatious too.

But Rudra looked into his cup of coffee and stirred it slowly. "The Press, my familiar world … Baba … They were all here. And of course Kailash."

Uma waited and then pursued. "Perhaps somebody special too?"

"The language. Yes, I missed being surrounded by the familiar sound of Bengali. Its rhythm, the formal intonations, the intimate nuances, the various dialects, the modern slang of street corners …"

"You mean to say that you were never tempted?"

"I can't quite say that. Strangely London reminded me of Calcutta in some ways. Architecturally at least, in parts anyway. And yet the naked hunger, the gaunt ribs, the grind of existence did not constantly force its way into your consciousness there." Rudra's spoon continued to slowly chase the brown liquid dispersing the foam and seeing perhaps in its dark depths a litter of the hopeless and the dying, recalling the desperate cries for 'fan', the starch thrown away when the rice is cooked. The sound was fused in his consciousness with the visions of the swarms of victims of partition in the city. Rudra was ten in famine-struck Bengal of 1943, 14 in 1947 when the country was freed and partitioned and only 14½ when he heard the cry 'Yeh azadi jhoothi hai' – 'This freedom is a hoax.' The procession was winding past their car raising the slogan. They had sat stiff and quiet, Baba, the old driver Hardulal dada and he, in the Studebaker. Rudra had come out of his school that afternoon to find that Baba was also waiting in the car and that there were many parents too who had come to collect the children. There had been talk of trouble in the city, as there was with increasing frequency. Idly he had noticed on the way that many shops had downed their shutters and then the car had turned a corner and come upon a procession. The men shook their fists. "Yeh azadi jhoothi hai". A lanky young boy with a few day's beard and a head full of dusty, unruly curls had looked straight at Rudra with wild eyes. 'Yeh azadi jhoothi hai'. Rudra had felt the heat of the gaze on his face. But inside the car they did not look at each other. Or discuss the anger that had throbbed in the street once inside Kailash.

"In London one could forget about the wretched of the earth. Or pretend to at any rate. There is an unfair distribution of wealth everywhere. But here it is so blatant, so hopeless, so, so…even justified by religion. The notion of karma. Think of the deviousness of the argument that you deserve to wallow in a life gutted with poverty because of unsettled accounts of a past life. In the meanwhile…"

"Are you a communist?"

Rudra put his spoon down. "In a Park Street restaurant finishing a meal with his wife clad in a new silk saree?"

"Isn't there such a species?" Uma recalled some of Kaku's friends.

Rudra side-stepped the question and startled her by quoting a poem in Bengali.

> Amra madhyam pathe bikeler chayaye rayechi
> ekti prithibi nashta hoye geche amader age
> arekti prithibir dabi
> sthir kare nite gele lage
> sakaler akasher mato bayesh |

> We are in the middle path of the evening's shadow
> One world wrecked before us
> Of another world's claim
> to resolve takes
> time like the dawn in the sky.

Uma looked at her husband who seemed suddenly very young, boyish, at odds with the sentiment of the lines that he recited.

Rudra said with a sudden smile, "I am not a poet either. Jibanananda Das. One of my favourites. Have you…?"

"I have heard of him but…"

"Would you like to read his poetry?"

"Of course."

Rudra looked around him. "There are other Calcuttas too," wryly he admitted, "but those require a different season."

The statement despite its context, held out a promise and thrilled Uma.

The grey and wet wind blew into the car and soon sheets of water cocooned them in. Thus followed the first murmurings of passion in their marriage.

So what if her day did not begin with Rudra – it did end with him.

Once after such an intimate moment Uma asked Rudra about his mother, hoping to know him better. He remained silent. Instinctively Uma knew that words or even gestures would be intrusive. She kept quiet too. She was good at that. Eventually Rudra spoke, "I was only five. And there was no talk of my mother in Kailash. Not much at any rate. Maybe…they…they thought it was best for me too. I was after all only five." Rudra pushed aside the mosquito net of the bed somewhat carelessly and got out. The room glowed for an instant in the flicker of a matchstick. The dark wood, the red leather of the writing desk assumed a different life in that brief spell silhouetting the framed photograph of Shashishekhar and Haimanti on the wall. The red glow of the cigarette contoured an unfamiliar face that appeared harsh planes and angles. Uma was suddenly aware of being in a strange house and perhaps with strangers too. It was raining outside but softly.

※ ※

Uma caught sight of the soft white form every now and then in Kailash. And the sudden sharp flash of green eyes.

Pishi was usually in the kitchen in the mornings when Uma helped set and clear the table in the dining room despite the protests of Khagen, the family's old retainer. Uma caught the flicker of the white saree in the evenings too as she walked with the priest who drew a monthly salary, up to the puja room on the terrace for a more formal offering to the deities. And sometimes she met Pishi walking up or down the stairs. They smiled at each other but never more than that.

Uma found out that Pishi stayed, appropriately enough, midway between the ground and the first floor. The room was tucked into a corner formed by the wide turn of the generous staircase. No one spoke of Pishi in Kailash. Even the room was hardly ever mentioned and if perchance one needed to, it was never in terms of its function or the occupant like 'the dining room' or 'Babu's room'. This was always and only 'the room on one and a half storey'. So apt, Uma thought later, of Pishi's own existence in Kailash with no clear right of occupancy. She was above the servants in status but certainly not a member of the family. In fact even the room that Pishi occupied would be noticed only if one had to pause in the process of climbing up.

There is a story here, Uma's heart fancied.

※ ※

Sunlight, even mottled, banishes fancies. The dining room downstairs caught the frail sunshine through its array of east-facing windows. Breakfast was a formal meal here. The men came down dressed for work to a table laid with milk and porridge, bananas (sometimes mango or jackfruit or some other seasonal fruit), toast and eggs. The spoons, knives and forks intimidated Uma initially. She was no stranger to them but she associated cutlery with eating out and was happy to learn that the Bengali cuisine at dinner was expected to be eaten by hand.

Rudra's aunt had instructed Uma to offer the ritual prayers, food and water to the household deities before breakfast with her stomach empty and her clothes fresh. Thus Uma too would be bathed and ready by eight thirty every morning. She glowed as though newly minted in a bright saree and gold jewellery, with vermilion in the parting of her hair and on her forehead and the red and white bangles of conch and lac gracing her wrists. Uma did not have to cover her head like the dutiful daughter-in-law. Here too Ashutosh had displayed his amazingly liberal attitude. He also wanted Uma to sit down and have her first meal of the day with them instead of merely serving her men.

Thus, slowly and steadily Uma began to know when to get up, when to pray, how to dress, how to eat, what to eat…. The ordinariness of the activities, the lack of repression and the lure of modernity created the illusion of freedom. As though these were not rules. As though she were not yet another element in the articulation of what Kailash was. Her joy winged its way to Delhi through weekly letters.

The father and the son left together, in a manner of speaking, in different cars and for different destinations to meet up later at lunch at the Press. After breakfast all Uma had to do was to wait for the men to return in the evening. The grocery was brought once a month, the fresh stock daily. Khagen visited the morning market at the crack of dawn to seek out the freshest fish, the crispest green and the just-ripe-for-eating seasonal fruits. The new bride had been asked by Ashutosh to also touch Khagen's feet as she sought the blessings of all the elders in the family to help her on life's new course. Khagen had shrunk back. His dark, calloused feet clearly visible under the new white dhoti seemed to curl in with embarrassment at the honour. Clearly overwhelmed Khagen had shaken his grizzled head vehemently. Everyone present, the Chattopadhyay clan, its offshoots and close family friends, had noted the graciousness of the family that honoured its servants so, even if they were low caste Bagdis. Khagen's wife, having served the family for almost forty years had gone back to the village with her eldest son and over the years she had made her two granddaughters and three grandsons join her. Khagen's second son stayed at the Press as caretaker and the youngest son drove Ashutosh's car. Khagen's youngest daughter-in-law Khema, the driver's wife, did odd jobs in the house and kept a strict eye on the women who came to sweep and swab the house, wash the clothes and collect the garbage. Khema's youngest son, nine and naughty, was already dreaming of driving the car for Rudra when he grew up and took an avid interest in the black Ambassador, looking down upon Ashutosh's older Studebaker.

Ashutosh, advised to take things easy like all well-to-do men approaching sixty, returned almost two hours before his son in the evening. He did not appear averse to feminine ministrations at the end of the day. Uma took in his tea to the parlour upstairs just as he emerged from his bedroom, washed and fresh in a sparkling white kurta and pyjama, laundered traditionally so that the long sleeves were crinkled. The standing lamp was lit. Uma poured the tea and handed him the day's refreshment: white puffed rice with grated coconut or crisps of white flour spotted with kala jeera or two tiny white luchis with spicy potatoes or two sandesh shaped like conch shells. The evening snack was always on the light side and always freshly made. Nothing was ever repeated in the same week. They chatted as they ate. Rather, Ashutosh ate and talked while Uma listened, sipping her tea occasionally. The hour, or two maybe, thus passed and when the sound of Rudra's return was carried through the open windows of the upstairs verandah from the porch downstairs, Ashutosh stopped immediately and dismissed Uma with a smile in his voice, "Go. The gentleman has arrived."

Uma did not grudge her time with her father-in-law at all. In fact she quite enjoyed it. If Rudra showed her Calcutta, her father-in-law peopled it with the past in the twilight of the evening. In fact, this is how she chose to remember her father-in-law later: sitting in a circle of light, wearing crisp white, balancing a cup on the saucer and talking about the past as he liked to remember it.

Thus Uma came to know that the first Bengali plays had been staged in Calcutta by neither the Bengali nor the English but a remarkable Russian scholar-adventurer called Gerasim Lebedeff in 1795, that the main edifice of the Grand Hotel was built by the Armenian Arratoon Stephen, and that the National Tobacco Company where Rudra went as a consultant was a Jewish firm and Shalom ben Aharon ben Obadiah Ha Kohen had journeyed from Aleppo to Calcutta via Baghdad, Basra, Bombay and Surat in 1798 to set up the Jewish community in Calcutta that was associated with some of the city's most imposing buildings. Catholicity and culture marked the city that Ashutosh brought into the drawing room of Kailash. He often recalled with pride that the famous Urdu poet Mirza Ghalib who stayed in Calcutta from 1828 to 1829 had said that it was better to sit in the dust of Calcutta than to grace the throne of another dominion.

There were days too when the reminiscences were more private in nature, tinged with Ashutosh's personal memory of the city. His nostalgia made them glow incandescent as they may not have in real life. The horse drawn carriages, the daily washed streets of Calcutta, the kerosene lit street lamps, the hawkers' – phiriwallahs – cry in the city of Ashutosh's childhood now fast disappearing, crowded into the parlour of Kailash even as dark clouds knotted thick or splattered rain outside.

Sometimes, but only sometimes, familial people featured in Ashutosh's pageant. Thus Uma learnt how Ashutosh's father from East Bengal, known as a 'bangal', was always given a small, silver bowl of fresh chillies with the meals supervised by his wife from West Bengal, a ghoti, known to favour a sweeter palate. She learnt too that Ashutosh's orthodox Brahman mother had started buying bread – paurooti – from the local hawkers at the insistence of young and motherless Rudra, half knowing that the hawker had put on a sacred thread so that the seller and the buyer could both pretend that the purity of the upper caste Hindu household was not threatened by the transaction.

Quirky, familiar or startling, the anecdotes seemed to bring the larger world to the private parlour of Kailash and sitting in the pool of light Uma was sometimes thrilled by a dim awareness of some hidden grand narrative of modern progress in Ashutosh's tales. It felt different, this past that was slowly unfolding for her in Kailash, from what she had actually seen once as a young child at home in Kashmere Gate, Delhi.

＊＊

Home. That's how Uma still thought of the house in Kashmere Gate which was a pale shade of green. Apparently the family had moved into it only in 1947, when Uma was five years old. Her grandfather had bought the house from a colleague of his in the Ministry. India had been on the verge of freedom and partition. Her grandfather had been asked if he would buy the house from his friend who was leaving, had to leave, for Lahore. It had been built with much love, and her grandfather's friend had wanted to leave it in caring hands. She had heard that they could not pay the whole amount immediately and Dadu's friend had said 'with a smile' that he would wait for the remaining 'small' amount. It would give him a reason to come back to the land of his birth, childhood and youth. Dadu's friend had also left behind a huge trunk full of books to be sent for later.

"Your grandmother was very upset."

Uma's mother dropped her voice even though there were just the two of them in their bedroom.

"Why? Did she not like this house?" Uma winced as the comb in Ma's hand pulled at a tangle in her hair.

"She considered the house to be sullied. And really, however worthy Dadu's friend might have been he was after all a … Anyway, your grandmother tried everything to make Dadu change his mind: words and tears. Even going on strike over food."

"Thakma? You are exaggerating ma."

"She did even more than that. When all else failed she reminded Dadu, in our presence, her grown up sons and daughter-in-law, of his promise to her. Thakma said that she had once left her village, her family, her friends and her land to come to far away Delhi with her husband."

"I know. She always says that her grief and her fear of the separation from the larger family had made her cry so much that she could not see anything on her first rail ride all the way from Calcutta to Delhi."

"But Thakma had come. She was his wife. And Dadu was in pursuit of a dream of a different India. Didn't he promise then that she would never ever have to cry so much on his account, Thakma asked Dadu in front of us."

"But Dadu did not relent?"

"No. Dadu who otherwise always let Thakma have her way refused to enter any negotiations. He would buy and live in the Green house built by his friend." Ma put the comb down. "Dadu's friend never came back to claim the remaining amount or his books."

"Didn't Dadu try to contact him later?"

"He did try but... anyway the amount stays in Dadu's bank, under instruction to his sons that it is never to be dipped into."

Uma knew that a trunk full of books occupied a corner of Dadu's bedroom.

Uma imagined a thin young man with a serious face, travelling to Delhi with his tearful young wife, two daughters and an infant son. 1911 was the year when the British had moved their capital from Calcutta to Delhi prompting several changes and possibilities, major and minor. One such minor, very, very minor change was the relocation of a promising young headmaster of a District school in Barishal – East Bengal then, East Pakistan now – to one of the many Ministries in Delhi. He later became Uma's grandfather.

Dadu. Uma remembered him as a man with gentle, myopic eyes. Later she learnt through Ma's stories that those eyes measured the past. Uma vaguely remembered playing a game with Dadu. It was like a ritual. She would push the door of his room wide, catch him reading and call out:

Dadu!

Dida?

What are you doing?

Trying to sort out the past.

Is it in a mess?

Terrible.

Who did that ?

Everyone of us.

You?

Yes.

Thakma?

Yes.

Baba?

Yes.

Kaku?

Yes.

The jamunkalekalejam wallah? Uma mimicked the cry of the man who sold berries in the streets during high summer.

Yes.

Mrs. Theophilus from my school?

Yes.

It would go on and on with little Uma casting her net far and wide. She named everyone she could think of, hoping one day to find at least one person who was not responsible for the mess that bothered Dadu so.

But Dadu died suddenly when Uma was seven. The doctor said it was a heart attack. But Thakma insisted that it was overwhelming grief at what was happening around him. This was not the freedom that he and the others had envisaged for their nation. Uma's aunts arrived with cousins for the funeral. The grief-stricken house thus also echoed with sporadic sounds of life and laughter. One afternoon Uma got off the double bed of her parents that she now occupied with her cousins for the afternoon siesta. The green house was quiet and dark. Every opening had been stuffed to keep out the scorching blaze of Delhi summer. Her mother was sleeping on the floor, much cooler than the bed, with her sisters-in-law. Uma tiptoed out.

Thakma, an ugly stranger in white, her jewellery and her curly ringlets gone to permanently mark her bereavement, was in the kitchen. She is a widow now, Ma had explained when young Uma had burst into tears at her first sight of Thakma's shaved head. Normally, Thakma was restless as a sparrow. But Uma saw her just sitting in the kitchen, staring down at her palms. An unfamiliar sense of sorrow overwhelmed the child and she rushed past the kitchen before she could be seen by her grandmother. The door to Dadu's room was half open as always, as she wanted it to be now, in the hope that everything else would be the same too. Uma's heart hammered. With utmost care she gently pushed the doors wide open. And then she stood petrified. Baba, her very own big, smiling Baba was crying softly at the writing desk. The room was dark as rooms in Delhi summer afternoons are kept. There was no Dadu.

But ever after Uma always thought of the past as a dark room with a man sobbing at a table laden with books even as dust motes danced in a thin ray of sunlight that had somehow found an opening. She tried though, she tried to shut the door on it in the hope that it would vanish.

※※

In Kailash, Uma took to dusting in the morning after Ashutosh and Rudra left for work.

Uma had always loved dusting in Delhi where the arid climate daily layered the house with very fine grains of sand. Now, as the daughter-in-law of the Chattopadhyays, dusting created the illusion of worthwhile labour. It also helped Uma get to know Kailash though slowly, ever so slowly. It was not an intrusion to open rooms and cupboards while dusting. And as she dusted the Dresden figures, the Belgian glasses somewhat fogged, the bare-breasted Venus, the clay lobster and the conch shells or even the books neatly arranged in the glass paned cupboards of the parlour upstairs or the formal library below, Uma felt that Kailash's past was rather different from her own experience of it.

Her father-in-law's bedroom appeared bereft of memories though. One day, driven by a deep curiosity, Uma opened the top drawer of the side table next to his bed. She was sure that there would be a photo of her mother-in-law there. It would be brown and scalloped and sepia tinged. Uma had been shown the family album and knew what Rudra's mother had looked like but this would be different. In looking for the photo Uma was actually hoping to know her father-in-law better and in keeping with her own expectations of him. He must be a man bereaved who grieved in private. A man who looked at his dead wife's photo and remembered her, as she was when the son was five or less. Her father-in-law must be opening the drawer by the bed in those intense moments of solitude to look at the young life so cruelly taken.

But there was only a neat pile of bill books and cash memos, cheque books and some letters. A bunch of keys too. All of it looked dull and official. A noise made Uma sit back on her heels. Her hands turned clammy and her heart suddenly started pounding. She was awash with shame and guilt.

But time gave her confidence and a reasoned righteousness. She was only cleaning her father-in-law's room. She would never, ever open the drawer of the big dark wooden almirah with a crystal handle, not even when she had to open it to put in his laundered clothes. These side table drawers were public. Her father-in-law knew that she dusted them. These were not locked.

She opened the second drawer of the side table. It revealed two fountain pens, two bottles of ink – black and royal blue – in a case with a soft cloth and a spare set of spectacles. She was touched to find that a copy of their wedding card lay below a stack of handkerchiefs with 'A' embroidered in one corner. The handkerchiefs were neatly ironed and kept with the edges alligned in an old paper case for Yardley's English lavender soaps. The case was beautiful still. Uma sniffed and felt, rather than found, the trace of fragrance. She wondered at this box being preserved in a house of plenty. Memories, she thought, were made of these.

It brought to her suddenly the mementoes of childhood and youth in the Green house in Delhi. And all that she had left behind in coming to Kailash. Uma sat back on the floor, lost.

She did not open the last drawer that day.

But two days later.

Uma was drawn back to the drawer in Ashutosh's bedroom though she argued with herself that perhaps it should not be opened. In fact she was about to leave the bedroom with a last flick of her duster when a sudden capitulation to sinful inquisitiveness took place.

Ah! Something at last. A stack of letters. At a glance Uma could make out from the faded yellow of the post cards, the green of the inlands and the mellow white of the envelopes that these were old. The enveloped lot had been sent to her father-in-law while he was in England. These were addressed in a thin, cursive upright hand, definitely male. Uma picked up one and turned it around gently. 'From Shashishekhar Chattopadhyay' was handwritten just above an embossed address of The Ganges Press. It seemed from the letters that Shashishekhar used to write quite regularly to Ashutosh in England. Next to this stack was another lot of envelopes, fewer in number and mixed with some picture postcards that Ashutosh had in turn received from his son while Rudra was studying in London.

Carefully Uma drew out the lot and had started dusting the recess when the drawer yielded yet another stack of letters. The letters of the alphabets on these envelopes were round with each character distinct as though written very carefully by one who had studied for a few years before being claimed by marriage and motherhood. Uma touched the letters, gently sifting the remains of a life. Her eyes caught the date on what was apparantly the last of the letters. It was the birthday of Rudra. The day he had turned five. Uma thought of the young wife writing to her husband in a far away land even as their son turned five. She rested her finger on the faded post mark that showed the date and felt herself to be a part of the intimate circle.

Of course Uma did not read the letters. She did not even think of it. Not then at any rate. But the guilt of having discovered a private self, though unread, gnawed at her. The sudden impatient clatter of rain at the window brought her to her feet and she turned to take one last awkward look at the room to check that she was leaving it as she had found it.

It was then that she saw it, her surveillance of the room perhaps made keener by guilt. It lay precariously between two pillows, half hidden by the heavy bed cover. Uma leant across and drew out the book that she had heard of so much. It was flat and rectangular, with the length almost the double of its width. The cover was light brown and an elegant archaic Bengali script read Neelkantha's *Chandimangal*. The oval logo of The Ganges Press anchored it.

Uma, for the rest of her life, remembered this moment in the bedroom of Kailash when Dvija Neelkantha, Rudra's great-grandfather and the legendary poet of *Chandimangal*, ceased to be a mere name and started taking shape as the person at the centre of darkness. It was a moment that would spread the dark staining her life. This too Uma remembered as long as she lived.

But at that moment she only knew that she held in her hand a story told in verse – a venerated and traditional story of the goddess. For thus are women revered in her land.

❊ Three ❊

CHANDI, ANNADA, UMA, KATYAYANI, GAURI, Durga, Parvati, Maya, Maharatri, Sati, Shakhamvari, Shankari, Suresvari, Shivani ….

The goddesses dark and fair, militant and domesticated, presiding over forests, fields, forts and families were familiar to Uma. They too had peopled her world from the beginning through stories and images, metaphors and movies, totems and taboos. Indeed she knew them almost as her family and friends. There had been five goddesses in Uma's class alone in school: Ambika, Sharada, Jaya, Aditi and Adya. The mother and daughter who swept and swabbed the Kashmere Gate house were goddesses too: Kali and Karali. And as Uma grew up she came in touch with many more. Familiar as well as distant.

"The goddesses are very different, Thakma."

"All these names refer to the Devi who is a manifestation of shakti."

"Ma, who is the Devi?"

"Wife to Shiva."

Thus the plurality of the goddess is seen as a play of her many forms. But the believers know that she is primarily a wife, gathering the knowledge from the very air that they breathe.

In Bengal, the most famous, and dearest, image of this Devi with multiple resonances was that of the resplendent mother goddess during the autumnal Durga puja.

Durga puja was special in Uma's memory too.

She remembered that Durga Puja meant a sudden burst of Bengali culture (for Baba and Kaku hardly ever wore the dhoti otherwise) in their daily Delhi lives. Come autumn, the religious and the carnivalesque coalesced in a five-day long festival of devotion, rich food, plays, films, new clothes, songs and books. Puja may be otherwise marked by abstinence but this festival of Bengal was an orgy of senses.

Gazing into the face of the goddess under the powerful light of the temporary marquee in the evenings, Uma always experienced a thrill of being. The goddess would glow in response to the pulsating passion of drum beats and clanging bells. The priest, stern and aloof, would move his right hand in a wavering circular motion as he propitiated her with different ritual offerings even as his left hand kept swaying a brass bell. The smoke arising from the resin burning with coconut husks in clay holders added to the atmosphere. Uma would wait, thrilled and impatient for the moment when the dance with the dunuchi, the smoking clay crucible, would be started by one of the watching crowd and then taken up by more. The observers would be asked to move back, yet maintaining a semi circle right in front of the goddess. The excitement would spread and inhibitions would be shed. More and more boys and men would break away from the watching crowd to join the dancers. The atmosphere would be thick with smoke and the sharp smell of smouldering resin. The marquee would pulsate with a happy excitement. The drummers would join the dancers. The goddess would look down on them all, the big red mark on her forehead, her wide kohl traced eyes, her shining nose ring, the vermilion in the parting of her dark hair, her jewelled diadem.... "She glows because of a special oil called 'garjan tel' with which the potters polish her face." Kaku had once wryly informed Uma but she did not want to believe that. It must be that the goddess comes alive at that particular moment when the dancers, the drumbeats, the smoke and the passion fuse into an incandescence.

Uma could never catch that glow later. She did try. The drums did beat. The bronze bells clanged. The priest moved the hands the same way. The devotees seemed transported. But inevitably as the passion climaxed Uma saw an old green eyed woman in a soiled white saree, bereft of jewellery, emerge from behind the goddess. She had no right to be there. The widow's presence would pollute the altar and she'd be hounded out if anyone saw her. But no one did. Except for Uma.

Uma's eyes smarted.

The green eyes of the old woman glowed.

The smoke rose.

The priest's hands, large and fair with tapering fingers, reached out to span the old woman's throat. And slowly the caressing hands turned taut, suffusing with blood the face that changed into a young girl's. But the eyes were still green.

"*Bolo bolo Durga mai ki jai*"

"All hail the mother goddess," the devotees thundered.

Uma blinked.

Smoke covered everything but the goddess's glowing face.

But the goddess herself appeared mesmerised by the movement of the priest's hand that offered her the rising flames of a lamp, flowers, a conch shell, clothes and the yak tailed chamar… one after the other. The goddess appeared impervious to all else. The Brahman priest held her captive as though in hypnotic trance.

The tears rolled down Uma's face. It's the smoking resin, she always told her family. But as she took the handkerchief from her husband's hand Uma was caught once again in a web of memories.

That night for instance when Uma had been a bride for only a week or so. Of course she had asked Rudra about the old lady in white. Her query though had been prompted by a sense of inhibition rather than curiosity. It was not easy to get into bed with a man who still seemed a stranger, though her husband. Uma always tried to stave off her rising embarrassment at this moment by striking up a casual conversation while tucking the mosquito nets into the bedding, unconsciously shaping an even more intimate world out of the draped bed. When they were more settled in marriage, and with each other, Rudra had laughed and said that for a creature who seemed rather quiet, Uma had been unusually voluble while getting into bed. It had, he must admit, worried him a little. "What would you know about coming into a strange house and having to make it your own? And the stranger too?" Uma too would retort and then laugh.

That night she had thought that she would ask Rudra about the lady in white. Uma's sense of intrigue had emanated from the old lady's proud demeanour which was evidently at odds with her social status in Kailash. There was the curious matter of the green eyes too that so rarely graced a Bengali face.

"A *lady* in white?"

Rudra seemed to be thinking which was a bit odd considering that the old woman was evidently a resident of Kailash too. It struck Uma then that her use of the word bhadramahila with its suggestion of the educated, upper class Bengali 'lady' may have misled Rudra.

"She has green eyes."

"Oh! Pishi."

"Your father's sister?"

Had Rudra drifted off?

"A cousin?" Uma found herself asking again.

"In a manner of speaking perhaps. I don't know. There is some sort of a village connection I think. You know how it is. My grandfather always helped people who came from his 'home' as he always thought of his village in Chittagong. I don't know when, or how, Pishi came to Kailash. She's always been here as far as I can remember. She helped my grandmother with the household chores I guess. Why?"

"Her green eyes…"

"Must have been some hanky-panky in the family …" Rudra's voice lost its force.

But Uma truly intrigued by now carried on regardless, "What hanky-panky…"

Suddenly Rudra turned towards her, "I thought you are the one who has studied English. Hanky-panky suggests hocus-pocus. I thought that the ladies of Miranda House knew all that." There seemed to be a smile in his voice in the dark. Uma felt Rudra's breath warm on her cheek, his fingers cool against her bared waist and his legs heavy trapping hers. But Uma's mind drifted elsewhere and it took a while to be one with her possessed body.

❧ ❧

The dark clouds drifted across the sky shadowing the afternoon which felt heavy and still. And so too Uma's heart. She was being silly she knew. But her heart refused rational reckonings.

> *durer ankhijal baye baye*
> *ki bani ashe oi raye raye...*

> Bearing tears from afar
> in waves what words waft over ...

The snippet of Tagore's song in Kaki's haunting voice, had been playing in Uma's mind since the morning. It mellifluously melded the dark of the rain clouds with her mood on the edge of tears. She had stepped inside Kailash for the first time on this day as a bride and nobody seemed to care. True there had been a trunk call from Delhi and other phone calls too from realtives in the city including an invitation to dinner at her uncle's but she had turned that down assuming that she would be with Rudra. Just the two of them, on their own. But Rudra had told her last night that he would like to meet his school friends for a 'boy's do'. Her father-in-law would also dine out at the Club as he did once in a while. Only Uma was to be at home. As was not unfair. Or unexpected. Or unnatural. But still....

She had nothing to do.

Uma picked up her wedding card that she was using to mark the page of the romance that she had been trying to read. And really how much can one read?

'...Rudrashekhar Chattopadhyay, son of Ashutosh Chattopadhayay... grandson of ....great grandson of .... Kynsa mati, Chittagong, East Bengal now residents of Kailash ... Dalimbagan ... Calcutta ... to wed ·Uma ... granddaughter of ... Kashmere Gate, Delhi formerly of ... Barishal ...."

Kynsa mati. This was the name of Rudra's ancestral village. The name rang short and sweet in Uma's ear. She had wondered about the name when she had heard it first. Later she had seen it printed in her red and gold wedding card, spiralling her to a past through an inventory of places.

"Kynsa mati. It is so lyrical. What does the name mean Baba?" Uma had asked her father-in-law one evening.

"I used to wonder too. Kynsa mati means the soil of Kynsa. The river Kynsa Khyong from Lushai hills of Mizoram flows through Chittagong before draining into the Bay of Bengal."

"Kynsa Khyong. It's such a pretty name for a river."

"The river is also known as Karna Phuli or the flower from the ear. There is a story to it."

"What?"

Ashutosh was visibly pleased. The questions suggested that his daughter-in-law was really interested. Rudra had always been an indifferent listener to tales of the past. "People say that an Arakanese princess fell in love with a tribal prince of Chittagong. They were enjoying a moonlit boat ride when the princess leaned forward to touch the glimmering water. A flower that the prince had tucked behind her ear fell into the water. She tried to reach it but the fast flowing current drew her in too. The horrified prince dived in and drowned as well. Thus the river got its name."

Kynsa mati. Uma repeated the name softly.

And Ashutosh thought of his stern father and the rare moments when Shashishekhar had talked of his life left behind in the village. Ashutosh had held on to the memory of those moments with his father, quite certain that he was being privileged in receiving the occasional nostalgia laced reminiscences. He had always felt that the way to know his father better was to understand his life in Chittagong. But there had never been time enough. Or enough unguarded moments.

"Once I wanted to write a history of Chittagong. But there was never time enough."

"I know this nostalgia for a lost homeland. Baba always talks thus of Barishal. But he was just a baby when they came to Delhi."

Ashutosh admitted, "And I have never even seen Kynsa mati."

"But..." But Uma paused, warned by the clouds in Ashutosh's eyes.

A whisper, a nudge, a smile or a sneer on the face of a relative. Sometimes his mother's tears in the dark or when she thought no one was seeing her. Oh yes, Ashutosh had known that his father had left behind a ... life ... .in Chittagong. But his father never talked about it. And Ashutosh who held peace dear had never thought of ruffling the apparent calm of Kailash.

Outside, the wind recklessly played with the gentle drizzle of rain.

A little later it was Uma who broke the silence, "You said that the princess was an Arakanese. The Arakanese are the Burmese aren't they?"

Ashutosh nodded again but seemed lost in another world.

The rain gathered strength.

Burmese. Burma. Thakma used to mention relatives who had settled in Rangoon.

Thakma.

Thakma and Kaki.

Kaki and Ma.

Ma and Baba.

Loneliness. It clouded upon Uma that afternoon, thick and fast. There came the faint sound of a song from the street outside. The twang of a string instrument that these mendicants in orange often carried, accompanied the song. The melody was monotonous yet soothing. Uma had heard and seen these Bauls from her Mamu's house too whenever she visited the city as a child. She and her cousins had loved to throw a coin or two down to the singing Baul who would pick it up, turn twice around the same spot in a strange ritual of acknowledgement and then carry on. There would be no pause in his singing.

But in Kailash the street lay beyond the wide verandah, the

driveway, the semi-circular garden and the high walls. Uma hummed the tune even as the song grew faint and then could no longer be heard.

The wind mussed the clouds letting in sudden bursts of bright sunshine. Uma longed for the afternoons of her past life of female companionship – in college with friends or at home with her mother, grandmother and aunt. She had always thought of the afternoon as 'women's hour', when there comes a pause in the day's occupation, after which the sun begins to lower.

With a sigh Uma got off the bed, rewound her hair to a neater coil at the nape of her neck, shook free her saree from where it had bunched up around her knees and went out of the bedroom.

The staircase had two long windows that let in the sudden splendour of the sun through a curtain of grey. She saw that the door of the room on 'one and a half storey' was partly ajar. On a sudden impulse she walked down and knocked on the door. Softly.

❦ ❦

"Yes?"

There was a firmness to the voice though of the aged. There was a lilt in it too, of echoes carried across rivers. It promised a dialect not of Calcutta, not West Bengal either but further east: the land of Padma and nostalgia. Uma was visited by a sudden hesitation. But it was too late.

"It's me, Uma, " she said, pushed the door wider and entered.

The small room was spartan. A bed, heavy and high, against the wall took up more than half the space. The bedspread was very clean but old, darned with neat stitches in a couple of places. A bottle of what appeared to be mustard oil rested in a little alcove set in the wall against the bed, alongside an oil lamp and a match box. A black trunk rested in the shadows beneath the bed. There was nothing else.

Pishi was getting off the bed with an achingly familiar movement of the hand on the knee that recalled Thakma.

"Are you in pain?"

The green eyes looked startled even before the owner could react.

"No. Old age. You need something?"

Embarrassed, Uma shook her head.

Pishi paused in the act of getting off the bed, looked at Uma and then moved back, "Come sit."

Uma sat, on the edge.

"Are you missing home?" The direct query found its mark in the heart.

"It is this afternoon."

"What did you do at home in the afternoons?"

Home? Yes home. Not Kailash.

"We chatted. Usually. Before the men returned as Thakma used to say."

It seemed like once upon a time to Uma even as she spoke.

"Tell me about your home."

How easy it was and how simple to begin to talk of oneself and of one's home. Pishi listened as though she really wanted to know and led with questions.

And Uma talked. Of the green house. Of Dadu gone. And of those who remained.

Gradually Uma moved back on the bed and then drew up her legs too as she carried on talking of Ma's anxieties, her younger brother's intelligence, Kaku's eccentricities, Kaki's music and Thakma's truisms. Uma peopled the afternoon with her past life even as the darkening sky lowered and slowly covered the pale sunlight just above the coconut trees visible from the barred window of the room on one and a half storey. Thus Uma and Pishi slipped easily, almost unconsciously, into a relationship of Pishi's 'tui' and Uma's 'tumi' – the familiar and familial pronouns making the propriety of the proper nouns and the uncertainty of social status irrelevant.

"It is a month to the day." Uma ended where it had all begun.

"Why that is so! It did not strike me. I did not remember the date. Wait, I will make something special for dinner tonight. What would you really like?"

Uma drew a deep breath and savoured the familiar offer. Thus the older women in her life had tried to erase the sorrows of childhood. "Nothing. Really. It seems just like yesterday though. My wedding."

A sudden silence enveloped the room as each travelled in her mind. And on her own. The sparrows twittered outside, no doubt in a frenzy at the fast fading afternoon light.

"Do you remember too Pishi?"

"What?"

"Your wedding day....?"

"No."

"What? Oh. I should not have asked."

"Why not?"

Uma stared. "Why not?" was an uncharted territory. Surely Pishi's widow's garb proclaimed a wedding?

"No, I mean..."

"Actually I don't remember anything about my wedding day."

"What do you mean?"

"I too have heard that it is the most important day of a woman's life. The day for which she has been born. There was a time when I dredged my memory daily for some remains of that day. But each time I came up with nothing. Now even that dredging appears to be a figment of my imagination."

And so it began one wet afternoon. The stirring of shelved memories. Thus the cracks appeared one after another and when shaken and stirred, the fragments floated freely before the pattern could be discerned. Of course Uma could have drawn back, chosen not to listen or listened without choosing. Not just that afternoon but in the several days through the monsoon. Yet she did. And more than that. Imperceptibly Uma so merged with the tale that it was difficult to bracket her own life out of it and remain safe and secure.

Thakma's bangle glimmered gold on her wrist as Uma settled a pleat of her saree. "My Thakma was married off when she was only five. She has often told us how frightened she was when she was finally being taken to her marital home. Dadu's family chose the waterway to take the bride home. The boat swayed upon the heaving river. A storm seemed imminent. Thakma says that storms always remind her of that day."

"Well, I remember nothing," said Pishi, "Neither a journey nor any storm. I knew I was married. I had known that almost ever since I was born it seems. I knew I was married because of the bangles on my wrist: red lac, white conch and dark iron. Oh and also the vermilion mark in the parting of my hair. How could I forget that? And if I ever forgot that water wipes the vermilion clean then I was made to remember it too. The sharp slap of my mother on my wet body really stung." Pishi smiled, unexpectedly. The moment seemed to be spinning, mutating. There was almost a childish glee in Pishi's voice, "I loved swimming. How heavenly it is to feel the water lift and carry you. I could swim for hours in the village pond."

"You knew how to swim?"

A broken tooth peeped through a pair of fine pink lips again. "How can you know the pleasures of frolicking in water when it comes through taps and is stored and measured! It's pathetic. Especially if you have known rivers, lakes and ponds. And our pond was something else altogether. It was so dark and deep. I thought it could easily rival our river. But Kynsa of course streamed out of the village to reach the sea. Girls were not encouraged to test the water there. Swim? But of course I could swim. For hours and hours. We swam in Padma pukur. The lotus pond. It did have another name too. But... anyhow it was reserved for the women of the village. Cattle were not allowed to bathe there. The boys were not welcome. But some young boys did come with their mothers. And some older ones too who came to fish but on the sly as they were supposed to leave this embankment alone for us women. But...." Pishi trailed off for a while, ".... The lotus pond. Did it really have any lotus? Or was it just water hyacinth, I wonder now." She blinked at the rustling coconut fronds outside her window.

Uma hunched forward. Some forgotten plot of rural romance glimmered faintly in her imagination. She could see a fair form, young and sleek, cutting the dark water of a deep pond. The girl's saree was wet and bright. Now clinging. Now floating.

"The water of Padma pukur used to wipe my vermilion clean. Ma always put it on for me immediately after a sharp slap for being so careless. Evidently I was married. But I remember nothing of the ceremony."

"Did not the others tell you? Your mother?"

"I believe I was very young. Three or less maybe. There was another wedding in the nearby village. Apparently the groom was of impeccable Brahmanical lineage, Kulin Brahmans as they called themselves. My father got to know of this from a friend of his. It must have been my lucky day. I believe my father hardly ever spent time at home. But he was home on that day. As luck would have it. He must have rushed over with his request to the man with the pure lineage of Kulin Brahmans. There were some other fathers too. Poor men all. But each a Kulin Brahman with the burden of daughters who must be married off to the right lineage. Well my father too did not shirk his parental duty and risk the hell fire that burns Kulin Brahman fathers who do not marry off their daughters to equally pure Brahmans." Pishi smiled yet again, "A new dhoti for the groom. Some rice. My green eyes were much closer to brown then. Also, the zamindar had offered a pair of cows. The day was auspicious. The marriage took place."

"The zamindar gave cows as part of your dowry?"

"Why not? He had plenty." The smile played about Pishi's lips without a trace of joy, "This was no simple act of charity. There was a family connection too I believe. The deed was a pious one as well, this act of relieving a poor Brahman of his daughter. It assures a place in heaven, don't you know? To help marry seven daughters means that you have acquired the piety worth an Asvamedh Yagnya."

"Asvamedh Yagnya? Like the one mentioned in the *Ramayana* and the *Mahabharata*?"

"You know those stories?"

"Yes of course I have read them."

"You read those stories? On your own? By yourself?" The green eyes turned to Uma, now eager and alert.

Uma knew the epics *Ramayana* and the *Mahabharata* but like most others had never really read them except the abridged children's version in Bengali called *Cheleder Mahabharata* and *Cheleder Ramayana*. Baba had bought the two books from the Bengali bookstall set up during Durga Puja. Uma's younger brother had quickly written his name in them in permanent blue black ink. Uma was very upset. "But it's *Cheleder* – for the boys" her brother had pointed out. Apparently there were no versions of the epics earmarked especially for girls. Or so Uma was told. But she knew them of course, like everyone else.

"Is not Asvamedh Yagnya the very important ritual sacrifice where a king's horse is let loose and it roams the country, entering neighbouring kingdoms where they either accept the sovereignty of the horse's owner or engage in a battle? Who can perform the sacrificial ritual of Asvamedh these days?" Uma smiled.

Pishi smiled too. "They could not in my days either. They married off the Brahman girls instead. Seven daughters shackled in lieu of a roaming horse. You earned the same worth of purity by these deeds, I have heard."

Uma wished to know more. But was uncertain if she should probe. The silence was not unpleasant. She looked at Pishi.

Pishi nodded. "Yes. The man agreed to help my father. All he had to do was to marry and thus earn a pair of cows. A pair of cows was not easy to come by. But there were plenty of Brahman girls waiting to be married off. So he also agreed to help the other fathers, for much less as well as much more. I believe he married many of us the same day. It helped save time too. He had to leave. There was work pending. It was the marriage season. Brahmans with daughters in other villages must have been waiting for him"

"Thakma used to mention an uncle of hers. He married sixty times. They called him Shattimoni – the jewel of sixty. He spent his life visiting each of his wives by turn."

"The jewel indeed!"

Uma wondered if she had spent time enough in the room on one-and-a-half storey. But there was no one waiting for her outside. So she asked, "And then?"

"So I was married. My father and my husband performed their sacral duties. Kanyadan, the gift of a daughter was given. The gods must have been pleased at this dutiful observance of their laws."

"And then...."

"Nothing. He took his dhoti and the rice. The pair of cows too. And all the other gifts from all the other fathers of the brides who were young and very young. And then he went away."

"Where?"

"Who knows. His home? The homes of the various in-laws that he must have acquired in his noble work of saving the pristine state of Brahmans? "

"And you?"

"I was one of the many he married in the process."

"He never called for you? He never visited you? You never went to your in-laws? He did not want to set up home with you?"

Pishi looked at Uma and spoke very gently. "Why should he? My parents were poor. He had much richer pastures to plough. My eyes had turned entirely green by then, the brown shrinking to flecks. He must have heard."

"You never set eyes on him since then?"

Even the sparrows were quiet.

"I did. Once."

Uma hesitated. Pishi looked at her and then looked away and out of the window. It was grey outside once again. The world seemed wet.

"It was a bright sunny day. A day that fills you with happiness when you look at the shining green world around you. There was already a nip in the air. But not enough to make you worry about all that you did not have. I went to the Padma pukur. The water was nippy too. But I did not mind that. I loved the way the body tingled and then the warmth that rushed through it when I emerged out of the cold water. You just needed the courage to take the initial plunge into the cold. Also many of my friends were there. Married.

Unmarried. Widows. Or wives-in-waiting. We filled the lakeside with our chatter. It was then that someone whispered to me. 'Have you heard? Your groom has come to the village?' 'Don't talk rubbish.' 'God promise. Didn't you hear anything at home?'"

"Did you?"

"Did I? I wondered. Were my parents whispering the previous night? Is that why I had been sent a little early to the pond today? Is that why my father left home in the morning? To make arrangements? The three coconuts that Ma gave my grandmother surely marked the day as special?" Pishi blinked and then looked at Uma, "There is no shame in acknowledging that my heart beat fast then. I thought that my day as bride had come. I left the pond as soon as I could without appearing to be in indecent haste. My friends were laughing by now."

"Was he there? Your groom?"

"In the village, yes. At my house, no. But I was fifteen and willed happiness. I wore the saree that I had got from my grandmother's house for Durga puja; the only new saree that we got once a year anyway. It was green. But darker than my eyes. My mother looked at me askance. But she did not say anything. The afternoon blazed. The household slept. I waited. Then began the slow decline of the sun. The kite called a sharp whistle high in the blue sky. I was seized with a restlessness. The sleeping household stifled me. I came out to stand near the hedge that marked the boundary of the homestead and scanned the horizon. 'Pssst.' I was expecting this call. But not in a girl's voice."

"Who was it?"

"Phulsai. My friend who had informed me about my fate that morning. 'Phul, your groom went to the zamindar's house on his way to some other village. He will be leaving now. He is with a friend. But your groom is the taller of the two. They have to pass the copse of bamboo beyond the pond.' I must have just looked at her. 'Go test your fate, stupid. And you are looking nice', said my sixteen-year old friend who had been a widow for more than half her life already."

"But how did she know?"

"I never really asked. But her father used to frequent the zamindar's house. She always knew more than us about village affairs."

"What happened then?"

"I went of course. My tryst with destiny I thought. I looked around for divine signs to let me know in advance that it was a turning point in my life. I walked alone all the way to the copse in my best saree. There is no shame in this I told myself. He is my husband."

Uma nodded.

"I stood deep in the shadow of the copse, gazing at the several paths that met and then led out of the village. I prayed. And prayed. I tried to recall my life to sort out if my sins were heavy enough to negate this chance encounter. Surely not, I thought. Surely not. Yes, I had stolen fruits from the orchards of others. Yes, I had let my mind wander while praying. Yes, I had cursed having to run errands for my mother. And yes. Yes, I had seen the handsome young groom of a friend of mine and I had wished he were mine. The thought had come unbidden to my mind. I am sorry God, I said. I am sorry. I am sorry…I am sorry…. Forgive me god. This once. Forgive me dear god….I saw the dust first, I think. And then the figures. Yes, one was definitely taller than the other."

Pishi lapsed into a silence holding herself straight and aloof.

"I have finished my tale. What else is left to say? They passed by the copse without stopping. The two men kept walking. I saw my life passing by. My life, my hopes, my dreams. I willed all shame away and came out of the shadow of the copse. I called out to them. Both men turned. The shorter one smiled. It was a terrible smile that stripped me entirely. He walked away a few paces and called out over his shoulder to his companion to hurry up with it. I knew then that it was over. My unformed foolish hope I mean. I looked at the taller man. The red evening sun shone on him. I could not see his face clearly. I can't recall his features any more. But I remember thinking how like a pincer he looks. He seemed so old. If we had met as strangers, I should have called him uncle. Certainly he looked older than my father. He looked me up and down. There was a sudden shout in the distance as though somebody was searching for lost cattle."

"And then?"

"And then he went away."

"You did not say anything?

'He was a stranger. I had called out to him as only wives can to their husbands."

"Maybe he did not recognise you?"

"I was the only girl in the village with green eyes. He must have heard that."

"He said nothing? Pishi?"

"The bamboo copse is infested with female ghouls."

"What?"

"He said that. Not to me. But to his friend as he caught up with him. Both laughed. I stood waiting in the copse. For the female ghouls if need be. But none appeared. It was a tranquil yellow and green inside the copse. But I knew that I had to come out of its dappled shadows eventually. And so I did. But since then I have never been afraid of female ghouls."

The room and Kailash were being gathered in darkness. Ma always said that there was something heartrending about the music of the shahnai at weddings. The wooden flute always seems to be a profound expression of the bride's grief amidst the festivities. Strange how I had forgotten that, Uma thought. But she was loath to speak.

It was Pishi who broke the silence finally. "It's almost dusk. Get your hair pins and the black ribbons. I will braid your hair." Thakma too had always insisted on women's hair being tied as soon as the daylight dwindled. She used to say that female ghouls prowled in the dark for women with untied hair. The dark evening had come upon them but Uma said, "In a while". There was no hurry. The men were not returning till after dinner.

"Pishi how did you come to Calcutta?"

"Shashishekhar brought me."

No kinship ties marked the name's prerogative in Pishi's narrative. It was not encased in familiar form – grading emotions, accessing rights. Shashishekhar. Not brother, father, uncle (maternal or paternal), aunt's husband or sister's. Not husband either for 'He' must not be named. Just Shashishekhar.

The name slowly coiled around the darkening room. A name that shorn of appellations was bereft of meaning. It was thus not an explanation but an infinite possibility of transgressed protocol.

Scandal, whispered the gathering dark.

Uma felt Kailash tremble, anxious and waiting and herself with it. She hovered on the edge of curiosity and caution too.

But this time the two women sat in silence though glad of the other's presence.

❊ ❊

"Baba, I saw the *Chandimangal* on your bed the other day when I dusted your room." Uma suddenly rushed into speech that evening, before Ashutosh could begin his day's anecdote.

"Neelkantha's *Chandimangal*. My grandfather's poem." Ashutosh settled back more comfortably in his armchair. Immediately Uma knew that he was searching the peripheral areas of what was to be the day's anecdote.

"He was fair. The colour of a ripe mango is how his complexion was always described. His features were chiselled. And he was tall with a sparse frame."

Ashutosh's tone today sounded different to Uma as he described his grandfather Neelkantha. And his language too. Yet it rang familiar, recalling the voices that had recounted for her the ancient myths and legends. She had not hitherto associated her urbane London-returned father-in-law with such stories.

"Handsome?" she asked.

"He would have been called handsome but for his stern ascetic bearing. In the coldest of winters he would still wear a thin dhoti and a cotton wrapper, even after his bath in the pale of dawn. People said that it was the effect of virtue – and the years of Yogic training in the Himalayas as a young man before he came to Chittagong. Or so I have heard."

"You did not see him? You never met your grandfather?"

Ashutosh looked a little preoccupied. Slowly he shook his head. "No. He was in Chittagong. He did not want to leave his village." The room fell into a silence for a while. "Chittagong. It is perhaps one of the most beautiful places in the world with its unique natural beauty of hills, rivers, sea, forests and valleys. Chittagong had been a seaport since ancient times. Sita kunda is a famous pithasthan there."

Uma recalled the dread rain of Sati's limbs from the sky which had been transformed into temples or so she had been told by Thakma as a child. In Kailash then Uma was suddenly visited by a hazy trace of familiar unease as severed limbs of Sati started their slow descent to earth.

Ashutosh, unaware, continued, "The right arm of the goddess Sati apparently fell in Chandranath in Chittagong. The raja of Tripura, Dharmamanikya, constructed a temple there. And this is where I think, our family history should begin."

A bloodied decapitated right arm slithered somewhere.

Uma swallowed hastily and asked, "It must be a very old temple?"

"I am not very certain, perhaps the 15th or the 16th century. Thousands of pilgrims would gather there during the summer month of Chaitra. Dvija Neelkantha came, with his elder brother, on a pilgrimage to the holy Sita kunda of Chandranath at Chittagong."

"And where did he come from?"

"No one knows. It must have been the early 1850s. He appeared like a flame of celestial fire amidst the congregation. Lesser mortals were drawn to him like moths. Such profound knowledge of the Holy scriptures in one so young was amazing. People insisted that this had to be the memory of a previous birth. His singing voice was divine too. They said he was aptly named Neelkantha. Blue-necked. It is one of the many epithets of Shiva. You know the significance of the name, don't you?"

Uma nodded. "Shiva drank the poison from the ocean being churned for amrita and held it in his throat to prevent the imminent destruction of the world. His throat turned blue. That's why the name Neelkantha is given to Shiva."

"Yes. Neelkantha was the young Brahman's name too. The name seemed apt to the pilgrims of Sita Kunda that year. He held the grief and worries of the pilgrims in his throat, through his songs. He absolved them of their burden. The pilgrims clamoured for him. His brother left but Neelkantha stayed on. The place evidently drew him too. A visiting zamindar also on a pilgrimage with his family was so moved by his presence and knowledge that he implored Neelkantha to take up residence on his estate and look after the temple of Chandi there."

"And did he?"

"Initially he refused. He did not want to grow roots he said. He wanted to have no material ties. But that night the goddess Chandi, in the guise of a young girl pleaded with him in a dream, to take care of her. And so he agreed to accept the Brahmanottar – the rent-free land grant from a zamindar to a Brahman. Thus Neelkantha came to the village in Chittagong called Kynsa mati."

Uma noted that her father-in-law hardly referred to his own grandfather with the familial appellation: neither the formal Thakurdada nor the affectionate diminutive Dadu. Ashutosh spoke of his grandfather as the Dvija – the Brahman as twice born. Born once like all mortals but born again when the sacred thread – the upavaita – is placed in a ritual ceremony of initiation around the young, male Brahman shoulder. Thus the Brahman is bracketed as superior to the rest of humanity who are born only once.

Like chickens. Kaku had once said to Thakma, biting into a hard boiled egg. "Born once out of the hen and then from the egg." Chicken and eggs had been banned from their Brahmanical household in Barishal as in most orthodox Brahman households. "Because we are cousins. Chicken and Brahmans. Both born twice,"

Kaku would say chewing the egg rather noisily. Thakma was always uneasy with the breaking of the taboo in Delhi by her husband. The comment could never raise a laugh out of her. But Kailash was clearly more emancipated than Thakma. Uma had observed no taboos being maintained in the house. Not where food was concerned anyway. Beef and pork were naturally not cooked in the house but she gathered that it could be consumed outside. Father and son had once shared some joke over 'tender sirloins' in her presence. Now the constant reference to Neelkantha as Dvija rendered askew the image of her marital home's westernised modernity. She felt uneasy. A little let down too, momentarily the niece of Kaku.

"When was this *Chandimangal* composed?"

"1857. At least he is supposed to have thought of composing the poem in 1857."

"1857? Really?"

"Yes. 1857. You know it as the year of the Sepoy Mutiny against the British though it is also when Calcutta University was founded. The Mutiny and the University mark the two faces of imperial rule. In our family, however, 1857 is also remembered as the year when the composition of the *Chandimangal* was started by Dvija Neelkantha, priest and poet par excellence, devoted to the goddess."

A moth fluttered around the lamp having foolishly broken through the fences of latticed windows. Uma suddenly realised that it had stopped raining outside. "But he also got married...." her sentence, uncertain whether to proceed as a statement or a question, trailed into nothingness.

"Yes he did of course. Dvija Neelkantha's brother did not bother to keep in touch with him after they parted ways in Sita kunda."

"But why?"

"Apparently the brother always wanted to be a wandering hermit. The Dvija, as the village called its most revered Brahman, realised that it was up to him to marry and beget a son to carry on the lineage. My father was thus born when the Dvija was well past forty, virtually an old man by the standards of those days. He went back to being an ascetic soon after."

And his wife? Uma wanted to ask about the woman who had ensured that the ascetic fulfilled his duties to his ancestors by begetting a son but Ashutosh got up suddenly and left the room.

Uma was about to collect the tray and leave the parlour when Ashutosh returned with the book, "Dvija Neelkantha's *Chandimangal.*" He held it out. "You and yours must be its custodians."

Uma on a sudden impulse bent to touch her father-in-law's feet before reaching out with both hands to take the book.

He touched her head in blessing, clearly moved too: "I know you have been taught to read Bengali even though you grew up in Delhi but you may find the language here somewhat archaic. I will help you through the difficult passages if you wish"

The room was quiet. Both realised that the evening had been special. But neither knew that it would be quite another who would take Uma through the difficult passages, using a different grid. Entirely different.

The moth was now fluttering inside the hot shade of the lamp casting huge shadows in the room. Uma smoothened the old book in her hand.

❧ ❧

Rudra climbed up the stairs with a light tread aleady seeing in his mind the parlour where Uma waited for him with Baba. A slight sound made him turn at the landing. But there was nothing. He stood still for a while with his head bent as though to catch some distant crying. Then he shook his head and walked into the parlour to allow its warmth to fold over him.

❄ Four ❄

THE LEE MACHINE. CRAB TREE. Black and white. Half tone. Multi coloured. Font. Heidelburg. Flat bed. Lithograph. Offset.

New words were beginning to seep into Uma's lexicon as the father and the son discussed the matters of printing at the dining table or in the parlour upstairs after dinner in Kailash.

"What do you print?" Uma asked Rudra, "Other than the *Panjika* I mean."

Chatto's Panjika was one of the most popular editions of the Bengali almanacs – a ready reckoner of rituals and festivals, standing in for the Brahman astrologer not just in Calcutta or Bengal but wherever the Bengali settled. It was indeed one of the bestsellers of Bengali publications. Uma was familiar with *Chatto's Panjika* which was kept with the household deities by Thakma. But it seemed somewhat incongruous to associate either her father-in-law or her husband with that garish pink almanac, a textual bastion of Bengali Hindu orthodoxy.

"A lot of prescribed and supplementary books on science and economics for the High School and the Undergraduate students," Rudra responded with an uncharacteristic alacrity, recovered, shrugged and added, "House Magazines for companies, cash memoes, bill books and multi-coloured labels."

"Labels?"

"Yes. For Bidis, soaps, umbrellas… Sorry. It does not sound romantic perhaps. But that's business for you."

Labels. Yes. That was yet another ingenuous contribution

to the business of The Ganges Press by Rudra's grandfather, Shashishekhar, who believed in seizing the moment.

❦ ❦

The world's rapidly expanding commodity trade had brought jute, known as Paat in Bengal, into immense prominence as packaging material. The heyday of the jute industry was between 1890 and 1940. During this period jute dominated the economic life of Bengal virtually monopolising the world's production of raw jute. The peasants in East and Central Bengal cultivated jute in their small holdings, initially using family labour but as labour cheapened, the holders of land and capital brought in hired hands. In 1855, the first jute mill of Bengal was built in Serampore, Rishra, by George Auckland, a retired tea planter from Ceylon. More mills came up soon enough: in Shyamnagar, Khidirpore, Budge Budge and Garden Reach. These were scattered on either side of the River Hooghly, as the tributary of Ganga is known in Calcutta.

There were also other mills dotting Calcutta and its neighbourhood: the cotton ginning, cleaning and pressing mills. Rice mills, Castor oil mills and flour mills too. These mills could depend upon a steady supply of workers from the increasing ruins of the rural resources. The men queued up before the mills first. Their women were left to retain the shrinking rural base: some land or just a homestead. But they too were forced to migrate when the rural resource was utterly exhausted. Sometimes these women accompanied their families. But often they came alone: widowed, deserted by the husband or turned out of the homestead by in-laws.

For Shashishekhar Chattopadhyay mills, jute and packaging meant labels. He was happy to seize the opportunity.

❦ ❦

Ashutosh was happy that evening. The dinner at the Calcutta Club with a group of old friends and acquaintances had been very satisfying.

The Calcutta Club, set up in 1907 with the express purpose of facilitating social intercourse between the British and Indians, was an elite bastion. It still attracted luminaries from different fields. Ashutosh had managed that evening to finally persuade an eminent Professor of Economics to compile a statistical overview of the Indian economy since Independence. It would not be a textbook but a companion. Ashutosh knew that there was, and would continue to be, a market for it.

Socially too, the evening had been relaxing. Ashutosh when asked about his new daughter-in-law could say honestly that she was a good girl. His gamble, of getting a bride for his only son from Delhi, had paid off. True, Uma's family was not the upper crust of the Indian elite but they hailed from the erstwhile well-to-do landed gentry. There was a dignity to the background and the promise of social mobility through the approved, and safe, means of education. So far, then, so good.

Ashutosh was grateful. It had seemed to him often of late that there was a sense of sorrow about Kailash. There were of course no visible signs of it. His mother, that amazing woman, had left behind a well oiled machine which still worked from the morning tea which arrived with two thin arrowroot biscuits to the lights downstairs being switched off at eleven sharp at night. His laundry was perfect. The beds wrinkle free. The silver, brass, bronze, copper and glass shone in the house with regular polish. The menu for four meals followed the seasons, his health and young Rudra's palate. There was absolutely no disarray. Yet some gossamer fine shadow seemed to hang about Kailash still. Sometimes Ashutosh found himself wondering why should it be so. His sins, if any, were surely those of omission? And arguably for the sake of peace.

He had not really started thinking seriously about Rudra's marriage when one of his sisters proposed Uma's name. Clearly she had thought it a suitable match. But then Rudra – well off, educated, London returned, good looking, not just upper caste but with a famous ancestry – had attracted several proposals over the years. That was inevitable. He had asked his son once, or twice maybe, since Rudra's return from London if he was ready to consider marriage: "So and so was mentioning a niece or a cousin or a neighbour. Do you want to think about it?"

"Not now", Rudra had always said.

He too had let it rest.

There had always been a certain degree of intimacy between the father and the son. Ashutosh still remembered how the five-year old Rudra had slipped his hands around the bed post and looked at him the night he returned from England. He had not expected his return to be thus. God knows how much he had thought and dreamt of the day he would return home to Kailash from England. But not thus. Never thus.

His five-year old son's eyes were bleak. No child should look like that, Ashutosh had thought, anguished. And not mine, never mine. For a moment there had been just the two of them in the room. And a shadow between. Of Shivani, his wife and Rudra's mother, who was now gone forever.

I will be here for you always, Ashutosh had thought that night of his return, gazing into his son's eyes though he did not remember being able to say anything. His parents were in the room too. Then Shashishekhar, his father, had gently taken Haimanti, his mother, who was crying softly, out of the room. It had been just the two of them finally. He and his son. Rudra.

Young and motherless Rudra had often appealed to him for licenses and liberties such as his orthodox grandmother would forbid. Father and son had always managed to work out a compromise. The older Rudra was also his colleague. Ashutosh respected, indeed valued, his judgement. He gave Rudra his space too, in the office and in life as well, he hoped. Ashutosh took some pride in the fact that his son respected him but it was not an awe that created a gulf, as had been the case between him and his own father.

But Ashutosh was surprised by Rudra's reaction to the proposal of marriage. He was somewhat taken aback when Rudra responded quite seriously to his aunt's suggestion that he should at least meet this girl from Delhi, saying "Why not? Let's meet them by all means." Ashutosh did not fail to notice that Rudra had already taken charge of the decision. "I did not realise that he was ready for marriage," Ashutosh had thought though he too voiced consent, "Let's go ahead. Let's meet them. At least. By all means."

One look at his son's face after the departure of the guests and Ashutosh knew. Oh it was not anything as coarse as calf love, but Rudra seemed to have made up his mind. There was a settled air about him.

Just before the guests left, someone had asked Rudra if he wished to ask Uma any questions. Rudra had smiled. Somebody else had insisted. Rudra had continued to smile and then had asked, leaning back a little in his seat, "Do you read poetry, modern Bengali poetry?" There had been immediate laughter from all around which drowned Uma's answer if any. The laughter covered up Ashutosh's reaction too – he had felt his skin crawl. The room had receded and another voice had come to him, a hesitant voice, a girl's voice that lacked the quiet assurance that laced Rudra's query, but asking the same question: "Do you read poetry, modern Bengali poetry?" Ashutosh had long forgotten the question that was buried deep within him. How did it travel through time and space to find an echo in their son's voice? Coincidence? Genes? Or nemesis?

Ashutosh was surprisingly shaken. He had wondered that night, alone in his darkened bedroom, if he should steer Rudra clear of this match. He felt as though the question was a premonition of the settled being stirred. But that would have been irrational, if not foolish.

He was glad now that he had not succumbed to the musings of a tired mind; glad too that Rudra was married. Uma's pleasant nature, her evident pleasure in being at Kailash appeared to have banished the fine cobwebs of gloom. Or what was perhaps just his fancy.

❦❦

It was a snack that Ashutosh fancied, this dish of boiled pigeon peas laced with ginger, where the palate savouring the tangy spice was occasionally surprised by the sweetness of small slivers of coconut. Ashutosh loved ghugni and felt that it suited the light drizzle outside. A heavier downpour went better with something crisp and hot like a plate of golden yellow telebhajha.

Uma was pouring out the tea.

"So have you started reading the *Chandimangal*?" Ashutosh asked and then added, "I hope I am not sounding like a tutor. It just means so much to me that someone is reading it in Kailash once again."

"Yes. But just about. I am afraid that it will be slow progress. I need to get used to the language. It is an older form, is it not?" Uma's tone was apologetic. She sought to steer the discussion away from exactly how much she had read. "Is there an original still?"

"Original?"

"I mean the handwritten punthi of Dvija Neelkantha. The book must have been printed from the manuscript much later?"

"Yes. Yes. But it's kept in the locker at the bank. The University had wanted it to bring out an annotated edition. I gave them the copy which my father had made for daily consultation, when it was being printed for the first time. I have to confess that I could not bring myself to part with the original. It is our family heritage after all. People keep jewellery in their bank lockers, but the Chattopadhyays keep their *Chandimangal*."

Dadu's soft face suddenly intruded like a shaft of pain. Uma remembered that Dadu too had once written a book. He had gone to Calcutta from his village in Barishal to get it published. He wanted it to be printed from the College Square in the city that he had roamed as a student. It was here that he had sometimes also chanced upon the Bengali luminaries in flesh and blood, who had heralded a renaissance in the colonised state. College Square represented for Dadu, as he himself said, a new and modern India. Dadu had believed that his book too had a place in the nation that was being formed. It was a belief, held dear like faith. But he had come back unsuccessful. There had been no takers. One publisher had told him that it was preposterous. Another had actually refused to return his manuscript saying that it was offal to be burnt. Dadu had retuned to the village, his broken heart encased in determination. He had his notes: pages and pages of thin scrawls in Sanskrit, Bengali and English. Almost a year later he had made another trip to College Street in Calcutta. With his new manuscript. And Thakma's jewellery.

Dadu's book was published but sank without a trace. A couple of copies remained on his bookshelf still. All of them knew those as the book that Dadu had written. The books were dusted regularly but no one had bothered to read it. Uma's heart suddenly felt heavy with pain for her gentle and unsuccessful grandfather even as Kailash resonated with Chattopadhyay pride.

Uma wondered if the publisher who had been so harsh with Dadu's work, thinking of it as 'offal to be burnt', was still around. "Were the printing presses in Calcutta always in College Street? All the old and famous ones, I mean?"

"Oh no! The presses before 1800 were naturally located around the residential and commercial area of the European community. It was called Tank Square then, Dalhousie Square to you and me today. In 1781, The Honourable Company's Press was inaugurated in Calcutta. In 1800 Fort William College was established to train the young British Officers of the Empire. Our English rulers needed books in 'native' languages on native religions, laws and cultures. William Carey the Baptist missionary started the Serampore Press with a second-hand machine bought from an indigo planter the same year. An amazing Bengali craftsman Panchanan Karmakar became Carey's right hand man. Carey's press brought out about 200,000 books in 40 languages between 1801 and 1832.

The rain heightened its tempo. A window banged against the wall and water seemed to be gurgling over the verandah.

"Do you know that the first printing press of India was actually offloaded in Goa by the Portuguese, and not the English, on the 6th of September, 1556."

"Goa? Not Calcutta?"

"The first printed book of this country, well, as far as I know, is *Compendio Spiritual Da Vida Christa*. This was printed in Goa in 1561. You see print, like trade, followed the coastal track from Goa to Hooghly or Calcutta, if you will."

"Which was the first Bengali book to be printed?"

"Technically the first Bengali book was not printed in Calcutta but in far off Lisbon."

"The Portuguese again?"

"I think it was *Crepar Xastrer Orth Bhed* or *Cathescismo da Doutrina*. In Lisbon. Yes, the Portuguese again. The first grammar and dictionary of the Bengali language was also published from Lisbon in 1743 – *Vocabulario em Idioma Bengalla und Poruguez*. It was in Roman characters though."

Ashutosh finished his ghugni and put down the glass bowl and the plate. Uma handed him his tea. A sense of well being, warm and satiated, slowly filled the room. Ashutosh carried on. The rain too continued unabated.

The printing press had rapidly proliferated – despite the initial orthodox suspicion that it was yet another attempt to corrupt the ancient Hindu culture. It appeared even in the Black Town of Calcutta in the northern part of the city where the 'natives' stayed. By the second half of 19th century printing was a spawning industry and a close second only to the jute industry. The cluster of presses along Chitpur Road, a large contiguous stretch, came to be referred collectively as Battala press. Hindu College, later known as Presidency College, shifted from Garanhata Street to Pataldanga next to a pond known as Goldighi in 1825. This gradually transformed the pond and the street adjoining it as Calcutta's College Square and College Street. The nerve centre of the publishing world of Calcutta also moved to this location sanctified by the new centres of academic learning.

The sky rumbled. Once and then again.

There was the sound of a car crunching into the driveway followed by a horn.

Ashutosh looked at Uma and said with sudden longing, "My father used to come home in his phaeton when I was a very young child. You don't find men like my father any more in this city. They were men who used western technology to help preserve the rich heritage of our own culture. They were men of vision and principles who learnt from the West without compromising their own tradition and heritage. I miss men like him and the Calcutta of my childhood more and more." Ashutosh sighed and let go. "This hankering for the past is an old man talking. But Calcutta has changed. No one can deny that. And unfortunately it is for the worse."

❀❀

Calcutta.

As the Brahman poet Neelkantha composed his *Chandimangal* in the quiet temple of the obscure village Kynsa mati in Chittagong, Calcutta was bustling with life and opportunities, providing for some a staircase to heaven but for many others a merry decline to hell.

The trading boats and ships dropped anchor at the Ganga here. The goods travelled to the great emporium or the Burra bazaar, the platform for the goddess of wealth while the human cargo from the impoverished ancestral villages scattered all over the city in search of a better life. Thus the bylanes of north Calcutta gradually got ghettoised in terms of various crafts and professions: Kansareepara, Kumortuli, Syankrapara, Tatipara, Darjipara....the colonies of the brass smiths, the potters, the conch shell craftsmen, the weavers, the tailors.... The patrons of these arts and culture in the city were the native elite compradors who were also the custodians of Hindu traditions. They conducted business with the English but maintained the sanctity of their homes, and their women, by observing all the rituals, and prohibitions, prescribed by the Brahmans.

The culture vultures of the new metropolis gathered in Bagbazar, often adapting the traditional forms of entertainment to suit the taste of the nouveau riche patrons. Cheek-by-jowl was the flesh market, Sonagaji. This was often visited by the same elite patrons marked by their wavy hair, the mishi darkened teeth according to current fashion and feather light dhotis. Of course coarser dhotis too were seen here as Sonagaji also provided for those with lighter pockets.

On the other side of Bagbazar stood the huge mosque of Reza Khan across the temple of Chittesvari, the churches of the Portuguese and the Armenians. The catholic character of the nineteenth century city was thus marked by the propitiation of the various gods and the ceaseless pursuit of wealth. No wonder they called her *Kolikata Kamalalaya* – Calcutta, the abode of the goddess of wealth.

By the middle of the 19th century, the spectacular and vulgar display of wealth by the comprador babus – the kite flying, the cock fighting, the foaming wine, the tinkling of nautch girls' anklets, the bawdy songs, the lavish funerals and marriages, the splendour of the religious festivals and the mindless consumerism – was beginning to be criticised by the next generation of the native elite population. This generation had received a different education and was aware of a world outside of Calcutta. Thus Chitpur now also housed the Adi Brahmo Samaj that critiqued the idolatory of Hinduism. The Hindu College had been founded. So too the Oriental Seminary, Duff's school and Bethune's school for girls.

❉ ❉

"I want to study in Kolkata," said young Shashishekhar.

Neelkantha opened his eyes and looked at his visiting son for a while without saying anything. Young Shashishekhar held the gaze but without arrogance.

The temple precinct was empty. There was still time enough for the evening prayers. The village knew that its foremost Brahman was being visited by his son and maintained a discreet distance between prayers.

The father and the son were seated across each other. Both

were handsome, fair and overbearing though one was old and the other young.

Finally Neelkantha asked, "Why?"

"We are Brahmans. Surely knowledge has been ordained as power for us?"

"But you want to study English?"

"I want to study English as well. As you learnt Farsi. The world is changing."

"It always has. It always will."

Shashishekhar looked at the sunlit river Kynsa for a while and then turned towards his father, "May I go then?"

"Where will you stay in Kolkata?"

"There are places for students, exclusive ones for the Brahmans too. But they cost money."

"And have your maternal uncles refused help?"

"I have not asked them as yet. Naturally, I will not discuss it with them till you give me your blessings."

Neelkantha looked at his son and felt something course through his veins very like emotion at the sight of the young and determined Shashishekhar. Young Shashishekhar was his father's entirely. The silly woman, fat and frivolous, whom he called mother, had been merely nurse to the sown embryo.

Neelkantha nodded. "I bless you my son. Go make your mark. Spread light as is the purpose of a Brahman life. Money will not be an issue. The zamindar here will be more than willing to sponsor you, even if your uncles don't. Go forth then and know that it is your destiny to rule the world through knowledge. Thus god made the Brahmans the head of the four castes, the head that thinks and by thinking, rules."

Neelkantha shut his eyes and recited a Sanskrit shloka in his rich voice which was a subliminal metaphor of the Brahman's superior existence. The sun glowed a fiery red lighting up the sky and the temple. Shashishekhar shut his eyes too. Both father and son were moved by the theatricality of the encounter, so reminiscent of rituals. Indeed they enjoyed playing out the prescribed roles. Thus must the gurus of yore have blessed their disciples who then spread out to fulfil their charted destiny.

The river Kynsa shone golden catching the sunlight.

※ ※

The river was a silver grey that appeared to merge with the moisture laden air. The monsoon magic vaporised the effluence in the water. A mossy boat swayed slowly as the water slapped its sides. In the distance could be seen the shadowy outlines of steamers, and launches. The big ships shimmered beyond them. It could be a ghost land. A loud shout from the shore broke the spell.

Uma and Rudra strolled slowly on the embankment. They were due for yet another dinner at a relative's but had paused on the way to look at the ships that so fascinated Uma.

"The ships look beautiful. It scares me though. To think of only water all around. I can't even swim."

"If the ship sinks I don't think swimming would help much."

Uma laughed, "Thanks. That's reassuring."

"Glad to be of help, Madam."

They stood together, staring at the watery expanse. The free end of Uma's saree gently fluttered against Rudra. He looked at his watch.

"I suppose you are above irrational fears," asked Uma.

"Hmm."

"Come. Confess. Do you have any?"

"Landings."

"What? Landing in a strange new country?"

"No. Just landings. In Kailash where I grew up."

※ ※

Shashishekhar had grown up in his mother's house, Mamabari, as they called it in Bengal. A bullock cart and a boat could bring him to his father's village in a day's time. Shashishekhar's maternal great grandfather was a subsidiary to a diwan to a salt agent. The East India Company had acquired its monopoly over salt in 1772 under

Warren Hastings which was leased over to private agents within four years. But since the agent was always British, an Indian go-between, the diwan, was required for the intricacies of the transactions. The diwan had, or formed, his own network of extraction in the countryside. Most prominent men of the 19th century, including the famous Tagores, owed their family's accumulated fortunes to this enterprise. The wealth usually translated into zamindari as land holding remained the safest, and the most prestigious, form of capital investment. Shashishekhar's maternal family had invested likewise. They were not just Brahmans but kulins as well. They were thus the purest of the pure.

Neelkantha having composed his *Chandimangal* wanted to fulfil his domestic duty by siring a son who could offer oblations to the dead ancestors. This was a religious duty. And Neelkantha did not believe in shirking from duties. He voiced his thought to the zamindar of Kynsa mati. Kulin Brahmans were not easy to come by. And a man was never judged by his age in marriage. Neelkantha had a proud lineage and a formidable fund of knowledge to boot. Undoubtedly this Brahman poet who presided over the temple of Chandi in Kynsa mati would be a catch. The patron of the temple, the zamindar of Kynsa mati, then suggested that his old family friend, Shashishekhar's maternal grandfather, should get his youngest daughter married to Neelkantha.

Neelkantha's looks and knowledge not only impressed but also alarmed the corpulent maternal grandfather of Shashishekhar. He didn't want to admit that of course and so he joked, "You want to be a father? Ha, ha….er… hmm, hmm." The coarse laughter was checked into a cough as Neelkantha turned and looked coldly at his prospective father-in-law. The cough, feigned at first became a real paroxysm as the man dragged too strongly on his hookah to hide his sudden nervousness. His dhoti climbed up to reveal a fat, white thigh.

Neelkantha asked just one question. "Is your family of the pure kulin lineage, that it is supposed to be?" The fat man nodded and took a deep breath before beginning on a recital of his lineage. The zamindar of Kynsa mati rushed into speech too to vouchsafe for the purity of his friend's kulin Brahman lineage.

Both were cut short by Neelkantha, "I would like to take a look at your Kulpanji. I presume you have one?"

Having thus vetted his prospective in-law and demanding the clan manual of him, Neelkantha got up, refused the hookah, nodded at his host, the zamindar of Kynsa mati, and left.

Contempt had its effect. Shashishekhar's maternal grandfather was convinced that he had found a true Brahman. Seduced by the honour that such a matrimonial alliance would bring and reassured by the knowledge that his daughter need not live with this rather frightening man but continue to be at his home even after marriage so as not to disturb the ascetic tenor of his son-in-law's life, the fat man agreed with alacrity. If the chubby seven year old object of transaction was frightened by her old groom, if his penetration into her life for a brief period, a couple of years later, resulted in tears or screams, nothing is known of it. All that is certain is the birth of a son in due course. The birth took place at her natal home. Her ascetic husband attended the due rituals of gestation, birth and all the subsequent ceremonies marking the growth of the male Brahman offspring. Her family bore the cost willingly. Neelkantha named his son Shashishekhar: Shiva bearing the crescent moon on his head. Thus it was ordained that in future all male progeny of the Chattopadhyays of Kynsa mati be named after Lord Shiva of the divine Hindu trinity. Hence Ashutosh and Rudra.

Shashishekhar grew up in a house marked as much by its tenacious observance of Brahmanical rituals as by coarse laughter and indolence. The house was large. The inhabitants numerous. The kitchen fire here was extinguished only very, very late at night. There was always milk: boiled once for the infants, thickened for the boys and thickened and sweetened further for the men. Milk was also always available for those who wanted to enjoy their opium in the evening. Thus the males marked their rites of passage in the family. And thus the family fortunes dwindled.

Shashishekhar's mother and Neelkantha's wife also matured here from a girl to a woman, from a daughter to a wife to a mother. The actual intricacies and labour of motherhood passed her by. There was always somebody to pick up the crying child. Her milk was thin. A wet nurse was organized as a matter of course. She played with her son, flirted with various cousins, gossiped with the maids and chivvied her sisters-in-law. Life carried on.

Shashishekhar visited his father more frequently in his adolescence. He was keen on education. His father approved his desire. His mother's family, her father and then her brothers, appointed the teachers and paid for them. His mother was relieved that she did not have to fulfil any other conjugal duties. But she enjoyed looking at her handsome son who was tall and fair. He was quiet, unlike his cousins. It struck a discordant note in her house. Shashishekhar's cousins, crass but assured of their place in the feudal rural society, sometimes sneered at him.

"Why don't you laugh? There is no tax on it."

"Go away. I am reading."

"Is this the poem that your father has written?"

"No. It is the *Ramayana*. Valmiki composed it, Brahman boys. You should have known."

"My father's got the punthi for you. What has your father…"

"Your father would have got it for you too. But it's meant for reading, not supposed to be used as a stool." Shashishekhar stood up, carefully placing the punthi on its short wooden stand. He was a head taller than the tallest cousin.

The cousins retreated. Then in a safe huddle, they hissed out: "Brahman boy, we have heard things about the great poet, your father."

"That indeed is a price of greatness. And thank god at least your ears work. But since the same cannot be said of what lies between those two protrusions, let's go and ask your fathers to decipher what you have heard."

The boys went away in a rush. They had all experienced their fathers' wooden slippers landing on their bare backs often enough.

They also knew that the uncles held Shashishekhar, though a young and dependent relative, in some esteem.

Shashishekhar looked thoughtful.

One day, soon after, he informed his mother that he was going to Calcutta to study further and that he had already discussed it with his father. She cried. Then she wiped her tears and asked that he marry before he left for that den of vice. She would ask her brothers to forbid it otherwise. And she herself would tie a noose around her neck. Shashishekhar agreed. The excessive display of emotion that his mother and her siblings thrived on tired him to death. It was easier to agree to marry. Indeed, it was the easiest way of achieving his purpose. It was also easy to find a bride. Her mother's cousin blessed with three sons had adopted the fourth daughter of her husband's sister, in the generous spirit of the blessed. Shashishekhar's mother and the cousin had grown up sharing secrets. They were happy to be able to share their children. The house too seized upon this chance to laugh and be merry, to gather around and find out what was happening in everyone's life. The ponds were dragged for the biggest fish. The jewellery cases inspected anew. The estate manager was sent to Calcutta to find the latest design in sarees and dhotis, despite the shaking of head of the old naib and the lighter coffers. The men vetted and voted for the dancing girls to grace the occasion.

Shashishekhar left his mother with her new doll and set off for Calcutta leaving not just them but that part of his life behind him. How could a man acquire knowledge if he remained fettered to the women of his family?

The women cried.

Shashishekhar's mother cried because she loved her son in her own way. His mother-in-law cried because she suddenly wondered what would happen to her daughter if this grim-faced boy did not return from Calcutta. His wife, the child, cried because everyone seemed to be crying.

But they also accepted that they had to let him go.

Shashishekhar's mother watched the retreating back of her

son amidst a procession of uncles, cousins and hangers on. Shashishekhar's father had said that the moment was auspicious for departure. Mahendra-jog.

"It is the steadfast devotion of the Hindu women, even when left behind by their men, that actually makes the world go round. We are Sati-Lakshmi, the household goddesses." Shashishekhar's mother cried some more after having proved her position as wife to the scholarly poet of the *Chandimangal* with the strong statement. The new bride joined in. She was very young and had been told by her mother to follow her mother-in-law in every way.

The other women of the family soon gathered around to take the weeping Sati-Lakshmis inside the house. "Our pain and misery purify us and that is why the world deifies us as Sati-Lakshmi," they echoed, thinking of their own lives.

❀ ❀

It was a Thursday. The day was held special for goddess Lakshmi by the Hindu Bengali. The goddess of wealth was also the beloved consort of Vishnu and therefore the guardian angel of conjugal bliss as well. Uma gently swayed and read out the verses from a booklet, *Lakshmi Bratakatha*, in the puja room on the terrace of Kailash. Or rather she held the booklet in her hand but recited from memory large sections of it. The bratakatha had slowly wound its way into her unconscious from the very first Thursday of her life as she lay on the big bed and her grandmother recited it in front of the goddess. She heard it when she toddled in the room, willingly ran chores for what she initially took to be her grandmother's dolls and then caught its echo from the various corners of the green house if she happened to be at home on Thursdays. Earlier Thakma used to perform this Thursday ritual. When she became a widow Ma took over as the chief housewife of the family with Kaki waiting in the wings. In Kailash Uma performed the Thursday ritual as the presiding lady of the household. Rudra's aunt had instructed her thus. Adding that her stomach must be empty, her state pure.

It was not a demanding duty. Everything was laid out for Uma.

The copper and the brass vessels, the lamps and the incense holder glowed warm, freshly scrubbed by Khema who had also placed the piece of sandalwood shaped like a pestle, the flat stone plate and a small copper container of water near at hand for Uma. Khema did not make the sandalwood paste as she knew that her low caste Bagdi touch would pollute the offering to the goddess.

Uma's voice was soft in the puja room of Kailash as she recited what was basically a moral tale with the promise of palpable, material awards for those who followed the prescribed path and agonising punishments for transgressors.

> *uccahaasi katukatha kahe narigan|*
> *sandhyakale nidra jaye haye achetan ||*
> *ramani bhushan lajjya diya bisharjan |*
> *jathae tathae kare svechaye gaman ||*
> *nahi deye dhup dvip prati shandhya kale |*
> *satir sindur shobha nahi pare bhale ||… … .*

> The women laugh loudly and harsh words they do speak
> at dusk you will find them still fast asleep.
> The virtues of women, shame and modesty, they kill
> these women go everywhere of their own free will.
> The incense and the lamp are not lit when it's dark
> with the good wife's symbol their foreheads they do not
> mark….

As always the monotony of the little chant soothed Uma with a remembrance of being at home with her mother, aunt and grandmother. Rudra's mother and his grandmother must also have thus read out the bratakatha.

The ritual over, Uma could now go down to a meal of fruit and sweets laid out by Pishi on a white plate made of translucent marble. An equally pristine white marble tumbler held the water of a tender coconut. It would be covered with a crocheted lace doily. The aesthetics of it filled Uma with a glow of immense happiness. Kashmere Gate had been far more utilitarian. She loved sweets too. This was compensation for missing out on breakfast on Thursdays.

❧❧

"So are you happy?" Rudra leaned against the parapet casually and tried to blow a smoke ring which was ruffled by the wind.

It was a Sunday afternoon. Lunch was over. Ashutosh had retired to his room for his afternoon siesta. Rudra and Uma were on their way up to the bedroom when the sudden darkening of the staircase suggested imminent rain. Uma wanted to check that the windows of the puja room were shut and secure and Rudra followed her all the way up to the second floor. He did not enter the puja room though but walked across the terrace and lit a cigarette. The creeping vine of Madhavilata drooped over the wall in delicate clumps of pink and white. The jasmine creeper from the front of the house had not made it to the terrace.

The sky was darkening rapidly though the clouds were still scattered and the breeze pleasant, promising a welcome respite for the steaming city. The agonising bleak monotony of monsoon had not yet set in. Rudra's white kurta billowed gently in the breeze. He is good looking thought Uma with a rush of pride as she too crossed the terrace to join him.

"There was a time when that house was full of children. I grew up playing there." Rudra gestured towards the garden that met their own boundary wall at the back. Amidst the mango, jackfruit, coconut and lemon trees ran a rich riot of weeds that spread on the ground and arrogantly climbed all over the ancient trees. The shuttered and barred doors and windows in the gathering grey of the afternoon only added to the dismal picture of neglect.

"There?" Uma knew it as the backyard of a godown of chemical products. Of course it must been a house once with a family living in it but its obvious air of neglect did not attract Uma.

"Hmm. It was not like this of course. A large family of innumerable children and cousins stayed here. The Seal house was the hub of Dalimbagan then. Look at it now!"

"Where is the family?"

"Oh, they moved to South Calcutta long ago. Some of the children have gone to America."

"Seal. That is an unusual surname."

"They represent Bengal's original merchant community. Baniks. The old patriarch was very proud of his lineage, like my grandfather. He often said that the Seals were the original merchant clan of Bengal, the Brahmans became merchants much later."

"Your grandfather could not have liked being called a merchant?"

"He did not. Certainly he did not see himself as one. A publisher and a book seller would have been for him the modern avatar of the Brahman. The person who really got riled though was my grandmother."

"What did she say?"

"She did not say anything. She hated what she considered to be Seal arrogance. The fact that their house was bigger than ours. The fact that old Seal always connected the Chattopadhyays with trade and saw the Brhaman as a merchant, like them." The smoke from Rudra's cigarette was becoming amorphous long before it could reach the Seal garden. "My grandmother lived in fear and trembling. The Seal girls were dark and slender. Nellydi, the eldest, was the toast of Dalimbagan. We boys just adored her. She used to play the piano."

"Where is she now?"

Rudra shrugged. "She got married while I was in school. What a wedding it was! My grandmother did not approve. 'Showing off money. Just like their caste,' she said."

The garden across the wall was being gathered in the growing darkness of the sky. The wayward wind raised a green tumult and the undergrowth could not be seen. Did the rustle of the leaves, the howl of the wind echo the laughter from the abandoned house?

"What was she like? Your grandmother?"

Rudra continued to smoke.

Uma peered down and caught sight of Khema in a bright orange saree scouring their lunch utensils. Her movements were hurried to avoid the approaching downpour. A fat blob of raindrop fell on Uma's nose.

"Let's go down." She said.

"She spent a lot of her time propitiating her gods. The rest was for us. Her son and grandson. Her husband too but he died before her."

"Most women of her generation were like that. They were taught to be like that, I suppose."

"I think she was a very insecure person. There was a time when all I wanted to do was to shake her pious assumptions and ways."

"Like wanting bread for breakfast?" Uma smiled recalling her father-in-law's tale of young Rudra.

"How do you know that? Yes, that was one. She had this peculiar thing against bread. The firangis had got it, she said, to make us lose our caste purity. She actually believed that they kneaded the dough – or worse still got the Muslims to do it – with their feet before baking it."

"But she bought bread for you."

"She also made a point of telling me how much she was giving up – or giving in – for the love of me."

"Well she did."

"Yes."

Rudra suddenly tossed the cigarette away in one graceful arc over the terrace. "Come let's go down." Rudra's hand possessed Uma's back in a warm, intimate gesture. But he paused once again, a little distracted.

"The terrace reminds me…"

"Of your grandmother?"

"Of my mother."

Uma stood still. More than surprised.

"Nothing tangible. Not an image. Not words. Just a feeling. I was only five. I wish I had at least memories. Something sharply defined."

Uma looked at Rudra and put her heart in her eyes for him,

wanting to make up for his loss, his sorrow, immediately and forever. And then overwhelmed by her own response looked away.

Rudra followed her gaze and saw the puja room.

"No. Not that room. Just the terrace. Just this space. Let's go."

"I…"

"I know."

Together they crossed the terrace and the puja room which was now shut and secure.

※※

"It smells lovely," said Khema, carrying down all the puja utensils to be washed and scrubbed into that glowing state again.

"What?" asked Pishi, looking up from her task of slicing potatoes very fine on a plate on the floor in the big kitchen with a bati; the curved knife gleaming out of a dark wooden slat that she held firm with her foot. Lunch was sent for the two men from home. Bamundi, the woman who cooked, a Brahman by caste though poor, would grind the various spices, prepare, boil, fry and cook the basics but Pishi always cut the vegetables, cooked the fish and the day's delicacies. There was an array of bowls with water in front of her. Each vegetable was cut differently for the different dishes. Those that would be used for the fish or mutton curry were kept separate lest they defile the vegetarian fare.

"The puja room with the flowers, the incense and the sandalwood is smelling really nice," reiterated Khema, as she went out into the courtyard at the back of the kitchen where she did her washing and scouring. The drizzle was thin, gently settling on her saree. But the door though open did not bring in any water into the kitchen.

"I heard you reading out to the gods." Khema's voice laced with wonder wafted into the kitchen as Uma came in a little later. "Can you not sometimes read here? We will listen to you while working? Will it be a sin, to read of gods and goddesses in the kitchen?"

"Will it be?" Bamundi asked.

Pishi wiped the bati clean.

Uma felt a little disappointed that Pishi did not echo the request.

"What would you like to hear?" Uma saw herself reading out to these women as they worked. She would be lightening their hour. "The *Chandimangal*?" she asked, inspired. It would help her get through the task of reading it too.

Pishi stood up somewhat stiffly and addressed Bamundi. "Is the oil hot enough now to fry the fish?"

Bamundi said that she thought so.

Pishi wiped her forehead with one end of her white saree before settling down again near the stove meant for non-vegetarian cooking.

Compassion flooded Uma.

"Why don't you come up and see the Puja room Pishi?" she entreated, "I have rearranged a few things. Nothing major but still I would like you to see it."

Pishi looked up and the green eyes wandered over Uma's face.

"The oil is beginning to burn Pishi" Bamundi remonstrated gently.

The acrid smell of the smoking hot mustard oil engulfed the kitchen. Hiss and splutter followed as the slices of fish were lowered into it.

❃ Five ❃

Bhaat maach kheye bache bangali sakal |
Dhaanbhara bhumi tai maachbhara jal ||

Fish with rice is Bengal's staple dish,
Where the earth is rich with paddy and the water's
full of fish.

BENGAL'S NETWORK OF RIVERS, STREAMS, canals, catchments, creeks, channels, ponds and a proto-Australoid influence have ensured that Aryavarta's injunctions about the impurity of fish and meat have never been strong enough to erase the prominence of fish in Bengali cuisine and culture. Brahmans elsewhere in India (excepting Kashmir) may lose their caste for eating fish but the Smriti scholars of Bengal like Bhavdeva Bhatta, Jimutvahan and Shrinathacharya argued that the consumption of fish (and meat) was no abomination for Brahmans except on certain holy days.

But food is also a measure of purity and the fish-eating Bengali Brahman had to be distinguished from lesser mortals. The white scaly fish, considered the best of its kind in Bengal, was thus sanctioned for the Brahman who was not to eat fish that lived in mud holes or had no scales or whose mouth and head resembled a snake's. Those were for men and women down the caste ladder. This too was stated by the Brahmans who composed the *Vrihaddharma Purana* in eastern India.

The widows of the Bengali Brahmans however could not have any. Neither freshwater fish nor fish from the sea. Neither from rivers nor from mud holes.

Purity and hierarchy were thus ordered and safeguarded.

Uma was not partial to fish. Her parents had complained often enough about the changing palate of the new generation of Bengalis in Delhi. Uma's brother had warned, in the true spirit of younger brothers, that she would probably have to eat fish every day for both meals if she married Rudra of Kailash, Dalimbagan, Calcutta, "Just see if they don't give you fish for every meal. And you will have to eat it too till your very skin reeks of it."

On the morning of her wedding Uma had been woken up almost before sunrise to have a mound of sweetened curd mixed with puffed rice thrust in front of her alongside a plate of sizzling hot fried fish.

"I can't."

"Just take a bite love, it's auspicious."

A little later the ritual gifts for the bride arrived from the groom's family. Two huge rohu fish were the prize display amongst a collection of sarees, sweets and two exquisite silver containers of turmeric and sandalwood paste. Of the pair of fish, one was trussed as the bride with a pink veil and a nose ring and the other carried the white ceremonial headgear of the groom with a cigarette dangling from its dead lips.

"Look at the size!"

"Goodness! How much do you think they weigh?"

"The Chattopadhyays have good taste I must say."

Once again plateloads of fried fish did the rounds of the house teeming with relatives. Uma mecifully was exempted from the meal as the bride and the groom were expected to keep a fast till the ceremony was over.

Uma in her red and gold bridal finery stepped into a silver rimmed plate of milk and alta – the red dye – as she entered Kailash. An elderly lady of the family gave her a fish to be held in her hand. The new bride was thus the talismanic icon of Lakshmi promising plenty in the household that she was entering. The cold, wet and slippery feel of the fish sharpened Uma's sense of isolation and loss as she stood in a circle of strangers. Her unshed tears blurred the edges. Voices and petals of flowers floated over her.

A huge silver plate was laid out in a ring of an ominous number of silver bowls for Uma's first ceremonial meal as a bride in Kailash. At a glance she could make out that there were fried fish, fish in lentil as well as curried fish of several varieties.

"Bride, you will have to eat everything."

Laughter.

"Especially the fish head."

More laughter.

"Begin the right way," said an old matron, "Let Rudra give you his share of fish too. Tell him,

> *tumi jodi hou bhalomanusher po*
> *tabe katakhan kheye mach khan tho |*
>
> If a gentleman's son you truly be
> then chew the bones and leave the fish for me.

"I can't," Uma had said and to her horror some tears escaped. She had meant that she could not eat that huge fish head gleaming on her plate next to a mound of rice. But the women deliberately took it to be otherwise.

" Is it a grossly unfair bargain?"

"And she has known our Rudra only for a day."

"And a night."

More raucous laughter followed and then some lewd comments too.

Ashutosh had enquired of Uma the first evening after the departure of all the guests, if she was settling down and eating properly in her new home. Unable to say that she had grown sick of the rich, festive food Uma nodded. "We'll soon start our regular home cooked meals", said Ashutosh as though reading her mind, "But I am afraid that you will have to eat fish. Your husband cannot do without it. In this matter he is a true blue Bengali Babu." Ashutosh's eyes twinkled as he uttered the words though. Uma cringed, stricken at the thought that the light-hearted bantering of the wedding festivities and her shamefully gauche behaviour had reached her father-in-law's ears.

She was beginning to like fish though.

※ ※

The frying of the fish was done. Pishi put another gleaming utensil on the fire. Then she leaned forward and wiped it clean with a folded cloth before pouring the thick and golden mustard oil in it for the curry. Thakma used to do this, Uma remembered as she watched Pishi. Thakma used to cook fish thus while Dadu was alive, before she changed into the woman in white and gave up eating fish and all non-vegetarian food. With Dadu gone, Thakma gave up eating even musoor daal, garlic and onion. She gave up everything that was to generate heat in the body. As a widow Thakma had to maintain a lean diet lest desire coursed through her, lest she enjoyed life in the absence of her husband. Thakma said that she did not mind it at all. Nobody was forcing her really. I have had enough fish to last me a lifetime said she. She who could never do without fish while Dadu was alive. Yet she just gave it up. Thakma had never liked vegetables except potatoes. She did not like milk either. Her stomach evidently did not understand the Brahmanical ideals of widowhood. It rumbled and grumbled and often let loose. The doctors said that it was the new diet. Her body was not used to it. Let me be, Thakma said. I just have to wait for death now she said.

And yet it was the same Thakma, who had told Uma of Shadu Thakuma, Dadu's youngest sister. When Thakma entered her marital home as a bride, Shadu was four years old and already a widow. But Shadu was lucky enough to have wealthy parents and indifferent parents-in-law who let her be at her natal home. Widows of Brahmans were allowed only one meal a day in those days. On the days when they did not have to keep a fast that is. With several taboos of course. Not this. Not that. Not thus. Not today. Not this month. So many taboos that reason could not quite fathom it all. But then when has faith been entirely encapsulated by reason? How can it?

But one meal a day was not enough for the child-widow. Shadu was perpetually hungry. A clay water container was often held to her stomach to soothe her hunger pangs. The older widows in the family told Shadu about the dharma of women who lost their husbands. But Shadu's stomach did not understand metaphysical ideals. It growled for food. Naturally. Shadu never walked. She ran. She was four...five...six and fleet-footed. Thakma's mother-in-law had cried, "The child's muscles, bones are pulling at her. Shadu is growing. Won't she feel hungry?"

A remedy was found. After her meal at mid-day, Shadu was allowed to fall asleep on the mat with her mouth and hand unwashed as though she had not finished her meal. She could eat some more thus when she woke up, without breaking rules. This went on for a while till some well meaning relative pointed out that it amounted to fraud.

"Shadu would always cry for a piece of fish. But that was forbidden. My mother-in-law would sometimes grind dal and fry it in the shape of a fish. She even put some shajne drumsticks in it to make up for the fish bones. That too had to stop eventually. Shadu herself gave up on it. Gradually Shadu became a white shadow in the house. She ceased to impinge on our existance." Thakma always wiped her eyes at this point. "But after we came to Delhi Dadu got a letter saying that Shadu had taken to putting kohl in her eyes and stealing fish from the kitchen on the sly. Someone had seen her tying a coloured saree over her widow's white. Clearly Shadu had lost her mind. What a life! Dadu did not eat that day." Thakma would wipe her eyes again and look at Uma, "Your Dadu wanted to bring Shadu to Delhi. But the next letter brought the news of her death. Who knows how she died!"

But the same Thakma who had cried for Shadu gave up on fish herself when she became a widow. And meat, musoor dal, garlic and onion. She only remembered that she was a widow. And a widow of a Brahman at that. And that there were rules as the gods had ordained.

Uma looked around the kitchen at Kailash. Pishi turned towards

Bamundi, "The fish curry will simmer for a while. Will you take it down when it is done? Shall I go?"

Khema entered the kitchen and gathered the used utensils.

❧❧

The drizzle of the morning had gathered a ferocious strength and poured over the city relentlessly for a few hours. But by late afternoon the rain had cleared the sky leaving behind only strips of orange-ribboned clouds. Uma and Pishi sat in the alcove just outside the puja room. The clothes lines glimmered with rain drops. Sodden leaves and petals from the scattered blossoms of the creepers littered one end of the wet terrace. Pishi drew her saree around her shoulders and breathed in the damp but sharp air. The smell of fish still lingered faintly on Pishi's saree.

"Don't you mind it Pishi?" asked Uma.

"Mind what?"

"Frying fish. Cooking it. And not having any yourself. Don't you miss eating it?" Uma asked remembering Thakma.

"I eat fish." Pishi's tone was rather dry.

The admission startled Uma though almost immediately she was also invaded by a sense of shame for feeling thus.

"Why shouldn't I?" Pishi looked at her straight in the eye. "I don't even know if I am a widow. Sure that man must be dead. He could not have lived to be a hundred. But I was never a wife, so how am I a widow?"

"But you wear…"

"My white sarees? Haimanti, your grandmother-in-law decided when she became a widow that I should wear white too. I got two sarees every month. Those came with the monthly grocery. They still do. Haimanti gave orders. The colours stopped."

"Why did you not say anything? Surely Baba would have intervened."

Pishi smiled.

Uma could not resist asking, "And your loha?" Uma's own iron bangle, given by the Chattopadyays, and covered with gold shone with the rest of her bangles where it would remain till she died or became a widow.

"I threw it away." Pishi smiled again. "I think there was a blister on my arm. Some oil must have splashed as I was frying fish. The iron rubbed against it. I took it off one afternoon. It did not seem worth my while to put it on again. Putting the loha back earlier had not brought me much luck either."

"Had you taken it off once before too?"

"Yes. That afternoon. When I was filled with rage that coursed through me like molten hot liquid. My heart pounded. How could that pincer just walk away, leaving my life behind?" Pishi's green eyes glittered in her face.

Uma suddenly felt a little uneasy. The terrace seemed very big and cut off from the rest of the house too.

"Maybe I was inspired by the female ghouls that day in the Bamboo copse. After my tryst with destiny." Pishi was almost puckish. It charmed Uma once again.

"Tell me." Uma said.

"A story?" asked Pishi.

But told her nonetheless.

"The sun was on the decline. I knew that I had to come out of that dappled green and yellow refuge of the Bamboo copse. So I did. First I walked. It was not enough for my raging anger. I ran then with my feet pounding with my heart. Thorns, broken shells of snails cut my feet. But that only helped spurt my anger. I turned towards Padma pukur. The orange glow of the setting sun danced on its dark waves. The water lapped the shore. The trees were dark and thriving all around it. I stood there for a while angry with its calm indifference and its beauty. I had to do something. I had been told that my bangles, the red lac, the white conch and the black iron protected my husband's life, that pincer. I took them off. All my bangles. One after the other. And threw them in the water. As hard, as far as I could. Some floated, others disappeared into the water's dark depth with small plops. Well, good bye Pincer I said, and may you drown too. I ran then, back to the house. I wanted to shake my bare arms at everyone. I ran even faster now. Almost looking forward to a roaring battle with my family."

Pishi paused.

Uma looked at the old woman sitting with her. She seemed frail but not forlorn. Yes something had endured. The remains were not rusted. Pishi was ready for wind and weather still. Uma could see the young girl. Running.

"When was this, Pishi?"

"A long time ago. A long, long time ago."

Uma reached out to touch Pishi's hand. The skin seemed dry and thin. Gently Uma held the old hand laced with fine blue network. Pishi was very quiet for a while and then said soft as a sigh, "We used to come up and sit on the terrace in the afternoons."

"We?"

"Shivani and I. Your mother-in-law," said Pishi and then lapsed into a silence again that seemed very private.

Uma thought of the girl in the faded photo in the family album where Rudra's mother sat next to a very young Ashutosh. He wore a suit and had thickly oiled hair. Her curls peeped out from the veil on her forehead and her feet dangled from beneath her saree and were incongruously encased in ankle length socks and shiny black strapped shoes. The shoes clearly signalled modernity and affluence as well.

Something inchoate passed between the old woman and the young on the terrace in Kailash.

"How did she die, Pishi?"

Pishi knew who it was that Uma was referring to.

"She couldn't."

"Couldn't what?"

"She just couldn't."

A cloud gently slid across the sun. The grey afternoon was quiet. On the terrace in Kailash at least. As though there was an intense straining. A suspension. A holding in of breath, lest it interfered with listening, lest the world intruded.

"You could." Uma said.

"I could. Yes I did. Why did I not think of dying myself? That afternoon by the Padma pukur? I could have thrown myself into its dark depths I suppose. I have asked myself that question several times. I don't think that it occurred to me at all then. Later I realised that I must have wanted to live. Just that."

"What happened when you reached home?"

Soft breath and silence again.

"Pishi?"

The green eyes blinked. "My mother was outside. In the courtyard. Sweeping the yard I think. She just looked at me out of the corner of her eyes. My grandmother shuffled towards me with a look of sheer relief on her wrinkled face. But I brushed her aside with the brute force of young angry arms. She cried out. I went inside and lay down on the floor. My breasts were flattened against the cool clay of the house. It hurt. I could feel my heart pounding still, threatening to burst out of the flesh and cloth encasing it. Gradually darkness descended in the room."

"Nobody came to you?"

"I heard my grandmother try once and then my younger sister. She was married too and had been sent back for an indefinite period by her in-laws. But I also heard my mother tell them to let me be. Her voice sounded cold and harsh. I hated my mother at that moment. She had helped barter my life away. She had bound me with chains. She had agreed to give me to that pincer."

"Poor thing, she probably did not even have a say in the matter." Uma whispered, aghast.

"I did not care then. Not then."

"And then?"

"The room grew darker still. I could hear the scratching of the cockroaches on the mud floor as they came out to forage in the dark. The coconut fronds rustled in the wind outside."

Uma could hear it too. She hugged her knees and felt the glow of moonlight on her self even in the afterglow of the afternoon on the terrace at Kailash, "You remember all that?"

"Who knows? Maybe I am making it up. Maybe it is memory

playing tricks. Maybe that is how I would like to remember my life. Anyhow, I don't remember falling asleep but I must have. I woke up with a start in the dark and felt a hand on my body. It moved the hair away from my forehead. It caressed my arms. The hand felt rough yet soothing. As though it wanted to heal me. I recognised my mother's hand and her smell. I lay still. There was the sound of deep breathing in the room too of those asleep. My grandmother and my sister were there in another corner. My father had gone away somewhere as he often did. A heavy hand seemed to squeeze my heart holding it captive. I could barely breathe. I willed my anger to return in a surge. But it turned treacherous despite my will. It was ready to melt in tears. I felt them hot and burning in my eyes."

Uma felt them too deep within her being.

"I was on my side. I could not see my mother. I did not wish to see her. But her breath stirred my hair. She must have felt the changing tensions of my body too, now no longer limp in sleep. She spoke then and her words came soft as the breeze that stirred the palm fronds outside, lest it woke the world. 'Toughen yourself baby. Harden your heart and your mind. You have to endure. There is nobody else for you. Not even God. He has no time for women. At least not for the deserted and widowed women of Bengali Brahman households. God knows I have called out to him often enough. You have to be tough. You just have to be. If you want to live.' My mother paused. Somebody stirred in the room. My grandmother got up and slowly shuffled outside. She suffered from incontinence ever since…. Anyhow my mother stopped talking. I turned towards her then. I felt my mother's calloused fingers in my hair, soothing my throbbing forehead, trying to ease my anger and my pain. If she could. I felt the warm flow of tears on my face. Hers and mine. Running down my nose, salt inside my mouth, so mingled that it was not possible to distinguish them."

The damp moved inside Uma, heavy and wet.

"Mothers…" She began.

"There were many days and many nights after that when my mother would beat me or curse me. For my wild ways, for being yet another mouth to feed, for being alive. But it did not matter to me. Even as she raised her arm or opened her mouth in a scream I willed myself to remember those arms soothing me and her voice in the dark. It is that voice that I remember even though she sent me away finally. I can hear that voice still. Sometimes in the daylight. Sometimes in the dark. But always echoing my anger."

Uma too caught the echo of a voice, wretched but strong, steadying a daughter in a hopeless world. The sombre sky seemed to have dropped low, more grey than orange now.

Pishi suddenly turned to Uma. The green eyes glowed in the wrinkled face catching the fading orange of the sky. "You have never felt it? Anger at your lot? Your life prescribed thus, because you are a woman?"

The words struck a discordant note. Sharp. Ballistic. It tore the tragic overtone of the damp and limp afternoon, pulsating suddenly with anger hard and cynical. Uma was not quite prepared to be jolted out of the rural retreat of the story in this manner. Or be drawn into the story. Surely everybody could see, even Pishi, that Uma's lot was different? Entirely and obviously different? Uma was educated. She was, well, she was modern. In some ways, some positive ways at least. Uma's world was a modern world with modern laws. Rudra could not marry again just like that. He could not just walk away from her. And … if he did … and … if he did Baba, Kaku, her brother, they would do something surely? If he did she could, she could do things, like … like … she could do things. She was educated. Her life, and her options in life were different, very different from Pishi's. Was that not so?

In the puja room across the threshold Lakshmi glowed golden next to Vishnu. The smell that had pleased Khema still lingered though now mingled with the stuffiness of a closed space. A silence stalked the terrace.

❀❀

Education. Vidya. By the end of the 19th century education had emerged in the city of Calcutta not only as knowledge but also as a mark of privilege. The recipients of the liberal education of the English were the new gentlemen of Bengal. They were not Babus, the compradors of yesteryear but the bhadralok. Refined and cultured, the bhadralok were removed from the world of vulgar physical labour as well as from any obvious means of coercion and oppression in acquiring wealth. The comprador wealth, which many of them now had from birth as a natural prerogative, was thus slowly rendered invisible even as it facilitated a certain lifestyle. And education of course.

No official policy barred the less privileged classes from education. But the turmoil caused in the city in 1853, by the admission of the son of Hira Bulbul, a well known prostitute, into Hindu College was symptomatic. Those who did not want their social purity to be compromised by the presence of a prostitute's son, broke away and founded the Hindu Metropolitan College though it is not known if at the same time they also stopped patronising prostitutes. The old Hindu College was re-named Presidency College in 1855. Distinctions of caste and religion were thus apparently abolished from the college, but the fee was ten rupees, marking the social status of education.

Years later, Shashishekhar, well aware that times were changing, chose Presidency College as his stepping stone in Calcutta.

Shashishekhar proved to be a middling student but then when did results measure accurately the agility of the mind? Haimanti's brother and a cousin were his classmates. Shashishekhar often accompanied his friends to their family owned press in College Street. It fascinated him and sometimes he helped with the proof reading. The Press fuelled his dreams. The development of the institutionalised education by the colonial government had increased the market for printed books. Sashishekhar knew that it would continue to grow. He always remembered, with a thrill of being, the day he was offered the printing press, alongside a bride, by his classmate's father.

The press was nondescript. Dukari Mukhopadhyay had bought it at a huge discount through his Marwari employer but could not really make a go of it. He heard that the handsome Brahman friend of his son was interested in it. Dukari saw it for himself too.

Dukari had four sons and a daughter. This daughter, Haimanti, was born in a rare moment of desire when the real need for copulation with the wife was over for Dukari's sperm had already shaped sons in the lucky womb of his wife. Haimanti was thus privileged from birth. She was that rare creature – a welcomed daughter. It also helped that she was fair and small built though adequately endowed and quiet. Haimanti's fond father wanted a groom for her who would stay in Calcutta but whose family should preferably live outside the city so as not to interfere in his daughter's life. He knew that it might help his daughter if the groom could somehow be beholden to him and his sons. Thus Dukari thought he would ensure a safe, and happy, marriage for his beloved daughter.

Shashishekhar fitted the bill perfectly. Of course he was from Chittagong, whose dialect was virtually incomprehensible to the Calcutta family. But he was no rustic Bangal. He was also an elite Brahman. His father was apparently a priest of some standing in their native village who had composed a mangalkavya of *Chandi*. Or so Dukari had heard. The boy's maternal grandfather had been a zamindar of sorts though it appeared that there was not much money left. But just as well perhaps. The boy would hold his wealthy in-laws in some esteem. Moreover Shashishekhar was very handsome. Intelligent. Apparently free of vices. He also appeared deeply interested in the press that appealed to none of Dukari's sons. The major portion of the dowry would thus be taken care of. And the boy was educated too. Good. Dukari knew that his sons, Haimanti's brothers, would never have agreed to marry their sister to an illiterate person, despite the kulin status.

Actually, Haimanti's brothers had thought that she herself should be educated too. Her parents had thought not. They knew that if educated, Haimanti's breasts would shrink, her womb turn infertile and the inauspicious inappropriateness of female education would eventually take her husband's life as the final chastisement. Everyone knew that educated women were destined to be widows.

"Enough. You don't need to make a mem, a lady, of your only sister. I will die before I allow that." Haimanti's mother raged at her sons.

The youngest among Haimanti's brothers had tried to teach her on the sly. But soon enough another young girl appeared in his life as his wife. It was a greater adventure to teach the wife to read and write. Haimanti's brother taught his wife at night which was the only time that they were allowed to meet. And then in the morning he would go off to college and ask fellow conspirators, "So, how far did you reach last night? Alphabets or words?" It was an adventure that thrilled many young bhadralok from the late 19th century. The education of wives became a staple of modern romance. It was done behind the parents' back; cocking a snook at old orthodoxy. It was the promise of a brave new world where the wife could read love letters from the husband sent on the sly during the day when they were not allowed to meet in self-respecting households. And then again at night they could read poetry together. Later, much later, it would help her keep household accounts too.

Haimanti had just about learnt to read and write her name when she was abandoned by her brother in favour of a more romantic pasture. She was quite glad to be free of those filial ministrations which were generously punctuated by cuffs and curses. Besides she did not see how reading or writing could help her further her interests. Haimanti had already learnt the three most important lessons in life: that men and women were different, that the men were the providers and spenders but women's piety ensured how much money was providentially provided and how much diabolically went out of the house and that as a Brahman woman she had a natural and greater claim on female piety. When Dukari fixed her marriage with Shashishekhar her mother taught her one more lesson: a husband was god on earth but a wife must keep her own counsel in domestic matters. Haimanti did not need to learn anything else. Or so her mother suggested.

The marriage was a happy negotiation. Both parties felt that a good bargain had been made.

"Why not?" wrote back Neelkantha, blessing the enterprise. But he asked Shashishekhar to verify the credentials of the bride's family as kulin Brahmans, the highest of the high caste Brahmans as they themselves were. As far as Neelkantha himself was concerned he would not attend the wedding as he hardly left the temple these days but Shashishekhar's uncles would be there, the letter said. Neelkantha would speak to them. Yes, Neelkantha agreed that it was better to get married, this time, from Calcutta. The letter then moved on to the production of books from the production of heirs. "Let your printed books be like the holy river that washes away the sins of the world, the river that Shiva carried on his head as she descended to earth for he alone could hold the tumult of the rushing torrent. "Not in vain have you been named after the God, Shashishekhar." The letter ended with a Sanskrit verse that described vividly the flow of the Ganga from Kailash, the epic home of Shiva, via Varanasi, Prayaga in Allahabad down to the Bay of Bengal. Shashishekhar liked the simile: 'like Shiva bearing Ganga'. The word Ganga however seemed to suggest a narrow perspective for his business venture.

But Shashishekhar had always obeyed his father. So he named his enterprise The Ganges Press. The name indicated for him an awareness of the glories of the Indian civilization but from a perspective that was familiar with the western, modern world too. How else could tradition be served? Shashishekhar forbade anyone to call the printing machine 'kal' (rhyming with ball) in coarse Bengali as though it was like the machines of the flour or the rice mills. Those had 'kal', or machines associated with petty labour and peddling. The printing press was a 'yantra': sonorous in Sanskrit. And his yantra made available the Sanskrit directives in vernacular. These, the *Ramayana* and the *Mahabharata*, selections from the *Vedas* and the *Puranas*, collections of vratas or acts of religious rituals simplified and translated into Bengali, found a ready and growing market in the modern metropolis. Also, these Bengali texts that Shashishekhar printed in his Press were generously interspersed with Sanskrit quotations for authority and sublimation.

"Will the public swallow so much of religious stuff?" asked Shashishekhar's friend who was now his brother-in-law as well.

"It will. I would not use the word swallow though."

The market actually gorged on it. Shashishekhar was a visionary. He knew that he had to make available in print what earlier the kathaks, or the wandering minstrels, had recited. The upper caste Hindu bought the books of The Ganges Press to be reassured about his privileged birth, the wannabes to learn the ways of the privileged, the scholars for the new-found pleasure of reading, the show-off to prove that he could, the conservative for stability in a changing world, the contemporary to learn of the past, the colonizer to know the colonized and the nationalist to locate indigenous spaces untrammeled by the colonizer.

"Your husband is a great business man," Haimanti's brother told her.

Shashishekhar frowned.

The Ganges Press printed. And reprinted. Thus Shashishekhar's yantra produced the ancient wisdom of the Hindu civilization. It also produced labels for the various products of the city's mills. But that was in another room.

Evidently the enterprise had divine sanction too. The goddess of fortune, Lakshmi, smiled upon Shashishekhar. He commissioned an oleograph and put her on his office wall. Thus Lakshmi beamed over the cash box of The Ganges Press, resplendent on a lotus smiling beatifically as she ruled the world. Her vermilion and her red and white bangles proclaimed however a more powerful husband elsewhere.

❦

"Would you have minded if I did not apply this red vermilion and did not wear these white, red and iron bangles that mark me a wife?" Uma asked Rudra that night in the cosy confines of the netted conjugal bed.

Rudra did not reply.

Uma spoke again afer a few minutes. "Would it matter to you if I stopped applying this red vermilion or took off my bangles?" She had been preoccupied throughout that evening, unable to step outside Pishi's story entirely.

Rudra had returned a little late from work. He had gone to meet some friends he said. He seemed tired and worn out. Somewhat distracted too. Conversation that evening at the dining table had not quite flowed. Uma realised that there was some disagreement over a project that Rudra and some of his friends were keen on but not so Ashutosh who felt that it was not in keeping with the profile of The Ganges Press. Soon both men seemed lost in thought. They may of course have also been listening very carefully to the news from the radio saying something about Aksai Chin and gradually a discussion on political accommodation along the Himalayan border between India and China started between father and son as Khagen brought in the steaming dishes one by one from the kitchen. Kailash was being lashed by rain again.

Uma ate quietly and thought of the ruined life of Pishi.

In bed that night, Uma held up her arm slightly, and ran a finger over her bangles remembering those which Pishi had thrown into the river in anger, challenging fate. "Would it matter to you?" she asked yet again. "If I took off these bangles? The red lac, the white conch and the loha?"

"Take it off if you want to. Why are you asking me? But can you?"

Uma had never heard such a dull note in Rudra's voice.

The timepiece clicked rather rudely in the room for a while. And Rudra turned over and fell asleep in an exasperating, maddening, frustrating display of the marriage having settled down.

Uma grew even more restless and lonely with her thoughts. She wanted Rudra to be awake. She wanted to tell him about a woman and her daughter in a village in Chittagong. "There is nobody for the women of Bengal. Not even God," Pishi's mother had told her daughter in Kynsa mati where one of Bengal's most revered songs to the goddess was composed. The mother and daughter's tears had mingled in the dark of the night. Uma could not erase the voice from her mind. Or its anguish.

But Rudra's breathing was regular. His arm hid his face resting on the pillow.

Uma's mother's voice shattered the somnolence of the bedroom, hissing in the dark. "Of course I will keep quiet. How else will your image as the dutiful eldest son of the family be preserved? Always there for every one in your family. In your family... what? Why do I keep saying 'your family' 'your house' even after so many years of marriage? Try. Try and reason it for yourself. It should not be too hard. But only if you are willing to try. But why should you?" A very young Uma lay between her parents in the house in Kashmere Gate. She stirred agitatedly sensing discord. Her mother's hand thumped her small body. It was not difficult for the child to make out even in the dark that her mother was breathing hard.

Uma sat on the floor. Some broken and battered kitchen utensils were strewn all around her. She could see Dadu's legs at the desk from where she sat. Thakma's voice came from somewhere above her. "Yes! Keep your face shoved in books all the time. But remember that I have had one two three four children. Not on my own. They have needed things, money, time and attention. But then their father was the scholar! Petty problems? Naturally. I was looking after the children. Not solving metaphysical puzzles. The past? Yes. I enjoy raking up the past. The embers remain because I fan them? Why not? Don't you rake up the past too? Yours is scholarship and mine ravings?" Dadu's legs seemed very stiff. As stiff as the knot in Uma's chest. She tried to hold her breath as long as she could. She bent her head over her doll and a cloud of wavy hair swung forward to curtain her face.

The kitchen in Kashmere Gate and Kaki kneading the dough. A brittle air of unease folded over the rest of the house. Kaki kneading harder and harder. The dough taken up and slapped down on the big brass plate. Kaki punching the dough and pressing her knuckles hard against its softness till they scraped the hard metal. "Don't get married. You are fine Uma. Fine like this." Uma in college was almost a friend to Kaki. Kaki pushed the dough all around the plate savagely. "If I go out in the evenings perched on a scooter it is only with my husband. He wants me to. He insists, even if I say no. In any case I do my share of household work through the day." Kaki rolling the dough up and down the plate. Up and down. Restless. Uma did not say anything but reached out and started breaking the dough into small balls. The embers of the coal glowed soft on the young face.

Uma turned restlessly. The green house in Kahmere Gate and her life in it had acquired a special sheen in her memory ever since her marriage. She saw it as the playing field of her innocence and she would like to remember it as such. What was rendering it askew tonight? Uma breathed hard and turned towards the sleeping Rudra. But the images stayed. Bright fragments. Precise and pointed.

How could Rudra just fall asleep when her mind was so unsettled and seething? Had she not listened for the last two nights to a project of his to bring out slim tales of Calcutta from The Ganges Press? 'The Other Calcuttans' Rudra wanted to call it. Was she not reading Jibanananda Das, Bishnu Dey and Buddhadeb Basu because Rudra liked them so?

Uma and Rudra. Made for each other. For ever and more. As the gods ordain. Uma remembered so much was made of their names and associations during the wedding.

"Uma and Rudra. My o my! This is what they mean by a match made in heaven."

Uma turned restlessly yet again.

❀ ❀

"Would you like to get Uma married this summer?" Mamu had asked.

And Uma had tried to make herself invisible at the dining table in Ballygunge place. "Rudra Chattopadhyay. The only son of Ashutosh Chattopadhyay, owner of The Ganges Press. Great grandson of the poet Dvija Neelkantha. Kulins. The upper crust of the upper caste Brahmans. The Chattopadhyay's of *Chatto's Panjika*".

"Really!" Uma's aunt, mami, had to sit down to digest the news better.

Uma was familiar with the *Panjika*, the pink almanac crammed with miniscule print in Bengali that was kept in her grandmother, Thakma's room with her household deities. It was constantly consulted for auspicious dates and festivities as in virtually every caste-Hindu Bengali household. The popularity of the *Panjika* was proved by the advertisements that it carried. These were numerous and eclectic ranging across cauliflower, cabbages, Homeopathic medicines, talismans, watches, football, cookbooks, detective novels and the *Gita* too. Thakma's early 20th century version was no exception.

Kaku with his usual licensed liberty, often apologized profusely after sneezing, for forgetting to consult the *Panjika*, if Thakma happened to be in the same room. Needless to say that it had not amused Thakma.

Uma's heart had plummeted. She could not imagine being married into a family that compiled and sold *Panjika*s. No matter how much money they made from it.

"But both the father and the son studied in London. You need not fear ignorant orthodoxy." Mamu had looked around triumphantly.

Uma's heart rose a few notches. And then soared as the conversation and the details about the Chattopadhyays flew around the room.

※ ※

The mosquito net floated above her in the breeze of the fan.

Uma turned around again. Restless. And turned again. There was a distant rumble of thunder. The sky was about to open up again.

Suddenly a hand snaked around her waist drawing her back. It was a man's arm, strong and firm. Uma put her hand on the arm almost about to push it aside. But it was warm. And so comforting in the dark of the night.

"Not feeling sleepy?" Rudra seemed wide awake too.

"Not quite."

"Is anything the matter?"

The arm was warm and strong around her. She slipped into the comforting crevice.

"Do you believe in fate?" asked Uma later for something had remained of the earlier turmoil.

Rudra took so long to answer that Uma thought that he did not care for the question. Or worse still, he had fallen asleep again. But even as she turned he spoke.

"Don't arguments about fate imply a turning away in cowardly compromise?"

"Why cowardly? It's a belief that gives strength too."

"Acceptance is not strength."

"Endurance is."

"Endurance is also letting the world go scot-free. It requires courage to want to know, and to probe and probe to understand why it had to be so. It can take an entire lifetime sometimes. The answer may be elusive even then. But endurance is to let it be."

"But how much can we know really? How much need we know? 'Humankind cannot bear very much reality.' "

Rudra got out of bed. The match was struck in a by now familiar post-coital ritual. A cigarette was lit. "I would like to have that courage though. Someday."

Uma was half asleep and felt the words traverse across the room in a soft haze. Or perhaps in a dream.

❋ Six ❋

UMA HAD ASSUMED THAT IT would be an innocuous act. How could she have known that just reading in the kitchen in Kailash could change her forever?

Khema had pleaded to be read out to by Uma. Bamundi had joined in, had indeed been the most vocal with her pleas. Pishi had said nothing. Pishi had only looked at Uma but there was a certain eagerness in those green eyes and a certain kind of watchfulness too. Not surprisingly it was that alert look that had both discomfited and driven Uma.

"Yes. Yes I will read to all of you. But of course," she had said.

What to read was not a problem. The consensus was unanimous. In fact if truth be told there was no other contender. It had to be Neelkantha's *Chandimangal*.

Where to read was a foregone conclusion. It had to be the kitchen. Naturally. Where else could these women meet? Where else could they have the right to meet?

But when to read caused hiccoughs.

It could not be in the mornings for that was for work. It could not be at dusk for that was for work too. It could not be in the evenings when the men returned. It could not be late at night for that was meant for the family, at least for those who had a family.

Then?

The late afternoon, Pishi suggested, her eyes flicking over Khema's despondent face and Bamundi's glazed look.

"But…"

"But…"

"We have to find a way," Pishi took charge, "Bamundi, can you not come somewhat early here and go a little late to the next house for the evening round? You can cook the evening meal for Kailash while you listen to Uma and whatever needs to be fried, I will take care of later. Will it be difficult to get permission from the other houses for the altered schedule?"

The mutinous turn of Bamundi's rounded jowls suggested that the other houses may not be given the choice.

Pishi continued, "Khema, you go off a little early to your own quarters after the morning chores and return a little early too. You can take care of the polishing in the kitchen as you listen to the tales in the afternoon."

Then Pishi looked at Uma.

Uma felt the pull of her mind.

"No problem at all," she said in a rush and then added a little defensively, "I never used to sleep in the afternoons in Delhi."

The green eyes seemed to twinkle.

A secret excitement throbbed in the kitchen in Kailash from a couple of days before the first reading session. Khema smiled everytime she caught Uma's eyes. Bamundi trembled with anticipation. "Please don't start if I am a little late. I will just pour two mugs of water over myself, grab a bite, leave the food covered for my son who has only a morning shift right now and come here, don't start without me, please," Bamundi reiterated again and again. Uma felt as though they had a secret assignation.

Uma's mother's inland letter arrived with the midday post and struck the first discordant note. It was obviously written as soon as she had received Uma's last letter. "It is fine, very fine that you want to read to those others but do not do so without your father-in-law's permission. His wishes must be respected. I hope Rudra approves too. I hope that they know...." The cautionary words tumbled out after a perfunctory query about Uma's state of being. Ma hoped that Uma was happy. But clearly Ma was also anxious that the proposed project of reading out to a community of dependents should not come in the way of her daughter's continued well being at Kailash. Unless it was approved of. In fact it *must* have the seal of approval.

And blessings. Or else. The dark abyss of the 'or else' was naturally not stated in the letter. But it fretfully circumambulated the two pages of Ma's missive.

Uma bristled. Approve? Permission? For reading out that which was written and published by the very same family for that express purpose; reading that which money could buy off the counter? Reading out to those who have been known to the household for years?

Uma took umbrage at Ma's tedious tone too. Did not Ma realise that Uma had grown up and that even mothers have to let go? She took an inland letter and began immediately on a brisk note: "I *do* know what I am doing. Why do you worry all the time?" But her irritation evaporated even as she wrote. The by-now familiar rush of nostalgia for her perpetually anxious mother engulfed Uma entirely and she ended the letter by reassuring her mother that she knew what she was doing.

But did she?

A canker raised its head in Uma's mind even as she enjoyed the heady sensation of being feted, to be pressed to read. "Why not?' she had thought. "Why should I not read out loud that which I am reading already?"

"Should not you tell the others? Your husband and your father-in-law?" The canker asked.

Tell and seek, approve and bless – the verbs teased her mind all through the morning, insinuating differences and refusing to be buried. Uma did not wish to address the invisible cankers in Kailash or even within herself. She turned to a P.G. Wodehouse. But an argument of insidious intent continued to invade her.

Uma had tried to follow the prescribed path though. She had tried it with her husband first.

Rudra had come in late once again. Apparently an old friend of his had come from Shiliguri on a brief visit. The 'boys' had decided to meet even though it was a weekday. Rudra had seemed preoccupied when he joined the family for a dinner that had been kept warm and waiting for him. There had again been some talk of publishing, or not publishing, a series of monographs called *The Other Calcuttans*. Clearly the father and the son had not quite settled their difference of opinion. Uma preoccupied too, had caught some words like 'the Signet Press', 'Modernist', 'Fidel Castro' and 'Communism' even as she listened to the falling rain.

She broached the subject in bed with Rudra that night.

"I am thinking of reading the *Chandimangal*."

"I thought you had started already."

"I have." Uma placed a tentative hand on Rudra's arm, "I thought of reading out to some others."

"Hmm…"

"Pishi, Khema and Bamundi…"

"I have told you haven't I, about my idea for a series of monographs called *The Other Calcuttans*? It would be about the city's forgotten artisans, craftsmen, petty traders and the factory workers." Rudra's hand covered hers and his head turned on the pillow to face her. Rudra looked into her eyes and Uma let him speak.

Much later she said again, "My plan to read out… Do you think that I should ask Baba…"

    ….

"I said that I should ask Baba…"

"Sure…."

Uma searched the crevices of that one word. Was it nuanced? Her trepidations were returning and she grew silent.

"Do you want to say anything else?" Rudra's voice sounded tired now.

Asked like that?

"No. Not really," said Uma.

"Goodnight then."

"Goodnight."

Uma tried with her father-in-law too. But it was difficult to say it suddenly without appearing as at a confessional. And she lacked the confidence to interreupt an anecdote in midstream. So Uma let it slide, wondering, "'Do I *dare*?', and 'Do *I* dare?'"

❖ ❖

Shashishekhar had dared and he was successful. Who would have known that a priest's son from an obscure village in Bengal, brought up by well meaning relatives but as a dependant, could prove to have the Midas touch?

The *Panjika* was Shashishekhar's first success. He had surveyed the market. The *Puratan Panjikar Parishishta*, 1844, the *Gupta Press Panjika*, 1857 and the *Bishuddha Shidhanta Panjika*, 1890 were already available and in circulation. But there was room for more. The city of possibilities was expanding daily and the gods needed to be propitiated. The educated class that was swelling continuously did not rid itself of religious rituals or of traditional caste hierarchies. The Brahman was still sought to present briefs to the divine, despite jokes about the sacred thread. But it helped if the Brahman priest carried the mark of modern knowledge: the printed book which in this case was the almanac. Moreover there was also a growing number of new readers and many more waiting in the districts and the villages. All of them were eager to accord the gods their dues, as the priests ordained. Had not James Long's report of vernacular printed texts of the year 1859 stated that the *Panjika* circulates where very few other Bengali books reach?

So Shashishekhar Chattopadhyay collated and edited *Chatto's Panjika*. The immortal pantheon was vast. The mortal needs varied. Shashishekhar made available a *Full Panjika* and then an abridged *Half Panjika*. By the time P.M. Bagchi and Butto Kristo Paul brought out their versions of the almanac, *Chatto's Panjika* had its own fatihful readership. Indeed many said that if the deity did not make it to *Chatto's Full Panjika* then he – or she – was not worth it.

Surprising many, Shashishekhar, and his Ganges Press, turned to novels next.

"Novels?" said Haimanti's brother and Shashishekhar's college mate and then laughed, "Remember I am the one who baptised you in novel-reading when you first came to the city from your village. But you are a deep one Shashi. I had not seen you hooked then."

Shashishekhar smiled too, "How could you see? You were immersed yourself."

The brother-in-law looked serious suddenly, "Shashi, you are doing fine as it is. Why take that risk? Your serious disposition will come in the way of chosing the right, and juicy, novels. We are talking about pleasure here. My brother, you have to admit that your disposition is, well, a little dry. I always suspected that you returned my novels unread in college."

True, Shashishekhar had started reading novels only in college, borrowing from friends who devoured them regularly. Haimanti's brother was right, he had not been intoxicated. But he had realised soon enough how many were, and not just college students. As Shashishekhar travelled home for Durga puja to his village, he noticed how his fellow travellers, also on leave from Calcutta, packed the festival in their tin trunks for their waiting families: colourful sarees, scented hair oil, dolls, toys and new novels.

"The *Panjika* and the novel? The sacred and the secular?" Haimanti's brother asked a little sardonically. He felt a little disconcerted by this man from rural Chittagong with a thick accent whom he had befriended in college and who was slowly lengthening his stride and bridging the gulf between them. "Should you be taking the risk, Shashi?"

"Give your brother a second helping of the sweet," Shashishekhar gestured to Haimanti, "He is turning acidic."

Shashishekhar added novels to his list of inventories. He knew exactly what he was doing. If the almanac offered traditional religious solutions to the general woes of the mortal world then the novels were modern tales of struggling individuals in a world that was rapidly changing. Shashishekhar recognized that there was some truth in the West's criticism of child marriage, celibate widowhood, polygamy and the cloistered, ignorant existence of Hindu women. But Shashishekhar also believed that Hindu society was, and must remain, very different from the dissolute western world, at least where domestic life was concerned. And so he published a small booklet for budding novelists, a guide to the art of narrating the modern tale: a list of dos and don'ts. Aspiring writers queued up outside The Ganges Press to buy it. Soon Shashishekhar formed a syndicated group of novelists who followed the Chatto's rules of novel writing. Of these the most important golden rule was that virtue must triumph in the end. The staple plot was perfected by The Ganges Press. The realistic description of the city and domestic lives quickened the novels to life while the poetic justice of the conclusions met with the approval of the vast middle order of a society organized along caste lines.

The Ganges Press did not really come out with a classic novel that triumphed over time. But most of its novels did brisk business. '*Grihalakshmi*: The Goddess of the Household', '*Bouma*: The Daughter-in-law', '*Model Ma*: The Ideal Mother', '*Grihastya*: The Householder', '*Paribarik Shukh*: Domestic Bliss' and '*Sati-Lakshmi*' were novels from The Ganges Press that went into several reprints. Vice lurked in these pages usually in female shape. She could be modern, educated and immodest, such as liberal English education was trying to spawn. Or she could be uneducated and shameless such as dotted the mills and factories of the city. Either way, vice was a woman who had to return to her destined realm, domesticity, or be punished. Bethune, and his scheme of female education notwithstanding, this was the land of Sita who had inadvertently crossed the boundary and look what a price she had to pay! Her husband Rama had to abandon her. The Earth had to burn Sita back into her womb.

The conservative as well as the progressive devoured the novels from The Ganges Press for both agreed that familial happiness depended on womankind. Men bought these novels to familiarize themselves with female vice. Satisfied with the moral, some emancipated men then bought the novels for their own women – the new readership that was slowly emerging in the early 20th century: the Bengali bhadramahila.

"You will be sued by husbands soon. The wives of Calcutta like nothing better than to read the novels from The Ganges Press. They care nothing for their household work if one of your novels is dangled in front of them," Haimanti's brother said with a laugh.

"As though the men don't read the same novels," his wife said with mock exasperation. Haimanti's sister-in-law's family had Congress connections and was considered to have modern aspirations. "Don't you read my copies before passing them on to me?" she asked playfully.

"That is duty. I need to know as a husband what my modern wife is reading."

The wife was pleased with the description. But the thrust and parry continued for a while much to Haimanti's envy and Shashishekhar's irritation.

But Shashishekhar recognized this newly educated woman too. The Ganges Press also published simple booklets for her. These religious tales, called *Bratakathas*, prescribed the feminine virtues of wifehood and motherhood and were narrated during rituals sanctioned for the upper caste Hindu woman. Shashishekhar sourced these religious tales himself from the Sanskrit epics, *Puranas* and from popular customs too. He added to or subtracted from the source material boldly and freely according to the need of the moment. And of course these tales were recounted in Bengali and not Sanskrit as they were to be read by women, however educated.

"So Shashi, you are contributing to the education of the modern Hindu wives and mothers?" the brother-in-law raised his eyebrow.

"Who else would hold steady the glowing lamp in a world that is threatening to change?" replied Shashishekhar in the same vein.

Soon Shashishekhar introduced a mail-order service with discounts for regular readers.

As the business expanded, slowly but steadily, Shashishekhar bought land. First in North Calcutta and then in the newly spawning South Calcutta. Yes, Shashishekhar helped expand the horizon of the metropolis. And his business too.

The Ganges Press was successful. The educated native elite of the city condescended to acknowledge that they had heard of it. Yet Shashishekhar remained restless and hungry. The Ganges

Press was not quite a revered name. Shashishekhar meant to make it so. He desperately desired success that would be of a different order entirely.

❦❦

"I hope this match is as successful as your son's."

A cousin of Ashutosh's had come with her husband to invite the Chattopadhyays of Kailash to the wedding of her husband's younger brother. The cousin anounced a little too emphatically, looking askance at Uma, that her future sister-in-law was a graduate in Bengali literature. "It is worth more than the two lines of English that everyone speaks these days," said the cousin.

"She is a little jealous. She always was," Rudra's aunt had called from Srerampore to warn Uma about the cousin that morning.

"Much was expected of this cousin's husband. He was touted as a very bright fellow when they got married. But all he did was party politics and that too only in the coffee house. Our cousin has become a little… angular… over the years," the younger aunt from Ballygunge had called later to add.

In due course Ashutosh let it be known to the visitors that his daughter-in-law Uma, though a graduate in English Literature, was reading Neelkantha's *Chandimangal*. He then looked at Uma who had been rather quiet so far, and said, "If you have any queries, Uma, about the poem you could ask my brother-in-law here. He may have a degree in Chemistry but his real love is Bengali literature and he knows as much as any professor of the subject I dare say. I don't know though if he reads it all himself or just soaks it up in the coffee house. What do you call it, osmosis?" Ashutosh laughed aloud with the unconscious ease of an older, and richer, relative. "Is your coffee house adda still going strong?"

"His lungs won't function without it," the cousin retorted with a sharp look at her husband.

"I used to run into Rudra sometimes at the coffee house but not so of late." The brother-in-law's adam's apple bobbed up and down. He was narrow-shouldered and fine-boned.

"And are you still supporting the comrades or have you grown wiser?" Ashutosh persisted with the gentle teasing.

The brother-in-law put down his cup of tea but his wife intervened smoothly again, "Don't you lead him on. No politics today please." She then turned to Uma, "Well, what do you wish to know about the *Chandimangal*?"

Uma thrashed about wildly in her mind. She could hardly say, "Nothing".

But darting a glance at Ashutosh, the brother-in-law said, "With all due respect to The Ganges Press, the first *Chandimangal* to be printed was Mukunda Chakrabarty's sixteenth century composition. This happened as early as 1819."

Uma gladly seized the opening, "But it's the same story?"

"Yes. More or less. The appeal of the mangalkavyas lies not so much in the novelty of plot and character but the re-presentation of familiar and circulating tales. These were sung in public over a number of days and nights. They were often called jagaran."

"But then it must have changed too, right?"

"The main story remained the same. The *Chandimangals* were composed in Bengal mainly between the 16th and the 18th centuries." The brother-in-law bent his shoulders in Ashutosh's direction in a cheeky impersonation of obsequiousness, "Neelkantha's was in that sense a late flowering."

"But..." Ashutosh began.

The conversation flowed freely and amiably aided by the platters of sweet and salted savouries that emerged from the kitchen.

A rumble sounded in the sky. Dark and deep.

The cousin looked pointedly at her husband.

But he was in full flow now, like a puppy, eager to play.

Another rumble and the sky opened up. The rain came down in a rush.

The cousin looked at her husband and pursed her lips which made her skin stretch across her face. They really should have left earlier, she thought, and then slowly her irritation gathered into a peevish rage with the drumming of the rain. She found it taxing too, this constant vigil over her husband's flow of words, lest it irritated, or worse still, amused, the more successful members of her extended family. But her husband looked at her, then looked away and asked for another cup of tea. The words, and the rain, flowed. As far as the brother-in-law was concerned the evening was a success.

※ ※

The first session was not a success.

Uma read.

The others listened, sitting intent around Uma.

Khema. The low caste Bagdi woman wedded to the service of the family in Kailash. A soft shining brown like the gentle hue of a freshly unfurled sprig of neem.

Bamundi. The cook. Her skin like a burnt toast tempered darker still by wind and storm. It must have been a jungle out there in the city when the deserted widow arrived with an infant son in search of life. She was upper-caste yes, but poor.

Pishi. Fair but fallen in some secret way and fading now.

And Uma at the centre. Like butter melting in the heat of the humid kitchen. With gold glistening on her. Uma was like the goddess herself in her avatar as Gauri – the golden one – who with severe penance obtained Shiva as her husband for he had earlier taunted the goddess's dark complexion when she was married to him in the form of Parvati. "Let me have a complexion resembling gold and let me be known by that name..." The dark goddess had prayed. And then she emerged as the golden one. The dark skin was exiled to the realm of the offensive. So Uma had been told as a child, so Uma had been taught to view the world.

Khema and Bamundi did not take their eyes off Uma as she read Neelkantha's *Chandimangal*. The sky dripped rain in drab driblets. The smell of leftover food hung heavy over the kitchen. A putrid smell, rancid and sweet, wafted in from the door that opened to the courtyard. The women could not afford to shut it and steam in the hot humid air of the kitchen. Nothing could be more dismal.

Khema and Bamundi had obviously dressed for the occasion and seemed stiff and ill at ease. The opening section of the *Chandimangal* was a long drawn out vandana; a formulaic eulogy of the important deities of the pantheon. Most of this was in Sanskrit or heavily sanskritised Bengali. Uma stumbled through the stanzas.

Then came the poet's personal explanation for composing the poem as it narrated the visitation of the goddess in Neelkantha's dream.

> *And so you chose me*
> *A poor priest of Kynsa mati*
> *To tell of your story*
> *And the glory*
> *Of those who revered you… ..*
> *Though this tale has been told*
> *As tradition holds*
> *By earlier poets, far greater than me…*

Khema's nine-year old son slunk in and all through the rest of the afternoon a silent tussle of will carried on between the mother who wanted the son to leave and the latter who mutinously refused to comply.

Everyone seemed relieved when the hour passed.

"We will meet again tomorrow," said Pishi.

Uma was not certain whether it was meant to patronise her or not. There was an oppressive feeling too that refused to go away.

She had not asked. Said. Told.

Whatever.

Her head was beginning to ache.

❀ ❀

Uma's head was throbbing. The memory of the afternoon, the smell of the kitchen, Ma's letter, her own constant worry that she was unable to hold the attention of an audience and a vague sense of unease, fear and guilt combined to pound inside her head.

Ashutosh too was rather quiet that evening in the parlour.

"Baba, I have started reading the *Chandimangal* today. I mean I have started reading it out in the kitchen." Uma half surprised her own self by the confession and then hoped that it would help ease the pressure at her temples and between her eyes.

Ashutosh looked at his daughter-in-law.

"I know." The baritone made the verb sound ominous.

Uma was more than startled.

"Khagen told me."

A glut of emotions, hot and putrid, threatened to surge up Uma's throat. You knew? Khagen told you? But when? It is less than an hour since you returned and Khagen told you? Why did you not mention it? Khagen told you? But why?

The questions pulsated through Uma's throbbing head. She felt sullied too, as though spied upon. Would Khagen have mentioned Rudra's doings as soon as the father returned?

Her head ran a beat: spied upon, tattled about, so there.

But in a moment she was contrite and defensive. I tried. I did try to tell you. And Rudra too. But the moments passed. I did not think it mattered. Was I not told that the mangalkavyas were recited over seven or eight days to entertain people, ordinary people, before novels, before radio plays, before cinemas came into existance? Was not the mangalkavya meant for everyone? I really did not think that there could be objections. Not serious ones at any rate. Not in this house at least.

Liquid hot the thoughts foamed in her and paradoxically a cold encased her.

Uma wondered, in bleak desolation, if there would be anger. And if so, in what form.

She voiced nothing of her thoughts though and as unobtrusively as possible she drew deep breaths to keep her gall from flooding out.

A smell of wet earth crept into the room.

The rain was drumming on the house when Uma finally reached the bathroom and was violently sick.

There was dinner to look forward to still.

**

The brown paper packet tied loosely with white string contained very slim volumes of poetry. This was Rudra's first gift to Uma; the first of what he himself had bought for her. The wedding gifts were not personal, being either heirlooms or bought by the aunts on behalf of the Chattopadhyay men. The occasional flowers for her hair when they went out together were not quite gifts in that sense.

Suddenly the world seemed to brighten. "You bought these?"

"These are a few of my favourite volumes of modern Bengali poems," said Rudra looking a little self-conscious. "You said that you would like to read some of these."

"Of course," said Uma touched, "but don't you have some of these at home already? I thought I had seen some in the parlour cupboard...."

Rudra looked a little surprised. "I thought that you might like to have your own copies. Poetry is very personal, is it not?"

Uma had never thought of it like that. She leafed through the books, reading a line here, a title there with a quiet sense of contentment while Rudra changed with careful, measured movements. "I think it will start raining again. It's so sultry despite the downpour," said Rudra neatly folding back the sleeves of his kurta.

As if on cue the soft patter of rain started drizzling Kailash.

Uma picked up the slim volumes, resting against the table and feeling ineffably happy. She wanted to say something if only to hold the moment a little longer.

"You know my brother was a little disapproving that I was giving up my studies to get married? I must let him know that my husband and my father-in-law are trying their best to educate me. *Chandimangal* earlier and now modern Bengali poetry." Uma smiled.

"Do you feel put upon?" Rudra reached out and held her wrist lightly.

"Of course not." Immediately Uma was contrite but the moment had dissolved.

There seemed to be shadows in Rudra's eyes too.

Uma said again with a pleading movement of her hands, "Not one bit. I had not meant it thus."

"But you don't have to." Rudra stiffened.

"What?"

"Be yourself. Don't let Kailash swamp you."

Uma spoke again. "I like it. Really."

"I'll go down. Baba might be there already. Coming?"

"In a minute…" said Uma.

But she stayed a while longer. Alone in the room.

The dull ache in her head was threatening to mount pressure again. Uma wished she was home. With her mother.

Seven

Daily the goddess grew in the loving embrace of her mother
Menaka and father Himavat.
Chandi, Sarbamangala, Gauri. Or Uma.
Call her what you will.
But know that she is born to rejuvenate Shiva, ascetic, immersed
in the grief of his dear departed wife. Sati.

Fair, shy and docile
Sweet as can be
Beautiful too
A daughter such as no one had.
Thus Uma grew
The one born for Shiva.
Chandi, Sarbamangala, or Gauri.
Call her what you will
Born this time to Himavat and Menaka.

Uma's mother looked at her fondly then sighed long and deep.
So much beauty
Such gentle demeanour
The star of our eyes
Will her husband cherish her?
Or if not cherished, let her know peace. At least.
Or if not peace, may she not know pain
Or if pain, may that be intermittent
Of one kind still
Not like the waves of sea
Hurling at the beach
Labour, child birth, poverty, other women, the cane

Desertion too perhaps.
Dear god keep her safe.

But wife, said her husband Himavat
However dear, daughters must be married.
My worry is of a different order
Not this feminine indulgence in grief.
I just hope to find
A groom of our kind
High born and esteemed
By all
So that we do not fall
In the eyes of society.
And luck may just shine on our house
For Shiva, the great god
Just might be
In need of a spouse.

IN KAILASH, THE LIGHT WAS on in the kitchen though it was afternoon. The scudding clouds had drawn a dark canopy across the sky. The kitchen door had to be shut as great lashings of rain would flood the floor otherwise. The women inside did not care. Uma had asked, requested, tea to be brewed for all. They sat nursing the warmth. Uma sipped from her cup, pausing from her reading for a while.

"But the groom would be a fair bit older than the goddess, no? It is Shiva's second marriage after all. There are those children too from Shiva's marriage to Sati." Khema looked worried. She was sitting, as always, close to the door.

"I had heard that the mother did not want the marriage to take place." Bamundi's hands for once were at rest.

"Menaka?"

"Yes."

"Where did you hear it?" Uma asked, trying not to smile.

"Why, everybody has heard that Menaka did not want the marriage to take place. This *Chandimangal* does not mention it?"

"Well, Menaka is apprehensive of the match but no more than that as of now."

"Why! Menaka had even threatened to kill herself and her daughter if her husband went ahead with his plan to marry Uma to that old groom. Haven't you heard the songs of *Shivayan* like

> *Khepa bura digambar*
> *dhakka maira bahir kar*
> *Aibar mor jhi thakur mor ghare*
> *Uma ke bandhiya gale*
> *jhap diba ganga jale….*
> *Bale jei bacha mor dibe ei bare|*
> *Stri hatya diba ami tahar upar||*

> The old lunatic gross
> shove him out by force
> Let my daughter remain a spinster for ever.
> Uma to myself I will tie
> and then plunge in the Ganges and die…
> That I should give my child to this groom,
> whoever proposes
> is a murderer of woman,
> upon him will be my curses.

Bamundi recited and then seemed a little embarrassed.

"Shiva is an old widower with children. No steady income. Many vices on top of that. It is not surprising that the girl's mother feels that way." Khema was belligerent.

"From where did you learn this verse?" Uma asked Bamundi.

"What's there to learn? Every woman knows these verses. Pishi don't you know any ?"

"Do you think I remember all that now in my old age? You want me to sit and recite poetry now?"

"Please do."

"One at least."

"Come Pishi."

"Do. Pishi. Please do."

> *Taal gaach katom bosher batom Uma elo jhi|*
> *Tor kapale buro bar ami karum ki||*

> After such labour Uma's the daughter I get.
> But what can I do now if an old man is in her fate?

Pishi blushed suddenly after reciting the lines. Everyone looked at her fondly.

The rain fell with a steady beat.

Bamundi drew a big plate towards her and started mashing the boiled potatoes that had been left to cool on it a while ago. "So at the end the goddess is like most other women. She has to marry an old man. A much-married old man. What hope is there for ordinary women then?"

The thunder growled.

The kitchen grew contemplative.

"I also know such a verse, " said Uma, suddenly wanting to belong to the group.

> *Mami kate saru suta*
> *Mama kate pat*
> *Satyi kare balna mami*
> *Mama ki tor baap?*

> My aunt weaves a fine thread
> My uncle cuts jute
> Is uncle your father
> Aunt, please tell the truth.

Uma leaned back to rest her back against the wall having recalled the verse, "Baba would make us say this to my aunt whenever we visited Calcutta in the summer. It was a joke. Of course we were children then and did not realise the pain in the poem, of young girls married to old men. It must have been awful to be married to these much-married husbands." Uma was watched in silence by the others. "My uncle lost his hair early – it runs in the family," she added a little defensively.

Bamundi spoke again. It was another verse.

> *Amli pata dudher sar*
> *kemne karbe parer ghar*
> *parer ghar na jamer ghar*
> *raat na poaite kame dhar*
> *caukher pani dardar...*
> *parer put raisya*
> *bet mare kaisya|*

> The cream from milk and Amli leaves
> In someone else's home how can she live?
> Another house or the house of death
> where even before dawn, to work she is set
> and her tears flow from eyes wet.
> The son of a stranger
> Then harshly canes her.

No one spoke.

After a while Bamundi said, "I don't know who composed this or when. But it has to be a mother. Only a mother can know the pain of having to give up your daughter to a life that is all too familiar. A life of labour and on top of that harsh unkind returns. It is a curse to be born a woman." She mashed the boiled potatoes to a smooth consistency, without any lumps.

"May I say something?"

"My! Since when have you sought permission to speak Khema?" Bamundi looked up briefly from her task.

"In our community you can get away from a husband and take another. Sengat. That is what it is called. I believe that the world looks down upon it. Many in the community have also started saying so. Low caste behaviour it is called. Or so I have heard. But why not is what I would like to know. Why remain tied to a man who makes life hell for you?"

"Why even the Vaishnavs can do it. That Haru's mother, do you remember her Pishi?" Bamundi suddenly sat back with a sigh, "She came back though. People laughed at her. But at least she knew happiness for a while and chased a dream. High and low indeed. It is the same grind as far as you are a woman. In fact the higher you are, the greater the grind if you are a woman. Yes, they say that it will get resolved in heaven. Tell me why can't we get a taste of it here itself. On earth as we live? Why does it have to be a living hell for most?" Bamundi sighed, looked at Uma and spoke again. "There are so many verses by women, of woman and her lot, that an afternoon is not enough to run through them all. If some woman could write those down, the poem will probably be longer than this *Chandimangal* too.

> *Tanka bhenge shanka dilam kane madankari*
> *Biyer bela dekhe elum buro chaapdari|*
> *Chokh khao go baba ma chokh khao go khuro*
> *Eman bar ke biye diyechile tamak khego buro|*
> *Nere chere dekhi buro mare royeche*
> *Phen galbar samaye buro neche utheche|*

> I spent my money on conchshell bangles and
>   rings for the ears
> At the time of the marriage I saw that the man
>   was an old greybeard.
> A fie on your eyes father, mother and uncle, how
>   could you not see
> that this tobacco chewing man was too old a
>   groom for me.
> I shook him and stirred him and then I said well!
>   He is dead
> but when I poured the starch from the rice, the
>   oldy danced down from the bed.

"Such is a woman's life and such it will be. Always. It is an endless pouring of the starch from the rice. And blisters thereby. Anyway, will you read some more today? If not then I will get going. Some guests are coming to the other house. There will be some extra cooking no doubt. The rain's let up a bit I think. Just check Khema. It will rain through the night though, mark my words."

The hot air rushed out as soon as the kitchen door was opened.

Bamundi stood up. But she had not yet finished for the day at Kailash. She addressed Uma, directly. "Look at you too. So beautiful. Educated. We have heard that you have studied English too. But at the end? Your father had to pay for your dowry too, didn't he? This house is stuffed with things. But even so. True you have got a good man. A good family too. And may you flourish always. But at the end that's a matter of luck is it not? I may be an illiterate woman, but am I totally wrong?"

"Maybe you should hurry Bamundi. It may start raining again." Khema had almost finished clearing the remains of the tea party.

"You go too Khema." Pishi said. "I will finish this bit. You have your household to take care of too. The men will return soon."

"May I? If it rains more there will be traffic jams. My husband will come home in a foul temper then. Don't you wash anything Pishi. I will come in later. I will clear up everything then," said Khema.

Bamundi and Khema stepped out.

The kitchen was quiet.

Pishi was stuffing the cooked and minced fish into the mashed boiled potatoes to shape a perfect oval. She worked very carefully with her frail frame bent over the big plate.

Uma, lost in thought, sat by her even though she meant to help Pishi.

Pishi looked at her a few times and then said, "Go shut the net door. The mosquitoes will come in a swarm soon." Pishi's voice was gentle as she continued. "Grief must let out sometimes. Her life has not been easy. Don't take Bamundi's words to heart."

Uma stood at the kitchen door, breathing in the sharp wet air. The row of chilli plants glimmered under the darkening sky along the kithcen courtyard. The green of the leaves and the red rounds appeared bathed and sparkling, if somewhat dishevelled.

O parete kalo rang brishti pare jhamjham
O parete lanka gachti ranga tuktuk kare

Gunabati bhai amar man keman kare
Haar halo bhaja bhaja mash halo dari
sadh jaye nadir jale jhanp diya pari

Across the river the dark clouds pour rain.
Across the river the red chilli plant shines
there is a yearning in my heart, dear friend mine.
My bones have become brittle, my flesh has
    withered
I really do feel like just jumping into the river.

That was one of Kaki's favourite verses, Uma remembered. Uma had liked it too. The melancholy had appealed to her in a distant sort of way. On an impulse she said the poem out loud leaning against the kitchen door of Kailash.

Pishi looked up. "Come away from the door child. This moisture laden air brings with it aches and pains."

Uma came in and sat down again.

"Shall I fry a fish cutlet for you? Lunch was a long time ago. Have one, hot and crisp," asked Pishi, her tone soft and caressing.

"Baba did not like it you know Pishi. My reading out the *Chandimangal*, I mean. No. I don't feel like eating. Not now."

Pishi had finished making the patties. She started clearing up and did not say anything. Uma looked at Pishi for a while and then said again in low tones as she reached out to help her, "I don't know why I felt so bad. No, not just bad, I was devastated really. I did not expect it of him and of this house. I did not think that I was willfully disregarding any... any... rules. I think of this as my home where I also... It was also the manner. I felt humiliated.... You have nothing to say Pishi?"

"What's the point? Ashutosh is not wrong perhaps. One day you will have to run the house. Maybe you should not allow the servants to get too familiar. It may come in the way of later reprimands, when Bamundi will take leave without prior notice, when Khema will cut corners, when I...."

"Pishi."

"Such is life."

"I felt I was married. A daughter-in-law. A stranger. Not of Kailash. And I thought I belonged. I tried."

This time when Pishi looked at her, the green eyes were sparkling, "But you are reading still."

"Yes. Yes. Initially I had thought that I would not. I don't know why. Hurt pride, anger or perhaps my cowardice. Maybe I want to be the good girl I thought I was. The good girl that I would like to be. The good wife. The good daughter-in-law." Uma looked down, "The hurt stayed all evening and all night. I cried too."

"Did that help?"

"I don't know. Finally I asked him, I mean that I asked Baba at the breakfast table the next morning. Rudra was there too but I did not look at him. I just asked Baba if I could carry on reading the *Chandimangal* in the kitchen with you people. Baba looked a little taken aback. That was my victory. A small victory. But I ended on an abject note again. I said I did not know the ways of Kailash and would be guided by them. He said, I was actually relieved that Baba said that it was all right. I managed to save my face. What would you people have thought of me if I suddenly stopped reading? What would you have felt?"

"We would have understood. Honestly, each one of us would have understood. Though..."

"Yes?"

"It would have saddened us to know that the rules still apply. Even to one such as you."

"'It is strange that in a publisher's house permission should be sought for reading books.' That's what Rudra said, interrupting suddenly. I don't think Baba liked the intervention. I was glad. But only partly. I did not want any more tension in Kailash. But you know Rudra. He just went on slicing his boiled egg and eating it after making that comment. I did not want Baba to think that I had asked my husband to intervene on my behalf. In fact I had not even told him. There was some hurt pride there too. When I had tried to tell Rudra he seemed entirely disinterested. Was I expecting too much from Kailash? Have I done anything wrong Pishi? Pishi?"

"Do you know your mother-in-law loved to read out too?" Pishi sat back. The shadows had lengthened in the kitchen and her face could not be seen clearly, "Haimanti could not bear to see her daughter-in-law with a book in her hands. But Haimanti was a true ghoti. She had to sleep after her lunch. Come what may. So in the afternoon she, Shivani, would steal upstairs to the terrace. I would be there. I would take my darning up there and look at the sky. It seemed the same still. It was as I could look up and see from my home in the village those many years ago. Shivani, your mother-in-law would join me there and then she would read out for the two of us."

"What did she read?"

"Poetry. Always poetry. She did not read as well as you. But she read with greater feelings I think. Shivani's brothers would supply her with books. She used to read some poems again and again."

"What did she read the most?"

"She said that she liked modern poetry. Rabindranath Thakur. There was one about a girl suffocating in the city…The poem described Calcutta as the city of stones. What was it now… *bela je pare elo* … ?"

There seemed to be a third in the kitchen. Listening. A yearning presence.

"Did Baba … ?" Uma stopped.

"Do you know that he used to grow roses up on the terrace? Your father-in-law was suddenly seized by this passion after his marriage. There was a gardener too but Ashu handled everything on his own. Manure, soil, pots, trowel and the watering can. Clearly it gave him a lot of pleasure. Haimanti did not like it. 'You look like a peasant with soiled hands,' Haimanti would reprimand him. Ashu was always gentle. 'The god I am named after was a peasant, ma. He carries the plough as well as the trident,' Ashu would tell his mother. 'Shiva is a peasant god.' Ashu would laugh, silencing Haimanti."

"I did not see any signs of a terrace garden."

"Oh that was over a long time ago."

The wet wind blew outside. The light flickered once in the kitchen.

Pishi spoke, her voice so low that Uma had to strain to catch the words.

"Rudra must have been a year or so. He was fretting. Your mother-in-law was walking him up and down on the terrace. Her saree had slipped a bit from where it had been drawn up to cover her head. There was a breeze blowing. And young Rudra was restless too. He was cutting a tooth I think. Apparently he had been irritable all through the previous night as well. Shivani and I had taken turns to hold him and walk. But I had to go down, there was work to be done. The evening was still young when Ashu returned. He was back home a little early from work and had come up to look for his wife and son. He had not even changed. But had come up to the terrace straight. Shivani turned to look at him with the baby in her arms. Ashu plucked a red rose from a pot and went to tuck it into Shivani's hair. She laughed at him, with the baby in her arms, now grown quiet. They looked so young and happy."

"Where were you?"

"I had come up to give something to your grand mother-in-law. She was in the puja room up there. I don't think Ashu knew that. I stood enthralled in the shadows of the stairs. Yes. Life can be beautiful, I thought, looking at them."

"And grandmother?"

"She came out too drawn by the laughter. Her face looked so tight. She asked me to go down. Not to spy upon the family like the shameless hussy that I was. I came away."

"And?"

Pishi sighed, "Ashu stopped gardening after that. Your mother-in-law went to her father's for a while. She had not been there anyhow after the birth of the baby."

"Was she … was she sent away?"

Pishi did not answer.

"But she did return?"

"Yes. Of course. But she seemed quieter. It was not the Shivani who had been with us earlier. Some may say she had grown up but I think of it as more…more weighed down. As though she was carrying something heavy all the time. Ashu left for London soon after that. His passage was paid for by his father-in-law, you know that don't you?"

Uma did not.

"Ashu was away for a long time. Shivani would keep his letters with her through the day. She never read it as soon as it arrived. 'It is nice to think that his voice is waiting for me this evening', she said. The next afternoon she would bring the letter up on the terrace. Sometimes she would read out bits and pieces. About the students and the teachers Ashu met, the new land and its ways. I did not know that there were so many countries in the world. Often Shivani and I would wonder if in another part of the world another woman was reading another letter like us."

Uma wondered if she could take to planting roses on the terrace upstairs. After all the family did employ a gardener still. The terrace was wide and open to the elements. The plants should blossom well there. She knew that the earth here was fertile.

Dark, red roses swayed gently in the evening breeze. Their sharp sweet fragrance slowly filled the kitchen.

"Can you find that poem for me? About a girl in this city of stones? The one that Shivani used to read so often?" Pishi's voice recalled her.

"What?"

"The one by Rabindranath Thakur. The one that your mother-in-law used to read out to me." Pishi drew her saree to cover her mouth. Uma thought she would cry. But Pishi coughed gently into the faded white folds.

❀❀

The lights had been switched on by Khagen as Uma went upstairs. But her bedroom was still half in the dark. She stood in the shadows. There seemed a crowd of women in the room. Crying, raging, laughing. Loving too. And loved. Oh yes.

Slowly the fragrance of roses filled the bedroom. Dark red. Smooth and heady. Sweet. Very sweet.

Uma recklessly threw open her own bedroom windows wide.

It had started raining again as Bamundi had predicted.

Uma started getting ready for the evening.

Words, phrases, stanzas crowded her mind. Yes it was a day for poetry.

> *Brishti pare tapur tupur*
> *Nadye elo baan*
> *Shiv thakurer biye habe tin kanye dan.*
> *Ek kanye radhen baren*
> *Are ek kanye khan*
> *Are ek kanya gosha kare baper bari jaan|*

> Pitter patter falls the rain
> A flood seems imminent.
> Shiva the god marries and is given three wives.
> One of them cooks and serves.
> Another just eats.
> The third one goes back home in a fit of peeve.

Really Bamundi had a point thought Uma. Who knows who composed these verses so long ago? About women cooking and serving and the lucky one who had it it all on a platter. But there was peeve too. Discontent. What happened, Uma idly wondered, to the third wife in the verse who had left her husband's home in a fit of peeve? Why were not there any verses about her?

Lightning streaked across the sky. Uma went to shut the window.

And as she looked up at the sombre sky she recalled her childhood nightmare of the rain of Sati's limbs from the sky. Sati, the goddess as wife, who had not listened to her husband and had gone back to her father's on a visit. She was humiliated and died and was decapitated by the discus of Narayan. The bloodied trail shimmered. Uma shut her eyes. And when she opened them the sombre sky above Kailash was only a blue black glow.

❀ ❀

She used to stare at the sky in a village in Chittagong trying to recall the face of the young man she had been married to those many years ago. But that day seemed covered in mist that rises over the fields in hemanta, spiralling up, thickening, knotting the world over with the white shroud.

Oh, she knew that her husband was tall, he was fair, he was a serious scholar and that his name was Shashishekhar. But she could not put a face to him or a voice. Sometimes she thought he must be like the gods the kathaks sang songs of who test the world in unknown ways; sometimes he seemed like the demons who held captive the princess with evil magical power. And sometimes she saw him as a man who returned home after a day's work and sat down to a meal served by a wife even as three children gather around. Yes, three children, two girls and then a boy. This she had heard, catching the echoes from the men of the family who visited him in Calcutta.

She rubbed her arm in anger and then winced. Her mother-in-law had pinched her hard that evening as she often did when vexed or lonely or irritated. Oh she held her in her arms too sometimes and said, "You have a burnt fate, what can I do?" but her right arm was still pock marked with pinch marks.

Once she had run away to her mother. But her mother herself told her to look to God.

Which god, she had wondered, Shiva? Husband to the Devi? Who sometimes bears the crescent moon upon his head and is called Shashishekhar?

Her face tightened.

Her mother wiped her eyes and said, "The Devi kills demons. We worhsip her for that for five days during Durga puja in autumn. But after that she is thrown into the river. Why? Because she must float away to Kailash to reach her husband, household and children. That is where she belongs. Even if she slays demons. And we are mere mortals."

"Throw me in the river then," she responded in a flash.

The next morning her mother sent her back to her mother-in-law.

❀ ❀

Uma stood by the door of the ante-room and watched Rudra as he took off his shoes. Rudra looked at her in the mirror as he pulled open the knot of his tie. "How was your day? Did you have a reading session? Did the women enjoy it?"

It is so easy to win over a wife.

Uma stepped in. Rudra turned around.

There was a smell of roses in the room and the night a dark velvet.

Or so Uma thought.

Or so she felt.

❀ ❀

"I have news," Bamundi looked up as soon as Uma entered the kitchen, clearly having waited for this moment since the day began.

It was raining outside. The drizzle misted the world with its steady and continuous fall. But a warm and dry smell held the room. The yellow moong was being slowly roasted to an even red on the fire under Bamundi's meticulous handling of the spatula which she turned and turned about.

"What?"

"Of the marriage. What else?"

"Whose?"

Pishi took the spatula from Bamundi's hand. The reddening of the moong dal was a fine art. It had to be just so. Bamundi was getting excited.

"Gauri. Uma. Whatever you call her." Bamundi wiped her hand on the saree, "The goddess when she is married to Shiva after Sati's death. Have you forgotten? Did we not say that the mother must have been unhappy with the match?"

"The goddess herself? You have inside information about the match?" Uma drew a low wooden stool, sat down and tried not to smile.

"Yes. The goddess. And why should she want to marry an old man with children from his first wife? Why would she want to enter a poor household? And her? So used to freedom? Roaming the mountains on her own, riding a lion?"

"But how did you come by this piece of information?" Khema asked. She looked a little tired.

The drizzle grew stronger. The heaven seemed determined to wear down the world slowly with the steady and persistent rain.

It can't be easy, Uma thought, looking at Khema, to live cooped up in a small space with her husband and son and father-in-law and especially when it rains so. Uma could almost see Khema's room with the beds on the floor, wet clothes strung in one corner and the blackened utensils and the stove in another. Khema was really looking tired as she sat with her head against the wall. Where was her son, Uma wondered. The small figure could usually be seen in the different corners of the garden even on a sunny day, sometimes with the gateman or near the garage. Clearly the boy did not go to school. This steady rain would hold the child captive too. He would be fretting. Should she ask Khema to bring in her son to the kitchen? But then it might become a habit. Uma held herself back. Young boys were restless. And they grew up so soon too. Perhaps it is better to let it be. But Khema looked tired. Her gleaming dark skin seemed blotched as though by weariness.

"Let us have some tea." Uma said instead.

Bamundi responded with alacrity, glad to be able to do something with her hands at last. Pishi coughed softly, holding her saree to her mouth. Bamundi took charge of the spatula once again.

"We have been getting together for Manasa pala in our area," Bamundi said.

A spark seemed to kindle in Khema, there was a lively note

in her voice, "Do you know Manasa, Boudi? She is the powerful goddesss of the serpents. The monsoon is her special time.'

But Bamundi took over again, "We are having an eight day session for her in our locality. Serpents are fierce creatures. We don't want to anger this goddess."

"Tell us about Gauri's marriage." Uma interrupted.

"Hmm. Well I was telling this neighbour of mine about us during one of our Manasa jagaran."

"Us?"

Did Bamundi look slightly embarrassed?

"Yes... No... I mean... I was telling people how we get togther in Kailash and how..."

Uma had this sudden vision of scores and scores of Bamundis scurrying through the underbelly of Calcutta who carried with them the intimate knowledge of the thousands of houses up above. No matter how high the house might rise, the network beneath held it captive; sharing, spreading news of births and betrayals, marriages and deaths, reporting the daily flow, whispering scandals or speculating a salary raise. Maybe she should... not...

"They named the goddess Gauri and Uma. The golden one, the gentle one, soft and docile. But so what? Was she not also Chandi and Parvati, used to roaming the mountains, being on her own, taking on demons and setting the world straight? How long would she be happy with domesticity?"

"What do you mean?" Khema asked.

"As if you don't know. How long could the goddess accept the drudgery of it all-waiting for her old man, cooking, cleaning, sweeping, swabbing. All the time the goddess remembered, surely she must have remembered, the other life that she must have led."

There was a brief silence in the room. All three remembered the icon of the goddess transfixed as she kills Mahisashura, the dark demon who had disguised himself initially as a Mahisa or buffalo.

"And then?"

"And then what? She told Shiva."

"What? That she had had enough?"

"Not like that perhaps. But she did say that she wanted to go back to being a goddess too. She wanted to be someone other than a wife. The goddess wanted to meet her followers. Lead them. Accept their worship."

"You mean that she wanted to have a life of her own," nodded Khema slowly.

"And she did. This *Chandimangal* that you are reading out to us Boudi, does it not say so too, does it not suggest that the goddess had had enough of being at home, of being tied down? Is not that why she comes to earth again, seeking her followers, strengthening her cult, wielding power as a goddess once again? Even though she is a wife with a husband, a household and children? Does she not, despite all that?"

The four women drew together. The greyish light of the afternoon grew darker. But the fire of the stove glowed golden.

☙ ❧

Uma felt her face glow warm as she made her peace offering. It meant so much to her to have her father-in-law's approval and affection. She also felt oddly protective towards him now, having known that he once harvested roses for his wife though Kailash had not allowed it for long.

"The *Chandimangal* is a kind of religious literature, is it not?" Uma began a little weakly, wanting to please her father-in-law once again.

"Well...yes...but not in a rigid sense. The mangalkavya traces the growth and popularity of a deity by recounting the primary tales of miracles associated with her."

"The surviving *Chandimangal*s usually contain three sections?" Ashutosh nodded mildly.

"The first section is called the divine section or the deb khanda. It gives us a sort of bio-data of the goddess. Then come the stories of two of Chandi's leading followers who helped spread the goddess's cult among their people, the Hunter's section or the akhetic khanda and the Merchant's section or the Banik khanda."

"There are no women poets of *Chandimangal* Baba?"

"Not that I know of. In fact most of the poets, other than one Krishnajivan Da, a Modak by caste probably, are overwhelmingly Brahmans. Naturally perhaps. Given the social conditions."

Suddenly the anomaly struck Uma. Why were the hunter and the merchant thus privileged in songs composed overwhelmingly by Brahman poets? Especially the hunter. Gently she intervened, "Why did the Brahman poets celebrate the hunter and the merchant as the prime acolytes of the goddess? I mean the hunter would be low caste, an untouchable, no?"

"The poems of this genre earned distinction, as they gave up the narrow communal arena to serve the higher ideals of literature," remarked Ashutosh. "We have to take a look at the historical and social environment of the *Chandimangal* in order to understand that the Brahman poet was trying to keep his flock together as his own power was threatened by Chaitanya's tolerant vaishnavism and the Muslim rule …."

The mutton croquets that evening were golden brown breaking softly to release their smoky fillings of mince in the mouth.

"When was Neelkantha's *Chandimangal* printed?" Uma asked her father-in-law.

" I have told you that my grandfather composed it in 1857, the year of the mutiny. My father printed it in 1907 during the height of the swadeshi movement."

"That's really quite interesting. It almost seems to be trailing the history of our freedom movement."

Uma knew of swadeshi, the turbulent five years from 1903 to 1908, not just from the history lessons but as it lived on in the memory of Bengal's bhadralok as their full-throated militant cry for freedom before Mahatma Gandhi's non-violent, non co-operation movement when the Bengali, often mocked as the effete intellectual by the colonial master, proved his martial valour to be no less than that of the Sikhs, Pathans or the Irish.

※ ※

The atmosphere in the formal parlour of Kailash was one of tense anticipation as when fate hangs uncertain over one's head.

"This is a moment for action. Not idle talk. We have to do something," burst out a cousin of Haimanti's.

Haimanti's brothers and cousins had come over to Kailash to meet Shashishekhar's cousins from Chittagong. No. Shashishekhar had not severed his ties entirely with his mother's family. Blood had proved to be thicker than water. And Shashishekhar liked the reversed role. He was no longer the poor dependant relative but the successful cousin in Calcutta, educated and enterprising. His star was rising as opposed to the faded glory of the cousins from Chittagong. Now Shashishekhar was sought out for advice and acknowledgement by his mother's family. He too was gracious. He allowed his maternal relatives as well as their considerably extended kin to look him up while in Calcutta. He advised them in city matters: where to find decent grooms or rooms, where to put in or, as was more often the case, borrow money, where to send the sons for jobs and in one or two rare instances, for college education. But this time the cousins had come to Kailash to gauge the mood of the moment. Discontent had been simmering for a while in the colonised nation. The partition of the province, or Bangabhanga, during the viceroyalty of Lord Curzon was the trigger.

The presidency of Bengal was to be partitioned into West Bengal and East Bengal comprising the Chittagong, Dhaka and Rajshashi divisions, Hill Tippera, Malda and Assam. Dhaka was declared the capital of the new province. The latter had a sizeable Muslim population. The ostensible reason for the portioning of Bengal, as given by the British administration, was the famine in Orissa in 1866. The Presidency of Bengal, then comprising present day Bengal, Bihar, Tripura, Orissa, Assam and Bangladesh, had an area of 189,000 square miles and a population of 78½ million. It was too large for effective management. Or so her managers trotted out as an explanation for the Orissa famine. A reduction in size would make for administrative efficiency, said her rulers. In private though other reasons were admitted. "Bengal united is a power," wrote one of the most powerful British administrators, H. H. Risley, in 1904, "Bengal divided would pull in several different ways."

The gathering in Kailash recognized the partition as a deliberate ploy of the colonial government to splinter along communal lines, the solidarity of the Bengali-speaking population and their growing nationalism. It was feared that the partition would encourage the growth of a Muslim power in eastern Bengal. Had not Lord Curzon in a speech delivered at Dhaka on the 18th of February, 1904, said that the partition would "invest the Mohammedans in Eastern Bengal with a unity which they have not enjoyed since the days of the old Mussulman viceroys and kings…"

Then appeared the fissures and the cracks. The swadeshi sentiment in the parlour of Kailash splintered into two recognisable streams, though with overlaps.

A select few, educated in England and among the city elites, wanted reform and colonial self-government. The cousins from Chittagong and some of Haimanti's kin wanted complete political independence. They rejected the method of 'prayers and petitions' and called for the social boycott of traitors, British goods, officialised education, justice and executive administration. They also acknowledged the possibility of aggressive resistance and armed revolt. If need be.

The servants moved about the parlour in silence, fetching and carrying refreshments from the kitchen; a good deal of which was consumed in that charged atmosphere.

Anger and voices rose in the talk of freedom.

※ ※

The voice in her head would not cease. Shashishekhar, Shashishekhar. The night was dark in Chittagong.

It was the night consecrated to Shiva. The fasting women prayed.

Her stomach churned acid, raging against the fast that she had to keep for the well being of her husband whom she had not seen since their wedding.

A cousin of sorts nudged her. See that you don't take your husband's name while praying to the god. Your lord shares the name of the god. But the lord must not be named. It is a sin.

Slowly she drew her saree over her head and whispered, "Shashishekhar, Shashishekhar," daring her fate, "may you have a burnt fate too. And all you men who do the same."

Her anger mounted with her chant, comforting her for the moment.

❈ Eight ❈

The goddess' anger was awesome. Rich and golden like molten lava. Her war cry bellowed across the universe.

"Where are you Mahisashura? Where are you? You coward!"

The earth trembled. The ocean receded. The clouds swirled in a hurry to get away. The deities gathered in a nervous huddle. The animals cowered in their jungle dens. The goddess's roar for the demon Mahisashura reverberated through the world again and again. The goddess swayed slightly as the lion that carried her surged forward.

Her hands exuded confidence. The rein that held the lion was slack but in control. Total and absolute.

The lady riding the lion laughed aloud. It was louder than thousands of thunderclaps. Lightning darted from her eyes as she searched for her enemy.

"Mahisashura, surely you are not afraid of me?" The goddess laughed. And then again. Waves and waves of it rippled all over. Exulting in its female self. Entering every nook and cranny of the world.

Wrath surged through the demon Mahisashura. His heart pounded with rage. He swelled his chest and answered the call. The sound emerged like an echo from a deep cavern in a jungle. Rumbling over the secret green.

The kettledrums rattled. Out rushed his Ashura legion. Like undulating black clouds.

The universe darkened. More terrifying than the pitch black in which nothing can be seen.

Was this pralay, the deluge that engulfs the world at the end of an aeon?

"So they have sent a woman to fight me, have they, your gods? World take note. The receivers of your daily worship, of your flowers and fruits, of the sacred smoke arising from your rituals of sacrifice, the devas, your gods are hiding behind a woman," countered the Ashura. Ah foolish pride!

Mahisashura's black eyes quickly ran over the golden frame of the devi swaying in perfect rhythm with the rippling golden muscles of the lion on which she stood. The goddess's feet, now seen, now not, were like lustrous lotus newly blossomed on a cloud of golden mane. Momentarily they diverted Mahisashura's attention, expert warrior though he was. Something flashed silver suddenly. His body tensed. He gathered himself, willing back the concentration with which he had defeated the devas led by Indra. Mahisashura had then taken charge of heaven.

But the defeated gods had complained to the mighty triumverate of Brahma, Vishnu and Shiva.

The male anger of the three blazed a pure flame on hearing of the sacrilegious temerity of the Ashura. Mahisashura was forgetting his place!

The flame flared and soared. The devas who had gathered around shielded their eyes from the glow of it.

But wonder of wonders! A female form emerged from this combined tejas of the three supreme male gods. She was golden and glorious. The other gods marvelled at the amazing sight.

Following the mightly three, they too willed her their shakti, their strength. Shaping her beauty and strength. A strength that could be terrible too.

Shiva gave her his trident.

Vishnu his discus.

Varuna a conchsell.

Agni a spear.

Maruta gave her a bow and quiver of arrows.

Indra a thunderbolt and a bell.

Yama, the lord of death, gave her his very own staff.

Brahma a string of beads and a water pot.

Surya poured his own rays into her skin so that it glowed like the sun in the cruel blue summer sky.

The milk foamed ocean gave her brilliant jewellery.

The lord of wealth, Kuvera, gave a wine cup that would be ever full.
Shesha gave her a serpent.
Kaal gave a sword and shield.
Vishwakarma gave her an axe.
Himalaya gave her a lion.
The lion loped forward.
The dark sky was illumined only by the flying silver of weapons and the hurling gold of flames.
She cut through the Ashura generals, Chiksura and Chamara.
She razed Udagra.
She devastated Mahahanu.
The mighty Ashuras Ashiloman, Baskala, Parivarita, Bidala, Uddhata, Durmukkha… all fell.
The goddess fought the Ashura legion. She split, smashed, shattered, severed or skewered them.
The enraged embattled Mahisashura was like a buffalo now. Death on his twin horns that could furrow the rockiest ground. Death in the mad lashing of his tail. Death in his thundering, pounding hooves. He charged forward. Excitement, expectation and the unknown mixed a heady punch in his body.
But what was this? Was he drunk or was the goddess wielding ten arms?
The snake hissed in one. Poison dribbled slowly down its horrifying fangs. The discus spun sharp shards in another. Eager to slice the skin, the sinew and then the flesh. The mace began its slow descent to crush his head.
Sweat.
Her arrow singed into his shoulder. His head was there a moment ago.
Blood.
The buffalo became a lion and the lion a man with a sword, the man an elephant and then a buffalo again.
Still she pursued him. And laughed. Though her eyes were red.
He threw his trident at her with all his might then.
It ricocheted off her shield with a loud clang.
All that lived covered their ears. Trembling, trembling all the while.

Laughter. Loud and defiant. Who would have known that female laughter could be so frightening?

How dare she?

Her broadsword was dancing. Playing with him. He thrust out at it. A foot swung through the air and landed on his chest.

Who would have known that the lotus could be like a mountain?

The trident in her most powerful arm flashed lightning.

Laughter.

And the universe sobbing in pure terror. Praying. Cowering.

Mahisashura struggled for lost splendour and in one last mighty heave half emerged from his buffalo form.

Her trident was forced near his heart.

Blood. Red and warm. Splattering the earth. Rendering the earth moist and soft. As though ready for ploughing.

She twisted the trident around. Ripped it out of the body, male and muscular. Trailing torn nerves. It was plunged in again. Deeper into the flesh. Troughing through to where the heart was beating. The proud heart that had once challenged the ordained order of the universe. And had succeeded too almost. Blast the gods for sending her was Mahisashura's last thought .

The trident reached and pierced his heart..

The red fountain glowed golden.

The dark disappeared.

The sun burst upon the scene.

Conchshells blew sonorous.

Flowers showered in a steady stream.

All came with folded hands. And bowed to her. The goddess.

Then the Devi spoke and her voice filled the universe:

Aham rudrebhivarsubhishchramyahamadityeru vishvadevyae….

I am the Devi, I am shakti. I am the divine force of the world….

I have created the world…. I am knowledge… I am worshipped by the gods…

The sky who is called the father

I am mother to him…

I move through the world as wind. As freely.

I manifest myself as the world. It's my own glory….

Uma turned the page, moved despite herself, despite her awareness that this was only a story, despite the fact that she had already read this particular passage once. And she knew that her audience was enraptured too.

Khema, Bamundi and Pishi. In the kitchen in Kailash.

Uma looked up.

"This is the passage that is perhaps the most quoted from Neelkantha's *Chandimangal*," she remarked, holding the place with a finger, "during the swadeshi movement, when India was envisaged as a militant mother goddess demanding the blood of those who had enslaved her. It was then that her children were exhorted to take vows to free the motherland from her colonial rulers. This passage was read out again and again in those days."

"Where?" Khema asked a little breathless, as though she had been in the battlefield with the goddess herself.

"In secret societies and in public places; wherever swadeshis – the freedom fighters – gathered, whenever they needed to rouse the ordinary who went about their daily routine without worrying about the nation. I have heard from my mother and grandmother that in those heady days the icon of the goddess was, in some villages, made to pierce an Ashura who was moulded to look like the local British officer. Of course the police would usually get to know and then the icon would be rushed out in secret and immersed in the local pond or river to the mingled cries of the swadeshis hailing the goddess as well as the motherland."

"Swadeshis?" asked Khema, a little diffidently.

And Uma said, "It was a heroic golden period of selfless devotion to the nation in the cause of freedom."

"Those days must have been different. And the people too," sighed Khema.

"Were they?" asked Bamundi, "How did these men who worshipped the mother goddess astride a lion treat their own flesh and blood women? Tell me, I would like to know that. Tell us honestly."

But before Uma could speak Pishi intervened, "We know, don't we, that most women of these devotees of the militant goddess were screened from the public world by blinds, windows, veils and taboos?"

Khema shot a sharp silent look at the others. Her fingers were busy though. A pile glimmered in front of her. She polished steadily as Uma read. Bronze, copper, silver, brass and glass. Each had its turn through the five days of the week. To begin again. An endless cycle. How else would Kailash shine?

Bamundi stirred and stoked. Sweat glistened on her face. The kitchen was sultry despite the door that was left open. August was almost over. But the golden glow of autumn was still afar.

Pishi sat surrounded by jars and bottles hauled from the store-room adjoining the kitchen. The monsoon also meant moulds and fungus. The pickles and preserves had to be tended to. Mangoes, berries, woodapples, tamarind in various states were inspected and given a fresh lease of life by being sunned or doused in mustard oil as the weather, and the recipe, ordained.

Suddenly Pishi said, "In the icons that we see, the Ashura being killed by the goddess is an obvious outsider."

"What?"

"The Ashura's black colour is absolutely opposed to the yellow and white of the divine mother and her children. Clearly he is not one of them."

So? The others asked, wondering.

"It suggests, does it not, that evil is outside the family?"

The four women mulled over the statement. But in silence this time and in the private recesses of their minds.

※ ※

Shashishekhar was a man of few words and hardly spoke as the mood in the parlour grew more and more fiery, escpecially of his cousins from Chittagong. It bothered Shashishekhar. He had always let it be known to his cousins, that he was there to give advice alone. They were welcome to visit him in Calcutta but no one was to stay in his house for more than three days and no alcohol or illegitimate fornication was to be tolerated within the premises of Kailash. He realised that he would now have to add that there was to be no 'politicking' from Kailash either. He would not say it in so many words of course but he would let it be known. As he had let it be known that no one was to talk about his first marriage.

No one did.

Such was the strength of Shashishekhar's character. And the measure of his success.

Haimanti was a wonderful hostess. Gracious and solicitous.

She too had been elevated in life. She had arrived in this world after four sons. Her parents had thus welcomed the novelty of the birth but nonetheless she was a daughter still. Now not only was she the ginni – the mistress – of Kailash but also the mother of three. Moreover the youngest was a boy. At last. The male scion was called Ashutosh, one of the names of Shiva as had been desired by the legendary grandfather years ago in far off Kynsa mati, Chittagong. The boy was placid and the epithet of Shiva, Ashutosh, that meant 'easily pleased' suited him.

There had been a time when Haimanti resented, hated and was even a little scared of anything associated with Chittagong. She knew, as the wind carries tales, that there was another woman there. She had also heard that women from East Bengal were different. They possessed a sharp palate, a harsh tongue and a strange dialect. Some said that they even knew magic. Of the black kind. What if her husband ….

Perish the thought, her mother had advised. For thoughts can take shape if a mischief-making deity happened to catch them. Pray instead, Haimanti's mother advised her daughter. Pray and fast. Take no chances. There were deities galore in the Hindu calendar. "Observe those bratas. Look upto your husband for he is the divine presence in female life. Look after him in bed and board for men are, let's face it, more corpulent than women. And try to produce a son. As my blood runs in you, you cannot fail," Haimanti's mother said.

Haimanti did not fail.

She turned to the gods, searched out bratas, observed fasts, ran a spic and span house as modern educated husbands desired, ordered special dishes in the kitchen to suit her husband's Chittagong palate, kept her voice soft all the time, covered her head, welcomed visitors from his side which meant that he did not need to visit them and never ever asked him questions about the other one. But her thoughts? Who has ever been able to put up barricades strong enough to sieve the flow of thoughts?

From behind the blind that screened the inner quarters, her face hidden by her saree Haimanti enquired softly of the visitors from Chittagong if they were comfortable and well looked after in Kailash. And then even more softly another question would follow.

"Is every one fine at home?"

The reassuring, affirmative answers always drove her to search out more bratas. Observe yet another fast to bribe heaven.

Lead me to peace, God, lead me, Haimanti prayed.

❊ ❊

"She laughs a great deal," remarked Pishi in the kitchen in Kailash.

"What?"

"The goddess laughs a great deal in this section about her battle with the Ashura."

"Won't she? She has left her old husband behind at last, no demanding children, no sweeping, mopping, gathering of firewood, grinding spices..." put in Khema.

"Given half a chance, I would too," Bamundi muttered.

"What! You would have gone off to the battlefield?" smiled Uma "Mmmm. Actually I can imagine your ten arms busy with the ladle, the mortar, the pestle..."

Kailash rang with female laughter.

"And your son? Who would cook for him?" asked Khema, half in jest. "Could you really leave him and go off?"

Laughter withdrew.

"I don't know. He was growing inside me even before I knew

what had happenned. Ever since then…He is his father's but where is that man? And the son? It is not my fault that the factory has closed down two shifts. But I am the one he bares his fangs at all the time. These days he has even taken to…" Bamundi's hand, at odds with her voice, gently sifted the sooji that was being roasted to keep safe from the moisture laden atmosphere. It heaved and settled smooth in the pan like fine grains of sand in a desert storm.

"She has to forget her former life." Pishi spoke again. "The goddess. Did none of you notice what Kuvera gave her? A cup of wine that never empties. You think that the Devi just holds it? Did you not read that her eyes were red?"

"Were they?"

The women quivered with sudden excitement. Uma was exhorted to look for the specific line. As she turned the page she felt a sudden tension in the air. The three pairs of eyes were fixed on her, as though they were about to discover something momentous.

"Here it is," Uma read, "*Kuvera, gave a wine cup that would be ever full.* Mmm *Her eyes were red….She laughed. Etc. It crackled all around.* Etc. etc." Uma looked up, "I have read this bit before. But it is followed by a couple of lines in Sanskrit. I did not read the lines because you won't understand that and…" Uma realised what she had said and quickly added, "…and I won't be able to read it well either. I thought it would break the rhythm." She finished weakly.

The kitchen was quiet for a awhile.

"Why use Sanskrit suddenly?" Bamundi asked, frowning.

Uma fingered the pages, "The sages used that language. And much of this section about the goddess is taken from the *Purana*s. I have been told so."

The women mulled over the problem. They had always accepted that Sanskrit was the language of the privileged, unavailable to women and the low castes. But in Kailash that afternoon it aroused their indignation. It did seem very mean to use a tongue that they did not understand for something that was meant for them. Or was it?

"What are the lines anyway?" Bamundi asked, her brows furrowed still. "Can you read them?" Then she added a little diffidently, "Let us hear them at least."

Khema nodded.

Pishi sat still and gazed at Uma.

Uma turned a few pages and then read slowly with some hesitation,

> "*Tatah krudhha jaganmata chandika panmuttamam.*
> *Papau punah punah punashchaiva jahasarunalochana.*"

I am not very certain if my pronunciation is right. I did not study Sanskrit beyond class eight."

"You studied Sanskrit?" Khema was incredulous.

"All of us had to."

"All the girls too?"

"Yes. Of course."

"You read it just like the priest," Bamundi said.

The adulation was heady.

Pishi spoke. "But what do the lines mean? Can you make out anything?"

Uma hesitated. "I studied Sanskrit only in school. That is very elementary."

"Still. Can you not understand any word?"

They edged forward.

Uma looked at the lines.

"Could you...?"

"Any word? Any?"

"Why are the eyes red? Is she crying?"

"I should not translate, I may make a mistake..."

"And what if you do?"

Uma suddenly gave in. "I think it means that the goddess is quaffing her drink in anger and her eyes are red as a result and she is laughing out loud... I could be wrong though."

Someone let out a long sigh.

Another said, "She is drinking huh?"

The women nursed the idea. Conspiratorial. As though they were part of some secret society. An excitement made the kitchen quite heady. Reckless too.

"The goddess has to forget the household that she has left behind. Her former lives. The philandering old husband, the crying children, the grind and grist of running a household." Bamundi stared at the fine white grains now cooling on a flat plate, "Who knows ….." The words hung midstream.

"Maybe the goddess is celebrating and laughing because it is wonderful to be on one's own, to fight for freedom?" Pishi continued.

Their minds trailed the success of the laughing martial goddess. Resplendent, free and powerful.

"But was it?" mused Bamundi. "Was it her freedom that she is fighting for? Or was it once again a clever plan to use her, to make her do the work for them?"

Her audience did not answer.

But they all knew 'them'.

Uma returned to the book. She started reading again and was soon carrying them all.

The polishing, stirring and sifting also continued.

※ ※

The Printers Union led the procession from Cornwallis Street to the Paikpara Rajbati. The air throbbed with heightened excitement and expectation. There was resolve too. Shashishekhar stood with a knot of professional friends and acquaintances and watched the strikers. He held his head up because he felt a little embarrassed and a little distracted too to be out on the street thus. The autumn sun was still strong enough and his skin glowed red from its heat. Onlookers nudged each other and asked who he was with his fierce good looks. He must be somebody!

The two big government presses in India, the Government of India and the Bengal Secretariat, had been complaining about the harsh treatment by white officers for a while. Discontent also simmered over inadequate pay and excessive hours. The government not only ignored it but also reduced the puja advance in the autumn of 1905. The workers retaliated by going on strike. The colonial context and the racial overtones only aggravated the inequalities of the employer-employee equation.

"There is a meeting at the maidan. You are coming aren't you?" Haimanti's brother was bubbling over with excitement.

"I have heard that the strikers are calling in barristers for advice?" Shashishekhar's voice reflected nothing of his inner turmoil.

"Of course and many of us will also be there."

"The clerks and compositors too?"

"Yes. The British do not know what a power we can be. I must leave, there is a lot to be done." He left.

"Look at my brother, he is looking so..."

"...exuberant," Shahishekhar finished Haimanti's sentence wryly.

Shashishekhar was a worried man. The Ganges Press had finished with its production of Durga puja specials. But labels remained. Already it was running a bit late because of the advance puja publications of bratakathas and novels. The work, once accepted, needed to be finished. There would be a long holiday for puja too. How far would the excitement spread? Or the demands? Who would the strikes touch finally, Shashishekhar wondered.

Shashishekhar's blood did boil when he saw the boisterous, inebriated or unthinking arrogance of the white men on the streets of Calcutta. Once one of them had halted his phaeton and said something in a slurred voice of which only the word, 'babu' could be understood. And the derisive tone. Irish scum, thought Shashishekhar though he had said nothing and asked the driver to move on. What they were doing to the coolies in Assam was inhuman too. Could these white men really belong to the race of Bentham and Mill?

But. And there was a "but". Freedom meant responsibilities. Freedom required maturity. Otherwise it could lead to chaos and disorder. What was happening was heady and exciting. But how far would they spread, these ideas of freedom and equality? How much would they touch?

Work must carry on. Freedom or otherwise.

Shashishekhar had a fine political sense though he eschewed politics. Could he afford to ignore the political mood of the times?

And the times, Shashishekhar felt, were changing.

Shashishekhar's fears were justified as the press employees probably were the first to organise a proper trade union in Bengal. The turbulence intensified in the third week of October,1905, as the Government of India Press sacked the leaders of the agitation. But the struggle only grew stronger. The colonial authorities tried to recruit workers from outside and get urgent matters printed by the convicts of the Presidency Jail. The strikers undeterred, formed a Printer's and Compositor's League. The workers appealed for a united front. Strike breakers were allegedly assaulted. The employers were also the colonial masters. A notice at the Bengal Secretariat Press calling for a workers' meeting showed the swadeshi impulse in exhorting a boycott of foreign goods as well.

The fund-raising procession for the strike wound its way very slowly through the streets of Calcutta, radiating a nationalist will. *Allah-ho-Akbar* and *Bandemataram* were shouted by many. And the voices were raised together. Passers by walked some way with the strikers. Women leaned out of balconies to throw down contributions. Some constables on duty chose to look away, defiant as well as furtive. Students stood in groups animatedly discussing what they could do now. The wealthy came out to feed the strikers royally.

But by then Shashishekhar, having done his bit, had left. He felt that India stood at the threshold of some great change. He could not afford to remain aloof. He believed in equality too. For some at any rate. But he did not wish to be seen as espousing the cause in any prominent way. Besides, it took very little time for a business to collapse. It could not be long before the Union extended its work to the private presses of the city, halting work. And work must carry on, Shashishekhar firmly believed. People must realise that they had jobs to do and that that came first.

❦❦

"Can you not find out?" pleaded Khema

"What?" Uma looked up.

"What really happened?"

"What was she like?"

"The goddess. Was she just a wife or was she another?" asked Bamundi.

"Riding a lion. Exploring mountains. Drinking wine," Khema recited.

"A loved daughter."

"A mother too. Nourishing the earth."

"A life before and after marriage."

"Maybe … maybe not married. At all."

"What?"

"Look, just between us, a lady who rides the lion and fights a battle, would she just marry an old man with a ready-made family. Or marry at all? Just between us, mind. And him so poor too."

"But he is a god. Shiva no less."

"Maybe that is made up."

"Maybe that was forced. Upon her."

"Because they did not like to think that a woman should be like that. "

"Powerful and independent."

"Can you not find out …."

"Why did they call the goddess an Ashuri, a dakini – a demoness, a witch?"

"Even though they worshipped her?"

"Even as they worshipped did they find it strange that a female should possess such power?"

"Well they could not deny her power."

"Maybe that is why they called her both devi and Ashuri. A goddess because she is powerful and a demoness because her power made her a stranger to them. They could not accept that a female could wield such power."

"They?"

"Them that wrote about her. For us."

"So that we could forget what else she was. It was a ploy by them. Them that held her captive with a husband and children."

"Them."

"So clever."

"Cunning I call it."

The pestle shuddered on the stone slab. The coconut husk scoured the brass. The water hissed and sizzled as it was poured over the shallow-fried vegetables in the pot.

"There must be hints. A whiff of it somewhere."

"The books?"

"There are many *Chandimangals*, are there not?"

"Of different poets?"

"From different parts of Bengal?"

"Yes Baba did say that this poetry flourished from the 15th or 16th century onwards. I mean a long time ago it would be."

"Can you not find out if they say different things?"

"Let slip a word or two?"

"Of a different goddess?"

"Of different goddesses?"

"Who are trussed up as wife to old Shiva."

"So that."

"So that."

"So that we are held too. In marriage, for ever and ever."

"Can you not find out?"

"Can you not?"

"Can you?"

"I will try."

Excited voices filled the kitchen. As though battle plans were being drawn.

꽃꽃

"Will swadeshi affect your work, your business?" Haimanti asked her husband. The anxiety that laced her query had very little to do with The Ganges Press though.

Shashishekhar was pacing up and down in their bedroom. Haimanti was on the bed gently patting her son to sleep. Her daughters were sleeping in the adjoining room. Shashishekhar had ordained a separate bed chamber for the children, wanting to instil discipline and self-sufficiency in them as they did in England. Even daughters. But Haimanti held on to the son still. "The British...." Shashishekhar's rich warm voice filled the room completing the circle of intimacy.

Much of what Shashishekhar said, Haimanti knew already. Her family was very sympathetic to the swadeshi cause. Her college educated brothers were attracted to liberal humanism and recognized the importance of the spirit of freedom. Much of their inherited wealth had also been invested in land in Bakhergunge that would now fall in the newly-formed province of East Bengal as a result of the partition of Bengal. Two of her brothers were lawyers and one a journalist. The family had business interests, especially in raw jute and the rice trade, that demanded a healthy Calcutta port. A new court of appeal at Dhaka, the rise of local newspapers, the imminent prominence of the Chittagong port that the partition of the province may ensure, were all apprehended as loss of business for Haimanti's family's Calcutta-based prosperity. A horde of cousins and nephews who coveted jobs in the Civil Service were also fuelled by popular anti-British sentiments. Did the Europeans not conduct a fierce campaign against the Ilbert Bill that allowed the Indian to judge white misdemeanor? Were the salaries and the pensions of the whites not draining the wealth of India? Should these jobs not be given to educated Indians like them? Would that not be the just measure against white racism?

Yes. Swadeshi had been the topic of discussion in the women's quarters as much as in the men's in Haimanti's natal home last week when they had gathered for the upavaita ceremony of a young nephew to initiate him ritually as a Brahman male. A sister-in-law's anglicised upper class family had Congress connections. She waxed eloquent on the method of boycott. A younger male cousin surrounded by a bevy of female relatives had talked about the Carlyle Circular that aimed to crush the students' participation in the Swadeshi and Boycott movements. Another had mentioned the racial convocation speech which proclaimed that the highest ideal of truth was a western concept. Tales of white arrogance and diabolical discrimination had been exchanged.

Haimanti knew that the British were awful and had no regard for Hindu rituals and customs. She knew that they were draining the wealth of India which had been a land of gold when the saints lived and scripted the *Vedas* and the *Puranas*. She had also been made to understand that the British were promoting the Muslims and the lower castes to undermine the superiority of the upper caste Hindus.

But Haimanti said none of what she knew already to her husband. She also did not say that in the secret recess of her mind she saw the partition of the province as ordained by the gods. The Hindu gods that is, to whom she had appealed through numerous bratas and fasts. The partition of the province meant that the other woman of her husband would now be on the other side. The gods worked in strange ways and this time they had chosen the British who were unlikely to revoke the drawn line. That woman, her husband's first wife, the other one, would remain in that side of partitioned Bengal now. A thanksgiving was in order. She must acknowledge the benevolence of heaven.

Her son turned around, half asleep. The child was big built and heavy on her arms. Mentally she spat for thinking of her healthy child as heavy. Who knows the gods might chance upon her thought and make her son fall ill this very minute. The child stirred in his sleep again. Something stirred in her mind too.

"Listen…"

Shashishekhar stopped pacing.

"Did not my father-in-law compose a *Chandimangal*?"

Shashishekhar looked at his wife.

"You print so many things, why don't you print that? Should the people of the country not know about her goddesses? I thought you were saying that swadeshi means 'of one's own country'?"

Shashishekhar sat down on the bed. Why had it not struck him before? Printing the *Chandimangal* would be a swadeshi endeavour. Even strikers and unions would recognize that. And The Ganges Press would be working and not be on strike. The Government could see that should there be a survey tomorrow or day after. His press had always printed religious matter. This need not be seen as departure. Or agitation. Why had it not struck him earlier?

Shashishekhar removed the sleeping child from his wife's arm and placed him further away on the huge bed. Then he thanked his wife who submitted as a good wife must. Later she went for a bath.

❧❧

"Mamu."

Uma's uncle's voice quivered over the phone from Ballygunge Place. "Uma! We have not seen you and Rudra in a while. Why don't you come over.... I know this wretched rain...."

"Mamu is there a public library...."

"Why, is there a shortage of books in the publisher's house or are they not good enough?"

"I want to read the other *Chandimangals*."

"The duties of a daughter-in-law?"

Uma waited for the laughter to subside and then tried again.

"There is the National Library. The very best place in fact. It's right next to the Alipore zoo. Do you remember Uma, the summer holidays when I used to take all of you there?"

Reminded thus, she did. Of course she did. But that was in another life. She mouthed some platitudes and then asked, "Can I just go there or do I need a membership?"

"You have to fill a form. There are some formalities."

"Is it difficult to get that done?"

"No. Not at all. Have you got a degree from Delhi University as yet? No? A provisional certificate would do too. Even that has not been collected? Well, you don't really need it but it's a useful document to keep. No, no, other ways can always be found. This is India. Your father-in-law would know it all. He would know the right people too."

"You don't?"

"I do but ..."

Uma could not let the 'but' grow.

"But of course. Okay mamu. Yes I am fine. Yes we will come one day. Yes we will stay back for a meal. Anything. Yes Rudra loves fish. Yes, I have started liking fish too. Yes. Yes. Yes."

Uma got her temporary membership.

But Ashutosh and Rudra were both tied up all through the next week.

The cars could not be sent back to Kailash to take Uma to the National Library during the day. And Uma did not wish to push her luck with persistence. Ashutosh seemed genuinely pleased with her interest in the *Chandimangal*. Her misdemeanour had been forgiven and forgotten.

Uma was also a little apprehensive of venturing out on her own. It had been a while since she had walked the streets. Or taken a bus. Or any other mode of public transport. It made her slightly nervous now to think of being on her own out there ... where buses arrived late, jostling crowds pressed their sweaty bodies upon you, taxis took streets that merged into others and yet others far, far from home where strangers lurked with false smiles and groping paws.

Uma had already forgotten what it meant to negotiate the world on her own out in the sun and rain.

But she lay awake in bed. A little uneasy. A little ashamed. Wondering if she was letting the side down.

❀❀

Shashishekhar lay in bed.

Yes. Yes. Yes. The time was just ripe for his father's *Chandimangal*. Iswar Gupta, the editor of the Bengali newspaper *Sambad Prabhakar*, had already feminised the nation as the mother. Bankimchandra Chattopadhyay's hymn '*Bandemataram*' – Hail the mother – had become a popular anti-colonial war cry already. More recently, Abanindranath Tagore had painted the nation as a Mother carrying the promise of food, clothing, learning and spiritual salvation. The painting enlarged, was being used in the Swadeshi fund-raising processions to the strains of Rabindranath Tagore's patriotic lyrics. The colonised nation was imbuing Bharati, Mother India, with Shakti. Yes. Shashishekhar thought that the time was ripe and right for him to publish his father's work.

Shashishekhar's body was relaxed. Satiated. Soothed. But it was at odds with his mental state of heightened excitement. His mind was teeming with ideas and possibilities. He would look at the hand-written manuscript of his father's *Chandimangal* tomorrow itself. It was a while since he had read it. But thank god he had carried it back with him when he visited Kynsa mati last for his father's funeral. He may have to edit it though and render it a little more suitable perhaps for modern taste. And the times. He could interpolate a section or two. If required.

Shashishekhar wanted to get up and start working on it immediately. But he held himself down. It was late. He needed to rest. He must. To work better and for a longer stretch.

Tomorrow will come.

"I should go to Kynsa mati though," thought Shashishekhar, "I must find out if there are any other hand written copies of the work. Who knows that fool of a zamindar may have got several commissioned as a form of obesiance to the poet. If I choose to edit or interpolate any section it's better if no one else knows about it. Who knows what some one else may make of the discrepancies in the days to come?"

The thoughts churned thick and fast in Shashishekhar's mind. He intended to read and edit his father's work himself before launching it into the world. And there must not be any rival claims. Or the question of an authentic version. A trip to Kynsa mati was imminent. He had not been there since his father's death.

A damp and fresh smell told him that Haimanti had returned to the room. Bathed. Shashishekhar felt her groping in the dark and gently dragging her son till he lay in the middle of the bed, between them. It's about time the boy had a bed to himself, Shashishekhar thought. The British knew a thing or two about instilling self-sufficiency in children. He must organize this after he came back from Kynsa mati. With the copies of his father's *Chandimangal*, if there were any. Shashishekhar felt a little impatient with himself. It really should have struck him the last time he visited his village. But then his father had passed away. The rites of the funeral had preoccupied him. He thought of his father. The whole village and several adjoining ones had turned out for the show. The funeral had been spectacular by the village standard. It would have cost a lot more in Calcutta.

It came to him then in the dark of the room, that strange encounter when had he last visited Kynsa mati. It had left him somewhat disconcerted too. He was walking to his father's temple cottage where he had stayed in austere seclusion for the stipulated days for the funeral. It was evening. Almost dusk. The village had never looked so beautiful. Its petty qualities, its increasing hunger was veiled over for the moment by the parting glow of the fast disappearing rays of light. Clots of white smoke from the wood fire lit outside the kitchens were settling over the trees in the distance. The variegated greens of the trees were slowly turning a darker shade. Shashishekhar took a detour through a more wooded path, sending his attendants away. He wished to be by himself for a while and think of his father now gone. He knew that no one would approach him. He was the son of their revered priest. He was in mourning. He was the successful man from Calcutta. The villagers would look at him with awe. They would remark how like his father he looked, especially with his head shaved for the ritual mourning. But they would keep a distance. At least for the time being. Good. He did not wish to suffer fools just then, even awestruck ones.

The wind amidst the coconut, palm and the betel trees was whispering a strange chant, replacing gradually the loud chirruping of birds returning to their nests for the night and the flapping of wings from the trees. The crickets grew louder by the minute. The glow worms twinkled in the rapidly deepening dark.

She emerged suddenly from the shadows. Old and thin, small and bent, her white saree was part of the chiaroscuro of the approaching night. Her head was shaven. The glazed eyes stared at Shashishekhar. Was it terror? He was taken aback by its intensity and almost reached out to tell her that he was not of the descending dark. She screamed then in a thin and whispery voice. His skin crawled. She put up her hands as though to ward off a blow. Like bird's claw he thought. Then, impatient more with himself than her, Shashishekhar took a step forward to pass her by. Alarmed, she trembled, spread her legs and bent at the knees just a wee bit, perhaps to keep herself from falling, he thought. The puddle was dark too. He turned away in disgust. It was then that another form came rushing out from the groves behind. The movement spelt youth. Her saree was hiked well above her ankles. The legs flashed fair, amazingly fair. She reached out for the old one with both hands. Something dropped. He could not but stare. She stared back too. Brazen and breathing hard, smoking anger. The smouldering eyes appeared a strange colour even in the grey light.

The older one was shaking on the verge of collapse. The younger one put an arm around the old waist. He noticed it then. A bulge around her waist where one end of the saree clearly held stolen fruits from the grove. A common thief he thought. He turned away. In disdain. And lengthened his stride. The animal like whimpering of the strange old woman, though soft, followed him for a surprisingly long time.

Later he made a joke of it. The attendants laughed too and told him that she was only a mad old woman. Not violent or anything. But not all there. She was the dead zamindar's daughter from the first marriage. The family clearly had not pleased the goddess. On their way back from a pilgrim tour to Sitakunda the zamindar's elder daughter had died and the younger one gone somewhat… loco. There were three old family retainers who had accompanied the zamindar's family. Of them one had been bitten by a snake and two never heard of subsequently. Not that anyone did much asking. The zamindar's wife had died too. Soon after. Some say that she went for a bath to the pond in the middle of the night. How could anyone hear a splash in the middle of the night? Naturally the old zamindar had to marry again. Mercifully a son had been born from this second alliance. The old man was not a bad father though. He did get the loony one married and settled in a cottage at the far end of the Brahman settlement of the village. She had once run off as she was being brought to the marriage altar. The next time she nodded right through the ceremony. Doped out of her mind no doubt. Opium has its uses! Fate. Fate. No one could fight it. Not even powerful men like the zamindar.

Shashishekhar recollected hazily some rumours from his past life.

And he did not mention the other one. The young one with the burning eyes like a tiger's. A tigress rather. It did not take much for a scandal to start in these places. Why risk it?

He also did not mention that he had turned one last time to take in the two women. The old woman had bent down. Picked up what must have been dust and thrown it at him. A pathetic gesture. But somewhat disconcerting too. Oh well! The villages of Bengal were littered with such crazy women.

"I have to go to Chittagong." He spoke in the dark to Haimanti.

The answering query took a while.

"When?" Haimanti asked at last though she really meant to ask 'why?'

"As soon as possible."

"Are you going on swadeshi work?"

"I suppose you could call it that."

She caught the sudden amusement in his voice even in the dark. I know, she thought with sudden bitterness, I know why you wish to go there. And it is not swadeshi work. Not quite. There is that one there. Your first one. I know.

Haimanti gazed in the dark and then reached out for her son. "When do you return?"

"As soon as the work gets over."

"Why don't you take my brother with you?"

"Don't be silly."

There may have been a sniff in the dark of the room but Shashishekhar was busy chasing his own thoughts.

Finally Haimanti spoke. "Be careful. Take care of yourself."

"And you too."

The soft warm breathing of the child filled the bed.

The cold heaviness was only around Haimanti's heart. She shut her eyes and resolved to perform the Sankat Mangalbar Brata from the very next day.

Shashishekhar lay awake for a while too. Already editing the *Chandimangal* – in his mind – for the nation-in-the-making.

❊ Nine ❊

THE MEN WERE DISCUSSING THE new nation in the making.

The words flowed around Shashishekhar. He nodded in an absent minded manner, biding his time and wondering how soon he could get up and leave without appearing to be rude. It was a gathering in the village in his honour after all, organised by the zamindar and attended by all the men, naturally upper caste, who mattered in Kynsa mati and its neighbouring villages. Shashishekhar realised that he was something of a celebrity in his father's village. It felt good.

Swadeshi and the state of the country were the topics of discussion.

"Preposterous."

"Outrageous."

"How dare they?"

"Anything goes these days, gentlemen. The British have sworn to defile our entire land."

"They want to educate and give jobs to the low born illiterate Shudras?"

"What will the Brahmans do then? Cobble shoes?"

"Death. The British are actually paving the way to their own death. To rule a country is one thing but to tamper with religion…"

"What do they think? Do they think that there is no god in heaven?"

"Hmph! Our gods were already old men when their Jesu Christo was conceived."

"Were our gods fools to say that of the four castes the Brahman is the head, the Shudras the feet and that they must serve those born above them?"

"Educate the Shudras indeed! Have the Shudras ever read the *Shastras*? Will they understand anything? Educate them indeed! Just crack open their skulls and all you will find is cowdung."

"Actually that is why I think the British want them to get all the jobs. The white men want to ruin this country entirely. It's a very, very devious plan."

"Absolutely. They want to turn the world upside down and make the low born Shudra sit on the Brahman's head."

"Why? Were the Muslims not enough?"

"The Muslims are to be held in the lap."

A cackle of laughter caused a mometary pause in the animated conversation.

"I believe they are making friends now. Calling each other brethren. The Muslims and the low castes that is."

"Naturally. It takes one low born swine to recognise another. But it won't last, this alliance. You mark my words. They will soon be at each other's throats."

"And then ...."

"Low born? You be careful of your words. The British will soon pass a law to punish the use of the phrase."

The voice came in a hiss from Shashishekhar's right, from somewhere behind him. He turned. The speaker, in his early twenties, was young, compared to the rest in the gathering. And perhaps that is why he assumed an expression of grim seriousness. The eyebrows were raised above a pair of horn rimmed spectacles that proved his modernity and an urban connection.

"So what do we call the low born? God's gift to mankind?"

"Namashudra," answered the young man, imbuing the word with a smooth mocking intonation.

A rude screech followed the comment.

"My nephew."

An oily voice whispered in Shashishekhar's ear, also from behind. He turned ever so slightly and recognised Abani Sarkar.

Abani used to be an estate manager in a neighbouring village. He had now bought a small zamindari too. Or so Shashishekhar had heard. There had been some legal wrangle but Abani had won. What chance did the young widow have against Abani Sarkar's cunning born of years of managing the estate anyway?

"My sister's son from Faridpur," Abani clarified again. He was clearly proud of his nephew. "He has come here to negotiate a marriage alliance for his brother. He studied in Calcutta."

Shashishekar looked at the smug self-assured young man who caught his eye and nodded in recognition of another urban intelligence in the rustic gathering, deliberately overlooking age and social hierarchies. Shashishekar grew rigid inside.

The men were leaning forward.

"Namo what?"

"Namashudra. Soon there will be a law that will force us to call the Chandals Namashudra. Low born is out." The nephew raised his confident voice.

Outrage and horror took possesion of the gathering. Jaws dropped. Many clutched their sacred threads.

"Since when has the low born shudra been 'namo'-worthy of respect? I have never heard …."

"Have you heard of all that goes on in the world? Have you heard of the Census? The British count and classify everything. Well in the next Census the Chandals will be renamed as Namashudra. Or so they are petitioning. Has not the land of Bengal been partitioned to suit them? Have you heard of representaion? The British have decided that the Muslims and the … low born swines … will now be given jobs because they are more in number in the new state that they have carved out from partitioned Bengal. It does not matter to our white rulers if there are educated upper caste men who are better qualified than these low born."

"What are you saying?"

There was a collective paroxysm.

"While you are merely pulling at your hookah and fingering your sacred thread these low born people are forcing their zamindars to repair old schools for their children."

Hookahs were hastily put down.

"What are you saying!"

"Tell us more."

"We do know a bit though."

The young man got up and moved forward, confident and self assured. "Sighing or beating your breast won't help. You must protest now. Please understand that the British want to ruin our tradition, our culture, our religion and our country. You must join whole heartedly in the …."

Abani Sarkar looked on with fond pride as his nephew held the village worthies captive.

Idiot! Shashishekhar thought. Abani Sarkar, are you not a jumped up caste too? I heard that you call yourself a kulin kayastha. When have kayasthas been kulin? At this rate you will soon declare yourself to be a Brahman. In any case your grandfather was not even a Kayastha. You jumped up so and so.

But Shashishekhar did not say anything out loud. He only looked more and more austere and aloof.

The nephew was holding forth still to a mesmerised audience.

"…The country is our mother. Do you want to see her begging and languishing? No. Once upon a time our mother was strong. Why else had the sages called her Devi – the goddess, who manifests herself as Shakti…"

Not such an idiot after all thought Shashishekhar recognising the impassioned plea of swadeshi politics, even in its mangled form, in the speech.

"The mother is asking for sacrifice. Of our lives and of the British goods…"

"Will the British allow us to boycott their goods?"

"Allow? What do you mean? You think they will say yes, yes come take your freedom, we will let go of our golden goose?"

"It has to be done by force."

"Yes"

"Yes."

"Yes."

"And even if some of our own don't listen…"

"They won't. I don't need to tell you who these swines would be. Well those who are getting too big for their boots would need to be taught lessons too. You know of the peasant who refused to buy swadeshi goods and had to see the foreign saree ripped off his wife's body?"

"What are you saying?"

"Where?"

"Where?"

"In public?"

"Was she young?"

"I must say that these women who work in the fields have remarkably well preserved bodies…"

"Oh yes, when the sweat shines on their black bodies…"

"Watch it! You are waxing eloquent…"

"And in any case when did you get to see a black female body shining with sweat…."

Shashishekhar saw no reason to stay on. He disliked the coarse play of male libido. And it was so much the worse in the crude rustic dialect. He knew that much was being made these days about drawing out and preserving the folk and indigenous cultures but villagers sickened him. Culture for him was in Calcutta, or rather, certain circles in Calcutta. Shashishekhar caught the eye of the zamindar, the pleasantly vacuous man who had once been his companion when he had come to visit his father Neelkantha as a young boy. Shashishekhar nodded at his host, managing to convey in one fine movement of the head both abhorrence and apology and got up to leave. Somebody came up in a rush as he walked towards his shoes and asked him to stay for dinner.

"I am not hungry." Shashishekhar clutched the manuscript of the *Chandimangal* that he had procured from his friend, the zamindar, and turned his back on the animated gathering. Well, he had guessed right. There had been a copy of Neelkantha's work in his village and kept with the zamindar patron. But now it was in Shashishekhar's possession alongside the original. So in that sense at least it had been worth his while to make the trip to his father's village in Chittagong. Another day and then he could set off from this place of pie dogs and skeletal bodies buffeted by cess, cholera and drought. Shashishekhar set his back to the zamindar mahal and kutchery that seemed tired and decrepit against the russet slowly turning to dark in the sky.

※ ※

White fronds of clouds floated aimlessly in a blue sun-kissed sky.

Sometimes the monsoon let slip such a day. In a month the drifting clouds would be massed together like the white heads of cauliflowers. The blue of the autumn sky would be sharper too. Agomani – heralding the time then for celebration of the goddess to come home. But there was time yet. Today the gentle foam and flecks of white clouds drifted lazily across the wide expanse.

The kitchen doors of Kailash were open. Sunlight streamed in. The brass pots and pans turned to pure gold as Khema dried them. A sharp scent invaded the space as Pishi and Bamundi pickled the tamarind that was threatening to turn mouldy in the store. Uma was the official taster. She had always been partial to pickles.

"But why did you have so much tamarind in the first place?" She asked.

"The garage roofs had to be fixed. They put a layer of tamarind there. These are the remains. There are some more in the store. Eat your fill."

"I have heard that there used to be a horse drawn carriage in the garage earlier. Did you know that?" Khema asked Uma. "Your husband's grandfather was a rich man. Well known too."

Bamundi was not one to be left out. " Well, now the garage has two cars instead of one carriage. That's not bad either. The Lahiri household, you know the one down the lane where I worked for a while, they used to have three carriages. And now? They have nothing. I have heard that they want to let out the garage space. But for that the brothers have to agree."

"Nobody likes to work there," Khema explained to Uma as the outsider. "It's a huge family of five brothers..."

"...who are always quarrelling and their wives are no better..."

"...and then at the end of the month nobody takes the responsibility for the salary."

"They talk big too. The old lady was alive when I worked there." Bamundi looked proud to be in possession of first hand information, "Well, this old lady would say all the time that they were not like us poor folks. They could not dream of going out of the house in public view. Apparently the old lady's mother-in-law, I never met her, was very religious. Whenever she wanted to take a dip in the Ganga the carriage would be washed and once she reached the riverside she would get into a palanquin covered from all sides. Two men would lower the whole thing in the river with the lady inside. The old lady would come back in the carriage, wet and dripping. Even in winter. Now that's called a holy dip," Bamundi paused.

Pishi coughed. The tempered spice for the pickle must have caught at her throat. Her face seemed a little flushed. Uma looked at her and remembered the girl rising with the water of Padma Pukur.

"My mother used to fetch water from the river. I loved going there with her," Khema sat back on her haunches a little straighter. "Well, she used to sell fish too. She would cut the bamboo reeds and mend the fence and the roof every year. We had only a small plot of land. But during harvest time my mother would help those with bigger plots with the husking of the paddy. You can't do all that and not be seen."

There was silence in the kitchen for a while. The clouds sailing in the sky were white still. The sun lenghtened its foray into the kitchen.

"Boudi?"

"Umm?" Uma sucked the tamarind seed and shuddered as the sharp sour juice filled her mouth.

"Is it bad for a woman to be seen in public?" Khema asked in a taut voice.

"Bad?" Uma rolled the seed inside her mouth forgetting herself.

"How else do you work? In the fields? Outside the house I mean," Khema looked embarrassed. "Why do you – I mean the world – call that low born-chotolok – behaviour?"

Uma took the seed out.

"I mean…"

Uma looked at Khema and then at Bamundi and Pishi. Bamundi lowered her gaze. The tamarind seed glimmered a transcluscent red brown in Uma's hand. Like the flush on Khema's young face.

"Fullora." Pishi said.

"What?" said Uma even as Khema cried out "Yes."

"Read that section from the *Chandmangal* again. The one that talks of Fullora," said Pishi.

"Yes, please Boudi. I really like it," nodded Khema relaxing again, "Read the story of the hunter and his wife. Let's hear the section that tells us that the hunter's wife Fullora is the first human being the goddess visits. Tell us how the goddess goes to a small broken down hut at the outskirts of the village where Fullora lives. Fullora! What a lovely name!"

Uma got up with alacrity to wash her hands, glad to be able to do something. Neelkantha's *Chandimangal* was by now familiar terrain. She found the section easily. She dried her hands carefully on her saree, pulled the book onto her lap and quite unconsciously pushed the small plate of pickle towards Khema with a smile. Pishi leaned across and put in another dollop and nodded too.

But Khema barely noticed the plate, "Begin from where Fullora tells the goddess what kind of a life she leads, Boudi."

"Here."

The first house that the goddess graces when she comes down on earth to spread her cult is hunter Kalketu's. The goddess had allowed herself to be caught in the guise of a golden iguana by the hunter. Kalketu leaves, leaving the goddess trussed on the floor of his hut. Once alone, the goddess changes from the iguana to a beautiful woman.

Fullora, Kalketu's wife, finds her thus when she returns to the ramshackle hut.

"Fullora returns home, tired after a day's wasted work," Khema added softly.

Bamundi nodded.

The goddess's beauty stuns Fullora. Fear clutches her heart. Has Kalketu, her husband got this lady by fair means or foul, to be a rival to Fullora? Fullora decides to tell the lady what it meant to be Kalketu's wife. Fullora knew that ladies were unware of the lot of wives like Fullora.

"Fullora thinks that the goddess is a lady who has caught her husband's fancy. So she tells the goddess what it would mean to be a poor low caste hunter's wife. Fulora knows that it would scare a lady for what would a lady know about a life of ceaseless labour?" murmured Khema as though talking to herself.

"Let Boudi read," Bamundi admonished gently.

Uma began to read the hauntingly moving baramasi of Fullora which catalogued a life of labour through the changing seasons of sun and rain, heat and cold, mist and fog as she went about hawking meat against the changing sky.

Baishakh. The angry sun in the sky beats down upon my head
The meat turns rancid and I can see no shade.
My saree leaves my legs bare, when drawn to cover my head.

But it's hotter still in **Jaishtha** and there is a threat of drought
A fire ravages my body both within and without... .
Buy, won't you buy the meat, still loudly I must shout.

Ashar brings the clouds and raises high the wind
Their eyes measure my body for my saree has so thinned
That my breasts lie exposed and they tell me I have sinned.

The leaky **Shravan** sky a steady stream does pour

day and night through our roof while I carry out my chores.
The water spoils the meat and provisions there are no more.

*In the month of **Bhadra**, ferocious clouds abound*
the streams run into rivers and there is water all around.
Buy, buy the meat I cry, but the thunder drowns the sound.

*In the festive month of **Asvin**, the goddess is worshipped everywhere*
Lambs, goats and buffaloes are sacrificed as her ordained share.
Nobody needs to buy meat then, our coffers are entirely bare... .

Uma paused in her reading. "Asvin. Whenever I hear this sound I feel that Durga puja is just around the corner. Agomani – it's time for the goddess to visit us. It is my favourite month of the year."

"When is Durga puja this year, Boudi? Early or late?" Khema surreptitiously wiped her eyes.

"A little late I think.'

"Will you go home this year? To your parents?"

"I don't know, it depends on ..."

"I know."

"But puja is not the same for everyone," said Bamundi suddenly in a harsh tone.

"Fullora says that, does she not?" Khema responded though softly. She found it the hardest to return to the kitchen in Kailash from the world Uma brought to them through words. " Does not Fullora say what for the others is a time of plenty and celebration, is a very lean month for her?"

"But who would pay attention to Fullora's baramasi, her cycle of struggle through the changing seasons? She is only a woman!" Bamundi again.

"A poor woman," nodded Uma.

"A poor vyadh woman. A hunter's woman, " added Khema.

The brief silence was amicable.

"Boudi, when are you going off in search of our stories?"

"What?" Uma came back. She had wandered off home to Kashmere Gate.

"Our stories." Khema lowered her voice. "The truth about the goddess and her marriage."

"Soon. When the sky lets up." But even as Uma said this a ray of sunlight streaked into the room.

And when they can send the car and I have the nerve to step out in the world again, thought Uma.

The sunlight cheered the room after a prolonged wet spell. The autumn of splendour and promise seemed round the corner. The green leaves of the row of chilli trees nourished by the steady rain now glowed in the sun. The world seemed full of hope in that bright light. And there was the promise of the ritual awakening of the goddess in autumn, the season to come.

"Will you read Fullora's story again?"

"Yes. But some other section, not her song of the seasons," Bamundi said.

"Why, I thought it was beautiful!" Uma was surprised.

"I thought she was crying," said Khema.

Uma read about Kalketu and Fullora, the hunter and his wife, Chandi's first worshippers, the dark man and his wife who work out in the open, under the sky, the outcastes of society.

And the goddess works too. The goddess leaves her home in Kailash to come down on earth to spread her worship and protect her followers. She roams the forests on her own and still she is worshipped. Nobody calls her a fallen woman for having ventured out of her home. The thoughts chased one another in Khema's mind. But she did not say it even in the charmed circle of the kitchen in Kailash. What was the word? Agomani. The promised visit of the goddess who slays the demon. And more. The goddess who visits the low born household first. And the low born hunters do not go hungry forever.

❖ ❖

The table was laden with food even though the meal was drawing to an end. Another cousin of Ashutosh's, a former District Magistrate had come on a visit. The evening had been spent in expressing shock and grief at the sudden passing away of the Congress chief minister of Bengal, the iconic Dr. B.C. Ray. The District Magistrate had eulogised the dead leader's vision for a modern Bengal while his wife held forth on how Dr. Ray had seen poor patients free of cost that very morning and how he had read a Brahmo prayer just hours before his death. With dinner being announced the mood was allowed to change and they turned towards Uma. The District Magistrate's son had married an Englishwoman (Scottish, Rudra said later) and lived in Golders Green, London. The couple had been in England that summer and had missed Rudra's wedding. Rudra had excused himself from the social occasion once again. He had one of his 'Boys' dos' that evening which he never missed and certainly not for visiting relatives.

The District Magistrate agreed to have another helping of dessert. Pishi did cook payesh rather well. His wife conceded to a second helping too.

"Has she been told about the family?" The District Magistrate enquired of Ashutosh and then addressed Uma, "You have been married into one of the Kulin families of Bengal. Do you know what it means?"

Uma nodded in a vague manner.

The District Magistrate cleared his throat. Clearly he had been waiting for this moment. "Adisura in 9th century Bengal wanted to perform a Vedic sacrifice for getting a son. He requested the king of Kanyakubja to send him five Brahmans but his request was turned down as Bengal was considered an impure land. An angry Adisura defeated the king in a battle and sent five Brahmans for the putreshti yajnya. The five Brahmans subsequently settled in five villages in Bengal and had 56 sons between them, each of whom was given a village. The names of these villages became the surnames of the 56 Brahman clans in Bengal. The five first came to Rar, the name obtaining from the tract of Bengal that now forms the northern portion of the Burdwan district. The Chattopadhyas trace their origin back to these five. Of the title, the first syllable, Chatto, is the name of the village granted to our Brahman ancestor by king Ballal Sen. The second syllable, upadhyay, means a priest."

He sat back, smug and small, perhaps palpably feeling the purity of the blood that was coursing through Ashutosh's, and his veins. He was also a Chattopadhyay, though a cousin from Haimanti's side.

Uma wondered what Rudra was doing.

"Did you know all this?"

Uma smiled again and lowered her eyes, refusing to disclose that she had heard this honoured history of the Bengali Brahman very many times. Prompter Bandopadhyay, with a cabbage nose, was a regular fixture of Kashmere Gate's Bengali Theatre group. He had loved telling stories too, particularly to young ladies. His tale of the pure lineage of Bengali Brahmans had been exactly the same but for one crucial difference. In his tale the original five Brahmans had settled first not in Rar but in Barendra land in Bengal, on the eastern side of the Ganges from where he himself came. Kaku had always flippantly deflated Prompter Bandopadhaya's upper caste litany with a mock admonition, "Shhh... Don't let the others know that we Brahmans in Bengal are really outsiders."

Uma's family had always identified people they did not like in terms of vegetables. The District Magistrate had a strong resemblance to a sun dried Indian gooseberry. Shukno Amlaki, dark and desiccated. It was a bit difficult to think of him, or Prompter (Cabbage) Bandopadhyay, as 'pure Aryan' as they saw themselves.

Did the Aryans know the cabbage and the gooseberry?

The District Magistrate was still holding forth on the cutural renaissance of the Bengali.

Uma looked absorbed.

* *

The wipers swung in an arc absorbing the water and clearing a patch on the windscreen that misted over almost immediately with the falling rain. Rudra watched the play of water on glass for a while and then turned ever so slightly to his companion in the car. "You are letting go of your job?" he asked again of Sisir, still a little shaken that the news should move him so. The rain continued to rattle with increasing vigour, on the car parked near the kerb in a narrow street in Manicktala. Sisir smiled. It was an amiable smile, almost innocent in its wide encompassing of the world.

Rudra and Sisir had known each other since class nine in school, they had studied togther in college too and were part of a larger amorphous group. They had been to the monthly reunion of friends earlier that evening. The nostalgia laced atmosphere had sharpened suddenly into a heated political debate over the efficacy and ethics of strikes and union activites. Sisir, and a few others had left then. Rudra had followed, called out to Sisir and offered him a lift in the rainy night.

"I hope you have given it some thought. You must have," Rudra turned towards his friend, letting his hands rest on the steering wheel. "We have heard that you are good at your work too, that you have quite a following amongst your students even though they call you Kakatua."

Both smiled.

Sisir had a striking thatch of hair that stood up from his forehead no matter how hard he tried to tame it and that, coupled with a hook nose which dominated the otherwise very pleasant face, had earned him the nickcame of the crested parrot from his friends long before his own students started using it.

"Most young lecturers tend to have a following, if they hold classes." Sisir's voice always sounded as though a cold was setting in, but it was rather soothing.

Rudra could imagine Sisir's voice rising and falling in a room full of young and impressionable minds. "It would require a little more than that, I should think," he said.

"No really," Sisir smiled, "The students just want someone who can relate to them, connect the classroom to the world in which they live."

"So then why are you throwing up your job? You don't need me to tell you about the economic condition of our state or the market situation as far as jobs are concerned?"

"It's only a temporary teaching assignment, in fact it has been so for a few years now," Sisir turned towards Rudra in the gloom of the car, "I can't do it any more, Rudra, not with any degree of honesty. Economy, state and society, that's what I talk about to these young ones. But I cannot carry on any more talking about change in the classroom without… without contributing to it myself. I believe you will undersand what I am talking about, how I feel."

Rudra gripped the steering wheel unconsciously and then slowly eased the pressure.

Two men pushing a hand cart covered with jute sackings gave the car a curious look as they splashed past in the rain. Rudra and Sisir sat in silence for a while.

"Why don't you come with us, Rudra?" the voice jeered.

There was as always a buzz in the coffee house. Rudra's class had finished earlier than expected and he had walked over to the coffee house which was the nerve centre of their college life.

Ashim was the most flamboyant one in the group. He studied English literature and wrote fiery poems in Bengali about Calcutta and its hunger. Ashim was already something of a cult figure in college and in the coffee house. He espoused anarchy to be achieved through the brothel, booze and the body. There was always an expanding group around the table that Ashim occupied in the coffee house. Rudra did not mind Ashim whom he had known since school too. Ashim's flamboyance was a little tiresome but his poetry already promised the greatness that was to come.

"Another time," said Rudra and started to get up.

" Is it fear or fastidiousness, kulin Brahman?" called out Ashim, "Look into thy heart and speak."

Guffaws and titters.

Rudra stood still, as though trying to catch an echo of something heard long ago.

He felt a hand on his back.

"Let's go," said Sisir. "See you, Ashim."

"Shall we go?" asked Sisir again as he and Rudra walked down the crowded staircase of the coffee house.

In a way it was Sisir who introduced Rudra to a city where he had been born and brought up and where Sisir himself had come much later. They were not best friends but they shared the magnetic pull of the city which they discovered in the afternoons of their college life when classes finished early. Sisir and Rudra would walk to the nearest bus stop, board one, usually the first one that came along, and thus they travelled all over the city jumping on and off from one bus to another. The two friends hardly ever spoke of, much less discussed, their personal lives or political faith, during these sojourns. But what they saw of the varied pasts and presents of Calcutta from their window seats of the bus, or sometimes a tram in those somnolent afternoons of the various seasons of their college days did create a bond of sorts between them.

Rudra checked in the mirror to see if his tail light was working in the wet night that enveloped them and then asked what was probably his first private question of Sisir. "This decision of yours to go and work in a village and live with the Rajbansi peasants, is it a Party command?" The question came out rather flat despite the stirrings of passion within.

Sisir's voice was even too, "We are a rice eating lot Rudra. Rice is our staple diet. But did you know that its leaves are sharp, sharp like a knife that can cut you with ease?"

"I am an urban beast, how would I know that?"

"Therefore."

"Look, I don't think…"

"Do you remember Rudra the afternoon we discovered Jibanananda's *Dhusar Pandulipi* thanks to Ashim?" Sisir said after a while; his voice filled the interior of the car for a brief moment and then he bent his head and ducked out of the car to step in the rain.

Silver rivulets on the windshield blocked the world entirely for Rudra.

The blood must have thus run from Sisir's body riddled with

bullets and killed in an encounter in the rice fields when he was declared an enemy of the state some years later.

There was no funeral.

Or a memorial service.

Nobody even knew exactly when it happened.

Rudra heard the news, in a chance encounter with an acquaintance from college days, amidst the jostling crowd of Gariahat market in a state of frenzied anticipation of Durga puja. For many days afterwards Sisir's voice played in Rudra's mind and a bleak desolation enveloped him.

> *Surjyer alor din chere diye prithibir jash piche phele*
> *shahar-bandar-basti-karkhana deshlaiye jele*
> *ashiachi neme ei khete;*
> *sharirer abashad-hridayer jar bhule jete.*

> Leaving behind the sunlit day
> letting go of the world's way
> City-port-slums-factory with a matchstick lit
> Has come down to this field
> The weary body – the fevered heart to forget.

Rudra remembered the rain streaming down the window and Sisir hunched forward and walking into it. Sisir who had said that day in the car that his father used to be in the Railways. Sisir as a child used to love walking on the tracks. Once on a cold winter evening he had come upon some railway gangmen huddled around a fire near the shunting yard. The men had drawn him into their circle. Sisir remembered the smell of burning coal. He remembered too that the men were talking and then singing about the fields and families they had left behind. Those were songs of peasant life. Sisir was amazed, having thought of those men, if at all, as belonging entirely to the railway tracks. The smoke rising from the coal was burning his eyes and he got up and walked away.

But not for ever, thought Rudra.

Gall rose in him at his own capitulation and for a few days Rudra knew the debilitating restlessness of his earlier life. He often thought of taking a bus ride through the city, alone, in memoriam. But eventually he just went about his daily business to return home to Kailash in the evenings at the end of his day's work.

⁂

Khema's work was not yet over though it was quite late. Kailash was already sluggish with sleep. Sleep was creeping over Khema's tired limbs too but her husband had gone to drop the visitors, Ashutosh's cousin and wife, to South Calcutta, where they lived half way across the city from Kailash. Khema's husband would be in late. The food must be kept warm.

Khema's son jiggled her arm, "Carry on with the story, ma."

"In the *Chandimangal* Fullora is the wife of Kalketu. They are Vyadhs – a vey old hunting community. Kalketu hunts with a bow and arrow. His wife skins the animals and then goes to the market with the skin, flesh, nails, horns … even Brahmans come to buy her wares. Where else would they get the rhinoceros's horn?"

"A rhino's horn? What do the Brahmans do with it?"

"They pour water from it to please their gods."

Khema's son saw a shadowy figure creeping through a jungle that was dark and foreboding.

"Kalketu is an able hunter and has been known as one even as a child. The animals are terror stricken. He kills so many of them. Finally unable to protect themselves from Kalketu, the animals of the forest appeal to the goddess *Chandi*. She is the lady of the forest. She is the one who must protect the wild. The goddess hides the animals. Kalketu can catch nothing. The hunter and his wife go hungry. One day, two days, three, four, five….Kalketu can barely move. His stomach hangs loose. If he stands his legs tremble and lights dance in front of his eyes."

"Does his mouth smell?"

"What? Yes, yes I suppose so but still he gathers his arrows and tells Fullora, "Wife, don't you worry, I will go to the forest again and bring home something for sure. Don't you worry wife. Don't you worry," Khema's voice trailed off.

"Carry on, ma."

"The forest is dark and deep. Kalketu flits from the shadow of one tree to another. Ever so quiet. Barely breathing. Was that a speckled deer behind the hanging roots of the tree or just a play of light? The forest seemed to be breathing with many lives and yet he could not see any. How could he? Had not the goddess hidden them all?"

Khema smoothened the rough hair on her son's forehead. He looked so vulnerable and soft as sleep slowly crept over him. He looked up at her with drowsy dark eyes, "Don't stop ma. You carry on with the story."

"The goddess sees to it that Kalketu is unable to catch anything. Defeated and worn out Kalketu is about to turn back when something shines on a heap of dry leaves just ahead of him. He opens his eyes wide, shuts them for a while then opens them in narrow slits lest it be a play of light merely. The animal is still there. And breathing. Can it be, is it, a golden iguana? Disappointment almost swallows his frame. Never mind he thinks. At least we can roast the blighter and have a meal. The svarnagodhika, the golden iguana, seems to be smiling."

"Why?"

"Listen. The iguana is our lady of the forest. The goddess *Chandi* herself. She had come to tell Kalketu and Fullora that they must not kill for a living anymore. She would give them another livelihood. She would give them riches. They were good people. And they were hers. Yes. The goddess visited Kalketu and Fullora. Even if the others called them the outcastes. The goddess came to them in their own hut that was broken and battered. She visited them first, before she showed herself to any other human being. Of any other caste. And she gave them riches."

Her son slept.

Khema looked at her sleeping son and recited the lines as best she remembered them from the sessions in the kitchen.

> *The story of Kalketu thus does clearly state*
> *That all of you then must the goddess propitiate.*

She had repeated the lines to herself several times. She thought they carried a secret message for her, and her people. If the goddess visited the hunter and his wife first, then how could they be lowly?

Softly Khema repeated the verse again, changing it ever so little.

> *The story of Kalketu thus does clearly state*
> *That the vyadhs first of all did the goddess propitiate.*

But the Brahman poet did not say it like this.

Gently Khema disentagled her son's slack arm and then, looking down at him, she added another line. "Bless my son O goddess. Look after him as you looked after Kalketu. May he not know hunger and want and pain. Bless him mother, for ever and more."

Khema sat up and leaning against the damp and cold wall, she thought of the sunlit afternoon in the kitchen to escape sleep.

❋ Ten ❋

No. Shashishekhar had not been able to make his escape. He should not have been wearing these wooden kharam as he no longer used them in the city. The wretched slippers had slowed him down. Shashishekhar sighed and waited in response to the call.

The three men caught up with him near the main gate of the zamindar's house.

"A word with you, Sir."

"If you so allow."

"Just a moment or two."

"Sure," said Shashishekhar but already rehearsing in his mind a polite but firm negation of any offer to get embroiled in the swadeshi fervour being stirred up in the zamindar mahal he had just left.

But it was something else altogether.

"Sir is from Calcutta. And is going back there. We were wondering if you would allow the women of our families to be escorted by you to the city. We would have gone ourselves but ...."

The voices droned on. And on.

Someone's mother wanted to visit the city. Another's daughter needed to. The third had a daughter-in-law who was now required to join the son who worked in the city. All three men were willing to pay the cost. The women would be received at the station itself. None would think of expecting Shashishekhar to extend hospitality in Calcutta. Even for a day. Letters of intent were produced to prove the point. In any case an old family retainer of one of them would accompany the women. He would oversee the journey. The women, and two maids, would have been sent with the retainer in any case. But now that Shashishekhar was also travelling, indeed as divinity had intervened favourably by sending him at that opportune moment, would he not allow the female group to be under his supervision? It was such a long journey and one had heard such tales of the city! And the retainer, though known to the family for ever and more, was still, after all not a gentleman like Shashishekhar.

There was no escape. Not if one was a gentleman.

"I will leave early morning day after tomorrow. Very early. I can't, won't, wait." Even Shashishekhar could not say any less.

The heads bobbed up and down. Of course they knew how busy he was. The women were packed to be sent off in any case. The carriages were ready and the boatsmen could be sent for whenever. True, the rail tickets were to be bought but the money had already been given to the old retainer. They just wanted, needed, Shashishekhar's benign protection.

"Fine," said Shashishekhar, a little abruptly but it did not seem to matter. He declined their offer to walk with him. "I will find my way back to my father's old place. On my own. If you don't mind. I need solitude." His voice deepened with the last sentence. They lowered their eyes in cosy consensus of refined feelings.

"No thank you. My man is there. Yes he will have some dinner for me. Yes, I am sure. No I don't need a lantern. It's not dark enough as yet. I do know the way. Yes I am sure."

Thus they parted ways. And Shashishekhar walked into the shadows of the trees.

Once again Shashishekhar's thoughts returned to the manuscript he was carrying and the work that lay ahead. His father had composed it for a village audience. But Shashishekhar needed appreciation from another: the elite of Calcutta. He would have to go over the composition carefully, mitigate the rustic flavour if required. The time was indeed fortuitous. Swadeshi was in fashion. You did not have anything like the militant mother goddess in Christianity. It would help state how alien the British were to this country.

Shashishekhar's thoughts flowed back towards the evening. Faces. Stray bits of conversation. His brows gradually met in a frown.

One of the protagonists of the *Chandimangal* was a low caste hunter. The goddess visits him first. Who knows in these turbulent times how that might be interpreted? Some jumped up low caste might cite that as his caste right to worship the gods on his own without the Brahman priest. Social reform was one thing but anarchy? His father would have followed the flow of the traditional tale and he could not have erased the character of Kalketu entirely from the *Chandimangal*. Two lines from the poem coursed through Shashishekhar's mind:

> *Kalketu and Fullora were full of joy,*
> *the wife and the hunter low born*
> *That the goddess came first to their house*
> *on that auspicious morn.*

Hmm. He would have to extricate the goddess from that low caste house. Subtly. To the extent possible. He would have to go over that section very, very carefully. Expunge what the new nation should not play with.

The crickets chirruped. And the fireflies glowed. The night was coming alive from between the ancient trees with clumps of gnarled roots. As once before. Shashishekhar shook himself mentally to get rid of fancies. He concentrated on the *Chandimangal* instead. So providential to have collected the remaining copy, he thought. He was really looking forward to getting it ready for print. He started the layout in his mind, it had to appeal aesthetically to a modern educated audience in the grip of nationalistic fervour. But it should also help evoke an immediate association with venerable tradition. Yes, the mood was right and ripe for such a poem. Shashishekhar enjoyed this process of shaping and formatting knowledge.

Not surprisingly he stumbled. It was rapidly becoming darker and darker. But a lantern would have meant an escort. Worse still, avid rustic curiosity. Shashishekhar gripped the manuscript hard under one arm and hitched his dhoti with the other. A conchshell blew in the distance heralding the dark. Another. And then another. Women were praying for protection from ghosts and ghouls for their households. He must be crossing the Brahman settlement of the village. Not very far now to his father's cottage by the temple. A couple of minutes perhaps.

The trees met and rustled over his head. And then a voice wafted over from the depths of the shadow. It was unmistakably a woman's voice. Shashishekhar did not believe in ghosts or ghouls. But he did start. As once before. He recognized that he was perhaps half expecting this. Hoping too?

"Please."

She came out from behind the grey pillars of the ancient trees.

Shashishekhar was really surprised that she was not the one. She was older for one thing. Were the eyes green? He thought not but then he could not tell in the rapidly clotting dark.

Instantly he was deeply ashamed. Mortified. At this inexplicable that he glimpsed within himself. This was the expectation that had haunted Shashishekhar throughout the village visit. And now he felt the damning disappointment that came on the heels of realisation that this was not her, the young woman he had seen on his last visit to the village, the very fair one with green eyes. This one was just another village woman. Or was she?

Clearly the woman in front of him was not used to accosting strange men in the darkening shade. Her entire body seemed to be cringing.

"Please. A moment of your precious time. If you will be so kind."

Shashishekhar sighed. Another one in need.

❀ ❀

The promise of autumn was clearly ephemeral. The truant clouds were back. But not in their dark splendour. They too seemed grey and tired. The weekend had been hectic. Ashutosh's sisters had visited Kailash with their families.

Bamundi was gently stirring the remains of the daal, allowing the water to evaporate. The daal would keep better this way. Moreover it could now also be metamorposed into stuffing for the daalpuri. Who could eat the same daal thrice over in a house such as Kailash?

Khema and Pishi were putting away the crockery in the store. The smooth creamy surface of the elaborate dinner set was edged at the border with tiny summer flowers, very English. Uma wiped each piece carefully and then handed it to Khema who in turn gave it to Pishi. Pishi layered each piece with a tissue paper before storing it. Uma was impressed.

Pishi caught Uma's glance. "Your mother introduced this way of putting away these English plates."

It did not register for a moment. Her mother? When did she step into the kitchen at Kailash to share this domestic detail with Pishi? Besides, tissues were rarely used in Kashmere Gate for this purpose. Or any actually.

Clearly Uma's face was an open book.

"I meant your mother-in-law."

The blush did not escape anyone either.

"But it is true," Bamundi finished ladling out the by-now-dry-daal and gestured towards Khema to take the utensil away. "A mother-in-law is not a mother even if you call her ma. But you can't call her oh-ma-goodness, can you?"

Uma felt that perhaps she should not join in the laughter. But she could not help it. And Pishi was smiling too.

"Will you read a bit today?" Bamundi asked.

"I don't mind. But which bit? Shall I carry on from where we let off? The story of the vyadh Kalketu and Fullora?"

"Boudi," Khema said a little stiffly, "You read in the beginning that Fullora and her hunter husband Kalketu were actually heavenly beings, that they were sent to earth as vyadhs to help spread the cult of the goddess.'

"Well so it said."

"But what if it's a lie?"

"A lie? What do you mean?" Uma smiled too. " It's a story."

"Yes, but in the story, as you read it, as it is written, the vyadhs Kalketu and Fullora are really not vyadhs. They are actually divine beings."

"How does that matter?"

"What do you mean? Then they are not vyadhs. Not real vyadhs. Then the goddess does not visit the vyadhs first. Not real vyadhs."

"Well…"

" But how do we know that they did not make it up. Maybe they put it in after the tale."

Kailash paused. But Khema carried on.

"What if that is a lie? What if all these Brahman men were consumed with jealousy and anger that the goddess came to be worshipped by the hunters first so they put in the bit about divine beings coming to earth as Fullora and Kalketu and took the goddess away from us?"

"Us?" Bamundi sounded slightly belligerent.

"Us low born people as…as… you people say. Kalketu and Fullora were one of us till the preface made them one of you, upper caste beings from heaven sent to earth"

The "us" lay fragmented in the kitchen of Kailash.

The dark was gathering its forces yet again in the sky.

No one said anything. Khema looked up finally. In a tight, stilted voice, she spoke. "Can I tell a story today?"

Uma nodded after a quick look at the others. Bamundi seemed a little belligerent, Pishi impassive.

Khema sat down slowly, "I remember that Ma Dombi was a popular goddess in our village Dopukuria. Ma listened to us. She helped us. Always. In her honour a month long summer fair was held from Baishakh sankranti. We villagers used to worship Ma on our own though a sebait was sometimes drawn from among us on special occasions. Everyone in the village knew that the goddess in the beginning was a Dom girl. Very beautiful she was." She looked at Uma and added almost to herself, "Though dark."

"One day as she was coming from the woods to her hut, she was accosted by a man who was young and good looking. His skin was fair and smooth. The eyes met and they fell in love. 'Will you marry me?' said the Man. The Dom girl's heart skipped a beat. Her bundle of twigs fell from her hands. The trees showered flowers. They held hands and stood. But not for long. A ferocious storm rushed over the village and reached the woods. The trees shook enraged. Lightning chased the clouds. 'Raja', said the Dom girl to the young man, 'Don't be frightened. I won't let you get wet.' She looked at his hands holding hers. His hands were smooth and soft especially next to her rough dark ones. 'You wait here under this big banyan tree.' She rushed out in the rain and gathered twigs, she cut and tore branches, she plaited the palm fronds and soon there stood a hut pretty as a picture. 'Come Raja,' she said. 'You are getting wet. You are shaking in the cold.'"

"But he did not," said Bamundi.

"No, he did not. He shook off her hand from his arm. "How can you work so? And a woman too! You must be a low born outcaste. You are a filthy impure Jhutha khai. How could I touch you! You foul bitch. Get away from me. Even your shadow will pollute my very being." He rushed out in the rain and did not look back even once."

Khema looked steadily into the fire. Shadows gathered in the kitchen. The sky was dark once again. The wind teased Kailash with her whispers.

"The Dom girl's tears formed a pukur, our pond. People called her Ma Dombi. Her spirit settled in the banyan tree by the pond and protected the village."

The rain started in a thin drizzle gently smudging the world outside.

"Ma Dombi was ours. Do you know who a Dom is Boudi?"

Uma knew that the Doms were considered the lowest of the low in the caste hierarchy and were associated with absolute ritual impurity. But how could Uma say that? She gave the ghost of a nod.

Khema sighed. "You are from Delhi. You have studied in an English school. I thought you might not know."

"This is not the end of the story, is it?" asked Bamundi in a tired voice, all belligerence gone.

"It is and it is not," said Khema. "When I last went to my village I wanted to thank Ma Dombi for giving me a son. But I could not reach her. No. A temple had been built for her. She was so powerful. How could they not recognise her?"

"Why couldn't you reach her?" asked Uma.

"Don't you understand? A temple has been built....a temple! A Brahman priest now presides over her. He did not let me go in lest I pollute her. But she was our mother till the Brahman took charge of her. Can it not be that they did the same with Kalketu, Fullora and their goddess? Taking what was ours and making her their own till no one remembered what she was once."

It was Bamundi who spoke first.

"I have to leave soon enough. Khema, give me the flour. Let me knead the dough for the daalpuri. Pishi can just roll it out and fry it when it is time."

Uma watched the fine white flour take shape under Bamundi's dark deft hands.

And Pishi sat gazing at the dark wet world outside the kitchen.

The wind rose and grazed Kailash.

※ ※

The daalpuri collapsed with a little hiss of steam as Ashutosh punctured it expertly with a finger. He scooped it elegantly in his mouth.

Uma seized the moment.

"Baba, should not the Hunter's tale be the first one? Instead of the *debkhanda*?"

Ashutosh finished chewing and swallowed. "Pardon?"

"I mean in the *Chandimangal* which has three sections, should not the Hunter's section precede the sastrik section?"

"Why?"

"I mean ... I thought that historically...The hunter would come before the priest."

"Poetry is not history."

The phone rang, Uma escaped for the moment.

❦❦

The ringing in Shashishekhar's ears receded. The night sounds filled the air again. A fox howled in the distance. Shashishekhar breathed deeply to ease the cold constriction in his chest. The woman was still speaking. Her cringing manner was entirely at odds with the tale that she told. "Please. We have not said it to anyone of course. I am saying it to you only because … only because our circumstances are such. I mentioned it only to let you know that we know but we have kept quiet always."

The wind carried the wailing sound of some small creature in pain.

The woman said again, "My daughter is a good girl. Maybe a little wild. But in the city she will behave herself. I am sure. She might make mistakes in the beginning, please forgive her."

Shashishekhar knew he had no choice. He had known he had no choice ever since the words had tumbled out in the dark of the night. The tale in itself was not quite devastating. No. No, it was not a bolt from the blue. This tale about his father, that the woman recited. Not quite. He had heard whispers every now and then through his growing years. He had dismissed them as the malice of the lesser born. No one had the courage to say it out in the open, least of all in front of his father. In fact very few dared to even open their mouths in his father's stern priestly presence. Shashishekhar had thus never wondered about the truth of it. He had chosen not to wonder about it. At all. It was irrelevant, entirely inconsequential. But to have to confront it now, now when he was about to make his father the pride of Bengal, was almost devastating. Bengal was shouting herself hoarse with *Bande mataram* – Hail the mother. What better moment than this to introduce her to Neelkantha's *Chandimangal* celebrating the Mother Goddess. This would be Shashishekhar's contribution to the cause of the nation. What a grim coincidence that he should be reminded of that gossip about his father, at this particular juncture when he was about to breathe new life into his father's work.

"We have said nothing so far. To anyone. Believe me." The woman said again.

It was also so coarse, so gross to have this illiterate foolish woman talk of his father in this manner. Shashishekhar had always abhorred the guttural sound of the village dialect. The account of the deed seemed even more offensive in that rustic, female tongue. For one wild moment he had wondered what would it be like to smother that thin reedy voice forever in this dark deep wood, to put an end to its dirty, muddied tale. But of course it was only a wild fancy. Shashishekhar knew that he would have to do what the woman wanted him to do. He would have to take the woman's daughter with him to Calcutta as the mother wanted. She wanted her daughter to be a domestic drudge in Kailash. Or as he fancied. He would have to pay for her too, for that is why this woman had come to him. And in exchange: silence.

Just as well. He will hold both in custody.

The manuscript and the girl.

Strange though how one had led him to the other, Shashishekhar thought.

Shashishekhar gathered his wandering thoughts and focussed on the woman in front of him. She was still droning on and on. "It makes us related in some way does it not?" said she.

The ingratitiating note made the blood rush through Shashishekhar and strangely enough gave him back his confidence.

"How much do you want?"

The contemptuous words reduced her to what she was in his eyes. A contemptible beggar. Loathsome.

✸✸

"Baba, do you know of a goddess who is a Dombi?"

Uma retuned and asked as Ashutosh finished the two perfectly fried daalpuris. He looked at her quizzically.

Uma hastily lowered her eyes. Tea was sipped in silence while she wondered if a dead end had been reached. But Ashutosh did respond, "I don't know. I don't think so. Is it not time for Rudra to be back?"

"I don't know. He comes back a little late these days, does he not?"

Ashutosh nodded. He seemed a little preoccupied. Uma allowed herself the luxury of letting her mind wander too.

Much later, in their bedroom upstairs when asked the same question Rudra said in an offhand manner to Uma, "Why don't you go to the National Library instead of depending on Kailash's resources?"

❦ ❦

When was the *Chandimangal* first composed?

The genre admittedly developed from older bratakathas, now lost.

And who composed those bratakathas?

Even the educated Bengali is likely to shrug and say, "*Ke jane? Mandhatar Amale!*"

"Who knows?*Mandhatar Amal.*"

Mandhatar Amal is assumed to be the hoary past before history. Before memory too.

Whose memory, now asked the kitchen in Kailash.

Whose? Whose?

❦ ❦

It was not dawn yet but a slight thinning of the dark as the night shroud was gently lifted from the world and the village, Kynsa mati. A cock crowed. A bird here and then another there recognised the approach of a new day. But the twittering was not a chorus yet. The stars could still be seen. The air was cool.

She felt tired. Her green eyes felt heavy and her heart too. This was to be her last morning in the village and what she called home.

She would be leaving with the Brahman from the city – the dead priest's son.

Oh no. Her mother had said nothing. She had heard it all by Padmapukur. She had walked back home from the pond in a daze. But the sheer absurdity of what was being said suggested that it might be true.

"You are going to Calcutta, with the Babu, the priest's son, we know," the women said at the pond.

"Really?" asked her friends.

Her green eyes shone bright but she said nothing and gradually the banter grew more malicious.

She returned to her battered and broken home straight from Padmapukur and found her mother sorting the weed from the green leaves that were to be cooked for their mid-day meal. The green eyes were hard as they took in the older woman and then dumping the pitcher that she had carried from Padmapukur with a loud clang, she turned away from the door. She had half hoped that her mother would call her back, that there would be a confrontation and that it would be loud and bitter. But then she was always looking for confrontations with her mother. She had them too.

This time however no voice, raised in anger, followed her retreating back.

She spent the rest of the day roaming her favourite haunts in the village on her own. Once she had companions in these sojourns. Now she was much too old for the new bands. Her younger sister at home was too docile. Why had the in-laws sent back such a soft biddable girl, the green-eyed one had often wondered .

Night saw her retreat though she was not afraid of the dark.

Was she awake through the night? It seemed so. Why else did it seem so very long? Why else were her eyes burning? She got up from the floor where she lay restless through the night.

Clearly she was not the only one unable to sleep. Her mother sat outside, leaning against the post. She walked past that crouching figure, holding herself straight.

She did not mean to turn back. But she did. At some distance though. Why did she feel so tired and heavy?

"How much did you get from him?" She spat finally, unable to let go without a fight. But was she not loud enough? Did not her mother hear her as she sat still with her head against the post.

She would not let her mother be. She spoke again. "What will you do with the money?"

Why did her mother sit so still? She raised her voice a bit more. "Will you buy a nose ring for your old withered face with it?"

Silence still.

She spat on the ground then and turned to leave.

Her mother spoke. "Yes. I need a nose ring."

Yes. She had been waiting for this. The bait had caught. Now for the play.

"I hope it's heavy enough to drag your face down. All the way down." She hissed at her mother. The green eyes glowed bright.

"Word has come from the in-laws of your youngest sister. They are considering sending for her. Her mother in-law is not getting any younger and has not been keeping well ever since she lost her child. But your sister's in-laws can not accept a shameless girl who wears no jewellery on her person."

"So?"

"So."

"So you are selling me to that man from the city for your youngest daughter. You hag."

Her mother held the green gaze as she answered, "I gave birth to five daughters. Two I have lost to death. One is with her in-laws. Alive I hope. I have not seen her since she got married. I suppose we would have heard had she died. Of the other two, one was never sent for. Another sent back."

"What is it to me?"

"My mother in-law is gentle but half crazed. My husband only visits his home now and then."

"Is that my fault?"

"No, it's mine. Your father comes and goes at will. Your

grandmother wanders off in her mind. I could not do either. I could die of course. But I never could bring myself to do that. I seem to be harnessed to this place."

"You could not die! Why should you? When you can sell your daughter instead?"

"Two daughters. Word has come for one. Her in-laws would take her back provided she is provided for. Somewhat. At least. Let's give it a chance I thought. Let one of us get another chance."

"And so you are disposing me off."

"They, this family of the priest, are like kin, in some strange way, to us. I have heard that the son is doing well, very well, in the city. They owe us something too." The old woman let slip a sigh, "Besides, people marry off their daughters too. At least here you will not have to…" Her mother seemed exhausted as she paused and swallowed.

The green-eyed one smelt victory though bitterly won. She leaned forward slightly, like a cat ready to strike, "Why are the words getting stuck in your throat? Say it. Let's hear it from you."

Her mother fell quiet.

But it was not enough for the younger one. She wanted to draw blood. She took a few steps and then gripped the post that supported her mother, bending down she asked then in a sharp, brittle voice, "How do you know that there won't be that? You would soothe yourself with such lies of course but, but how can you know? How can you be so sure?"

Yes. She had won.

Her mother jerked her head up, "Should he…approach you… you tell them that you know, that you will then tell the world. You remember, don't you? You know what I am talking about? You recall your grandmother's ramblings? Don't you?"

She did then but the harsh tension in the voice of her mother suddenly changed the incoherent tale of her grandmother into something menacing. Suddenly she felt frightened. Her anger and grief had left no room for terror earlier. She meant to ask, should I really worry about that? How should I say it? Who will listen to me in that big place? She meant to say that she was beginning to feel scared, very very scared of leaving her known world behind. Perhaps for ever. She wanted to drop down by her mother and lean against her body.

But she did not and when she spoke her voice sounded steady if a little high pitched. "But why me? Why are you sending me away? Is it because I am the middle one, because I am the one with green eyes, because I am wild, because I don't deserve a chance…"

"No." The shrill cry of the mother frightened the flapping birds in the rafters. "No. I am sending you because you are my brightest and best." The older woman let go of the post then and looked at her daughter. "I am sending you to the city so that you can tell them."

"Tell them what?"

"Tell them about us. Tell them how we live. Ask the people of Calcutta if we don't deserve better? Ask them if we should not live? Perhaps they don't care because they don't know. You go and tell them of our lives. Of all my children only you can do it. That is why."

The sun had stolen a march on them unseen.

The glow of dawn, and more, warmed her, keeping terror at bay.

She spoke finally.

"Ma, can I go for a last, quick round of the village? I will be back."

"Don't take too long." Did the voice catch? "I have kept some food for you. You must eat before you leave. You did not have anything last night either."

"I will be back." She turned then and walked out of her home. But this time she felt her mother's eye caressing her back, keeping her warm.

❋ Eleven ❋

"**B**ABA, WHO IS PISHI?" asked Uma seizing a lull in the conversation as Ashutosh paused to sip his tea.

Every window in the parlour had been shut to keep out the great lashings of water that heaven poured on the city.

Clink. The cup was set on the saucer. The baritone was pure bass. "What do you mean?"

Why is she shrouded in white? Why is she so, so very fair and green eyed? Why does she call your father by name? Why does she live in that indeterminate space, the room on the one and a half storey? Why does she keep your house without salary or acknowledgement?

Why is there so much anger in her frail breast?

"Her green eyes," said Uma. Rapidly sifting and seizing the obvious, the most innocuous and the farthest from home. "It's so rare in a Bengali. I don't think I have ever seen one."

Silence.

'Did I dare shake the universe?' wondered Uma.

But Ashutosh spoke. "Bengal's colonial past. There will be residues of all kinds. In this case the Portuguese. Perhaps."

"Portuguese?"

"Yes." The tone was rich and fruity once again. "The English have so dominated our lives in the region that we have forgotten that no less than seven European nations fought for supremacy over Bengal between the 16th and 17th centuries. The Portuguese, the Dutch, the French, the Danes, the Flemish, the Prussians and of course the English have all bid for Bengal's mastery and at one time within a range of a few miles along the river at Hooghly. But the Portuguese were the first of them."

"Tell me more."

This time the saucer made no noise as it came to rest on the marble of the table.

"The Portuguese arrived in Chittagong in 1517 naming it Porto Grande or the grand port. Chittagong in fact was described by the early Portuguese visitors as the entry to Bengal. It was at that time a prosperous cosmopolitan port with traders and mercenaries from all of Asia. The descendents of the Portuguese settlers still continue to live in Chittagong – at least they used to – as Catholic Christians in the old Portuguese enclave of Paterghatta. They are known as the Firingis. It all began a long time ago… "

The words moved through the room smoothly, possessing it. They coalesced with Uma's memory recalling the Atlas as well as the buried History classes of schooldays. The rain that hurtled at the windows and gurgled down the gutters of Kailash, turned to salt sea sprays, drying rough grains on the beards of men whose eyes were screwed small, scanning the horizon.

The four ships cutting the deep, moved steadily away from the south western corner of the Iberian Peninsula. Away and further away the ships moved from their Lisbon harbour where the caravelas with the exotic lines of their hulls and triangular shaped lateen sails were anchored.

They were the Portuguese whose name derived from the words Portus Cale, a possible mix of Greek and Latin. Or Celtic and Latin. Or Phoenician and Latin. Who can say with certainty after all these years? Whatever be the origin, Portus Cale meant beautiful port, marking a predilection.

The Portuguese were the first Europeans to reach Sri Lanka, Sumatra, Malacca, and Timor. The first to find the mythical Spice Islands, the Moluccas. They were the first Europeans to reach and trade with both China and Japan by sea. The first to view Australia. The first Europeans in America to 'discover' Brazil.

Yes, they were Portuguese whose Prince Henry set up the first school of navigation in Europe in the 15th century, earning the nickname Henry the Navigator. Or so it was said, and particularly by the English who thereby staked a nebulous claim in the Portuguese maritime enterprise. The Portuguese Prince Henry's mother was after all the sister of Henry of Lancaster, Henry IV of England.

Europe discovered the entire coastline of Africa from the Portuguese and perhaps something else too. In about 1501, was not the first batch of African slaves to be exported to the Americas from Lisbon, Portugal? In which case the Portuguese also spearheaded an efficient commerce in human beings.

In the drawing room in Kailash the Portuguese ships navigated around the Cape of Good Hope. The men aboard the ships were moved by myriad feelings on sighting the stone pillar set up by their fellow countryman, Bartolomeu Dias. Saluting him, they sailed on. On and on. All along the eastern coast of Africa. Along the deep and what was once, the boundless, to reach the western coast of India.

The Portuguese were the first to sail directly from Europe to India.

The flagship of the small fleet was called St. Gabriel. It was commanded by a man from the lower nobility of Alentejo in South Portugal. They called him Vasco da Gama.

On May 20, 1498, Vasco da Gama dropped anchor at Calicut, in the southern coast of India. The Hindu king was not interested in his goods. The Muslim merchants were not happy with this new arrival. But da Gama managed to acquire some gems and spices to prove back home that he did reach the fabled land of India. He returned again and by 1500 Portuguese factories were established in Calicut, Cananore and Cochin. Then the first Portuguese fort came up in 1503. Goa was conquered in 1510 and its Muslim population was massacred.

Many Portuguese, especially from Malacca, had come to Bengal in Moorish ships as roving traders drawn by rumours that the land was a rich source of textiles, rice, sugar, saltpetre, opium, cotton, clarified butter and oil. In 1514, the Portuguese settlers in Pipli in Orissa visited Hijli in the Midnapore district of Bengal. Three years later Joâo de Silveira commanded the first regular Portuguese expedition to Chittagong. From then on a Portuguese ship was sent to Bengal every year.

In 1536, Mahmud Shah allowed Martim Affonso de Mello to build factories in Chittagong and Satgaon in Bengal. And it came to pass that the Portuguese so dominated the sea board from Orissa to Chittagong that no alien ship, not even the Bengali ones, could touch at the Bengal port of Satgaon without a Portuguese pass.

When the sky turned grey and the clouds chased each other before lashing the water below with rain, the Portuguese ships glided into Bengal with their goods. They spent the rainy months in buying and selling. The Portuguese traders operating from Chittagong conducted a slave trade in the Bengal estuaries with Arakan or Magh pirates in their rapid rowing boats and they managed a varying average of 1500 to 5000 slaves a year from this region. Some of these were qualified artisans, some agricultural labour force. When the monsoon clouds dissolved entirely leaving fluffs of white in the sky, the Portuguese ships too sailed away on the swollen water, laden with goods including the crying or petrified merchandise.

Just opposite the city of Chittagong on the southern bank of the Karnaphuli river there grew a Luso-Asiatic settlement of Portuguese-Christians, Topazes or half-castes and slaves, known as Dianga.

In 1607 the king of Arakan welcomed the Dutch merchants, soliciting their help against the Portuguese who now dominated the ports of Bengal. Together they massacred several hundred Portuguese in the Port of Dianga, twenty miles south of modern Chittagong.

Other winds of change were also blowing.

In 1575, Munim Khan defeated Daud Karrani in the battle of Tukaroi. Thus the Afghan sultanate of Bengal was incorporated into the Mughal empire.

In 1580, Bengal got her first English visitor, Ralph Fitch.

The rest is history.

"Portuguese at one time was virtually the lingua franca in the coastal area of Bengal. The earliest Portuguese word to enter Bengali is predictably harmad meaning pirate. It derived from armada." Ashutosh leaned back, clearly having enjoyed the attention of his audience.

"I did read once that Lord Clive could speak Portuguese fluently though not any Indian language," nodded Uma.

"Yes. The English East India Company wanted all their officers to learn Portuguese within six months of their arrival in Bengal. It was of course only a matter of time before the English almost erased Bengal's memory of the Portuguese. What is this?" Ashutosh asked suddenly. Startling Uma.

"What? The table?"

"And this?"

"The chair!" She laughed. A little uncertain.

"When we were growing up though, we called these mej and kedara. We assumed that's Bengali. But both derived from Portuguese. The me'sa and the cadeira. English has replaced these words. Perhaps it will be Hindi next. Now that's history for you."

"Tell me some more. The Portuguese words, I mean. The ones that we still use perhaps." Uma was enjoying herself. It brought back the memory of Dadu too who had thus tried to enrich the vocabulary of his grandchildren.

"Oh there would be many. Let's see now... if you can get the Bengali word that we use? I will give you the Portuguese original. These would be objects and ideas that the Portuguese introduced in Bengal."

"The English equivalent too. Please."

"Okay. Here goes. Cupboard. Armario."

"Almari"

"Soap. Sabao."

"Shaban."

"Ribbon. Fita."

"Phita. Really?"

"Pitch or Tar. Alcatrão."

"Alkatra."

"Bucket. Balde."

"Balti."

And thus Rudra found them when he entered the parlour, for once unannounced by the car horn which the pelting rain and crashing thunder had drowned. Ashutosh and Uma turned towards him with the unfocused eyes of those lost in another world. To Rudra the old man and the young woman suddenly seemed vulnerable and exposed. A soothing sense of peace slowly coursed through Rudra drawing him into the cosy confines of the room after days of tortuous restlessness. He allowed himself to be drawn. This was the alternative he thought, for mere mortals like him: family life, warm and snug. The slush, the putrid smells, the traffic snarls, the petrol fumes were already draining away from him. And the past as well.

"Finish. Acabar."

"Wait … wait. Kabar … Really?"

Ashutosh and Uma laughed.

And Rudra asked, "What's this all about?"

"When did you come? We were discovering the Portuguese. In Bengal." Uma was about to get up but Rudra gestured her to remain where she was.

"Why don't you take Uma to see the church at Bandel this weekend, Rudra? It's one of the finest that the Portuguese built near here. It is the oldest church in Bengal perhaps."

"Where do I get a boat from? The roads are water logged."

"Oh the prosaic! If the weather lets up tomorrow, the roads will be fine by Sunday. As fine as they ever will be any way. I am afraid that the romance of the weather or history is lost on your husband."

"I studied Economics. Had to." But the smile took the edge off the remark and Rudra added, "Let's see. If the rains let up…"

"You come too Baba," Uma added in a spontaneous gesture.

Ashutosh was moved and tempted to give in too and join the

young who have the world before them still. Yes, he thought suddenly, it would be nice to see the world once again in the company of those who love you. But he said, "Of course not. An old man like me…" His words were certain but something like longing may have brushed them a different hue.

Rudra spoke. "The maudlin does not suit you Baba. Just come. It was your idea. But remember that when you and Uma push the car through the mud. I, of course, will be dry and clean behind the wheels. Your wheels. We will take the Studebaker."

Every one laughed. As happy people will at mere statements of mundane facts.

※ ※

The old woman seemed to be crying.

The sun glittered on the water of the river that led away from Kynsa mati. The haggard and emaciated figure in white tottered and stumbled but still she ran along the embankment shouting and shaking her fists. Occasionally she stooped to pick up clods of earth which she flung into the river. Her mouth dribbled spit and garble, "Di, di….save…save…again…help…again…help…come back…give her back…"

The knots of people by the riverside did not pay much heed. She was the familiar village idiot. Besides most of them were looking at the two boats that glided into the river and slowly drew away from shore.

The young girl with the strange green eyes held herself straight in the narrow boat. Her throat felt dry. She looked steadily into the sunlight drenched water which the sinewy, swaying boatsmen cut with long logs. Someone nudged her, another whispered, "Your grandmother." But she did not look up.

It did not take long for the wind to carry away the feeble unsteady voice. She knew without looking up that her crazy grandmother had vanished from sight as well when the boat moved along the gentle curve of the river.

The village receded. The water held the sky.

❦

The sky was flushed pink despite the grey when Calcutta woke up on Saturday. The day progressed confident and golden. The treacherous world welcomed the sun just as it had celebrated the rolling dark across the golden halo in May.

Sunday was clear. It could have been the onset of summer once again but for a certain slant of the sun, a certain softness in its warmth and a hint of a breeze too. It promised autumn: Bengal's special season for the agomoni of the goddess.

There was something very like joy in Kailash too, at least in its upper quarters.

Uma got into the car carefully, holding her saree clear of the puddle that had not dried yet near the porch. The light Murshidabad silk was now blue now green like the season. But the border was a slim and a steady yellow. Ashutosh got in beside Rudra and they set off.

A quick glance at the windows of Kailash assured, reassured, Uma that no one was there, waving goodbye or just gazing. She was glad; relieved too. Pishi and she never met during weekends though they did run into each other in the kitchen, near the landing or outside the room on one and a half storey. It was an unconscious agreement to avoid a greater contact when the men were at home. Uma was glad she did not see Pishi at the window, or at the door as she set off for the day with her husband and father-in-law. If she did, then she would have to tell her that they were off, off to discover Pishi's history but without her.

Her eyes met Rudra's in the driving mirror.

With a sigh she let go of those who had remained behind.

We will have a good time she thought.

And indeed they did.

Nourished by the steady monsoon, the green, on the drive to Bandel from Calcutta was amazing. It was shining on stately trees, growing mossy on mute old buildings, drawing deep into the rickety wrought iron verandahs in the guise of the Aswath, creeping up with confidence where tram tracks ran and lush with life even on corrugated tin roofs.

"Somewhat different from Delhi roads?" Rudra asked.

"I like it."

"Indeed? This is just the beginning."

"You mark my words, I will like it," Uma sat back with a smile.

It took a little over two hours to reach Bandel. A few kilometres south may have been the first Portuguese settlement in Satgaon. Ashutosh turned slightly from his seat in the front and said, "It is not possible today to mark the first Portuguese footfall here exactly. But we do know that they called Satgaon, Porto Pequeno which means the small port. By 1579-80 Antonio Tavares founded Ugolim or Hooghly at the mouth of the river Ganga near the first settlement of Satgaon. The town grew rapidly and in 1603 it had about 5000 Portuguese inhabitants. The religious orders erected many churches including the one at Bandel where the Order of the Augustinians built a friary in 1599. The church of Nossa Senhora di Rosario was attached to it."

"Did you read up all that last night?" Rudra laughed and asked his father.

"It's a question of interest, my dear."

Rudra hummed softly as he drove.

The Bandel Church was crowded. Devotees and day trippers lit candles to Mother Mary with equal enthusiasm. The bright sun spurred hope. Uma learnt that the church was built in 1660 by Gomez de Soto though the key stone of the old church still bore the date 1599 over the eastern gate of the monastery. In front of the church stood a ship's mast presented by the Captain whose vessel was saved from a storm in the Bay of Bengal by the grace of the Virgin.

On such a ship must have come a man with a pair of green eyes, thought Uma. The ship anchored in Chittagong, Porto Grande. The green spread. Slowly. By force and stealth. Perhaps love too. But whatever be the means or mode, it insinuated itself into the very blood of the land. And then one day, years and years later, the green reached Kailash.

"Shall we go?" asked Rudra.

His father and wife looked at him. Clearly the wanderlust had seized them for the day. One old and distinguished and the other young and beautiful. Both dependent on him. Rudra felt oddly protective of them. Indulgent. But somewhat impatient too.

"Let's go," he said again but added, " I will show you my bit of Portugal in Calcutta now. If you wish to see it."

"Barkis is willing," said Ashutosh.

"But where?" asked Uma.

"A grave and a temple."

The return took a little longer. Calcutta was festooned in colours. Clothes of every size, shape, age and hue hung over every available space to catch the sun. Faded and fluttering, starched and stretched, the clothes celebrated the sun after days of rain. The city steamed from every nook and cranny.

The Park Street graveyard was quiet. In its south west corner rested Henry Louis Vivian Derozio of Portuguese descent. He was one of the pioneers of the intellectual movement that had marked Bengal's renaissance.

"He was only18 when Hindu College appointed him," said Ashutosh.

"But orthodox backlash got him dismissed from the College. He was only 22 when he died. He was the first, or one of the first, Indians to write a patriotic poem in English, 'To India – My Native Land." A burst of cawing overhead silenced Rudra.

"Now where?" asked Uma.

The Firingi Kalibari was built by yet another Portuguese. Anthony Heusman had competed with the professional Bengali troupes of the 19th century that composed impromptu verses on erotic or religious themes for the Babus of the city. Calcutta remembered him as Anthony firingi, a poet and a singer devoted to the dark goddess Kali.

The temple was small but evidently a centre of faith. Uma almost tripped over a young man who suddenly measured his length on the ground in front of the goddess. Ashutosh said sotto voce to the young couple, "Girlfriend's getting married to the groom chosen by parents. Mark my words."

"Maybe he just needs a job," Rudra was much louder.

The Brahman priest leaned forward and marked Uma's forehead with the wet dark vermillion.

"And now for a meal. On me," said Ashutosh. "We will go to the Grand."

The Grand! But the vermillion is streaked all over my forehead, thought Uma. And it clashes with my saree too.

※ ※

The limp saree clung to her. Her stomach felt empty. Her head light. Her mother had given her some parched rice and a small chunk of jaggery for the journey. The other women travellers had offered her food too. But she could not accept food from those whose curiosity she had rebuffed. Besides, her body seemed to be heaving in constant motion and she was not certain that it could keep the food down. She could not bear the indignity of it. There were shadows under the green eyes by the time they reached Calcutta.

She had not wished to reach when the boat had heaved off from the bank, drawing her away, and further away, from her village, her family, her friends and her world. She had not wished to leave. But now she longed for destination. Oh! To be still and not to be in motion.

※ ※

The clouds returned with a vengeance as they headed back towards Kailash. The potato, cashew nuts and pineapple that the Portuguese had introduced in India churned inside Uma's stomach. In the back seat of the car she sat, feeling heavy and tired. An elegant tree nodded from the boulevard as the car picked up speed. "You have been seduced by my red blossoms and named me after the most romantic of your gods, calling me Krishnachura, the crowning glory of Lord Krishna," the tree whispered, "but I could be from Peru or Portugal."

The sky, a turgid red, was rapidly turning black. There seemed to be a traffic snarl as most people realised that the clear Sunday was about to be dissolved in a flood of water once again. The windows had to be rolled up against the petty but insistent splatter of raindrops. The smells trapped in the rich leather of the car did nothing to ease Uma.

"Do the Portuguese have green eyes? I always thought of them as dark. Dark by European standards that is," Uma opened the conversation in a brave bid to forget her rising nausea.

"I don't think that one can draw such pure racial examples," Ashutosh said.

"*Ojos verdes*…Green eyes. The green eyes of a passing stranger, green like the basil, green like the wheat, green like the lemons," Rudra hummed a few bars, "A Portuguese classmate of mine used to sing it all the time." There was a smile in Rudra's voice. "Affonso, my Portuguese classmate, was going around with an English girl with green eyes those days." He looked at his father and added, "It's a fado, Portuguese's melancholic answer to the Blues. Amalia Rodrigues was quite a rage in London in the early fifties."

They seemed to belong to another world, the two men in the front. Uma sat in isolation at the back. She rolled down the window a bit and breathed deep the damp air.

The dark sky flooded the city with heavy, incessant rain. They had reached home in good time indeed. Uma glanced at the room on one and a half storey as she went upstairs to change. It was dark as she knew it would be.

※ ※

Sunlight and shadow played in the room. She stood behind Shashishekhar, holding on to a pathetic bundle. Loose limbed she seemed as though ready for flight. But clearly she was tired. It showed in the green eyes. She had never travelled beyond her village. Her body could barely remain steady now having coped with the varied motions of cart wheels, oars and rail tracks.

Haimanti stood before Shashishekhar. Her saree was drawn low over her head. It hid her face entirely. Shashishekhar was a little surprised. Hem never wore her saree like this for him, not even in the public sections of Kailash. But he did not wish to ask her anything here beyond the perfunctory. He knew that there were other curious eyes and ears peering into the room from the nooks and crannies of Kailash though no one was visible. One must maintain a certain distance to command respect.

"So, is everything all right here?"

Shashishekhar sank into a deep chair and stretched his legs out. How could it be? How could he ask the question?

But all Haimanti said was a soft "Hmm."

Actually even if she wished to, Haimanti could not have said any more right now. There was that familiar constriction in her chest once again. The stones had settled within Haimanti ever since a maid had slithered into the parlour upstairs to inform her that the master had returned. And that there was a woman with him.

"She is so fair. Just like a *mem*. She has strange eyes too." The maid prattled on, clearly very excited.

Haimanti's heart had tumbled then. But she caught the naked curiosity in the maid's eyes and asked her to go down while she herself stood holding the bed post for a brief while. Oh God. It was bad enough to have her in Chittagong but to have her in Kailash itself! Oh God. Haimanti rubbed her hand around the bed post in despair. There seemed to be a burning in her palms. Oh God. Oh God. Why are you doing it? Why are you doing this to me? What have I done? Or not done? True I produced two daughters before the son arrived but I have given him a son finally. Why then? Why? She smiled wryly in one brief moment of rare cynicism. What would God know of such despair? Was he not a man too? Married to so many? Was he not ever ready for secret assignations with the Patanis and Kuchnis, the low born women who sashayed in public? What would he know of the agony of sharing your husband with other women?

Haimanti pulled up her saree to cover her head and walked down the staircase to meet her husband. And the other one.

Shashishekhar stretched again. "I am getting old. These journeys are beginning to tire me."

Young Khagen stood at a respectful distance from the couple. Alert. Waiting to slip on his master's house slippers at the slightest gesture.

You won't need to any more, thought Haimanti. With her here.

But was it her? Would the other one wear such an old, stained saree? But Haimanti stifled hope not wishing to be dealt a blow unaware.

I won't need to any more, thought, Shashishekhar.

With his father gone and the manuscripts in hand it was as though his last link with the village had been severed. He did not regret it either. The thought of his father's village reminded him of the girl.

"Hem. This is a...a girl for you." Even to him it sounded cliched and false even though he had started to believe that it was the truth. Suddenly the tiredness of the journey surged through Shashishekhar too. It made him irritable and he assumed authority. "Her family is distantly related to ours in the village and they are destitute, like so many there. Her mother asked for succour. You have been overworked and tired of late, with the children and the house. Let her serve you. She is raw like all villagers but most of them are honest and faithful. Teach her what you will." And then having finished his speech, Shashishekhar nodded at Khagen

Khagen kneeling down, gently slid Shashishekhar's feet in the slippers.

Shashishekhar allowed his tiredness to show and he said to Khagen, "Get my bath ready." Calcutta had started getting piped water since 1870. But Shashishekhar preferred his bath water to be drawn fresh from the well in the house. It was his daily ritual. The water had to be drawn a few minutes before his bath in summer and an hour before in winter to warm in the sun. Oh, he had no superstition about tap water. He was all for science and technology. But this was, how should one say, a foible. Shashishekhar had grown up in his uncle's house as a dependent, though his father was a respected and a remarkable man. Shashishekhar had not been neglected. But there had been no question of idiosyncracies and foibles. This ritual of bathing in water drawn daily from the well when he could have used tap water, made him feel that this was his house and he could do what he wished to.

Khagen gathered up Shashishekhar's shoes.

Shashishekhar turned then to Haimanti, "Take her," he said.

Neither Haimanti nor Khagen spoke.

Both turned to leave.

She followed though nobody had said anything to her. Her feet seemed a little unsteady. She wore her saree high. Like the village belle that she was. Her feet glistened pale. Shahishekhar frowned.

"Hem." They all stopped. Shashishekhar looked at Khagen who melted out of the room and it was only then that he said. "Let the girl have the room on one and a half floor and not the servant's quarters."

The constriction in Haimanti's chest had started to dissolve slowly. Surely this could not be her. Not her. The other one. Not this bedraggled creature.

The instruction jolted her.

But if Haimanti's reddened eyes started watering once again nobody got to know as the saree covered not only the eyes but also a good part of her nose that morning.

૦ ૦

"Who could have known that the wonderfully clear morning would end in such a deluge", thought Uma as she came down to the dining room in a soft cotton saree with her face scrubbed clean of the grit and grime of the journey. Rudra and Ashutosh were there already. Neither Ashutosh nor Uma had wanted any dinner after that late and heavy meal at the Grand. Pishi was in the kitchen stirring their Horlicks to keep the skin from forming on top. Uma put her chin on Pishi's shoulder stealing a brief unscheduled moment with her as she went in to fetch her cup.

"Do you know from where your green eyes have come?"

"I know where they have brought me."

"Where?"

"The kitchen in Kailash."

※ ※

The kitchen swayed gently. She steadied herself with a great effort, trying not to think of her home in Kynsa mati.

Haimanti had asked a maid to show her the room on one and a half storey and then disappeared upstairs having given the order. She exchanged no word with the stranger to her house.

The maid, a round small thing, very young and clearly newly-married, looked at the newcomer with avid curiosity, clearly taken up by her fair skin and the green eyes. But before she could ask anything of the green-eyed one, a voice wafting from downstairs claimed her.

She stood in the room on one and a half storey alone. All she wanted to do was lie down and die. Her body seemed light. But she seemed scarcely able to carry it. And she needed to empty it too. Urgently. She looked around. Surely she was not expected to do it here. She had heard that white men and women did it in the room. But surely she was not expected to do it? There seemed to be a weight welling up behind her eyes.

Need drove her out of the room finally. She looked up from the landing to where she could hear voices. But she felt terribly uncertain. Kailash made her feel raw. There were so many things in it. Small and strange. Big and dark. Looking down from the landing she caught sight of the dark lanky fellow called Khagen. He crossed the hall and disappeared into a room. Carefully she came down holding tightly on to the banister.

There seemed to be a buzz in the kitchen. But it stopped as soon as she entered.

"I need to... wash up." She looked into their eyes to combat the shame of it.

In the confines of the dark, dank slithery bathroom of the servant's quarters her warm tears mingled with the cold water poured from a tin can.

There was food on a brass plate in one corner of the kitchen when she returned. She noted that the amount was generous. Two elderly maids sat in one corner while the young maid with the round face who had shown her the room scoured some brass and copper jars with tamarind at some distance from them. The older women looked at her with sour curiosity on shrunken faces. Another face peeped in from the door leading to the courtyard. She heard water splashing from there.

One of the older maids looked her up and down and said, "Sit. Your place has been set aside. The mistress asked for a new plate to be taken out from the store because you are a Brahman's daughter. So what brings you here?"

The peremptory note riled her. She had always loved a challenge.

"Do you people get coconuts here?"

The round one's mouth formed a perfect O. Her hands, smeared with tamarind pulp hung motionless in air.

The sound of water splashing from outside ceased abruptly too.

"If you can't swallow your food without grated coconut then your mother should have sent a couple of trees with you." The voice of the old maid was like metal rubbing against metal.

"I am talking about coconut husk. The bath room needs to be scoured."

"Here we make do with what is given to us."

"Us?" The blast from the green eyes was quite something. She sat down. "I don't eat so much. Remove some of it."

They responded to order. Impressed despite themselves by the lack of appetite. Or need.

Khagen entered the kitchen just as she was leaving it. On her way out she heard the hard metallic voice of the older maid say to Khagen none too softly, "Get coconuts tomorrow. The cat faced woman wants them. And get ready to take orders from her too, from now on."

She met Haimanti on the stairs and stood aside silently. But she did not lower her eyes. Or fall at her feet. Or sob piteously. She only waited to be told what should she do now, do next, do for ever.

"How arrogant," thought Haimanti. "Just because she has that pale skin and strange eyes. But I am the mistress of this house. And I won't let her forget it."

And she did not. Ever.

As for the green-eyed one, she hung onto her dignity which prevented her from seeking compassion or companionship either upstairs or downstairs in Kailash.

※ ※

Upstairs in Kailash, Uma had just finished tying her hair in a tight plait for the night when Rudra came to the bedroom. Uma had switched off the main lights and only two lamps were on in the room, one by the bed and the other on the study table, casting soft patches of intimacy.

Uma saw Rudra's reflected image in the dressing table mirror first as he pushed the bed room doors shut. He seemed alone, preoccupied, in that brief moment as he stood with his weight against the doors and his head bent at a slight incline. On a sudden impulse Uma went up to her husband and put her arms around him.

Rudra drew her into a closer embrace but without passion for the moment.

"It bothers me so," she mumbled into his kurta.

Rudra withdrew his arms and walked towards the table by the window, "What's bothering you? Tell me."

"Print, potatoes, poets…if we have accepted so much in our relationship with the Portuguese, then what sin did a pair of green eyes commit?"

"Are you talking in general or particular?" His tone was light.

How could green eyes in Kailash not have a particular reference thought Uma with a certain degree of uncharacteristic asperity but it had been a wonderful day and she wanted it to end on a soft happy note. "Pishi had once suggested that she was probably abandoned, or never accepted, after marriage because her green eyes showed that she was somehow sullied. Baba said that given

Chittagong's history, green eyes could signal an...alliance...with the Portuguese." She kept her voice light too.

"The Brahmans have always argued fiercely for the purity of upper caste blood lines. Miranda House in Delhi could not have been so removed from the rest of Indian reality that you would not know this."

This time Uma was truly baffled. The assault was unexpected. Uncalled for too, she thought, feeling hurt. "It's not that one does not know. I just wonder what manner of men were those who graded relationships and interactions with another people so finely. One could conduct business with those others, the firingis, for instance and make profit. One could learn from them too. But one was not supposed to marry them. Then you were sullied. For many women it was probably not even marriage but brutal coercion." Having held her ground, Uma moved towards the bed then seeking closure.

But Rudra spoke from where he was. "Why? It makes perfect sense. Perfect business sense at any rate. You go where, where ever, there is a chance of profit. But you ensure that your fortune is in safe custody. With your own kind. Of your blood."

Years of living in a large family had left Uma with finely tuned antennae that could spot domestic discords from afar. They erupted out of apparently innocuous situations and obscure statements and then transfigured, monstrously feeding on dormant and dusty resentments and slights. Uma had resolved long ago that her marriage would not sink into that petty realm. Genuinely bewildered, she sought to abstract herself, as well as Rudra, and make peace, "Anyway, your grandfather did rescue Pishi in a manner of speaking. He brought her to Calcutta. Rather Kailash than Kynsa mati I am sure. For Pishi at least. It was rather decent of him, your grandfather I mean, to intervene like that for a poor girl and in those days. He must have been an extraordinary man."

"He must have been, I am sure. I did hear a fair bit about that all through my growing years, about his lineage and his individual genius."

Uma on the verge of a question, hesitated, uncertain of Rudra's strange mood.

But Rudra carried on. "He used to come home with a gift for me everyday when I was a child. Sometimes it would be just a pencil or some pieces of coloured papers from the Press but it added some excitement to my evenings. But for all that he was a formal man and somehow we spent much less time together as I grew older. Baba always addressed him formally as 'apni' rather than the familial 'tumi'. As for my grandmother she would probably have it that he was not a man at all but a demigod."

"Then it must have been a happy marriage."

"That's what we would like to believe. Certainly, Kailash would have it so," Rudra shrugged, "As a child I always thought of him as a tall man. Tall and big, dwarfing us all. But when I joined college my grandmother said that she had kept some of his suits. They were made of fine English cloth, I could perhaps try those, she suggested. I did though really more out of curiosity. I had no desire to enter adult life in Edwardian suits."

"And?"

"They were too tight for me. It was such a revelation. The big demigod was actually much smaller in real life."

Uma looked at Rudra standing by the window with the darkness of the night in front of him and she felt that he was talking about a Kailash different from the one with which she had fallen in love one balmy summer evening.

And Rudra thought of his grandparents, now portraits on the wall above him.

"You are the poet Neelkantha's progeny. We are kulin Brahmans. It is not done so in Kailash. Look at your grandfather," thus Haimanti would always begin whenever there was a clash of will or way with her grandson. And that happened often enough.

"What is it to me? I don't care," once Rudra had replied rudely with adolescent aggression and then suddenly Haimanti had turned towards him and said that it was this stubbornness of his that had killed his mother.

"No," he had protested through lips that suddenly felt very taut.

Haimanti was immediately contrite too and caving in she did say, "Do what you will, do as you think best."

"Why did you say that?"

"What ?"

"You jolly well know what," Rudra raised his voice fully aware that it rattled Haimanti. Baba never did so. The demigod had not either. The bedroom doors were open. "Will you tell me or not?" He asked again

"I made a mistake."

"So you have made a mistake but tell me."

"There is nothing to say."

"Tell me, "Rudra's tone grew harsher still and then he added, "tell me why you said that or else I will ask Baba. I will tell him what you said. I will."

This was soft, marshy ground. Both grandmother and grandson recognized that this was where they must call a truce.

Haimanti's eyes filled up.

"I will tell Baba." But Rudra lowered his voice now.

The stubborn set of her grandson's face seemed alien to Haimanti, and with the tears slowly coursing down her cheeks Haimanti said in a soft reassuring voice that how could a five year-old boy know that he must not make his mother run all the way across the terrace on a hot summer morning for that is how the sun touched Shivani and the fever came so relentless upon her that she had to leave all of them for ever. How could a five year-old have known that he should have stayed with his grandmother in the puja room and not made his mother run after him all over the terrace in the hot sun in a show of stubborn will. But he was a child after all, Rudra must remember that. Rudra must not be too harsh on himself. Haimanti should not have brought it up. "That's all," Haimanti said through quivering lips, lifting a shaking hand to caress her grandson who at twelve was already taller than his grandmother but Rudra moved his head away and it was to his retreating back that Haimanti said, "That's all, forget it, forget it."

Of course Rudra did not. The knowledge lay between the old woman and the young lad whenever an argument erupted between them and each time Rudra wished he had something other than his grandmother's memory to help him access that fateful day when he turned five. In the beginning he had thought that there was something. He did remember a small room with a latticed window, a few streaks of sunlight on a red floor, Pishi with something green and gold around her and laughing. And then the light changed and his mother's white face looked up as she dragged herself up the stairs and his grandmother stood stiff against the wall, watching. He knew that his mother was looking at him as she heaved up the stairs past his grandmother and though he could not see himself he knew that he was waiting on the landing above and that his heart was beating fast and he was gripping something hard. He thought for a while that his mother had fallen down the stairs, in fact he thought that he knew that was what had caused her death and that there was a great conspiracy that called it fever. But then even Baba returned from England and said that it had indeed been fever.

Rudra loved Baba from that very first day after his return from England.

It also slowly dawned on Rudra that Pishi never ever smiled, leave alone laughed. She never wore anything bright. He took to avoiding her almost guiltily at first, as though something tarnished lay between them, and then, given the nature of Kailash, he grew almost entirely to forget her. His memory faded too, as memories will, his grandfather died and then years later his grandmother too passed away leaving him with his father, but in Kailash still.

"Kailash!" Rudra said half to himself, "Kailash has taken from others only what suited it. Like the successful everywhere. And like the successful, it can hold others. Why else are we here?"

We. The pronoun hit Uma with a sharp force. Her heart thudded suddenly, entirely discomfited. What did Rudra mean by that? She had never asked herself why she was in Kailash. It lay fathoms deep within her and was allowed to filter through only as romance. The water rose. Uma blinked. "What do you have to say about my presence in Kailash? Why do you think I am here?" she asked of Rudra but silently, only within herself. And finally, "Do you regret that I am here?"

The rain ran crazy paths on the window pane. Rudra drew the chair close to the window, and switched off the table lamp in an unconscious gesture and then let it be in case the light bothered Uma. Uma responded without thinking and turned off the bed side lamp too and lay down, waiting, on the bed, in the dark.

But Rudra stayed where he was and she did not call out to him either.

The rain remained persistent. The room silent and dark.

♣♣

It was an alien darkness. Not soft and shadowy where her home nestled in the village. Kynsa mati.

Kynsa mati with so many shades of green and some like her eyes. She lay on the red cemented floor of the room on one and a half storey and chanted unconsciously the name of her village even as she listened to the strange sounds of Kailash. Thus she fought despair.

Mercifully however her body was too tired and sleep soon erased everything.

❊ Twelve ❊

THE NIGHT WAS ROUGH.
Uma took a long time to fall asleep and then dreamt of crashing waves and green trees. Her bedroom appeared to have no walls and people gathered at the far end of it. Faces crowded her dream. Some she knew but soon they merged and blurred. Someone started shouting unprovoked obscenities. She knew the voice but could not place it. The harsh voice grew louder and louder. The faces wavered.

Uma woke up with a sharp sense of fear. Relief flooded her as she turned to see the shadowy outline of Rudra sleeping by her side. She moved a little closer to his warm, breathing body in an attempt to calm herself. A sense of unease stayed with her though and would not dissolve with the night.

❊ ❊

The green-eyed one was the first to wake up in the morning in Kailash. The sun was beginning to rise. The coconut palm gently swayed outside the window as it had in Kynsa mati. But the village was far, far away, as though a distant dream. Her body felt bruised still. Her eyes felt tired.

But it was morning and she had to meet the day.

❊ ❊

In the morning, Uma did not wish to inspect the scaffolding of her dream or its contingent causes. Why was Rudra so distant last night, so abrasive? Had she betrayed her marriage in some way? The tap water ran through her fingers to gurgle down the sink as she stood staring at the slightly swollen face in the bathroom mirror, thinking of her marriage and oscillating precariously between self righteousness and guilt.

The mighty storm of Sunday evening had settled down to a steady drizzle by Monday morning. Rudra's whistling, mainly tuneless, as he got ready for work grated on Uma's nerves. She wished to be by herself for the first time in Kailash.

Eventually the two men left the house.

Khagen shuffled around the dining table clearing the remains of breakfast and brisk sounds drifted in from the kitchen. The day was in progress. Uma slipped into the library and shut the heavy doors on the world.

※ ※

Thick maroon drapes gave a stuffy feeling to what was called the library. The room ran the length of Kailash downstairs. Clearly doors had been knocked down to incorporate the connecting passage between two rooms to house the vast collection of books. Walls on all sides were lined with dark bookcases. The English books were classified according to subjects while Bengali followed chronology. Sanskrit occupied one tall cupboard next to a shorter one of German publications most of which related to printing, though there was a copy of Kalidasa's *Shakuntala* as well.

Sorrow lingered here not just of nostalgia but neglect. Uma had drawn aside the curtains but the rain-sodden mossy wall rising up too close to the windows and the tired and leaky slice of the visible sky only added to her vague sense of despair. Uma thought with sudden longing of the fierce glow of the summer sun as she switched on the lamps in the still, grey room.

She had noticed the usual Books of Knowledge, the *Encyclopaedia Britannica*, *Rabindra rachanabali*, Saratchandra and Bankimchandra *granthabali* during her earlier forays into the library with the duster. But today she had come there to look for the old Bengali poems that might contain references to the goddess as a low caste. Her heart was not in it anymore though. And yet she was also shamed by this discovery that she could so easily think of sacrificing commitment to convenience. The animated anticipation of the kitchen echoed in her ear. Uma longed for some legitimate distraction.

Old paper cut-outs of fighter planes, Daniel Defoe, Walter Scott, all kinds of books on football, the World Wars and Perry Mason marked the rites of passage of Rudra. The glass front of the cupboard gleamed in the lamp light. Uma squatted down, opened it wide and was glad to immerse herself in this past of her husband left behind in the library downstairs. Cobwebs softened the wood at the back of the cupboard and she wondered uneasily if the dark recess hid lizards as well. The feathered duster was clearly no good. She would need her rag.

The clock on the wall carried on ticking.

Imperceptibly Uma's heavy, unhappy mood of the morning lifted. She was almost happy.

※ ※

The pursuit of happiness, Shashishekhar considered to be a feminine occupation. He sought worth and satisfaction in keeping with his station in life. His identity, as he would have it, was encrusted by his father, his printing press and his son: his past, his present and his future.

His father Neelkantha's *Chandimangal* had become the pride of Bengal. Shashishekhar regretted not having interpolated a catchy refrain in it such as *Anandamath*'s '*Bandemataram*'. But anyway it had done well, remarkably well. People, at least those who matter, could no longer afford not to know of it. His father represented Bengal's proud culture and tradition. Shashishekhar was satisfied with the reflected glory. Indeed anything more ostentatious he would have found distasteful. He had toyed, for a while, with the idea of getting a portrait painted of his father. There were no photographs of course. But he could describe his father's appearance to the artist who would also naturally have to glean his character from his poetic composition. The result could be something like

Joshua Reynold's representation of an individual – a confluence of the ideal and the actual – as one of Shashishekhar's 'English' teachers in college was fond of saying. But Shashishekhar let go of the thought. Better to leave certain things unsaid and unseen. Legends are thus fostered.

The Ganges Press was doing brisk business and expanding. Shahsishekhar had managed to buy the space next door (which even in his mind he never thought of as a shop). He had also bought more property in Entally and Ballygunge. Some of his acquaintances had mentioned other diversifications: the rice trade or even jute. Someone had suggested moneylending too. Shashishekhar did dabble a bit with jute. But he saw no need to share his life or its means with others. Thus he always shook his head at these suggestions and said, "I am a Brahman's son." So too were most of the advisers, and many in the business too. But Shashishekhar liked to state the difference, especially in present times.

And the present inevitably led to the future. His son Ashutosh, a post-graduate from Presidency was a competent and intelligent assistant where the press was concerned. Some day there would be Ashutosh's son too to look after The Ganges Press. Shashishekhar felt that his son's marriage would, should, brighten the Chattopadhyay future even further. Almost all of Ashutosh's friends were already married and many were fathers too. Haimanti who had been on the lookout for suitable grooms ever since the daughters were born seemed to be dragging her feet over Ashutosh's marriage though there was a steady stream of proposals. But Haimanti's standards where her son was concerned seemed to be rather exacting.

"I suggest you place an order with the potter," Shashishekhar had laughed once when Haimanti told him that she had rejected her sister-in-law's niece as the girl's two nostrils did not seem to be symmetrically aligned.

"I will do so if required. And why not? My son is perfect in every way. Just show me another like him in the city."

Shashishekhar was rather proud of his son too but sometimes

he wondered if Ashutosh had his own burning passion within to succeed. But such comparisons inevitably led to his own past with its alleys and shadows that he did not wish to traverse any more. Shashishekhar wanted his son to go to England to study printing. Now that was something that he himself had not been able to do. But he also thought that Ashutosh should go after marriage. England had too many temptations for a young unmarried Indian. Besides Shashishekhar's fine business sense balked at the prospect of spending money on his son's edifying trip to England when several families in Calcutta would gladly oblige, if Ashutosh was made their son-in-law. Ashutosh had come of age long ago and while it was true that a man was never too old to be married, it would not be prudent to let things slide.

"The ideal groom is from a rising family, the ideal bride from a sinking one. The former looks up, the latter down," Haimanti had always told Shashishekhar. He knew the proverb of course but he would not stand by it. Marriage was an alliance. Did not Krishna advise Arjuna so even before the great battle of Kurukshetra? Where would the Pandavas have been without Draupadi's father and brother by their side? Besides, why ally yourself with those with needs? Shashishekhar had never wanted a brood of dependents in Kailash. He had had his share of living with a crowd in his early life. He had no time for such sentimental nonsense. He never did.

The Ganges Press's novels of sentiment were doing well. But the romance of jute was fading. There was a slump in agriculture too. Both might affect him in the near future. His business had survived the anguish of the riots of 1926 and the turmoil of labour unrest of the following years but a second line of business, through marriage alliance, would be a sound investment. Ashutosh would have to marry into a worthwhile family of his father's choice.

Shashishekhar chose the bride for Ashutosh or rather he chose the family. He met them at a social gathering at Haimanti's brother's. They seemed to be related to the sister-in-law with Congress connections. The men were discussing national politics, as they always did these days. The deliberate insult of the all white Simon Commission still stung. But the upper caste Hindu gathering, self-assuredly superior, sought solace from the fact that it was communal difference that had broken up the united Indian front. You could not trust 'them' was the common consent. The absent 'them' came in for a long bout of chastisement. The efficacy of compromise formulas were being deliberated when a gentleman with broad genial features and thick coarse hair turned towards Shashishekhar and said. "We try to run before we can walk. We should concentrate on the Calcutta Corporation elections first."

"Equality…"

" … is an absurd idea in a country like ours right now but we need to be alert to the problem of exploitation."

Shashishekhar looked around. One of Haimanti's brothers hastened forward to introduce the two. Shashishekhar learnt that he was talking to a Banerjee of 'Banerjee Brass Founders'.

Through the course of the evening the two men critiqued British economic policies, agreed that educated upper caste Indian men must have democratic privileges, exhorted the need for scientific education for the enslaved nation and wondered about the possible personal rivalry between the two young stars of the Congress: Jawaharlal Nehru and Subhash Chandra Bose. While discussing the immoral gap between the millions of pounds that the British were draining annually from India and the meagre rupees that was the per capita income, Shashishekhar also learnt that the gentleman had four sons and a daughter.

It was not difficult to find out the rest.

The Banerjees were from Barrackpore near Calcutta that used to be the summer residence of the viceroy. It was here that a sepoy Mangal Pandey had refused to bite on cartridges greased with animal fat thus allegedly triggering the revolt of 1857. In 1864 Shimla took over formally as the summer seat of the imperial government, eclipsing the possibilities of Barrackpore's potential growth. Uncannily, in the same year a storm devasted the trees of the main avenue of Barrackpore and was seen as a powerful portent from heaven signalling its decline. The same storm is said to have broken the main Banerjee residence too. Two of the many brothers of the sprawling family made up their minds then to leave Barrackpore for Calcutta. The main branch of the Banerjees gradually withered into genteel poverty but the offshoot in Calcutta grew strong and bright; with the aid of gas first and then electricity.

'Banerjee Brass Founders' in Calcutta arranged gas lights at weddings and later at meetings. They dealt with carriage lamps too. Initially there had been a partner called Dey but the Banerjees moved on without him with the aid of electricity.

Electric lights were first demonstrated in Calcutta in 1879. The first Calcutta street to be lit by electricity was possibly the Harrison Road in 1891 though in 1905 the authorities reverted to gas. But the Banerjees had faith in electricity and gradually came to be known for their electric fans, for the table and the ceiling; devices which were also being popularised by the Calcutta Electric Supply Corporation from the early twentieth century. They still called themselves 'Banerjee Brass Founders' though.

A couple of the Banerjee boys attended Presidency College but the clan flooded the three institutions in Calcutta that taught modern science in English: the Medical College of Bengal established in 1835 where Madhusudan Gupta caused a sensation as he dissected a human body ignoring caste Hindu strictures against touching corpses, St. Xavier's College established by the Belgian Jesuits in 1860 and the Calcutta College of Civil Engineering started in 1856 and renamed as the Bengal Engineering College when it moved to Shibpur in 1880. The genial gentleman with four sons, and a daughter, had studied in the last institution and had been with the Bengal Nagpur Railways for a brief while before immersing himself entirely in the family business.

Shashishekhar had been happy with Haimanti. The association had been a fortuitous one. He thought it a lucky omen that he should chance upon the alliance for Ashutosh at Haimanti's and that like Haimanti this girl too was the only sister in a family of four brothers. But he never did discuss his deals at home.

❀ ❀

Uma looked up and saw the frail figure in white standing unusually hesitant at the threshold of the library. Pishi came in a little stiffly and then asked, "Can you read all these books?"

"At least the ones in English and Bengali I hope." Uma smiled.

"Yes." Pishi coughed softly. "We could not find you, lunch is ready."

"Give me five minutes? Let me finish this one shelf that remains. Why don't you sit here? Wait, the floor is dusty from all these old books that I have taken out." Uma wiped the patch of the floor close to her for Pishi and then carefully pulled out the remaining books from where they nestled on the last shelf that remained to be dusted. "I think that this must have been 'his' cupboard," Uma smiled at Pishi again, unconsciously inflecting the masculine pronoun so that the world would know that it refered to her husband. Pishi seemed lost in another world and Uma wondered if she had ever been inside this room earlier.

The *Sanchaita*, perhaps the most popular collection of Tagore's poems, was pushed to the back of the cupboard as though someone was trying to hide it from prying eyes. Uma was a little surprised. She knew that there were at least two other volumes of this collection in Kailash: one upstairs with Rudra's poetry collection and another as part of the Tagore collection in this very room. Besides Rudra's habits were rather neat and meticulous and of an order that must have been so from childhood itself. So who could have crammed the thick volume behind other books in this cupboard thus?

The spine seemed a little cracked. The thin pages of the *Sanchita* were a creamy yellow.

Pishi came and sat quietly behind her.

Uma opened the book and turned the page.

❈ ❈

In Kailash thus another woman came into Haimanti's life without her consent. She could only say to Shashishekhar in her soft voice, "The family is too westernized. A poetry reading and piano playing girl can never make a good wife or daughter-in-law."

"The world is changing and besides she need not do either in Kailash if you don't like it."

"Then why have her here at all?"

"You won't understand."

There was nothing left to be said after that.

The marriage took place.

Haimanti knew that she was right. But she also knew her place.

Ashutosh stood next to the trembling young bride in red and gold at the threshold of Kailash. Haimanti ululated with the other women and touched the bride's forehead with the winnowing tray in a symbolic gesture of fertile prosperity. She had to hold aloft the tray, the bride was taller than her. Ashutosh smiled at his mother. Like a sheep, thought Haimanti. It was in that instant that the amorphous dislike took shape and possessed her. Of the new bride and her life ahead with Haimanti's handsome son who had always been so considerate of his mother. She knew all that would change now.

I have spent all my married life on the edge, for how could I tell when that other woman might not appear and take my husband away? He has already brought home that arrogant creature with green eyes. I have done my duty as best I could yet I have no say in Kailash. I have no say in Kailash, the house that my father bought for me. It is being taken over by other women.

The chant rose from deep within Haimanti as she waved the winnowing tray in the prescribed manner to welcome home the new bride.

Then she stood aside to let the couple enter. Ashutosh and Shivani.

The women blew the conch.

Laughter.

Only Haimanti's heart seemed heavy. Her thoughts continued their chase.

And so a new life was set in motion in Kailash.

※ ※

"He nutan esho tumi sampurna gagan purna kari…."

Let the new dawn fill the sky entire. …

Uma peered at the ink written words that were faded but legible still on the fly leaf of the *Sanchaita*. Clearly the book had been a gift. Below that penned message another hand in rounded characters proclaimed ownership of the book.

'Shivani ~~Devi~~ Dasi'.

Shivani, Rudra' mother and Ashutosh's wife.

In the book now held by Uma, the middle word, Devi, had been crossed out and Dasi added in a different ink. Obviously marriage had ordained the change and 'Devi' had become a 'Dasi', in the manner of Shivani's time. Shivani had followed the prescribed path to reach Kailash: from a goddess to a serving woman. Yet 'Devi' remained in the middle, under erasure but not gone.

Uma recalled that Ma had mentioned a ritual question that would be asked of the son when he first brought home his bride.

"What have you brought son?" the groom's mother would ask.

"A maid for you, Ma," the dutiful son would reply.

Kaku in his inimitable style had said, "A blister for you Ma," causing nervous laughter.

And she, Uma? She had taken to calling herself Mrs Rudra Chattopadhyay, unthinkingly abandoning twenty years, consenting to travel by the earmarked path to live in Kailash. Uma touched the alphabets of her mother-in-law's name gently and recalled the letters in Ashutosh's bedside table.

"It is her book." Pishi's voice stirred the silence in the room as she suddenly peered over Uma's shoulders in the unfocussed manner of those who cannot read. "Can you find the poem in it? Her favourite? The one that I told you about? Of a girl in a city of stone? She used to read that very often. Even I learnt to recite some of those lines. I thought I would remember them forever. But I don't now."

"In the end one forgets everything." Uma thought of the green house in Delhi.

"Almost everything," Pishi sighed consent.

There seemed to be something inserted between the pages of Tagore's collected poems. Very carefully Uma drew it out. A young Ashutosh smiled from an old photograph clearly sent from England. Unmindfully Uma turned it over and saw the scribble, '*mone pare*? – Think of me?' She put it back very carefully and in so doing looked at the page and read the title '*Bodhu*'-Bride.

"Have you found the poem?" asked Pishi.

Uma knew she had. Pishi touched her arm gently, "Will you read it aloud? For me?"

And Uma did.

> "'*bela je pare elo, jalke chal'|*
> *Purano shei shure*
> *ke jeno dake dure-*
> *Kotha she chaya shakhi, kotha she jal!....*
> *Haye re rajdhani pashankaya!*
> *Birat muthitale*
> *chapiche drira bale*
> *Byakul balikare, nahiko maya|...* "

> 'The day declines let's go get water.'
> That old refrain
> does sound in vain
> The shade and the river, my friend, where have
>   they gone!...
> Alas! Capital stone city
> Its giant's fist
> with force does grist
> the girl perplexed, without pity....'"

The clock ticked.

"Tell me Pishi, have you ever been happy in Kailash?"

Pishi looked around the library as though she too was seeing the room through another lens, in another time.

Uma asked again. "Tell me Pishi, have you ever been happy in Kailash?"

❦❦

Haimanti stood in the dark parlour, cloaked in unhappiness. Kailash slept. Or it should. Why was there still the tinkle of bangles and whispers from one room? Haimanti was not eavesdropping, she had come out of her own room as had become her habit, as she often did to check if her children were sleeping all right. She had never liked her husband's new fangled notions of forcing the children to sleep on their own.

"It builds their character. The nation's too. Europe is what it is because of this," Shashishekhar had said years ago.

"How?" Haimanti had asked, alarmed and upset.

"You won't understand," Shashishekhar had admonished.

How do you negotiate that inflexible statement?

Haimanti had taken to visiting the children while they slept, drawing a sheet over tender bodies slack in sleep, shutting a window, straightening a limb. Sometimes stroking to calm the wild terror of a nightmare or putting a glass of water to parched lips. It was not easy to be a mother. Fatherhood was different. You won't understand.

A laugh in a deep male voice was quickly smothered. A female voice whispered something.

Haimanti's ears burnt in the dark. She moved unthinkingly towards the stairs. Ashu had never shut his door so firm. Her son had never laughed like that. The marriage was not even a month old and already he seemed a stanger. She should not have left him a bachelor for so long. Stifled desires break out with much greater force.

Haimanti held on to the banister.

Her son was born after two daughters. She had been worried. Her husband's family had a tradition of naming sons after Lord Shiva. She had fretted. What if she failed? Would he then go back to … ? Shashishekhar did not say anything about wanting a son, not even when her second child was a daughter again. But then who could tell what was going on in a man's mind?

Haimanti's own mother was more explicit, "How can you be my daughter and not produce a son? You must try harder. Pray to Shiva. Observe all the bratas of Sashthi who presides over childbirth and children."

Haimanti did. Fasting practically through the week at times.

Ashutosh had made her proud. Fulfilled her being.

Haimanti treaded the stairs unseeingly.

Ashu fast asleep with traces of milk on his lips, a soft heavy weight against her breast. Ashu held up, kicking his legs in the air, standing shyly by the door and then running into her open arms. Ashu held by the cheek to get his thick curls combed, wiping his hand on the end of her saree. Ashu looking up from the landing to see his mother as soon as he returned home, from school, college or work. Ashu reading a book lost to the world yet looking up with a smile when she got him a glass of sharbat of the golden yellow bel, a favourite fruit of the god he was named after.

Haimanti stopped in the dark landing.

Ashu always asked, 'Is there enough for you Ma?" whenever he wanted a second helping.

Ashu never said, "You won't understand." He came home and told her of his school and college. He told her and not his father that he would rather teach history than look after the family business. And when he did join his father at The Ganges Press, he told her about his work and the world outside. He walked back home to her after attending a public bonfire of foreign cloth where he caught a glimpse of Gandhiji. He talked to her of the Mahatma, heroes and martyrs with dreams in his eyes. It had frightened her, though she did not show it. Keep him safe, she had prayed, when he returned home after walking with the long procession that followed the bier of the revolutionary Jatin Das. "He died on the 64th day of a hunger strike to improve the status of political prisoners, Ma," said Ashu. His eyes had looked wild that day. Her heart had lurched. She had not asked him if his father knew how he had spent his day.

Ashu shared his life and his thoughts with her. But he won't any more. How could she match one who could read his books and write letters to him? How could she fight the charms of youth? It is nature, Haimanti told herself. The old gives way to the young.

But still the tears came. Feminine tears, her husband would have said. But would he be able to hand over his office keys without a backward glance? One fine day? Would he make way for a younger one just like that? Would he not wonder if the usurper was honest, able, trustworthy? Should he not find out if his business was in safe hands before retiring?

Haimanti stood on the landing on one and a half storey and pressed her fist against her mouth to check the cry of anguish. She had not meant to be thus. She had meant to be happy for Ashu, for all of them. Her god knew.

❀ ❀

"Tell me Pishi, have you ever been happy in Kailash?" Uma had asked Pishi and she had only smiled but later in the quiet of her room on one a half storey Pishi allowed the question its play. Happy? She could not say that but certainly it was a lightness of being. Pishi could describe it in no other way, that bright patch of three days in her otherwise blurred life in Kailash. The three days when she had treaded the air.

It all started as she consoled the young bride of Ashutosh who missed her home, its familiar ways and chiefly her mother. "Don't you, don't you miss your mother too?" Shivani had asked again and again the lady with green eyes who seemed to be a kindred soul in the alien space of Kailash. A friendship, warm and sustaining, grew between the woman and the girl despite differences.

And then one afternoon, which had become their hour, Shivani looked into the green eyes and said, "I have thought of something. I have been waiting and waiting to tell you. But how does one get you alone in this big house? You are always downstairs and I am not allowed to..." She did not finish the sentence. She did try to be loyal.

"What is it?"

"Shut your eyes. Oh dear, no. Not yet."

The excitement touched Pishi too.

"You are happy today." She looked fondly at the young bride of Ashutosh. "Tell me. What is this mysterious plan that you have hatched? Will you go to England with your husband?"

A shadow flitted across Shivani's face. "These people won't allow it. My father had asked." But soon she perked up again. "I have been thinking why don't we get your mother here?"

Her heart lurched caught off guard. The world stood still. Shivani prattled on.

"One more person won't matter so much in this big house and in any case I have asked my mother. I have told her about you. She said that if Kailash can't, or does not want to keep your mother, she will be only too happy to let your mother stay with her. She does feel a little lonely now that I am married, she says. But isn't this a grand idea?" Shivani put her arms around the green eyed one.

The green glittered. She tried to steady herself and remember who she was. And where. And how. But the birds twittered. The coconut palms gently swayed their leaves and the sunlight glowed golden. Throwing pride to the wind then she asked, "Will they allow it? Can she come?"

"I will ask myself," said Shivani as though taking an oath but looked a little nervous.

The green eyed one carried on with her life as usual but it was not the same. Her mind was abuzz with other sounds and images.

Ma this is the staircase. My room is half way up there. Why are you scared? It is just like climbing up the bank from the river.

Ma would stay in her room. She would get the food up. Together they would eat it, sitting on the floor and pretending it was home. But what if they didn't allow cooked rice to be brought up? It would not matter, she would take her mother down after everyone finished in the kitchen. In the late afternoon, the house would be drowsy with sleep. The two of them would eat then. How much would Ma eat anyway? They did not ration her food and it would be enough for the two of them. Ma's saree would be worn thin but she could wear hers. Ma would not wear a blouse though. 'You have become a memsahib', Ma would say in wonder looking at her daughter's blouse. And the taps? Would she agree to bathe with captive water? She could not take Ma to the river, how could she, when she herself had not seen it since the day that she entered Kailash? She would show Ma the curve of the drive from her window. But she would tell her that beyond the shaded green and the iron gates lie the streets. She would confess that she had not been out herself ever since she entered Kailash. But when the house would sleep at night she would take Ma up to the terrace. They would sit under the starry sky. A soft wind would rustle the leaves. After a while they would go down to her room on one and a half storey. Not the bed, not for me, Ma would whisper. Not for me either, she would reply and spread the sheet on the floor and lie down beside Ma and talk in whispers, perhaps into the long night or till a gentle sleep drifted down upon them. And in the morning Ma would still be there and she would quietly slip down to begin another day in Kailash.

Thus she lived on in her mind seeing Kailash anew through her mother's wonderstruck rustic eyes, recalling her mother through the loving haze of nostalgia, with a longing that had been layered over in time, frozen and hidden. And so it came to be that she who had always been so very sensitive to her surroundings, lost touch with reality. She did not even see those significant registers of hope dashed: Shivani's embarrassed smiles and downcast eyes.

❦❦

She could be on an island and not at home. Grey water cascaded from the sky relentlessly. Uma had worked her way through the library, dusting and looking for the goddess as the low caste. It held reading Neelkantha's *Chandimangal* at bay.

She had gone through all but the cupboards at the end of the long library which rested in the darkest alcove. Uma drew back the curtains from the nearest windows but they refused to let in any light, conspiring with the sky. This close, she could make out that there was a door behind the cupboards. Clearly the kitchen could once be approached from here. But now three cupboards blocked the way. The one at the centre was tall and heavy. The two shorter ones on either side were full of novels carrying the oval logo of The Ganges Press. The shapes in the tall cupboard in the middle were different. These were long and flat. Intrigued, Uma opened the cupboard.

The files were classified as literature, philosophy, religion, etc. Clearly these were manuscripts sent by aspiring authors to The Ganges Press. All were marked with one word in red ink: 'Reject'. Yet someone had carefully catalogued and preserved them. Surely there must be something special about these rejected manuscripts to have been brought to Kailash from The Ganges Press?

The dust tickled her nose. One by one she took out all the manuscripts and rubbed the shelf clean.

The rain continued to fall. Sweat trickled down Uma's scalp and back. It ran down her legs under the folds of the saree and petticoat. The fan was faithfully stirring the confined air in the room but even that did not quite reach where Uma sat. Two shelves were done. She got up to open a window but a spray of water splattered a vase. Carefully she wiped it off and returned to her position by the cupboard. The window was left partly ajar. She took down more of the rejected manuscripts and paused to look at the titles, reading a line here, a comment there.

"You are alone here. Don't you feel scared?" Khema's voice sounded hollow at this end of the room and startled Uma.

"What's there to be scared of?"

"I don't know. All these books that stare at you silently? You don't know what they contain."

Uma asserted herself, "Books never harm anyone."

"I would not know that," Khema came a little closer. "Have you found it?"

"What?"

"The books which say that the goddess was ours. Once upon a time."

It was beginning to irritate Uma a little, this assumption of familiarity on Khema and Bamundi's part. She merely shook her head and turned to her task. Or rather turned away from Khema. A mild smell of mildew forced Khema's presence upon her consciousness though. It stayed. Finally Uma turned again.

"Do you want something?" But she felt mean even as she finished her curt question and tried to take the sting out of it with a smile.

"Oh yes. I came to ask you if I should clear the puja room upstairs? Have you finished your lakkhi *puja*?"

It was Thursday.

"Hmm. That is why I am here," Uma was brief.

"You finished early today. Usually you take much longer."

There. That familiar tone again. Instantly Uma regretted smiling. This time she kept quiet and carried on with the files.

But Khema was looking at her. "Are you feeling all right, Boudi? Your face is flushed. Would you like to eat something? Or drink some lime water? Or coconut water? You like that, don't you? Shall I get it here?" Uma turned again from where she sat on the floor. Khema's fine head of hair glistened with rain drops. Sweat ran down her throat to plaster the faded blouse to her body. Uma recalled the girl in Khema's story who had been discarded by her upper caste lover because she worked like a menial. Had she sweated like this when she built a hut for her man? Something like shame flickered inside Uma. She wished she was a more resolute person. She could always be easily persuaded.

"No, I don't want anything. I did not feel like reading the bratakatha in such detail today so I finished with lakkhi *puja* early. I wanted to find the other books. Our books. The ones that may have the poems about the goddess as a…a Bagdi or a Dombi. I don't think that the gods would hold that against me." She added with a smile again, "My Kaku always teased my grandmother about reading the same bratakatha every Thursday. 'The goddess must be bored of it too.' He would say 'Why don't you read the newspaper to your goddess instead, to let Lakkhi know what is happening in her world?'"

"Your uncle sure knows how to rib."

The library rang with their laughter. But Khema had other chores waiting.

Silence engulfed the dark corner of Kailash, and Uma, once again.

※※

She shut her green eyes for a brief while, gutting them of their dreams. She felt foolish, utterly so, and exposed too. She should have known that it was a ridiculous suggestion. She had lost her bearing for a while. She gathered herself stiffly, forcing her heart and mind to be absolutely blank. "It is all right. It really is," she said though she wished that she did not have to speak just then.

Shivani's contrite face was red. She would not look up. She shook her head looking down at her toenails still. A tear escaped. Shivani rubbed at it, like a thief.

"Don't take it so. You did try," she said and the words were dry.

"But that is not enough. I try but it is never enough."

"For me it is. I never thought that you would actually ask your father-in-law."

"What does it matter who I ask if the answer is no? Maybe it was my fault. I should not have asked him in the morning when he may have been preoccupied, worried about his work. But I could bear it no longer. I had thought of it all night long. I tried talking to my...." Shivani paused. There were certain things that one could not share with anyone. Not even with one's best friend. Shivani turned her face away to hide her failure and looked at the green of trees in the big garden on that side of the terrace. She had heard women laugh there. 'I don't know about your family but we don't mix with people like the Seals,' her mother-in-law had said. Shivani turned her gaze away from the garden and looked into the tired green eyes of her friend who said, "Let it be."

In the evening Khagen halted Pishi near the staircase, "You have been called. Babu wants to see you." Khagen kept his voice low, ever alert that the kitchen was full of ears.

"Where?" She did not raise her voice or lower it either.

"The library. Now."

Shadows danced on the wall.

Shashishekhar was sitting behind the big table with Haimanti standing by his side.

"I will leave." Haimanti was gone soft as the wind even before he could say anything.

"Come in." Shashishekhar invited Pishi across the depths of the dark room to where he sat in a pool of light.

She held Shashishekhar's gaze steadily.

"You asked the new bride if your mother could come to Kailash."

Not quite but it did not matter. And in any case it was not a question.

Silence.

Shashishekhar cleared his throat. "That is not possible."

She spoke then, "I have heard that."

The green eyes were burning into him. It made him uneasy and Shashishekhar, about to shuffle the papers on the table in an awkward gesture, caught himself just in time, "Your mother can not come here because she is no more. I am sorry. I did not tell you earlier because I saw no point. You are here. The village is far away. There was nothing that you could do."

Someone opened and shut a door in the depths of the house rather loudly. Then there was only silence again. She stood erect, waiting.

Shashishekhar finally looked at her again, "I too got to know of it much later."

"I will be required in the kitchen now. Dinner is being cooked."

"I gave her money on your behalf. I would like you to know."

She walked out of the room.

He looked at the manuscript on the table for a while and then dipped his pen in the pot of red ink.

❦

I must ask Khema to shut doors a little gently, thought Uma. But her rancour had vanished. The library seemed to bring in some sunlight with Khema's laughter. The rain had thinned.

Strange how Kashmere Gate stole upon her at such odd moments. It was almost lunch time. Did her place at the table stare her mother in the face? Rudra had said that they might visit Delhi during Durga puja. But autumn seemed very far. No letters had come last week from Delhi. Even the post takes rainy day holidays, Rudra had joked. Uma had felt a little let down that he did not ask her if she would like to book a trunk call to Delhi. And she felt embarrassed to suggest it on her own.

The rejected manuscripts lay heavy on her lap and around her. A few nestled in the cupboard still.

A weak ray of sunshine peered in through the window and splayed across the glass pane of the cupboard. There must be a rainbow in the sky. 'A fox is getting married to a dog', Thakma would always say on seeing that colourful arc spread against the pale blue sky that drizzled. Vibgyor. Dadu had taught her the word. Uma had taken it to be a mystical one that let her into the secret of nature. Violet, indigo, blue, green, yellow, orange and red. Vibgyor.

With sudden vigour Uma wiped the shelf as far as she could and then reached inside to take down the last lot.

The Evolution of the Mother Goddess.

The red ink had slashed the proposed title with some force and then written with a flourish: 'Goddesses do not evolve. They are.'

It was Shashishekhar's arrogant, aggressive red.

Uma knew the title though not the book.

"*Dadu?*

Dida?"

There was a tiny brass catch set in the shelf at Uma's eye level. How come she did not notice it earlier? She sat still, absolutely still, staring at it. The rain dripped now not from the sky but the eaves to run through the sewage pipes. She did not want to look at the manuscript and confirm what she knew already, what she knew she would confirm anyway.

"*Dadu?*
Dida?"

Did she really play that game those many years ago? The tiny brass catch glistened dully at her. What if she put the manuscript, the rejected manuscript, back? Who would be wiser? Who would know? Who would want to know? She was used to playing hide and seek with herself.

"*Dadu?*
Dida?"

Her grandfather had gentle myopic eyes behind thick glasses. Over the years Dadu had merged with the photograph in the drawing room. She remembered no other but what they told her of him. A nice husband, a nice father, a nice father-in-law, a nice grandfather, a nice neighbour, a nice man. Nice. Nice. Nice. And a failure too? A gentleman and a failure. Did they say so? Was it in the air? In the dark of the night hissed across the eldest son's marital bed? Hurled as an accusation by the wife from the sweltering kitchen? A snide remark? A casual joke? Never meant seriously but there in the shadows in arched back insinuations? Entirely made up like the rhythm in her ears?

"*Dadu?*
Dida?"

The Evolution of the Goddess. The few copies in the book case in Dadu's room were part of her childhood and youth. She had dusted them, used them as paper weights, held them to draw straight lines, mentioned it occasionally to some friends and once after marriage to Rudra. But she had never thought of reading the book that Dadu had written, the one for which he had sold some of Thakma's jewellery. Nobody else had read it in Kashmere Gate as far as she could tell.

"*Dadu?*
Dida?"

A pair of bicycle clips. Kaku kept them in his drawer now. Dadu used to clip his trousers before setting off on his bicycle. Thakma had cried when Baba bought his first car. It was a second hand

Baby Hindustan. The family had gathered round it in excitement when Kapoor uncle from Baba's office had driven it home for Baba was still taking driving lessons. "Your father would have been very happy," Thakma said looking at the car. Baba had held his mother in a gentle embrace. But, sitting in Kailash now Uma wondered. Would Dadu have been happy? Would it have mattered to him if none of them cared about what mattered to him? Not even those who loved him?

"*Dadu?*

Dida?"

No one seemed to have read Dadu's book, not any one whom she knew at any rate. Except Shashishekhar, Rudra's grandfather. And there it lay rejected in the cupboard in Kailash where she lived now. It pricked at her, this revelation that Rudra's grandfather had rejected hers, that the Chattopadhyays had won in some secret way, that they were superior. True, she herself had granted Kailash a superior status on her own. But to have it stated thus?

Uma looked down then at the manuscript, as she knew she would eventually.

Dadu's name gently lapped the arrogant red, like water, as was his name.

"This is offal to be burnt," the red ink said. Shashishekhar would have been new to his profession when he read Dadu's work but clearly he knew his mind already. He also knew that he would make up the minds of others. Dadu had been told that his manuscript could not be returned. It was that bad. He had gone back to Barishal broken. But there he had put the pieces together again. He had published his own book with Thakma's jewellery.

Uma turned the pages and noted that the red was everywhere. Sometimes as question marks, sometimes as ticks but predominantly as crosses. Page after page she turned, following the red. She could not bring herself to shut either the manuscript or her eyes.

※ ※

Ashutosh looked into the red rimmed eyes of his wife. He cupped her face and then spread his fingers slowly on that smooth surface as though to drain out her sorrow.

Shivani reached up and held his hand against her face. "I have to go to her."

His thumb was on her lips.

"I have to go to her, you do understand, don't you? Her mother is no more. I did not know that. She did not either. She is alone in her room. All alone. I have to go to her. Shall I go?"

The words caressed his fingers. The breath tingled all through him from there. His passion smouldered.

Thus no one came to knew if a vigil was being kept in that small room on one and a half storey, whether the green eyes shed water or burnt through the night, whether a head banged the inflexible wall of Kailash, leant against the cool iron bars of its window or simply lay on the pillow exhausted and defeated.

But the sun rose as usual and the afternoon followed.

Shivani put her arms around her and said, "But I am here. I will always be here for you."

She nodded slowly, a little preoccupied.

"Shall I read?" Shivani asked after a while.

She nodded again, it was easier to agree. One did not have to talk then.

Shivani read.

> 'bela je pare elo, jalke chal|'
> Purano shei shure
> ke jeno dake dure-
> Kotha she chaya shakhi, kotha she jal!....

> "The day declines let's go get water.'
> That old refrain
> does sound in vain
> The shade and the river, my friend, where have they gone!..."

A kite whistled. Somewhere in the sky.

A few months later, Rudra arrived.

One morning, carrying a bundle of washed nappies to Shivani's room, she suddenly caught herself in the mirror. She had never noticed the silver in her hair before. Or that the beds in which the green eyes rested had fine wrinkles.

Shivani looked up at her with a smile, tickled a chubby toe and said to her baby, 'Look who has come. Pishi!'

Thus she was drawn into the family years after she had come to Kailash and made Ashutosh's honorary sister in one easy gesture by Shivani. And thus when hardly any trace remained in Kailash of the engrossed mother or that gurgling baby, the word remained as an echo of that moment for gradually everyone took to calling her Pishi.

❧ Thirteen ❧

Pishi and the others were already in the kitchen by the time Uma forced herself to finish a late lunch.

"Did you find the books?" Khema asked.

"Did you?" Bamundi repeated.

'The book?" Uma repeated looking up with lost eyes but the sudden sharp green gaze made her gather herself. "No. Not today."

"Aw." Khema and Bamundi's disappointment merged and clouded the kitchen.

"I will look again. The books will remain in the library if they are there. They won't run away." Uma tried to make light of her dereliction of duty.

"We know a lot of stories too but we can't read any. If you don't find it for us then …"

Uma looked up then, "I will."

"But supposing it is not there?" Khema persisted.

"Then I will go to other libraries. Bigger ones. The National Library where the government has collected all the old books." They all looked at her. They had heard her say it a few times before but not with this degree of resolution.

Khema looked at the others and then asked a little suspiciously, "This, this government place that you talk about, they keep *all* books, all *the* books? Even those about Dombis?"

"Almost all." Uma, shaken by what she had found in the library, found it a strain to carry on with the conversation, yet she hesitated to just get up and leave. Pishi's watchful silence bothered her too and she wondered uneasily if Pishi was already aware in some strange way, of what Uma had found in the library. So she said, "Shall I read for a while now?"

"They have kept our stories also? The government? Really?" Khema was still not convinced.

"When did the government listen to us?" Bamundi intervened. "Are you sure that is the place where you should begin the search?"

"We have to begin somewhere."

Years later Uma wished she could remember who had said that. Pishi? Khema? Bamundi? Or in one burst of unfamiliar drive, she herself?

❊❊

There was a burst of red on the terrace. Ashutosh had taken to gardening with a vengeance when he learnt of his imminent fatherhood, handling it all on his own: soil, manure and trowel. He grew just roses. Dark red and velvety. The roses grew all along the terrace and in clusters too here and there.

"We did not know this Ashutosh," Pishi told Shivani who looked a little wan. Rudra toddled back and forth. The child was irritated and rosy hued. He threatened to put everything in his mouth.

"This child did not sleep well again at night. I felt so worried that his crying would wake up the household. It was not this bad with his first tooth."

"Everyone knows that children have teething trouble. They will understand," Pishi tried to reassure Shivani again.

"I wish I could go home. For a while. My sisters-in-law went home each time they had a child," Shivani sighed again.

Pishi said nothing. The first born, and the several thereafter, were traditionally born at the mother's family out of consideration for the finer feelings of the nauseous and swollen mother-to-be. It also helped to let the natal family pay the expenses and fend the hazards of childbirth including death. But the Chattopadhays had kept Shivani with them in Kailash. They knew how to shoulder responsibilities.

"She is ours as much as yours," Shashishekhar had told Shivani's father genially.

"But of course. More so," Shivani's father had responded with equal grace though he had come to ask formally if his daughter could be with her parents for a while till the baby was born. The gifts he had got as appropriate acknowledgement of the news that his daughter would give birth in the near future to the next generation of the Chattopadhyays, were taken inside by the family retainers who had accompanied him. A conch blew from within Kailash.

Tea and trays of snacks arrived for the two gentlemen in the parlour who were soon engrossed in a deep discussion of the finer points of the Gandhi-Irwin pact, whether Irwin had really treated Gandhi as an equal and whether Willingdon would eventually be willing to meet the Congress demands. Gandhi's increasing love for the harijans, the lower castes, caused some caustic comments and both wondered if it had anything to do with the British behaviour with Ambedkar.

"But the day will come when this land will be ours once again, the English will return to their own," said Mr. Banerji as he took his leave.

And Shivani remained in Kailash.

"Don't look like that," Ashutosh consoled his wife that evening, "You may call me selfish but I am glad you are still in Kailash and not gone with your father. I can't meet you everyday if you go to your parents."

Shivani feeling heavy in more ways than one leaned against the window frame.

Ashutosh touched her gently on the shoulder and said, "Don't you know that the God I am named after could not stay without his wife either and went to her parents' house once in the guise of a bangle seller? Would you have me do that?"

"Did you then tell your mother that I should stay in Kailash till, till the child arrives?" The last bit was said in a rush. It was only extreme frustration that drove Shivani to refer to her indelicate state.

"No," said Ashutosh and then added, "Not quite. But mothers understand without words being exchanged."

* *

"They did not let her come?" asked Shivani's anxious mother as soon as her husband returned.

"What's the hurry? Ashutosh will go to England soon. Shivani can come and stay here then, with the baby."

"If they let her come then. Did they like the tattva?" Shivani's mother had spent a frantic few days putting together the appropriate gifts for this visit. Priests and ladies of the family had been consulted and each item vetted.

Her husband nodded absent-mindedly. He did not grudge having to pay for Ashutosh's edifying trip to England. It had been part of the marriage deal. It was also overdue. He liked his serious son-in-law. He wished he could pack off his youngest son too, far away from the turbulence that increasingly threatened even the middle and upper class homes where the young, steadily growing disillusioned with Gandhian constraints, were seeking alternative roads to freedom: terrorism, mass struggle or communism. There were some passionate advocates of these alternative modes within the large Banerji clan itself.

"Has your youngest son returned home or is he attending some rally again?" Shivani's father sharply cut short his wife's comparison of their own behaviour with the daughters-in-law with Kailash's.

The answer came just as sharp, "Why does he need to go out? There are enough people to incite the young ones within your family itself, in this very house," but then Shivani's mother lapsed into silence and thought of her daughter who could not visit her when she needed to, when she was about to become a mother herself. Her husband grew silent too thinking about the nation and his youngest son's growing involvement with the struggle for its freedom.

* *

The civil disobedience movement, the flaming agitations, the counter repressions and the increasing attacks on British officials in the city and the country could not wind their way through the heavy iron gates and the curving drive of Kailash. Occasionally a rumbling from the streets or a faint disgruntled murmur of a mob did try to invade its recesses to draw out its inmates. But Shashishekhar was an able guard.

On the terrace of Kailash however these matters of the nation were sometimes aired.

Shivani looked at Pishi who was carefully stitching a spread from the used and softened sarees for Rudra, "My mother stitches very well too." And then, "Ma used to send my brother to Kailash earlier to meet me but he told me the last time that he has to work for the country now. He cannot waste his time on these visits. 'Do you know that a District Magistrate of Tippera was assassinated by two school girls, Santi and Suniti Chaudhuri? They are fighting for the nation and you just worry for your baby,' my brother said the last time." Shivani was clearly proud of these filial admonitions. "He said that he would not come here at all but for your cooking."

"I thought he was complaining about salt the last time, or so word carried to the kitchen?" Pishi smiled. The blue thread in her needle was spreading an undulating river on the soft white spread.

"Salt? Really? Salt? Oh that must have been my brother talking about Mahatma Gandhi's earlier Dandi march to the Gujarat sea shore. It was a protest against the salt tax of the Britsh government. A tax is…tax…"

"I understand tax."

"The Mahatma is amazing," Shivani lowered her voice, "but two of my cousin brothers disagree with the Mahatma and his ways. There is some tension in my family over that. These cousins feel that there should be a mass upsurge. The British should be terrorised into leaving our country. You know there was an armoury raid in Chittagong…"

"Chittagong?" Pishi loked up sharply.

"Yes. A group of revolutionaries, lead by Surya Sen, seized the local armoury and fought a pitched battle on the Jalalabad Hill. They issued a proclamation of Indian Independence in the name of…."

Chittagong.

Chittagong with its mountains and rivers. The sea. The villages. And of the villages none so dear as Kynsa mati where the dark water of Padma pukur lapped its shore and women gathered in groups talking in a quick tongue that echoed the flow of the many rivulets and rivers which rushed ahead to meet the sea.

Pishi interrupted Shivani, "Tell me, when this nation of yours is independent will everything be different?"

※ ※

The rains seemed loath to let go, autumn a reluctant debutante. But an occasional cool morning breeze, a sharp blue sky, the solitary swaying soft white head of a precocious kashphool, a mellow glow of the sun or a mass of white cloud did tell the world that come she will. And the goddess with her.

In the kitchen in Kailash each of the four women seemed somewhat preoccupied. Discrete. Different.

Bamundi worried about her son. He was almost always at home either in a restless bad temper or stupefied with cheap country liqour. She had mentioned the autumn festivities to him once, only in an attempt to cheer him up, but he had snarled back at her. "Puja? What puja? The factory itself may shut down. Some other drum will beat then. Don't bare your teeth at me in a smile. Old fool. Puja indeed!" It went on then, his vitriolic litany of woes whose still point was his mother for bringing him into this world.

Khema worried about her daughters. She had wanted them to be with her but her mother-in-law had taken them to the village. A letter had arrived from her the previous morning. Her mother-in-law wanted money. The rains had trammelled the roof in one part of the house in the village and the wind had blown the cowshed off. No one could say yet if the harvest would see them through the year. They hardly had any rice in stock, her mother-in-law's postcard said. The children should be grateful that even in old age their old mother was able to hold the homestead together. The least they could do was to send her money regularly without reminder. And look after their father who had stayed back in Kailash. The letter, dictated to the village post man, did not mention Khema's daughters. The young girls who stayed with the grandmother in a hut with a part of the roof gone. Khema's girls who were young and budding had only an old woman to mind them in a world of uncles, cousins, nephews and neighbours.

Uma thought of her grandfather's manuscript nestling amidst her unwanted wedding sarees. The rejection of it by Kailash rankled and made her feel now small, now resentful. It was a heavy weight in her heart and she carried it alone, unable to share it with either Kailash or Kashmere Gate. She was curious too. Why was the file marked 'offal to be burnt', preserved? What did the ticks mean in a sea of crosses? Uma could not bear to put it back in the cupboard where it would lie lost, forgotten, dismissed. She could not betray Dadu thus. Not any more. Not here. Yet she did not want other eyes to chance upon it either. She longed for a space of her own for it. Entirely her own. Not mysterious or secretive but just her own. But there was none in Kailash. Not even a cupboard. And she had found it so very romantic.

A few days after the wedding, Rudra had opened the cupboard in their bedroom and then turning towards Uma had said that he liked seeing her clothes in it. "It just had the ubiquitous black, white and grey earlier. You brought colour into it."

Uma's being had taken a roseate hue.

They shared cupboards: the older heavier one in the bedroom that had come with Rudra's grandmother as well as the lighter, modern one that came with Uma and was kept in the anteroom next to the one with the mirror that had come with her mother-in-law, Shivani. The last shelf in this contained those sarees that came to Uma as wedding gifts and were waiting to be redistributed on suitable, similar occasions for she did not like them.

Carefully Uma slid Dadu's manuscript beneath the rejected sarees now kept in Rudra's mother's cupboard and then she wrote in a rush, to her grandmother. She knew that Thakma would be pleasantly surprised to get this unscheduled letter. How are you, Uma wrote to Thakma. How is your life? Your knees? Your stomach? Thakma, will you please send me Dadu's book? I don't know if there are more than two copies. You may wish to keep them with you. I will understand that. But should you feel that a copy may be given to me, I will be very happy. I would like to read it. I only wish that I had done so earlier…..

Thursday was not a day for posting letters in Kailash. If Khagen was surprised at being asked to post the letter as soon as possible he did not show it. If it reminded him of another afternoon, indeed if he remembered another afternoon such as this with its urgent plea to catch the post, he thought it best not to recall it. He was a servant of the house after all. Grown old in faithful service but a servant still in Kailash. He knew that.

And Uma was beginning to know that a woman, like a Brahman, was born twice. One life before marriage. Another after. She had assumed a smooth flow. The crack had appeared, thin as a knife's edge, but there.

And Pishi? Pishi looked at Uma who used to smile so easily, a little too easily perhaps. Was the smile less frequent? Had the glow dulled a bit? Was she beginning to know her place as had happened once before in Kailash with another wife?

※ ※

"Shall I read the last section of the *Chandimangal* today? The Merchant's Tale? We have spent a lot of time on the Hunter's section," Uma asked.

"The Merchant's Tale?" Khema was suspicious again.

"She means Lahana and Khullona's story," Bamundi added sagely.

"They may call it the Merchant's Tale but I think of it as the wives' story," Pishi spoke unexpectedly.

"You mean the errant wives' tale," Bamundi cackled loudly and then lowered her spatula, "Let's hear it," she said.

The red chillies crackled and spluttered in the pan.

Khema settled down to listen too but a little uneasy, a little edgy. The hunter's tale, his travails, his wife's ways, now that was the story of her people. She could relate to that story. They were her kind of people. Those who knew poverty and want. Those who worked with their hands and knew the sun and the rain. But the upper caste poet had given the hunter's story a twist. He had made Fullora and Kalketu the creatures of a higher heaven come down to earth for a while to live out a curse. But she, Khema, knew that was a trick. Duplicitous. As the Brahmans always were. The Brahmans had always taken everything from her own people. Their labour, their stories and their gods and goddesses too. Khema wanted to talk about that betrayal instead of listening to the merchant's tale. But she was one against three in Kailash's kitchen. So Khema restrained herself and thought that if the section of the *Chandimangal* that was going to be read was about wives then that was a different matter. Perhaps. After all, the world over, women knew similar pain. Look at the goddess herself, thought Khema, look at her marriage, her household and her truant husband. Khema could relate to those too, what if she be a housemaid. So she too settled down to listen to the third and last section of the *Chandimangal*, the Merchant's Tale.

※ ※

Dhanapati was a handsome Banik, a merchant of Ujjain, married to the beautiful Lahana. One day he catches sight of a young girl frolicking in the river. He falls in love with her instantly.

> *Water from her body caught the sun for a while*
> *Silver and gold*
> *The arms rose and fell as though in a dance*
> *His heart was sold.*
> *He wondered long by the riverside*
> *How to fix the deal.*

> He must possess this young nymph or his
> Heart won't heal.

Dhanapati finds out that the girl is Khullona, the young niece of his own wife. He resolves to marry her against the tears and entreaties of his first wife whom he had loved once.

> The moon was glimmering when to the river bed
>   came
> Lahana, the merchant's first wife and she said
> To her own image in the rippling waters that
> She might as well be dead.
> My tide's out leaving eddies and swirls.
> My husband dear
> No longer wishes to plough his old field
> It is quite clear.

Young Khullona's mother, ill at ease, did not wish to marry her young daughter to the already married Banik Dhanapati either. She thought that,

> A woman's life knows many perils
> But greater none
> Than a co-wife who is also aunt to the
> Bride young.

But marriages are made in heaven and when has heaven taken note of female tears? Or dissent? The groom came and took Khullona away. She sat quietly with her head bent, her palms folded in her lap. Her heart beat frantically.

Her groom promised to look after his new possession. The Brahman presided over the ceremony.

Lahana, the older wife, spent days cleaning the house for her husband and his new wife. Her own niece. He had eyes for none other now. He had no shame either. Drawing Khullona into his arms for all to see. Lahana too had carressed her niece once, carried her in her arms, fed her milk and rice. But now whenever Lahana saw Khullona, she saw her in the arms of Dhanapati, her husband. Happy. Smitten.

> *Then rose pungent envy, though pleasure*
> *She did fake*
> *But her heart grew putrid as her own life*
> *Was at stake.*

Would her husband spend his entire life thus? Following Khullona
with his eyes. Reaching out for her. Whenever. Wherever.

But a man unlike a woman has a life beyond emotions. He must
work and Dhanapati was a Banik too. So one day he set sail leaving
Khullona at the mercy of Lahana. Lahana made Khullona sleep
on the floor, gave her rotten food to eat and sent her out to graze the
goats.

> *Khullona cried, tired, worn out*
> *And full of fear*
> *But no one heard her or could*
> *See her tears.*

Her skin lost its glow. Her hair its glaze. Her eyes were dull. Her
stomach empty. Her heart heavy.

Look at her now thought Lahana with malice, just look at her.

And then one day a tired Khullona fell asleep while grazing. Her
goats wandered away. She was terrified of Lahana's wrath. She
wandered about in the forest, crying out for her goats and for herself
too. Suddenly in the middle of the shaded green she came across a
group of women observing a brata of the goddess Mangal Chandi.
They dried her tears and led her to the goddess.

They sang:

> *Sister join us. Dry those tears.*
> *Pray to Mangal Chandi*
> *The goddess will hear*
> *All your woes*
> *Khullona did so*
> *And observed the brata.*
> *The goats returned of their own accord*
> *And from his journey*
> *Came back Khullona's Lord.*

There was a soft silence in the kitchen as Uma's voice died.

But there was a turmoil within Khema. Khullona had learnt of the goddess from women in the forest, Khema thought. What manner of women would be in the forest in the first place? What manner of women would teach and draw a stranger amidst them without worrying about caste or creed? She thought of Neelkantha and Kailash. Not their kind. Certainly not. Mangal Chandi cannot be a Brahman goddess. Khema looked around the kitchen and felt that the bond of intimacy that had been forged maybe a brief one. She must be ready for the inevitable rejection.

"If you have finished with the cutting and chopping I will take the utensils outside."

They looked at Khema, a little amazed that she should interrupt the moment thus.

Khema looked back at them. Her eyes seemed to be burning. "I have to start my evening chores," she said, "It is getting late."

※ ※

Rudra was returning home rather late these days. And then after the family dinner he immersed himself in work in their bedroom. It seemed that Rudra was determined to bring out the series on *The Other Calcuttans* and that it involved a lot of archival and editorial work.

Uma too carried books from the library to the bedroom upstairs. Sometimes as she passed it, she found that Ashutosh's bedroom door was open and he seemed to be holding a book or a magazine in the still room but not quite reading it. Uma remembered the nights in Kashmere Gate which were always full of clatter. Compassion would make her pause then in front of her father-in-law's bedroom and she would wish him a good night once again. Nodding, smiling, Asutosh would turn back to whatever he was holding in his hand and Uma too would move away after a moment's hesitation.

And then in their own bedroom Rudra would sit at the table and she on the bed, reading quietly. Occasionally they read out a line or two to each other. She asked him the meaning of a Bengali word or phrase, he sought help with the syntax of a sentence in the manuscript that he appeared to be proof reading. Thus though neither knew exactly what the other was reading, there was no sense of being entirely shut out. The silence in the room was not brittle. It helped heal Uma's sense of frailty, buried but there since the night of storm, the sense that by living in Kailash the profit was all on her side. Or so Rudra had implied, she thought, even though he had used the pronoun, 'We'.

"Come, tell us ladies, what are you going to do now?" The Head had exhorted them to speak one by one at the farewell party in college. "Other than get married I mean", she had added, and had been rewarded by the expected laughter.

Uma had gone home and narrated each moment of the event to a rapt circle of female audience – her grandmother, mother and aunt – that afternoon. "What does she mean? She wants you to wear high heel shoes and go to office every morning, swinging your bag?" Her grandmother had visibly bristled, her short, grey widow's mop almost standing up at the edge of her scalp with indignation. Ma and Kaki had laughed too. But had wonder laced their amusement?

Uma had drawn out the query once again in the privacy of her mind that night.

"Other than get married?"

There had been some predictable chorus: "Teach like you Ma'am." Only a few, three or four maybe, had indicated their desire for an entirely different path. But truth to tell, most like Uma were only waiting for marriage. Where else would they find a legitimate affiliation with romance, the security of finance, an arena for the display of uplifting feminine virtues? And yet they were the modern women of independent India. They would retain an individual singularity in their unique combination of domesticity and aestheticism. Thus they would arrange their rooms, thus they would pack the tiffins, thus they would lay the table, thus they would dress up in the evenings and ask their husbands as they returned home from work, "Did you have a good day?" Surely her dreams had come to pass and more?

Rudra shuffled some papers, gathered them neatly and put a glass paper weight on them.

Uma looked up, "The house behind Kailash. Remember you had mentioned the dark and slender Seal girls?"

"Yes?" Rudra seemed a little wary.

"Seals are from the Banik caste, merchants, no?"

"The Seals were gandhabaniks. Spice merchants. The Baniks are the merchant heroes celebrated in mangal kabyas," Rudra laughed suddenly. 'We have been merchants long before you Chattopadhyays', old Seal always told my grandfather. I always liked that crusty old man for telling Shashishekhar Chattopadhyay, the Brahman, that he was a merchant ultimately. Making a profit in the city, like so many." Rudra seemed a stranger again, his voice hard.

Profit, profit again, the unspoken word wriggled between them like a worm. Uma's gaze sliding away from Rudra was caught by the portraits of Shashishekhar and Haimanti on the wall. The vermilion in the parting of Haimanti's hair had been coloured red in the otherwise black and white portrait. Thus the men conducting business in the city had demanded the brightened purity of their secluded and chaste domestic realm lest their upper caste privilege be defiled.

Rudra drew another sheaf of papers towards himself. Uma returned to the book on her lap, she had been reading Kabikankan Mukundaram's *Chandimangal,* the eminent predecessor of Neelkantha. In this 16th century composition, some of the Hindu merchants who come for the feast at Dhanapati's house after his return bore the Muslim title Khan:

> *Panchrar banya ailo Chandidas Khan|...*
> *Vishnupurer Banya ailo Jasamanta Khan |*

> Panchra's merchant came, Chandidas Khan...
> Vishnupur's merchant came Jasamanta Khan.

A Hindu name and a Muslim title. What can it suggest but an alliance? What can it be but a social recognition of economic exigencies? The norms of society were very clearly different for men and women. Profit, profit again. Yet the same men had demanded that the Khullona who had gone to the forest to graze the goat be put through a chastity test.

Suddenly on an impulse Uma reached out for Neelkantha's *Chandimangal* from the bedside table and opened the last section, where the merchants had come to Dhanapati's to demand a chastity test of Khullona. Yes, it was as she had thought. Unlike the earlier 16th century composition, none of the merchants had individual names in Neelkantha's narrative and certainly not a hybrid Hindu-Muslim name. Had Neelkhantha overlooked his heritage? Or had Shashishekhar edited it thus while preserving the nation's culture? Could she, Uma, ask for the manuscript? The one that stayed safe in the Chattopadhya's bank locker where ordinary families kept jewellery.

Would Ashutosh comply?

Would he be angry?

&❧&

But the angry merchant clan, demanded a fine from Dhanapati.
Khullona had left the confines of the domestic realm to graze the cattle.
The circumstances did not matter.
She had gone out. Out of her home.
Was she chaste still? Pure? Good enough to remain a wife?
A woman is not strong. Her duties as wife and mother, time and again
She has failed
When prompted by her feminine self. Find out if Khullona was chaste
While you sailed.
So said the clan.
Khullona declared that she would not allow Dhanapati to pay the
fine. She would rather face a trial of chastity.
Arrogance, arrogance went the whisper. Retribution would follow.
Every one knew that.
But Khullona triumphed over every trial. She could not be burnt or
buried or drowned. Naturally. She had the goddess on her side.
And so happiness is restored.

"Whose?" asked Bamundi.

'Whose?' echoed the kitchen in Kailash.

Uma read.

> *The merchant clan justified their concern, reminding Dhanapati of*
> *Sita and Radha. Though goddesses, both are known to have crossed*
> *the sacred threshold*
> *the pain and the shame that followed the sages have described*
> *for all to behold.*

And the women remembered their own lives once again.

❀ ❀

Pishi tried later to remember how the day had begun. But there was nothing to mark it as out of the ordinary. Nothing to show that the dark clouds were gathering somewhere out of sight. It was late April. The sky was clear and blue. The sun bright and merciless, battering the world with its heat. Furious and terrible. Fierce. Rudra.

And Rudra was five.

The mingled aroma of freshly ground green cardamom, fine rice, milk and sugar filled the kitchen. The creamy mixture thickened and bubbled gently on the stove. Pishi stirred it from time to time. Maids walked in and out of the bigger kitchen in Kailash. They knew it was the grandson's birthday. They knew that they would get something too. But not now. Their turn would come after the gods, and the family, had eaten. Still they turned their heads ever so slightly following the heady aroma that came from the recess set aside from the main kitchen and then carried on with their chores. The recess was the vegetarian section. Pure vegetarian. Meals were cooked here for the household deities, the priests and the widows of the family but on a separate fire, when they came on visits. And on special occasions.

And today was special. Rudra was turning five today.

Shivani came into the kitchen. The starch in her new saree crackled and made her sweat. The day was still young but the sun was rapidly drying the dew on the grass, burning up the cool morning air. It promised to be a blazing day.

"Is it ready?" she asked Pishi

"Almost." Carefully Pishi drained the water from a small bowl and added the raisins to the payesh.

"Did you use the fine rice, Pishi? My mother-in-law sent me down to check. It's so difficult to get hold of good quality rice these days."

"I did." Pishi stirred the payesh and looked at Shivani, "You are looking nice. Where is Rudra?"

"On the terrace. It's already burning up there but he kicked up such a fuss! I had bathed him and now he is wet with sweat."

"Is someone there to keep an eye on him?"

"His grandmother is there. In the puja room, waiting for the priest. She said to let him be and not to make him cry on his birthday. She will feed him the payesh after offering it to the gods. Rudra can come down with her then. So she said. But it is so hot up there. If he falls ill, then it will be said that it is my fault."

The sun glinted at the window. Amidst the din of the early morning kitchen came the sounds of another world to Pishi, leaving behind a yearning she thought she had quite forgotten. Or curbed. "Never mind. A little sun never hurt anyone. We used to roam the village under a sun much hotter than this."

The raisins were slowly swelling in the hot mixture. The small recess was already quite stuffy. Pishi lifted a white arm to wipe her forehead.

Shivani caught her arm. "Don't. Don't feel sad today for what's behind you. It is my Rudra's birthday. Let's be happy."

"And you too."

Shivani's sigh was long drawn.

Pishi turned to look at her. "You are thinking of Ashu. And your parents."

Shivani sighed again.

"Never mind. You can go home during Durga puja. Don't feel blue. Keep that in mind. Shivani will return home to Menaka this autumn."

It drew a wan smile from the younger woman.

The payesh was carefully poured into a big silver bowl.

"He used to love payesh. He can't have it in England I am sure. He would have returned by now but he stayed back for some work experience," Shivani said and blushed suddenly.

"We will make it the day Ashu comes home."

"Yes. Nobody makes it like you. My father-in-law said yesterday that arrangements for his return are being made. He will be home soon."

"Can you take it up? Mind it's hot," Pishi asked and then added, "Can you set it in a plate of water in the puja room, it should cool a bit."

"I can," Shivani flushed. "I don't like it."

"Payesh?"

"No. This bit. You cook it and I take it up. Why can't you take it up to the puja room today? You are constantly running errands, going to that room. Why not today? Why have I been asked to take it up? Everyone knows that you have cooked it. And in any case the gods would know. It's this that I don't like."

"Your brother has been talking about Gandhiji again to you," Pishi carefully scraped the pan. She knew all four of Shivani's brothers well though she had met, rather seen, only the youngest, senior to Shivani by four years who was a fervent follower of Mahatma Gandhi now, having briefly flirted earlier with more revolutionary ideals.

"Again? My... my mother-in-law says that my brother need not come here till 'He' – her son – returns."

Pishi sought to distract her once again, "He did not talk to you about any poems the last time? Your brother?"

"He did. Several. I have not read any of those out to you yet. But I marked them in my *Sanchaita* . They make you think, he had said. I read one last night again and again.

> sabare na jadi dako ekhono sharia thako,
> apanare bedhe rakho chaudike jaraye abhiman-
> mrityu majhe habe tabe chitabhashye sabar saman.

If you do not call out and still stay aloof from all
Shackle yourself all around with arrogant faith
You will be made their equal then in the pyre ash of death.

"And this is your poet? Rabindranath Thakur?"

"Who else would write like this? My brother said that the poet had written this after the swadeshi movement. You remember those days?"

"Neelkantha's poem was printed then. By your father-in-law," said Pishi. And I came to Kailash.

"Yes," Shivani said a little dismissively and then in a rush, "My brother said that we failed then because we could not carry the downtrodden, the poor and the peasants with us and we should learn from past mistakes and this time forge a nation of equals."

Pishi turned around and smiled, "Are you surprised then that your mother-in-law does not want you to visit him?"

Shivani looked at Pishi and laughed finally.

A maid came in and said somewhat archly, "But your mother-in-law wants you upstairs."

"Tell her I am coming this minute." Shivani watched the maid's retreating back as she adjusted the saree over her head.

Pishi set the bowl on a gleaming silver plate. "Mind you, pour some water in this plate when you set it in the puja room."

"I would like you to be part of the celebration today," Shivani added suddenly.

"I am part of it. I have cooked the payesh."

"As family. As one with us."

"*'Sabare na jadi dako?'* If you do not call all? But that is poetry."

"One has to begin somewhere. Is not Kailash part of our enslaved nation?"

Pishi smiled as she gathered the used vessels, "And others have sowed and winnowed the rice, milked the cow, cut the wood and mined for coals. The silver has been battered for this bowl which has been scoured by yet others. Are you going to call everyone?"

"I would if I could. If I had the means and the courage. I don't.

But I do believe that is my own failing. I don't think the gods have ordained it so."

"So you are inviting me to curry favour with your gods?"

"Don't say that. Don't. Don't. You know what I mean."

"I do. But go now. Your mother-in-law must be waiting. Your father-in-law has to leave for work too."

"It's my Rudra's birthday. We will have the payesh together."

Pishi smiled.

Shivani faltered and then added, "We will have payesh together this afternoon, not on the terrace upstairs but in the house."

"Go up. It is getting late. Someone will come looking for you again."

"We will have it together this afternoon. Let me make a beginning at least in Kailash. Let me possess the courage for a brief act at least. For myself. For my country. You will come. To my room?"

"Is this you or your brother speaking?"

"Does that matter?"

"No and no. I won't come."

"I will come to the room on one and a half storey then. In the afternoon."

"No."

"I know. It is insulting to do it thus when the household sleeps. But I can't do it any other time. Not yet. But you know that I want to. Don't you? You know I would if I had a house of my own? But I don't. And I don't have any one of my own here today. Except you and Rudra. Let's spend the afternoon together, in your room and not on the terrace. Don't say no again."

Pishi looked at the earnest young face. And held her tongue. And pride.

And the day rolled forward. Regardless. Careless.

॥ ॥

Carefully Uma drew out the manuscript from within the cupboard.

Kailash was quiet. It was late afternoon but still she had shut the bedroom door and locked it too.

Uma was acutely aware of her surroundings. These days she often was. Suddenly. In the middle of the day or in eventide. The sunlight falling on one side of a sofa, the shadow in the room where two walls met, the pattern of light on the banister or the swaying green outside her window where a bird sat alert with its head cocked – everything around her would become sharply clear. It seemed as though she had seen it before, this slant of light, the play of shadow or the angle of vision. She would take it in, standing still, for as long as she could bear it, wondering what magic made it appear as though she had seen it before. Just as clearly. Just so. And then the realisation would course through her slowly that she could not have seen it earlier. She had never known of the existence of Kailash and its inhabitants before this summer. This was not her home. Yet it would be so. Till she died. It cast a bleak glow.

Uma sat quietly in front of the open cupboard that had once belonged to her mother-in-law. Had she felt like this too in Kailash? Did her mother feel thus too? Her kaki? Thakma? Did every married woman feel this tightrope walk of being where they did not belong? Trying to make it their own. Belonging. And yet a stranger. This was female fate.

And yet.

Uma turned the pages of Dadu's manuscript and suddenly she caught her name nestling in a grid of red. And as she looked at the page Dadu's soft voice came to her from the secret crevice of Kailash.

"The Babylonian word for mother is Ummu or Umma. The Accadian Ummi. The Dravidian Umma. Ommo, Uma and Amba. These words can surely be connected to each other? Etymologically, it is unlikely that Uma derives from Sanskrit."

Dadu had given her the name. Uma. And Thakma had told her its meaning. Uma was born to be Shiva's wife. Uma's mother had recounted how the *Puranas* and the *Ramayana* describe the divine Uma as the daughter of Himavat and Menaka. Uma was born, it was always clarified, to be the wife of Rudra-Shiva. Uma was born for her husband, Uma had to leave her parents and her natal home for Kailash, the austere abode of her much older, much married husband. But every year during the autumn months Uma, the much loved dear daughter returned to earth, from her marital home Kailash, to be united with her parents for a brief period of five days.

This is woman's destiny and even the goddess cannot escape it. Even if she slays demons. Ma had repeated the story as she had heard it from her mother and had held her daughter, as yet a child, a little tighter knowing that she too must marry and leave one day.

Uma looked around. The thin gap in the curtains suggested that a gentle sun had perhaps lit the clouded afternoon sky. The light inside was mellower still in the ante room where she sat surrounded by cupboards and a dressing table. Uma thought she felt something. As though someone had come to sit by her side. Kailash was breathing softly. And nothing stirred. Uma read on from Dadu's manuscript.

> *... The goddess as we know her today was not always thus entirely. In the first phase the goddess is the earth personified by the primitive mind. Like the earth, she delivers life. But the goddess in this stage is without an owner. In the earliest texts the goddess is not married. It is at the very end of the Vedic period that Uma is recognised as Shiva's wife. ....*

The cross next to the paragraph was small. But firm and red.

❊ Fourteen ❊

WITH A FIRMNESS OF PURPOSE Shivani opened the heavy cupboard that had come as part of her dowry. The mirrored front of the wood reflected a listless form and a pale face. She wished that her head would not hurt so. She should really lie down for a while but there was a promise to be kept this afternoon. She was excited about it too. If only her body could rise to the occasion.

The lower section of the cupboard contained some new sarees. She knew that there was a saree in green with thin gold lines running through it. A duri saree. The green was meant for Pishi of the green eyes. Shivani wanted to give it to her. Today. With the payesh. She wanted to give her much more. But what did she have here that she could call her own and give without feeling that she was presuming? Shivani leaned against the shelves of the cupboard, tired and lost in thought. The drawer dug into her stomach and idly she moved, opened it and took out a Yardley's lavender soap from the box kept there. A cousin had got the box from England for her. Ashutosh had laughed at her for hoarding it so. She held it in front of her nose and inhaled deeply. And thought of her life before marriage. Slowly her body seemed to rejuvenate.

On a sudden impulse Shivani emptied the cardboard container of the remaining soaps. Another drawer was opened. Carefully she picked up a stack of white handkerchiefs from its depths and settled them in the box. There was still some time for him to come home from England. The handkerchiefs would be infused with the fresh smell of the soap by then. Her past and present would mingle thus. The embroidered **A** in one corner of the white linen spoke to her of her lonely existence in Kailash and the long wait for her husband's return. She had embroidered a handkerchief for each month of his absence even though she had always disliked the needle.

"That is not much, is it, Hindu wives have done much more for their husbands?" Ashutosh may smile.

"But I have always hated embroidery, take that into account," she would tell him.

"I have made you do that which you hate then?"

"I won't embroider any more."

"You won't need to."

She would hold him to his promise.

Already Shivani was feeling better. Her morning blues had lifted. But her head felt heavy still. Rudra had insisted on being up on the terrace even as his grandmother propitiated her gods in the puja room. She was doing it for him because it was his birthday. Rudra was told that several times by Haimanti. Slowly the child had grown truculent. It did not help that the priest came late. The April sun warmed up a scorching day. Shivani had to drag the child back to the safety of the shaded section of the terrace every now and then. "Your father was very biddable. He never disobeyed me," her mother-in-law had said to Rudra from within the puja room.

Shivani joined the maid and ran after the child once again all the way across the terrace silently accepting that Rudra's waywardness must have come from her.

The sun blazed. And blazed. The city glimmered in the heat. Kailash dozed after a grand lunch.

Shivani picked up a small bowl of payesh, tucked a soap in the saree and put it under her arm and called out to her son engrossed with a toy train set that Shashishekhar had given him in the morning.

"Let's go to Pishi. Can you carry that fat book for me?"

Rudra's head remained bent over the toy set scattered on the floor.

Shivani lowered her voice and said in a staged whisper, "We have to go very quietly. No one must know. We will have some payesh there. Or do you want to stay here?"

Rudra reluctantly got up and then with a quick change of mood, put Tagore's fat volume of poetry, the *Sanchaita*, on his head like a hawker and followed his mother.

Shivani laughed, "Not like that. Are you going to sell the book?"

"My grandfather sells books."

"Not quite like that. Don't say it like that. Don't make a noise," Shivani cautioned.

"I know," the child whispered enthralled now having caught his mother's nervous excitement. He had initially resented being kept at home on a school day but his grandmother had insisted on his presence for the puja in the morning. The day had not been too bad so far. The afternoon was promising to be even better.

He started walking on tiptoes with the book still on his head.

"It's a book of magic," he whispered to his mother, "It will take us where we want to go."

※ ※

Monsoon had lost its magic. It was simply monotonous now. Through the listless wet afternoons the women listened to the tales of trials in marriage from the Merchant's story of Neelkantha's *Chandimangal* where the old wife was being abandoned and the young being broken. All awaited the grace of the goddess.

"Tell me..."

"I will."

"Jokes apart. Tell me do you think she really minded it?"

"What?"

"This going out to the woods everyday to graze the goats? What would Khullona have done at home all day long? Lahana would not have left her in peace."

"And really one can't blame her. She will seethe and burn on seeing the lust on her husband's face for the new wife..."

"...and one who is her niece too, almost a daughter." "And him, that old goat Dhanapati! It could not have been much fun for the young wife to have him constantly lust for her when at home. How do you say no to your tormentor when he is your husband?"

"So was it not a boon for Khullona in a way to go out of the house, to roam on her own, pick up a fallen fruit and eat it, sing a song, lie down on the grass and stare at the clouds floating in the sky?"

"I think you are right, Khema. She would have had to cook, clean, stitch, wash, fetch or carry in the house under Lahana's eyes all the time without respite. Her punishment seems much better than being stifled at home. Does it not?"

"The goddess had got bored with domesticity too, had she not?"

"You are right. The goddess also wanted a break from her household work."

"She came down on earth to spread her cult and roamed the forest too. She too wanted to get away from her husband and children for a while."

"If not forever."

"The poet does not quite say that."

"How can he say everything?"

"How can he say that with him being a man and all?"

"How is he saying even this much?"

"Is he saying it or are we?"

Khema said suddenly, "It is clear though, don't you think, that they find the goddess Mangal Chandi strange initially?"

They would not have, if the goddess had been one of their own kind thought Khema, though this she kept to herself.

"Huh?" Bamundi looked at her.

Khema had everyone's attention suddenly.

She swallowed and carried on, "Well, initially Dhanapati does get very angry with Khullona for worshipping a strange female deity. So does it not mean that the goddess came from elsewhere? From people who are different, with different lives? She who is found in the forest is not one of their kind."

"Perhaps, but…" said Bamundi.

"Shall I read that bit again?" intervened Uma.

"Yes."

Bamundi seemed lost too till Pishi gently told her to mind the cabbage which had to be "shredded very fine."

> *The king orders that merchant Dhanapati must once again set sail on the sea*
> *which is full of peril thinks Khullona and prepares for the brata of Mangal Chandi*
> *for her husband's safety.*
> *The day arrives, the sailors ready the ship, their women come with lamps and flowers*
> *to observe the traditional rite , so that the deity of voyages showers blessings on their husbands' enterprise.*
> *It is time, cries a sailor from the top mast whose eyes the water's mood do gauge. Where is that wife of mine? Asks Dhanapati of Lahana.*
> *She must pray for my voyage.*
> *Where is my wife? shouts Dhanapati enraged.*
> *Bewitched man, what I am then? Not a wife? Seethes Lahana. But she bends her head*
> *Swallows her pride, her tears, and then cunningly says,*
> *I am afraid I have to confess that Khullona is engaged with a strange goddess.*

❈ ❈

The burning sensation in Haimanti's chest would not go away. Really she should not have had that second helping of fish. Her husband had always been partial to this dish of small fish cooked to a fiery consistency with a paste of green chillies, coconut and mustard. Haimanti had not much cared for it earlier but now she found herself asking Khagen every other day to get some fresh fish that was small and full of bones. She always added, "Babu loves it," in case anyone thought that Kailash was driven by her appetite.

Rudra's birthday had been the occasion for many special dishes at lunch. Haimanti had asked for this too. Rudra had taken after his grandfather. He loved fish. Already he could manage a bony ilish on his own.

"He is five today. Get five kinds of fish from the market,"

Haimanti had said that morning to Khagen and then wiped her eyes as she thought of her own son in that faraway land where they ate only boiled vegetables.

Haimanti burped once again. She would not be able to get her afternoon nap like this. A headache would follow as the night the day. There were some English medicines in the sideboard of the dining room. She looked at her maid fast asleep on the floor beside her bed, her mouth slack and open. Haimanti was disgusted. It seemed so gross.

Should she ask the maid to go down? But she may get the wrong medicine. Sighing, Haimanti got up. A daughter-in-law should always be available for such errands she thought, never having lived with a mother-in-law herself. Another burp.

On her way out from the bedroom Haimanti nudged the maid gently and said, "Shut your mouth and sleep. It does not look good."

The maid got up with a jolt. "Can I get you something?"

"No I will manage," Haimanti added gently, "You go back to sleep."

Haimanti walked downstairs with the uncertain befuddled maid following her.

The dining room was dark with drawn curtains.

Ashu would drape his tired frame over the chair here and ask, "So what are you feeding me today, Ma?"

Haimanti's eyes welled up again. Ashu has been away for so long. Why did one wish for independence and yet send one's sons to the same master country to study? She had not asked this of her husband. She knew his answer would be, "you won't understand." And Shivani's father fuelled it too, insisting that he make all the arrangements for Ashu's stay in England. He had paid for it too. Haimanti's grievance against her husband mutated into irritation with Shivani's father who had, in her eyes, propelled Ashu's trip to England.

Haimanti measured the mixture. The maid took the tumbler with sleep still in her eyes. An ever alert Khagen had silently come in and was standing in the shadows of the curtain. Haimanti adjusted the saree over her head and treaded the stairs. Her heart was burning still. She thought of her son alone in England and Kailash bereft.

It was unmistakably laughter. In the afternoon. From the room on one a half storey. Shivani's voice. Laughing. And then the other one's voice echoed the laugh. The green eyed witch.

Haimanti's breath suddenly came sharp and deep. The burning seemed to spread all through her body. She looked at the maid trailing her, "Go down to the kitchen. I will call you if I need anything."

The maid went down reluctantly. The kitchen was much hotter. There was no ceiling fan there.

Haimanti watched the retreating back till it disappeared.

She climbed up the first flight of stairs then and pushed open the door on one a half storey with a firm hand though she stood at the threshold still.

The green eyed witch and Shivani sat on the floor. A saree, evidently new, lay half open by a bowl of payesh, a silver bowl, a fine silver bowl, Haimanti's fine silver bowl, in one corner of the room with a bowl of water. Shivani had a book in front of her. It was as though a strange ritual of propitiation was taking place.

And Rudra was on the bed. Her grandson. Sprawled on that green eyed witch's bed. Fast asleep with sweat on his brow. This room had no fan either. How could Shivani do this to her grandson and on his birthday too! And then to be laughing with the witch without a care in the world while Haimanti's son was alone in that strange land sent by none other than Shivani's own father.

Something burst within Haimanti.

"The older generation was right," she said soflty from the doorway and then added,

> *"Jat marley tin Seney,*
> *Kehsab Seney, Wil-seney, Isti-seney –*
>
> The caste purity has been ruined by three Sens,
> Keshab Sen, Wil-son and the sta-tion."

Keshab Sen was a leader of the progressive and reformist Brahmo samaj, Wilson's was the hotel where caste Hindu men allegedly ate forbidden meat and *Istisen* referred to the railway station as the space where strict caste barriers had to loosen up somewhat because of the exigencies of a railway journey. Shivani's father had worked with the Bengal Nagpur Railways for a brief while. The connection was quite lost on Shivani but she understood the criticism well enough and stood up in a rush. Trembling, though she tried to hold her head high. Was she not doing that which was right?

"Come in," said Pishi from where she sat on the floor with the ghost of a smile on her face. At least that is how Haimanti recalled it later.

✿ ✿

An enraged Dhanapati stomps inside the house and finds Khullona engaged in the brata of a strange female deity, as informed by Lahana. He kicks all over the sacred space. Khullona is dragged by her hair and beaten for worshipping Mangal Chandi, the goddess of the women in the woods. Be like the other women, our women, or else. Dhanapati thundered, his breath coming in shallow gasps, as he rained blows and kicks on Khullona.

Don't tire yourself so just before the voyage, said Lahana.

It is time Sir, said the sailors and their wives, who had followed Dhanapati.

Dhanapati sets sail. Leaving behind the broken remains of propitiation. And Khullona. Bruised and battered.

"He won't get away with it."

"He can't."

"Foolish man. The goddess's wrath will lie in wait for him. How could he behave so?"

"But he did not know that. He did not know that he was dealing with her and that she is powerful."

"Yes, that's why they think that they are strong."

Dhanapati's ships sink first. He has a strange vision. In the middle of the ocean, a goddess alternately swallows and throws up an elephant. Dhanapati reaches Sinhala where the king imprisons him for lying about a strange goddess.

Khullona in the meanwhile gives birth to a son, Shrimanta. Lahana holds the small and soft body against her dry breasts. Khullona sees her wet eyes.

Lahana, Khullona and Shrimanta.

Peace prevails in Merchant Dhanapati's house.

Coming of age Shrimanta sets sail in search of his missing father. His mother reminds him of the power and grace of Mangal Chandi. Shrimanta's journey repeats the fate of his father. He reaches Sinhala, like his father, having lost everything and being granted the self same vision at sea which he cannot conjure for the Sinhalese king to prove his innocence. He is sentenced to death.

At the cremation ground, a frightened Shrimanta prays to the goddess Mangal Chandi who appears in the guise of an old woman and subsequently calls forth an army of terrifying female companions who savage the king's company. The king recognises the power of the deity, as does Dhanapati. Shrimanta is married to the Sinhalese princess Sushila. The father and son return home with riches.

Dhanapati now permits the goddess to be worshipped, but only by women.

❀ ❀

The book had tumbled from Shivani hands when she got up in terror on seeing her mother-in-law enter the room. She bent and picked it up and placed it on the bed next to Rudra, after touching it to her forehead. Shivani's hand trembled. Pishi nodded gently to Shivani as though in reassurance.

The scene burnt its way into Haimanti's heart. She tightened her grip on the door.

The green eyed one still sat on the floor.

"Come in," she said again.

Ignoring the impertinent words of the she-devil, Haimanti looked her daughter-in-law in the eye as she hovered uncertainly near her sleeping son and knew in a flash just where Shivani was weakest.

"From tonight my grandson will sleep in my room."

Haimanti could almost feel Shivani's heart lurch and then turn cold. The feeling was familiar and now oddly comforting. Haimanti had been there herself many times.

"Why?" asked Shivani, licking her lips.

Haimanti could have told the younger woman that it was a futile question. Still she said, "The very fact that you need to ask the question shows how inept you are."

"But…"

"This is a Brahman household. Of the highest order. We observe a certain decorum here. Perhaps you have not been taught that in your family. Perhaps they do not follow them. It does not concern me. But my grandson is the descendant of the Kulin Brahman poet Dvija Neelkantha. I cannot afford to have his heritage frittered away by you. And certainly not in the absence of my son, his father."

"No," said Shivani. Her voice was not just low but pleading, almost abject.

Haimanti crossed the threshold, stepped inside and then looking at the one on the floor said, "I would not enter your room but to take mine own away."

How easy, Haimanti thought, how easy it is to take charge of one's own. She should have done it years ago and not been afraid. Was Kailash not hers too? Her god would have seen her through and given her strength. Was she not doing that which was right? Rama had entered Lanka too, had he not, to rescue Sita? Haimanti bent down to pick up the sleeping Rudra.

The child woke up as Haimanti's grip tightened on the small frame. Haimanti tried to gather her grandson in her arms, "My golden one, you will sleep in my room from now on. Come."

"I don't want to sleep," said the child squirming and wriggling free and then in a rush of pure id he added, "I am hungry."

"I will get your milk, come," said Shivani gratefully, seizing the escape route. This is why you need sons at your in-laws, she thought.

"No, leave him," said Haimanti and again noted with a surge of power that her words halted Shivani. How strange, she thought, she had not known her own strength all these days. "You don't need to bother yourself with him any longer. Your ways are not the ways of this house. Your family knew that they were getting their daughter married into the house of Dvija Neelkantha. They should have instructed you better." Haimanti could not resist adding, "I knew this was not the right match. I had said so then."

"Mother," Shivani started not knowing how to go on.

"You must not argue with your elders," said Haimanti, "you have not even been taught that. How could I expect you to maintain the sanctity of Dvija Neelkantha's family?"

"God knows I have not done anything wrong."

"We don't eat or sit with just about anyone from the streets. Certainly not one whose origins are muddied. And I think you know that too, else why have you come here like a thief while Kailash sleeps? And how dare you bring my silver bowl into her room, how dare you feed her greed," Haimanti glanced at the green eyes, almost revelling in the excesses that she was uttering, "And how dare you make my grandson lie on her bed."

"But," said Shivani.

"Forgive us. This is not a Brahmo family. We are caste Hindus. Brahmans. Kulin Brahmans. Proud of our lineage. Careful with our reputation. This your family knew. You should not have forgotten it here." The words came in a flow from Haimanti.

"But," said Shivani again.

"There are no buts."

A thin pesistent voice cut the heavy silence of the moment sensing, perhaps as animals will, the throbbing tension. "I am hungry," said Rudra.

Shivani moved towards him.

"Don't!" said Haimanti.

The figure sitting on the floor moved.

"Go down child," said Pishi. "Khagenda will be in the kitchen. Or Dashidi. Go down. They will give you something." She looked at Haimanti then, "I don't suppose you will sit in this room, but I suggest you stay. I have something to say to you."

"I am not interested in anything that you may have to say."

Pishi looked at the child still lingering in the room. Young Rudra seemed uncertain now. He looked at his mother. Gently Pishi spoke again addressing him, "What's the matter? Why are you still here? There are goodies in the kitchen. Go down." The child looked at Shivani who could only nod. Rudra slowly walked out of the room sliding his hand over the bed, uncertain but unable to override the authority so evident in the voice of Pishi. Something on the bed suddenly caught his eye and the child ran back, gathered the book close to him and left the room with a smile at his mother.

Haimanti walked towards the door too. She would have liked to leave with her grandson's hand in hers but still, she had managed to show them their place, and hers, in Kailash.

Pishi spoke. "No, no Haimanti, don't follow him. You have spent your precious time, and breath, in this room. Not my room perhaps but where I stay. Yet you are still breathing. Your pure blood is still flowing. A few minutes more won't harm you. Or your purity."

"I don't expect you to know anything about purity. Your green eyes let out the dirt in your blood."

"Does it? This blood, this purity of blood that you talk about constantly, let us stir it then and see what we find in it?" Pishi stood up and moved. She was now between the door and Haimanti.

Haimanti's mouth slowly turned dry. The burning in her chest had returned with an increased intensity.

"I am not interested, " said Haimanti. And she spoke the truth. Shivani could not speak or move even if she wanted to.

"Why not?" continued Pishi, "You said that you were interested in the sanctity of blood. The purity of your Brahman, your kulin Brahman grandson's blood. Let us stir it then and see if it reveals that which is other than the eternal and pure. If lying on my bed defiles him then …"

What was the monster threatening to do, wondered Haimanti, horror stricken. Would she reveal herself and her relation with Kailash? Tell the world that which she, Haimanti, had only suspected all these years but had never been able to catch red-handed? The she-devil would not. She could not. No woman, however low, could actually talk about her relationship with … to his wife and his daughter-in-law, in his house. Kailash cannot be made to sink so low.

Haimanti willed her legs to move and brushed against Shivani in the small room, "If you have any sense of decency left, girl, you too will leave this room this minute."

"Don't go," Pishi's voice arrested Haimanti. "For your own good. Don't make me raise my voice. You would not want this echoing in Kailash."

"What do you want?"

"To stir the blood. To have you tell me Haimanti, what do you do if you find in your blood not the eternal and the pure but …"

"I will not listen to a mad woman's ravings."

"You call it so and shut out the truth about yourself and your kind." Soft as breath the words came then, "She was not mad either. But the horror of the deed made her so."

"Who are you talking about? What does it have to do with us in Kailash?"

"My grandmother. No, don't look like that. You cannot afford to be so dismissive."

"Your grandmother has nothing to do with us."

"I wish so too. I wish she had nothing to do with your family. She wished it too all her life. But the dark deed, that she witnessed, connects me to you and your Kailash."

"There are no dark deeds associated with Kailash."

"You think so? Then let me tell you today of Dvija Neelkantha, Kailash's ancestor, worshipper of the goddess and revered poet. Your husband's father, Haimanti. Dvija Neelkantha. Let me tell you about that Brahman poet who sang of the goddess and held death like poison in his throat."

※ ※

The car returned to Kailash for Uma after dropping Ashutosh at the Press. Uma would then be seen off by a motley group: Pishi, Bamundi and Khema. Sometimes other women would join them if they happened to be around, women who came to sweep and swab Kailash, wash clothes and collect garbage.

Khema's husband behind the wheels was a little disgruntled as this new mid-day duty dragged him away from his morning sessions with the mechanics and drivers at the garage near The Ganges Press. But he knew that it was not for him to question why the lady needed to go to National Library every day.

Uma had not realised that she had missed it so. Or that she had loved thus the business of reading and taking notes and seeing an unknown world unfurl bit by bit and meanings made. But she returned to it as though the memory had returned of a past life. The first few days at the library were chaotic. It took a while for her to get into the rhythm of knowing what to look for in the catalogue, how to access the books and how to minimise the period in waiting. Now she sank gracefully in her marked wooden seat with the books waiting for her, the fan whirring above and the scratching of pen on paper all around in the huge hall of the National Library. As Uma read and wrote she sometimes thought of her college days and of all that she had taken so lightly in her earlier life.

Uma left the library at two fifteen sharp. The car came to fetch her after carrying lunch for Ashutosh and Rudra. It usually reached the library about two thirty but Uma always stood ready on the steps. The car must never be late because of her.

It was wonderful to be received by her three women in Kailash in the afternoon. Uma took to having her late lunch in the kitchen instead of the dining room which remained drowsy with the curtains drawn across the wide windows. The puja room on the terrace upstairs was soporific too. In the mornings Uma rushed through the rituals and then shut the door on the gods and goddesses in order to be ready for her tryst in the library.

She told the women of all that she learnt through the day even as she ate her lunch. A lunch much fussed over because she was having it so late and because she had been working. Because, unlike them, she was not used to working and also because she was one of them. Thus it had been with Thakma, Ma and Kaki when she returned from college.

"Who is the goddess then?" asked Khema. One of you or one of us? But it could not be articulated thus. Not in Kailash; not even in its kitchen.

"She is mother earth, corn mother, warrior goddess, protector of cattle, children, forts, fertility, health, happiness and the destroyer of 'evil.'"

"We know that but is she always a wife?"

"The *Devimahatmya* where Chandi kills the demon Mahisashura does not say so."

"So there."

"But this composition is now part of the *Markandeya Purana* where they call her the wife of Shiva."

"Who are they? Who composed this *Purana*?"

"Must be some Brahman man."

Everyone laughed with a grudging admiration for the cunning of their opponents, no longer in awe of the sacred thread.

"What else?"

"One of her names is Shakhambari, she who bears vegetation."

"The goddess must be then as old as the earth herself."

"And is she married, when she is called Shakhambari?"

"No."

"But no one remembers her thus, do they, the goddess growing vegetables?" asked Khema. Her mother, dark as the earth, was forever scattering seeds around the small hut. The creepers grew soft and green on their roof. Khema had always wondered how the black earth could yield the brilliant orange of the pumpkin or the bleached white of the gourd.

"Is Shakhambari dark?" the question escaped.

"I don't know. But in the *Mahabharata*, the goddess is also called Krishnachavisamakrishna, dark as dark can be."

Khema nodded, "The earth is dark." And full of despair as well.

Why do you want to stay with me, her mother had consoled her, I cannot even give you a fist's measure of rice each day. And so Khema had been married and sent to the city.

"Does anyone know Shakhambari in the city?" Khema's eyes glittered.

"The goddess resides in a bunch of nine plantains, the nava patrika. The ritual bathing of these crops marks the beginning of the Durga puja, the bodhan," Pishi responded but with a distant look in her eyes, hazily recalling a tall, spare, fair-skinned man ceremoniously bathing the tightly bound plants in front of an excited village crowd. Her grandmother clutched her arms in terror as they watched too but from a safe distance. As the priest held up the plants, the old woman's crazed terror escaped in a shrill cry.

"I have something to say, something to say" Her grandmother had dribbled.

"Go away nutter. Not now."

Someone picked up a stone to throw at her lest her ravings distract the meditative silence of Neelkantha. She had to drag her away from the impatient crowd.

Perhaps it lacked coherence, this past that was now unfolding in the kitchen in Kailash, a past so different from the one charted in the parlour upstairs that they scarcely seemed to be of the same world, but it held the women.

Pishi ladled some more food for Uma before she could protest.

"And the hunter's goddess, did you chance across something, Boudi?"

"Some say that in older times Oraons worshipped a goddess named Chandi who is associated with young and unmarried hunters. The iguana is the totem of several aboriginal tribes in Madhya Pradesh. The goddess is associated with the nomadic

Abhiras, Sabaras, Pulindas. The *Harivamsha* describes her as a goddess of the outcastes who bring her cocks, goats, sheep...."

"Steady. You will choke on the food," Bamundi reprimanded. Like Thakma.

Our dearest Uma, Thakma had written in response to Uma's letter sent that Thursday when she had discovered Dadu's manuscript in Kailash. Our dearest Uma, I have never missed Him as much as I did when I read your letter. I wish I could let Him know that you had asked for His book, that you want to read it. He was always a quiet one. He never shared his feelings. He did not show them easily either. But I know how much the book meant to Him and how hurt He was that no one wanted to read it, that no one cared. He got nothing out of it. Indeed He got far less from life than he deserved....

Very carefully Uma had cut the brown strings that held the parcel containing Dadu's book and Thakma's letter. Baba had written the address on the parcel. Uma drew out the sheet of paper. Thakma's writing on the enclosed note was shaky. Uma could visualise the knots of green nerves on the hand that moved the pen. Her Dadu had insisted that his bride should know how to read and write. He had taught Thakma the alphabet himself. In one rare and unguarded moment Uma had heard Thakma shyly refer to her husband as 'amar mastermoshai – my teacher'. The parcel seemed to come to Uma from another life. She longed to go home to her parents. But it was not time yet. Uma looked at the book that the parcel from Kashmere Gate had brought to her, so familiar and yet a little mysterious, now invested with fierce emotions and alien meanings. The oval logo of 'The Ganges Press' did not mark the spine of Dadu's book. The paper was cheap. The cover simple, ordinary. But the title still read *The Evolution of the Mother Goddess*. Uma recalled that the red ink had slashed the proposed title of the manuscript with great force and then written with an arrogant flourish: "Goddesses do not evolve. They are."

⁂

Her tale was distorted. It had to be. It must be. But the entire world of Kailash seemed to have changed since the afternoon in the room on one and a half storey. Everything had altered since the green-eyed one had spoken.

Haimanti sat on the heavy double bed. She was small built. Her feet did not reach the floor from the bed which in any case was very high. Haimanti was very conscious of the fact and always took care to tuck in her feet after getting onto the large bed of dark mahogany wood. But today she sat leaning against the raised curved section at the foot of the bed, unmindful that her feet were pathetically dangling from the side.

Seven. The girl who was killed was only seven. Somehow Haimanti could not get that out of her mind. Six. Seven. Eight. She herself was a bride at ten. Your groom looks like a prince, her sisters-in-law had said. Lucky you. "Yes, lucky me," Haimanti had thought. No one had told her that he had a wife elsewhere. And when Haimanti came to know that, gradually as you come to know the seasons, they said so what? He is a man. A Brahman. A kulin Brahman. He has to fulfil his duties and marry as often as required in order to ensure that Brahman households do not suffer from the sin of having unmarried daughters. Is he not a good husband, an able provider? He gives you your dues too, does he not, they said. Besides the other one is in faraway Chittagong. Why do you worry unnecessarily?

How would they know that distances are deceptive. How far would Chittagong be if Haimanti failed to please her husband? Failed to soothe His weariness, to match His palate, to ensure the continuity of His lineage? Only Haimanti knew that she had to be vigilant all the time. How could she tell the others that she lived perpetually under the fear of failure in Kailash? Oh He never complained or said anything sharp but how long does it take for a man to change?

Turn to the gods, her mother had said. Haimanti had, with a vengeance. Kailash had been safe so far. Safe from the rage and curses and tears of a woman curdling over from Chittagong. An abandoned woman. Shahsishekhar's first wife. Haimanti expected to hear the other one's curses all the time. But so far Kailash had been silent. But now she heard in it the smothered scream of a child, another bride. A child bride screaming to be heard. The thin scream waited below the bedroom, beneath the landing, deep deep in the ground made damp with water, water that lapped Kailash's foundation and flowed out to Chittagong to mingle with the tears of another bride. Sitting on her bed, Haimanti saw again a dark room and a man bent over a small figure, a bride, and then a pillow descending on that soft, vulnerable face. Haimanti shut her eyes. And the smothered one was only seven. Six. Seven. Eight. Gauridan. The gift of Gauri. That is what the Brahmans called the marriage of very young upper caste girls, before the girls developed breasts, before their blood flowed out every month. Gauridan they called it, referring to goddess Gauri married to a much older, much married Shiva. Was the goddess terrified too? Of marriage? Of the act? Oh, the horror of the act. Did he do it to the girl before smothering her? Is that what drove the younger sister out of her mind. Dear God. Dear God.

A wave of nausea overtook Haimanti. She got off the bed unsteadily. Dear God. Tell me what I should do with the knowledge. Show me a way.

Haimanti prayed, kneeling on the floor near the bed.

Her skin crawled when she heard the shuffling sound outside her door. But almost immediately she also heard the soft familiar cough of Khagen. "A moment of your time, Mother," Khagen said from outside the door. What now, Haimanti thought in a flash of irritation. Is there no respite from the running of Kailash? And then she stood stock still. Why, this was it. This was the answer. Her God had shown her the way. Her duty lay in running Kailash. With honour, pride and most of all, devotion, whatever be the cause or the cost. As she had done so far. As she would continue to do.

Here was the message sent to her by no less a man than God.

The housekeys jangled from one end of her saree as Haimanti

rose to the call of duty in Kailash: the house of Kulin Brahmans, servants of the goddess.

⁂

Why did they choose to sing of the goddess thought Uma. Why did these Brahman male poets infuse an older narrative, perhaps by women, perhaps by other castes, lower castes, with a fresh and vigorous lease of life?

Khema had been quite belligerent the other day. She had asked how could they know for certain that the hunter's tale was not composed by those who knew that way of life? How could they say that it was not a purloined tale, a purloined goddess?

And she a woman. Bamundi had added, though not looking at Khema. Would the men who believed in giving gifts of daughters and burning widows have thought of a warring deity as a woman who was powerful? And with a life outside marriage?

It must have come from elsewhere.

And if there are poems that describe the goddess as a low caste, even a Dombi? The lowest of the low? What then? No Brahman would conceive of a goddess thus unless she already existed and existed with such a powerful hold over the people's lives that even the Brahman could not erase her entirely, Khema had carried on. Mutated. That's what they must have done. These Brahman male poets had so transformed the goddess that her own kind failed to recognise the echo of their own power in her; seeing instead in her only the mediator's power who worshipped goddesses but suppressed flesh and blood women.

In the National Library, the two men working behind the counter noted even amidst an animated discussion of varied stomach ailments, Uma's soft beauty.

"Is she a teacher?" The stomach was briefly suspended.

"No. I checked."

"Oh. Research."

Long hours of interaction with researchers, giving out and

collecting books, had left the two with nothing but disdain for the species.

A fresh deluge of books separated them for a while.

Uma was still working when the two, at the counter, came together again.

"What is she working on?"

"Don't know. She has been reading a lot of those *Chandi-mangals*."

"Really? She does not look the sort. What is she doing with them?"

"Anything goes in the name of research these days."

"I know."

They returned happily to the states of sick stomachs.

❦ ❦

Haimanti's stomach was beginning to burn again. She shifted the heavy curtains and stepped out.

"Forgive me, mother. I did not mean to disturb you mid-afternoon like this. Do you need anything from the market?" Khagen asked, looking down at the floor.

Had Khagen lost his mind? Haimanti wondered. He wanted to go to the market in this scorching hour of the day when the shops were shut and he had come up to find out if she, Haimanti, too had lost her mind and would think of things to buy now!

But before she could say anything, Khagen produced a letter. The envelope was long and white. It was ready to sail across the seven seas carrying tales of Kailash. It was clear to Haimanti that Shivani had lost no time in writing to her husband of the afternoon in the green-eyed one's room. And of the dark deed revealed there.

Regard. Honour. Duty.

Did the new wives know nothing of those values? Did they not know that you married not a man but a family? Or that you had to serve them, in life and unto death?

A bitter scorn for Shivani, and her poetry reading, piano playing modern kind, steadied the ground under Haimanti's feet.

Khagen spoke. "I was asked to send this letter immediately. Since I have to go to the post office, and I knew that my lady was up, I thought I would ask if there are other errands."

Yes. Get some hot coals and heap them on this letter.

Haimanti looked at Khagen and then at the letter in his hand again and felt helpless and frustrated. She could not reach out and take the letter from Khagen's hand when it was clearly not meant for her. Kailash never stooped so and certainly not in the presence of servants. "I cannot think of anything at the moment," she answered with unconscious honesty.

Khagen left. He was relieved. He had been in a quandary ever since Shivani had come down to ask him to take the letter to the post office. Immediately, she had said, it still might catch the post. Khagen whose eyes and ears missed nothing in Kailash, knew something odd was about. Today was not the day for catching the mail. Should he take it? His mistress, the older one might not like it. But then the young one would be his mistress some day. It required the skills of tightrope walking.

But now Khagen felt easier as he stepped out in the hot sun. He would go to the post office but those who should know, knew. His was not to wonder why.

Close by, Shivani, in another room, looked at her son. Her head felt hot and heavy, her breath a little shallow. "I have written everything to your father. He will know what's to be done. Don't worry," she said to the child but more really to reassure herself.

Rudra nodded in an absent minded manner trying to twist the funnel stuck to the black and red railway engine from the set that Dadu had given him that morning. And then still not looking at Shivani he said in an offhand manner, "I have hidden the book. No one will be angry with you for reading it in Pishi's room now."

Suddenly Shivani felt an overwhelming sense of gratitude that her child was a son and not a daughter who would be seven in two years time to be married and sent off to a strange house to be at the mercy of a stranger. A stranger who looked like a god and took life.

The contours of her own bedroom seemed to waver.

Shivani knelt then and held Rudra in a tight embrace. "Don't worry. Baba will come and everything will be fine in Kailash."

Rudra suffered the embrace for a minute and then he pushed his mother away and asked, "Will he get something for me?"

❀ Fifteen ❀

KAILASH LAY IN DEEP SLUMBER under an indigo blue night sky. Khema sat on the steps that led to their quarters. She was alone. A swarm of mosquitoes whined all around her.

The sharp acrid smell of burning tobacco warned her of her husband's presence even before she felt or saw him.

"What's the matter?" he asked squeezing in beside her.

"Did horses stay here earlier?"

"What?"

"Bamundi was saying the other day that horses were stabled where we sleep now in Kailash? Is that a fact?"

"I think not. And even if it were so how does it matter? Will it dent your rating in the kitchen? Do you know how many people sleep out in the open in this city? That Bamundi of yours is just a jealous old hag. I saw that vagabond son of hers the other day. Pissed out of his mind he was."

"I know that too. She told us herself. Poor thing." Khema added after a while, "There is a lockout in his factory."

"Hmm."

Skin rubbed against skin, slippery with sweat.

"Khema Majhi let's go inside." But he did not seem to be in a hurry either.

"Do you know from where we have come?"

"Kasbak village in Manbhum. Or so I have heard. The family moved from there subsequently when it did not rain and famine followed, bringing the moneylender in its wake. You know it too. And in any case how does it matter? We belong to Kolkata now. I have grown up here and so will my son. I cannot speak for you though."

Khema was used to being teased about her rural background. Her mother and her mother-in-law had grown up in the same village. Her mother-in-law in some moment of unguarded childhood generosity had promised to make a daughter-in-law of Khema. Khema's mother had grumbled when her friend returned from the city with its ways. "She wants a dowry now. Why? Is not the girl enough? We just sat face to face, daubed a paste of turmeric, a sheet was thrown over us, an iron bracelet put on me and that was that. The marriage was complete. Where does this dowry business come from, I would like to know." But the city had greater prospects and the groom might be a driver some day. Khema's mother who had never seen the insides of a car could recognise still a good bargain. The dowry was put together. The village girl Khema came to the city, like her mother-in-law before her.

"I know that too. I mean where have we come from? Originally?"

"What?"

"The Brahmans say that they have come from the gods, so where have we come from?"

"I don't know and I don't care."

"I believe that they say we come from the feet of the gods whose head produces the Brahman. But that is what they say. Do you think it is true?"

"Are you going to worry about all that nonsense sitting out in the wet night. Come." But looking at the despondent droop of his wife's shoulders the gruff voice added, "Has anyone said anything to you? About your caste? Has anyone insulted you? I told you from the beginning that you should keep a certain distance from your employers. And talk less too. But would you listen? I think you should stop going to these…these parties in the kitchen."

"Shh. Don't talk so loudly. No. I was just thinking."

"Don't strain your brain so much. Let's go in. And remember there are only two castes in this world: employer and employee."

"My mother used to say that Lord Shiva was constantly playing the field with other women so his wife once tested his fidelity in the guise of a fisherwoman. He gave in to temptation but later when confronted with the truth Shiva too got angry and said that the child born of that union would be a Bagdi and live by fishing. That's where we come from. Do you think that is true?"

"What do I know of gods and goddesses except that they do not have to work for a living?"

"They do too," Khema cried out triumphantly. And then she lowered her voice. "How do we know that it was a disguise? Perhaps the goddess was a fisherwoman. What do you think?"

"I think it is nonsense. What is it to me anyway? I am not a fisherman and I am not going to be a peasant."

"Why do you always say it in that manner? If I had a choice I would go back any day to the village."

"And then die of hunger."

Khema was quiet for a while.

Her husband said again, "Nobody cares about villagers or farming in the city. Have you heard of Durgapur? They are building a steel city on the banks of the river Damodar. The future is in the cities." He bent a little more towards Khema, "I would like to have a small shop in Kolkata some day and repair cars. I think I am quite good at that. In the office area drivers always seek me out to tinker with their cars. I think I will speak to Rudrada one day. I won't leave this job of course but...." He sat there, drawing on his cheap and pungent bidi, flinging and spinning out hope with the soft weight of his wife by his side.

And Khema heard the distant echoes of old toothless women talking in the village, telling the young ones that they came actually from the heron or the jungle cock, the fish or the grass that existed even before the Brahmans. But why did they not speak out? Why did they not tell the Brahmans to leave their stories and their gods and goddesses alone? What compelled them to allow others to take charge of their lives?

Khema sat soft and quiet against her husband but wandering elsewhere in her mind, in search of meaning. A part of her longed for the moments in the kitchen where the fable of identity was not dismissed summarily so.

The mosquitoes whined and drew blood.

❈

The last bloodied rays of the fierce summer sun lit a fiery glow on the curve of the staircase of Kailash. The crimson light of the setting sun coming in through the big windows near the landing, torched the door to the room on one a half storey. In a few moments the door would be encased in dark. Shivani looked at it from the landing above. The bloodied hue did nothing to soothe her raging headache. Her breath seemed shallow and hot. Her legs trembled.

It had been hot on that terrace upstairs. All through the morning she had run after Rudra over that burning expanse till her mother-in-law finished her special puja for her grandson's birthday. But the morning was a lifetime ago.

Shivani gripped the banister quite unconsciously.

Slowly the sun withdrew. Softly the shadows began to creep in. Gradually they enfolded the door to the room on one a half storey.

A room where Kailash's horrific past was unfolded by Pishi.

Shivani saw again a room lit by a lamp. A room with two windows. The window on one side was now shut. When opened in the morning it gave a view of the temple of the goddess at Sitakunda in Chittagong. In the evening the window carried in the sounds of bell, conchshells and music: all the sounds of the goddess being worshipped. The house's proximity to the temple was one reason why the zamindar from Kynsa mati on a pilgrimage to Sitakunda had rented it. But now the window that let in the sights and sounds of the goddess's worship was shut. The louvred shutters were down on the window on the opposite side of the room too but for the last two slats which were a little unhinged. And with her eyes to it stood the five year old child transfixed, held there as though by some evil spell to watch her sister being smothered to death by her groom.

The younger girl had run when at last she could to what she thought was sanctuary to unburden her horror. But no one wanted to listen to her. No one wished to remember. But she could not forget her sister's small body thrashing and thrashing about under the heavy hand of a grown man, her groom. And her crime? She was not a Kulin girl. Her family was not the purest of the pure. Her father had not shown the kulpanji – the family tree and had not mentioned that the family had firingee dosha – that their pure blood had been sullied in intermingling with the Portuguese once upon a time. No one knew how or where or when. But occasionally a pair of green eyes appeared in the family. Someone had taken the trouble to inform Neelkantha and his brother in Sitakunda after an ecstatic session of devotional music of the goddess, of this thinning of the blood of the zamindar of Kynsa mati who claimed kulin Brahman status and trapped the divine Neelkantha into marrying his daughter. True, the daughter's eyes were black. But the green lay dormant deep within her and waited to uncoil and strike. Thus the marriage defiled the groom, the pristine Brahman groom, Dvija Neelkantha.

So. One child was killed. The other slowly went out of her mind. How could she relate to a world that denied what she had seen, that slapped her for saying that she had seen it and that told her that it would happen to her too if she did not forget it? Would it, she had wondered, trembling. Would the pillow come down on her face blotting out everything even as the hand rubbed and rubbed her tiny nipples as had happened to her sister? In daylight then, darkness would descend on her. She would feel the terror anew and the liquid trace of it escaping through her eyes and nose. Often, even down her legs in a stinking yellow mess. Forget it, they said, looking into her eyes. Shutters downed the eyes then but forget she did not. I have not forgotten you Di, I have not, she cried to herself. And when she saw the murderer revered, when she saw her father bringing him and installing him as the priest of the village temple, she banged her head against the old gnarled tree that Di had loved to climb. She said nothing when they found her with a bleeding forehead. She avoided the temple entirely as she saw the hands coming down to smother life when others saw it raised only to bless.

Her mother died. Her father remarried. She was free to be on her own with her nightmare. They tried to marry her off. But she ran away with the cunning of a crazed mind. But they won finally, drugged her and held her. Luckily her first born was a son for they let her be after that.

The shadows sketched strange figures in the approaching gloom. Shivani pressed her head with one hand. A muffled clattering sound came up from the kitchen. She should go down now, thought Shivani. She had stayed up in her room for far too long. The sun had withdrawn leaving only an afterglow in the sky. Soon the lamps would be lit in the streets. Thus man fights the dark. And careering down that man made path husbands and fathers would return home in a while.

Her father-in-law Shashishekhar, Neelkantha's son, would be returning home too.

Shashishekhar. Her father-in-law. The custodian of truth. He knew. He had known. And yet … Shivani's mind brought down the shutters too and sought the safety of the well trodden path.

She had written to her husband. She had done what she could. She had done the least she could for the time being. And the safest, the easiest, said a tiny voice from somewhere within her.

But now I must go down. I must, Shivani thought. Her head pulsated and thundered. The muscles down her calf seemed turgid with tension too.

Earlier, writing the letter at the sunlit table had brought some relief to Shivani. She had turned to her husband for she knew that in this matter she was a married woman and could not look to her father or her brothers or even her mother for succour. She was a Chattopadhyay now, however she felt.

I don't know if I should be writing all this to you so far away from home but I am so very upset. The deed was terrible and to conceal it so…

For a long while there had been nothing in the room but the brush of nib on paper. Rudra too had been quiet, playing with his new toys near her feet.

Shivani stood still on the landing lost in thought.

It was dusk.

Dusk when lamps are lit and by that light deeds of the night are witnessed, thought Shivani.

Her husband's grandfather had killed her friend's grandmother. A child. A bride of seven. Innocent and tender. Yet smothered out of existence.

Kailash had to atone for the life thus taken. It had to. It must. How could there be a God in the world otherwise?

A hand tugged Shivani's saree; a small pair of hands. She felt the goosepimples prickle her skin. But it was only her son come out of the bedroom to find her. He was tired now and perhaps a little uneasy too.

A noise made Shivani lean over the banister. Her mother-in-law was coming up the staircase. Haimanti would go up to the puja room now to finish her evening prayers before her husband returned home.

Haimanti seemed tired too.

Shivani prised open her son's hold on her saree and walked a few steps. Rudra remained where he was, perhaps remembering the threats of the afternoon. But he stretched upon his toes to look over the banister.

"Mother," Shivani called rather softly but even that made her head reverberate with pain. She lifted her hand and pressed her hot temple for a moment's ease.

Haimanti was tired.

But she was carrying on. She had to. The green-eyed one had come down to the kitchen too. There had to be a special dinner. It was the grandson's birthday after all. Haimanti had looked into the green eyes and issued orders for the evening. Then she had left the kitchen. Haimanti was glad for once that her daughters were not coming to dinner tonight with their families even though it was Rudra's birthday. She could not take that added strain of entertaining tonight and her daughters would have felt her sorrow. Providence then that they were not coming for the birthday. One had a husband down with fever and the other had fever herself. The ague seemed to be doing the round of the hot and humid city.

The shadows of the evening frightened Haimanti with the dark of the night round the corner. It threatened to bring back the horrors of the afternoon, carrying the choking cry of a young girl being muffled to death in a lamp-lit room.

Was there a shuffle of small feet from the shadowy depths above? In Kailash?

Haimanti forced herself to look up from the staircase. In the name of God.

She saw Shivani coming down, slowly, smoothening her hair. Shivani, Haimanti's daughter-in-law who had lost no time in carrying tales of Kailash to Ashutosh, her son far away from home. Tattling; thinking only of herself.

The demons of the night vanished for Haimanti.

I must tell her, thought Shivani, I must tell my mother-in-law that I have written to her son, my husband. He would know what to do, how to expiate the sin and how to relieve Kailash. Shivani knew that her mother-in-law too would find it easier to turn to her son rather than her own husband.

Her husband, Shashishekhar, who had brought the manuscript and Pishi from Chittagong and held truth in custody.

Haimanti and Shivani would turn to Ashutosh instead, the 'easily pleased', benign face of Shiva. He would lead them to penance and bring peace to Kailash.

Shivani's gaze embraced the door to the room on one a half floor as she crossed it and then she reached out her arm to reassure Haimanti as well.

Haimanti noted the flushed face of Shivani. She saw the arm reaching out in front of the room on one a half floor. For the green-eyed one she thought. The green-eyed one again.

Shivani saw the unhappy face of Haimanti. It mirrored her own state, she felt. Why! Kailash holds us both captive, thought Shivani in a sudden flash of compassion that wiped out her desolation for the moment. Shivani let go of the banister and took a few steps down. Towards Haimanti.

And then she leaned forward. Reaching out still.

Instinctively Haimanti turned ever so slightly. Away from Shivani, towards the wall.

Shivani's arm found nothing but air. Which you cannot clutch.

The head bumped against the steps all the way down.

Haimanti went numb except for her heart which heaved with each hollow thud that marked Shivani's fall. Haimanti tried to force her mouth open, to scream for help and in terror.

But amazingly Shivani got up at the bottom, pushed herself up and then hanging onto the banister slowly, started climbing up with crazy clumsy steps.

She lurched past Haimanti who now stood quivering with tension against the wall.

Shivani thought of nothing but to climb up to her bedroom. To reach sanctuary and Rudra whose eyes were large in a face dredged of all colour. Shivani looked only at that small face pushed against the rails of the banister up above.

I am coming child. I am coming. Shivani forced her eyes to remain on Rudra.

And Haimanti standing petrified near the landing of one and a half storey thought, as Shivani climbed past her with glazed unseeing eyes, that she did not matter to this chit of a girl at all; she who was Shivani's mother-in-law.

Rudra stood in the shadows of the upstairs landing with his heart in his mouth. He watched and waited for his mother to reach him.

Why, why was she walking thus? What did it mean?

☙❧

Meaning seemed to be elusive; full of contradictions and incoherences as the books of poetry and politics, history and divinity, Sanskrit and Bengali meshed a tangled web. But Uma carried on. Was a map of intentions and effects emerging?

The developed Chandimangals start appearing about the same time when the Afghan sultanate of Bengal is incorporated into the Mughal empire at the time of Akbar. The conquest is consolidated by early 17th century and Bengal rapidly develops into the richest subah of the Mughal empire.

"But why did those who had known the goddess as powerful and independent, Kalketu's goddess and Khullona's, allow her to be shackled in marriage?" Uma asked the women in Kailash in desperation when it seemed that the library would fail her too as had Kailash.

There was silence for a while.

Jumped up castes thought Bamundi. Mimicking our ways. Upper caste women don't work in the sun or roam the forest. But then she looked at her own dark, work-gnarled hands and was quite lost.

Khema spoke, "I have heard it said that there was a shift in the course of the rivers of the Delta, as a result of which many took to cultivation. I have heard it said in anger and jealousy how these people acquired riches and broke away from their clan's ways."

And Uma recalled then that she had read that the period of the growth of *Chandimangals* was also the period when there was a rapid growth in the European and Asian markets for Bengal's cotton and silk goods and food products. The period, from the middle of the 16th century to the middle of the 18th century that roughly coincided with the rise, spread and silting of the *Chandimangals* was thus a proliferation of possibilities for many people.

"And with their new money the people chose to follow the Brahmans," added Pishi in a tired voice, "Handing them their goddesses…"

"And their daughters…"

" …to become domestic drudges."

"To enhance their caste…"

"By handing over the freedom of their women..."
And women come cheap.
They looked at each other sharing the bitter gall.

※ ※

Life could not hold him so cheap. It could not. It should not. The
refrain hummed in Shashishekhar's head making him slightly
nauseous. The city rolled by him: Calcutta, a proud metropolis
of independent India. Independent but partitioned so that the
ode to freedom was sullied by the howls of the homeless and
shattered.

The car braked suddenly to avoid crushing a skeleton. The
skeleton moved. The city itself seemed to have become a relief camp
with refugees swarming everywhere, thought Shashishekhar. He
had always been a little suspect of the passion for independence
and look at what it had brought in its wake. Another skeleton with
a fly spotted infant at her hips scrabbled at his car window. He
was glad that he had warned his mother's family of the imminent
partition of the nation. But he was relieved too that most of them
had chosen to move to Silchar in Assam where a son-in-law had a
powerful family with land and political connections rather than to
Calcutta. Calcutta seemed to be growing old and tired before his
very eyes. Shashishekhar had heard of the forcible occupation of
deserted plots and houses by refugees in Jadavpore, Kasba, Garia
and Behala. Jabardakhal, seizure by force it was called blatantly.
This was the price of independence then. But sometimes when
he heard from the pavement the cry for succour in a Chittagong
dialect from some wretched victim of the Partition, it did pull
at some hidden heartstring of his. Well, if truth be told, he too
had come from Chittagong to Calcutta as a poor Brahman boy
dependent on others for survival. It was here in this city that he,
Shashishekhar, had learnt about the world and earned his place.
It was for him the city of opportunities and yes, of joy. Calcutta
was home for him. His only home. He did not like to see it
swamped thus.

The stalled car honked and then moved forward. Shashishekhar looked out of the window and the dread cold held him again in a fearful grip.

How could it be? How could he have been stricken thus? Of course he would seek a second opinion. But he felt that the diagnosis was right, absolutely right. He was certain of the impending doom. He had felt this certain of success when he had set out to print his father's work.

Cirrhosis of the liver. But that was the nemesis of alcoholism. Cirrhosis was the just retribution for the weak and base. He, Shashishekhar, had always been firm, meticulous and careful. Besides he had never touched the stuff. How could his liver, a part of him, betray him thus?

Shashishekhar had been suffering from indigestion for a month or so. "It is overwork," said his son. "It is all those chillies," said his wife. Just old age, he himself had said, not believing it for a moment. He was in the prime of his life. His mind was teeming with ideas. Independent India would need books. More books. Ashutosh was an able partner. True his manner was different and some of his ideas too, but he would be able to take The Ganges Press forward provided Shashishekhar was there to guide him for a while longer. Pity about Ashutosh's wife though, thought Shashishekhar. The girl, Shivani, was quite nice. Shashishekhar had chosen her himself. Or rather he had chosen the family. They had seemed to come from sturdy stock. Shashishekhar had great faith in those who left their ancestral locations to branch out and survive. How could he have guessed that the girl would have such a weak constitution? How could she die after a day's fever? A day after Rudra's birthday too and without knowing that in a month her husband would return home from England. Pity.

Of course Ashutosh could have married again. Maybe he should have. But he seemed not just reluctant but firm. Anyway, there was a grandson. Rudra. Now that lad seemed to have more fire in him. Shashishekhar smiled at the thought of his grandson.

Something had turned inside Shashishekhar that night after

Shivani's death when Haimanti had lain the sleeping Rudra between them. His daughters had come with their children on hearing the news, to be with them in this hour of grief. Haimanti had brought Rudra to their room, asking Khagen to pick up his sleeping body from the tangle of cousins from the next room.

"Let him be," Haimanti had said to Shashishekhar, adjusting the bed clothes over Rudra's small frame, "His father is not here. His mother just dead. Let him sleep with us. Don't start on your theories of bringing up strong citizens."

Shashishekhar had said nothing but gently smoothed the hair from his grandson's forehead. He did not remember trying to heal his children thus. The child looked tired and there were blue shadows like bruises under the eyes now shut in sleep.

Later in the middle of the night Shashishekhar had woken up to see Rudra staring wide eyed in the dark.

"Do you want water?"

The child shook his head. And then shut his eyes.

But Shashishekhar knew that his grandson was feigning sleep to avoid conversation or contact. Oh he knew this need to avoid. He had known it so often in his own childhood. So he let his grandson be. But he lay awake himself, keeping vigil.

He was glad when Haimanti turned in her sleep and placed an arm on the child. But Rudra stiffened. A little later the child carefully picked up the arm and placed it away from his body.

Haimanti was upset when Rudra refused to return to his grandparents' bedroom to sleep the day Ashutosh came home from England.

"Come my golden one," Haimanti had said when darkness gathered in Kailash and the visiting relatives had left. "Come to your grandparents' bedroom. Let your father rest. He has been travelling for many days to reach home." Haimanti had wiped her eyes too.

Rudra laced his arms through the intricately curved poles at the foot of the bed and looked at the man who was his father though he scarcely remembered him as a person.

"Come." Haimanti said again. "Let your father sleep undisturbed tonight."

Rudra tightened his grip on the bed post.

Ashutosh looked at the child through the slats at the foot of the bed.

"Let him be with me," said he.

Haimanti stood still. It was Shashishekhar then who gently steered her away from the room.

Shashishekhar never returned home without something for his grandson.

Haimanti teased him sometimes. "You never did all this for your own children."

"That was the principal amount, one had to be careful. This is the interest. One can just enjoy this – the grandson's childhood."

Shashishekhar's own childhood was different. He had not known want of course. Not at all. But he had not known assurance either. Not in that gross house which belonged to his maternal uncles, those creatures of flesh. But none of them had died of cirrhosis. As far as he knew. Why him then? Why? Was it not genetic? Was he not his father's?

His father Dvija Neelkantha knew no excess, no indulgence either. He was an ascetic. He was self sufficient. But his family? A voice whispered. What did Shashishekhar know of his father's family? He had heard that his father had a brother but he had never seen him. His father never talked of his family. No one knew where he came from or what he had left behind. No one asked him either. No one dared to. Dvija Neelkantha was Svayambhu – self-generated. Like the gods.

Shashishekhar suddenly tapped his silver-headed walking stick on the floor of the car in frustration. The driver looked back, Shashishekhar shook his head. Why cirrhosis? Why him? His feet were swollen and soft. It was this that had finally driven him to visit the family doctor. Ashutosh had threatened action. But Shashishekhar did not want the doctor to come home to proclaim a fatal diagnosis.

Had he known it then, known and not known, that he was stricken? But why him? Why? He had been a good man. Motivated. Principled. He had never harmed anyone. Why, that Bagdi family was on the verge of death on the pavement outside Kailash when Shahsishekhar had asked the skeleton-like mother and son to be given succour in the servant's chamber. It was the usual story. The father had left the homestead and the tiny parched piece of land to come to the city and join the stream of mill workers. The family had waited for money and news. The wife and the son had been driven out when neither came.

It was a sound investment too. Look at Khagen now. Shashishekhar had helped get him married, buy a plot in his wife's village. The snotty, scrawny boy had grown up to be a pillar of Kailash. Khagen was tireless and faithful. Shashishekhar always knew how to hedge his bets. Slowly voices and faces filled the car of those he had helped and those who had been left behind.

"We have reached Kailash, babu," said the driver finally.

Shashishekhar got off slowly.

It was his heart that failed him finally.

Which is often the case with cirrhosis.

※ ※

Their heart was in the right place whatever be the states of their stomachs. The two men at the counter of the National Library, after some confabulation, led Uma to the man who sat by himself at a table at the far end of the hall.

He was thin with a crow's nest for hair. Some of it appeared to have got disentangled to settle over his upper lip. The white kurta could do with a wash and ironing. But the eyes that gleamed behind the spectacles were sharp. Uma almost lost her nerve.

"The gentlemen at the counter directed me to you. They said that some of the books that I have requisitioned are with you, if you don't mind could I take a look at those please?"

Crow's nest seemed reluctant but it was difficult to say no to a lady, especially if she is beautiful and humble.

Uma repeated, "That's my table, may I just see what you have got?"

"What is your area of research?"

"I am just reading about the *Chandimangal*."

"I am working on *Abahatta* – the *laukika* pre-Bengali linguisitic formation. Don't take more than one book at a time from my lot. Please return the book today and as soon as possible."

Reaching out for the pile before the self-assured scholar Uma paused suddenly. "Can you tell me if there is a *Chandimangal* that talks of the goddess as a Dombi or a Chandali?"

"Not *Chandimangal* but *Carjyapad*."

Uma knew she had fallen in Crow's nest eyes forever as a scholar.

Crow's nest jangled his feet beneath the table, "The *Carjyapad*, the earliest literary composition in Bengal mentions a female deity who is the low Chandali or Dombi."

"How come nobody talks of it?"

"Who talks of old Bengali literature these days?"

Uma got up.

"Excuse me."

Crow's nest held out a slim volume brown with age. "*Hajhar Bacharer Purano Bangla Bhashaye Baudhyo Gaan O Doha*, a collection of Buddhist songs and Doha from the thousand year old Bengali language. This was put together by Haraprasad Shashtri almost half a century ago. This should have what you are looking for."

Uma reached out. The volume was pulled back by Crow's nest.

"I am working on it. I have to finish my work and get back to my job. I teach Bengali in Behrampur. In a school." The last was hurled at Uma almost defiantly.

"My grandfather was a school teacher too, in Barishal," Uma looked out of the ceiling-high windows of the library. Two gardeners were dragging a thick, black pipe across the emerald green expanse. The library was earlier the palace of the Lieutenant-Governor of imperial Bengal. Did Warren Hastings also watch his gardeners thus?

"Well, you can have it for a brief while tomorrow afternoon," said Crow's nest softening, "But I need it too, let me tell you. I have to finish my work and leave soon enough. You can't keep me waiting."

"I will come tomorrow just for it."

※ ※

When Shashishekhar died many came for his funeral. The publishing world and the men of letters were well represented. He would have been proud of the gathering but perhaps a little disconcerted too on hearing some of them say in soft murmurs that he was perhaps a little conservative, a little reactionary and a little behind the times.

Why? Shashishekhar would have wondered. Was he not the one to give Bengal one of her finest literary masterpieces? Had he not propagated the modern novel? Did he not recognise the newly educated woman and print booklets for her? What else should he have done?

Haimanti shaved her head, removed all her jewellery and wore stark white. She had never looked so serene, said some, as she sat with folded hands amidst wailing relatives inside Kailash.

The rituals of death were observed in accordance with the rules.

Gradually the relatives stopped their well meaning daily visits. Shashishekhar's daughters departed from Kailash to pick up the threads of their own lives with their husbands, children and in-laws. The servants went back to their routines. The sun and the wind carried away the lingering smell of the funerary rituals: flowers, sandalwood, incense and ghee. And Haimanti knew peace at last. She knew that she deserved it too. She had done her duty. She had served Kailash faithfully.

Oh yes. Haimanti also asked that Pishi be given only white sarees, the widow's garb, to wear from now on. She did not have to deal with the green-eyed one herself. The sarees were ordered with the monthly grocery. She just decreed the colour. Haimanti prepared to suffer furtive glances and sly whispers. But better that the world think this of her husband and the green-eyed one, the usual masculine failing of the flesh, than the truth about the green-eyed one's relation with Kailash, thought Haimanti. She, Haimanti, was now the custodian of Kailash's honour after all. Her husband would have preferred this too. Haimanti understood that now. If eyebrows were raised and whispers echoed at the white on Pishi's person, they did not ascend the higher reaches of Kailash.

A big photo of Shashishekhar graced Haimanti's bedroom. She changed the garland each morning and increased her bratas and fasts. She visited temples and even attended some sessions at the Ramakrishna Mission, founded in 1897, with her sisters-in-law. Shashishekhar had been a little chary of the Mission as it drew too many followers from the ordinary middle class, gryhastya, families. But Ashutosh did not ask any questions and always sent the car whenever Haimanti asked for it. Sometimes he asked in concern, "Should you really be fasting so much?" Haimanti was fulfilled once again.

Marking the pale green shadow gracing Rudra's upper lips and hearing his voice on the verge of breaking, Haimanti suggested that Rudra move out of his father's bedroom to occupy his grandparents' room. "My grandson needs his own space, his grandfather would know peace too if he sees a growing Rudra now occupying the same room from where we started our life in Kailash," she told her son and grandson, "As for me, I really don't wish to be in that room any more. In earlier days at my age, people left the household for the forest. I will move to a smaller room on the same floor."

Rudra said that he would not mind the puja room upstairs with the terrace thrown in. The family of deities could come down.

But the gods and goddesses remained where they were and it was Haimanti who moved laterally. She left behind the big framed photo of Shashishekhar on the wall though. Her own companion piece nestled in the cupboard for future use.

Rudra moved with his books, chess board, gramophone and records to the 'master' bedroom.

Kailash settled down to a new rhythm. Mother, son and grandson.

On the terrace upstairs, Pishi sometimes paused to think of the girl who had also come to stay in Kailash. A smell, a smile and snatches of poetry wove a presence and then was gone in an instant as the puja room was tidied and latched or the dry clothes were picked, folded and brought down.

❧ Sixteen ❧

"Yes?"

It was Rudra who picked up the phone at The Ganges Press instead of Ashutosh.

Uma, speaking from Kailash, was actually quite relieved. She had not quite realised how nervous she was.

"Oh, you are at the press already? Aren't you very early?" she asked a little breathlessly.

"I had to discuss something with Baba. But I find that he has gone out," said Rudra.

"Baba did call home earlier to say that the car can't come for me today as he has some urgent work to attend to...." Uma paused but there was only silence at the other end. "Actually I was getting ready to go to the library and could not take Baba's call. Khagenda told me. But I do need to go to the library today. I could not tell you last night that I found a very important book there." Uma paused again but still there was no response. "I must go today. Can I? I will take a bus. Shall I go? It is rather urgent." Her anouncements trembled uncertainly and became queries seeking sanction.

"Sure. Why not? And why don't you take a taxi?"

"I feel better in a bus. Safer. There is a direct one too. I know that."

"As you like."

"Tell Baba too won't you? Do explain to him why I need to go to the library today even though the car is not available. He must not misunderstand. Tell him about the book."

Rudra's impatience crackled over the telephone line.

Uma repeated nonetheless, "Don't forget to tell Baba."

"I won't."

"See you in the evening then. Will you be late again?"

"I just might. This work has come up and…I will give a ring if it gets very late."

"Okay. I am going then. All right?" Mortified Uma found that the hand that replaced the reciever was sweating. But it was all right to go, was it not?

Rudra thought of Uma as he stood staring at the black instrument now silent in its cradle. She had turned out to be somewhat different from his expectation. Just as well perhaps, he thought. That had been a silly reason of his for wanting to marry. One cannot escape like that, using one's wife. Not from Kailash.

The door opened with a familiar creaking noise.

Mrs. McCluskie, Ashutosh's personal secretary put around a grey head in a stiff bob and asked Rudra if he would like a cup of tea. Rudra shook his head. He used to call her McClue aunty once. She called him Rudra baba when he visited the Press with his father and gave him biscuits from her drawer from a round tin box inlaid with Buckingham Palace guards. Mrs. McCluskie's short hair, frock-clad figure, the clacking of her typewriter and the fluid gesture with which she pushed the piston back at regular intervals used to fascinate Rudra as a child. The relic of a community forged out of an alliance between the white ruling man and the black native girl, Mrs. McCluskie with her fair skin now a patchwork of wrinkles and freckles, seemed to be shrinking like her community. She no longer addressed him as Rudra baba though she did not call him 'Sir' either as yet. Rudra too did not call her 'aunty' any more. He could not even remember the day he stopped.

Ashutosh's office echoed Rudra's sigh. The walls on every side were covered with book-lined shelves here. Some books were piled on the floor too while another lot lay on Ashutosh's desk with new proofs and copies. Every book carried the oval logo in gold of The Ganges Press on its spine. The smaller room to the left of this one was Rudra's at the moment. There too the walls were similarly lined with books. A leaden weight seemed to hold Rudra to the spot.

Slowly Rudra became aware of a sound from the street filtering into the room, thinning its viscous air. He walked across his father's office to stand at the window.

> *Inquilab, zindabad. Amader dabi, mante hobe.*
> *Amader dabi, mante hobe.*

> Long live the revolution.
> You have to agree to our demands.

A tram, like an engorged worm, stood still in the distance. A motley crowd was crossing the track in a procession raising slogans. The placards that some of them held could not be read from the upstairs window of The Ganges Press though.
Inquilab, zindabad.
Some passers-by raised their fists to the slogan.
Rudra felt his blood beginning to churn slowly with the sound from the street.

※ ※

The street lay innocuously open before Uma, gleaming black under the morning sun of mid-September. Fifty steps or so from the gates of Kailash, she thought, one by-lane, not that, another by-lane, not that either. She must carry on walking till she reached the house with the high pink walls. A third by-lane curved out from there which would lead to the main road. A small cigarette kiosk would suddenly come in view as she moved forward along the curve.

Uma had been on these streets many times before but always in a car with someone else navigating. Her own senses did not need to be alert then – not in this way at any rate. Today she felt tense, a little like a fugitive, aware of the solemn presence of Kailash behind her.

Uma lifted her saree and stepped over a puddle. It had rained again last night but a pleasing shower, not the ferocious monsoon downpour. The sky was now a clean blue festooned with massive white clouds. It was an autumn sky, a puja sky. But she would not be going home this puja. Rudra had told her that he could not take a break now. He had work to do. She could go on her own or they could go together in December. He had heard a lot about the Delhi winter, Rudra had added. She would wait for winter then, naturally. And in the meanwhile she too had work to do.

A rickshaw tong tonged gently from behind and Uma crossed the road quickly. The small clusters of white flowers on a dark green plant hung over the pink wall of a corner house marked by a graffiti of the hammer and sickle. At this hour the area was quiet, taking a brief respite from the rush of the day. Early morning shopping was over. The office goers and most school children had left home long ago. Two maids engrossed in conversation walked past Uma with the flip flop of plastic slippers. An old gentleman under a black umbrella stopped suddenly in front of her as though he had forgotten something. A little boy ran out of the partially ajar rusted iron gates of a house even as a thin reedy voice called out a warning from inside. Uma smiled at the child and her nervous tension at being out on her own after so long began to dissolve.

Now she could hear the hum of traffic from the main road. Ah! The cigarette kiosk.

The two young men chatting lazily by the kiosk looked at Uma from across the road. One said something and then the other immediately turned his head to look her way. They were saying something about her, Uma was certain. What could it be? There goes the new bride from Kailash, the girl from Delhi? But this time she did not flounder. Her mood had changed imperceptibly. Uma took out her cats-eye dark glasses, put them on and in a new surge of confidence reached the main road. The bus marked 'Alipore Zoo' trundled along almost immediately. The conductor leaned out. Three senior schoolgirls in white sarees with green borders, got off the bus chattering happily. Uma climbed in.

There was no going back now.

The city rolled by her. Calcutta. Kolkata. The city that she was beginning to love and know. It was her city now; she could not imagine belonging to any other.

A woman with a small child touched Uma's wrist lightly to

indicate that she would be getting off now and that Uma could take her seat. The insignificant gesture warmed her. Uma smiled and then sank into the seat still steamy with the press of human contact. She would get off at the terminus. The National Library would be just across the road. There was nothing to worry about even though she was on her own like never before.

* *

Rudra refused to acknowledge that he was worried. Instead he opened the windows wider still to catch the sounds of the street but the procession had moved on. Impatiently Rudra chucked the butt out. As though on cue, the familiar bonnet of the Studebaker nosed its way into the street. A little boy in long faded grey shorts holding a kettle of tea in one hand and small clay cups in the other stood stock still on the pavement staring at the car. The tea stall across the road sent tea every two hours to the Press through its midget workers. Its supply of little rickety boys from the suburban hinterland of the city seemed to be endless. Rudra could not see the boy's face but he could imagine the expression of wonder and desire on it. Ashutosh's elegant figure emerged from the back seat of the car. He said something to the boy with a smile and then looked up, saw his son and after a moment's hesitation, or so it seemed to Rudra, raised a hand. The sun glinted on Ashutosh's greying hair and from above his tall frame appeared very spare. Baba is growing old thought Rudra, his heart contracted and he stepped back into the room and felt once again the familiar pattern of the past shading his life.

But not this time, Rudra thought. No 'buts' this time.

The little boy followed Ashutosh into the Ganges Press balancing the clay cups on top of each other carefully.

* *

Uma chose her words very carefully. She did not wish to offend Crow's nest.

"Please, I have been looking for this lead for a long time. I know

I am not a researcher like you but I have come today especially because you said you would lend me this book." And I have come on my own.

"I will, I just have to finish one section."

"It was difficult to come today but I came because you said…"

"I don't underdstand why you are rushing me like this."

An elderly gentleman looked up from the next table, his pen poised over a notebook. Uma felt the glow of embarrassment warm on her face, tingling her ears. How could she explain to Crow's nest that a nervous impatience had taken hold of her? If the goddess was referred to as Dombi somewhere in some old verses then the Mother Goddess was layered as Khema had argued. The goddesses had evolved as Dadu had suggested. There was something forged as Bamundi suspected. There was something forgotten. As with Pishi.

But Crow's, nest was intractable. Uma returned to her table.

Her watch seemed to be keeping time to a slower beat. The book of poetry that she had picked up while waiting for Crow's nest to keep his word could not really hold her attention. Uma drew a deep breath and then started copying some of the poems from the collection. She formed the letters carefully in an attempt to curb her nervous impatience. It was then that she noticed what she had been reading:

> *Prithibir shei manushir roop?*
> *Sthul hathe byabharita hoye-byabharita-*
> *byabharita-byabharita-byabharita hoye-*
> *byabharita-byabharita*
>
> The earth's feminine self?
> In coarse hands being used-used-
> Used-used-being used-
> Used-used

The day seemed miraculously sprinkled with meaning.

Soon perhaps, she would lift the cover off a conspiracy that had escalated a deity beyond the reach of her people, ensconcing her in Kailash.

But Uma had to go back to Kailash too. Before it grew dark and the men returned.

"How much longer?" Uma asked Crow's nest an hour later, leaning over the table.

& &

Bamundi leaned over the fire and stoked it again. She was tired. It had been a long day but she had just been asked to fry luchi for the unexpected visitors of the young couple for whom she cooked early in the evening. It meant that she would get late for the last port of call where she cooked dinner. This couple often made these sudden unreasonable demands on her time. Bamundi had thought that she would give up her work in this house but instead she would now have to look for yet another house to work in. She needed more money. Her son had not contributed anything towards the household for months now. She could squeeze in another house in the afternoon perhaps. But not right away, not while the reading sessions lasted in the kitchen at Kailash. It was something that she looked forward to all day long, a moment's peace in the backbreaking drudgery of her life.

There was a burst of laughter from the drawing room. Bamundi lifted a tired arm and wiped the sweat gathering on her forehead. I will look for another job after puja maybe, after Lakshmi puja perhaps that comes in the wake of Durga puja. The sessions in Kailash would come to end by then.

It stirred within her again, that sense of a guilty unease. Why had she not shared what had come to her mind that day in Kailash when Uma had mentioned that the *Harivamsha* describes the devi as the goddess of the outcastes and then had spoken of a devi who was dark …

As Uma spoke, Bamundi's memory unbidden, had yielded an image.

Lakshmi puja in the village. The mud and thatch home. She still a wife and the granary, if not full, full enough. The golden moon was slowly rising in the autumn sky and she was getting ready for the worship of Lakshmi under her hawk-eyed mother-in-law. But before Lakshmi could be propitiated, a rival of the golden goddess had to be ceremoniously evicted from the house. This was Alakshmi, a dark skinned deity with black open hair, who wore iron ornaments and whose ritual involved the use of winnowing fan, cow dung and the hair of women. Alakshmi had no husband. She had to be thrown away to make way for the golden domesticated Lakshmi.

"Whom did we throw away mother, in ignorance?" Bamundi miserably asked in the steamy kitchen. She remembered that Alakshmi was given the epithet Jyestha or the eldest. But older than whom Bamundi wondered now. Could she have been the goddess of an earlier time? Was she Khema's goddess?

But she had not been able to voice her thoughts in the kitchen at Kailash, hanging on for the moment to the honour, the only honour she could now claim, of being a Brahman, though a poor working widow. She could not bring herself to share her misgivings with Khema in the kitchen, overcome suddenly by envy of Khema's strong young body, a husband by her side, her assured roof in Kailash and yes, of Uma's obvious affection for her.

"Am I reduced to this, thrown out of my house, to be a hired hand in another's kitchen because I evicted Jyestha? But I did not know you mother, like all the others, I too accepted what I was told, so why am I being punished thus mother?" Bamundi softly wept in the kitchen for her lost life though her hands carried out the task of rolling out the luchi and the careful frying. "When will it end, Ma, this trial of mine? When?"

"They are not being fried right. The luchis are not properly swollen," someone called out from the dining table inside.

࿓ ࿓

Father and son faced each other across the table as they did every day.

Ashutosh opened the conversation. "You have asked the office to do the costs, give an estimate, for your series called '*The Other Calcuttans*'?" a pause, and then, "Mr. Rakshit told me."

"I just wanted an estimate," Rudra looked at his father. "I did tell you about the project. I did not deliberately keep it from you. If that is what you think."

Inquilab, zindabad.

Is it that finally wondered Ashutosh.

"What I think does not really matter. It is what the others in the office may think. We have a reputation to look after," Ashutosh held up his hand as though in anticipation of Rudra's dismissive rejoinder.

Rudra shrugged. "I just wanted to know how much the series would cost. I did not think that required a clearance too. We had not decided that The Ganges Press would print it."

"We?"

"Yes. My friends and I."

"Your comrades?" Ashutosh said a little sardonically and then grew silent, gathering strength, waiting for that despondent sense of loneliness. He had been preparing himself for this, to be left out, to be left alone. He thought he was prepared like the stoics.

Rudra laced his fingers casually on the table. As always the drawn face of his father began to dissolve his resolution and bring in its wake that familiar feeling of frustration.

Echoes.

I want bread.

Thrice a week then.

I don't want her to arrange things in my cupboards.

I will tell her. But your grandmother lives for us.

Why their bedroom? Give me a room elsewhere. Kailash is big enough.

She is moving out for you. She has lost her husband.

I won't go through the initiation ceremony of a Brahman. I won't wear the paite – the sacred thread is nothing but nonsense.

Throw it away later.

I want to study literature.

Economics is better. Your grandfather came from the village and built this business.

I will join St. Xavier's.

But Presidency has such a faculty! Besides I went there too and so did your grandfather.

I don't believe in funeral ceremonies. I refuse to shave my head.

I have lost my father. Just be there by my side.

The moments were stamped indelibly in Rudra's mind. How often, how many times did he and his father sit together negotiating desire and duty? Don't. Don't negotiate this time Baba, please, thought Rudra. Don't bring love and family into it. Don't say who has done what, for whom and therefore.

The moments stabilised. It was Rudra who broke the uneasy silence finally, "Baba. There is a world outside Kailash."

"Rudra, we…"

"At least for me there is."

The cold hand of loneliness slowly reached inside Ashutosh's ribcage. He smiled a little and said, "As there is for everyone, as there should be. But maybe we should discuss our social lives at home. What concerns me here is that *The Other Calcuttans* is…" Ashutosh paused.

"…about the midden heap of our city? Tiljala, Tangra, Topsia and the shanty slums exist too Baba. We have to move beyond the charmed circle of our families." Again Rudra's voice hardened.

"We can do what we wish to without denigrating our families, Rudra."

"Not us, Baba, you know that. Let's not pretend that our family, with its Kulin Brahman claim, does not dig its claws into us and drag us back into Kailash."

The echoes caught up with Ashutosh too.

Let's liquidate love.

His brief sojourn in London was as a student after having become a father and manager of The Ganges Press. It had not been easy to leave but he knew what was expected of him. The Ganges Press required a stamp of western expertise. It was what his father desired. And so.

Yet despite the heavy heart London cast its own spell on him.

Ashutosh could still see the rooms neighbouring his London digs bursting with posters and leaflets. He could still recall the passionate talks about the Spanish Civil War. Once he was taken by friends to a small snack bar, Marie's café, to the left of the main entrance to the London School of Economics. He could still hear, if he wished to, the lusty young voices singing to a Cole Porter like tune,

> *Let's liquidate love*
> *Let's say from now on*
> *That all our affection's*
> *For the workers alone …*

There was a mesmerising sense of youthful purpose in the air. A promise of universal brotherhood. But Ashutosh remained on the fringe remembering Kailash: his father's dreams, his mother's loneliness, his wife's farewell words, "*Kobe ashbe*? – When will you return?" And his son's wet sloppy kiss.

Ashutosh walked alone in the cold and foggy roads of London, dreaming of Kailash and his country's warmth to which he longed to return.

Ashutosh looked up and saw that his son's eyes were on him. But guarded. It cut him to the heart though what he said was, "The Ganges Press never has printed agitation and propaganda literature."

"Hasn't it? " The sweep of Rudra's hand took on the whole room carelessly, "What is this then? If not fodder for upper caste, middle class values?"

Careful, careful warned Ashutosh's heart. "Rudra it is not that I don't understand. But…"

But. Yes. There had always been the but. Always. Negotiating. Conforming.

"If you *know* then there is no but." This time Rudra was abrupt too.

Except for a sharp intake of breath, Ashutosh refused to show that the cold hand now gripped his heart entirely. He leaned forward a little to ease the pain. The words flowed all around him.

Rudra was speaking passionately. The words wavered and mingled like the buzz of bees. No. He could not let the words sweep him away. Ashutosh intervened rather abruptly again, "Business runs on different principles from politics."

"Does it? I thought that the question that must always be asked in both, before we do anything, is 'What's in it for us'?"

"These are fine words Rudra, if a little jaded. I am sorry but perhaps the problem is that you never had to scrabble for a living. You had a career handed to you, a roof over your head and so…"

"When does the debt get over, Baba?"

This time Ashutosh expressed no emotion or words.

Father and son sat in silence for a while as though the silence was a natural calm. A pigeon fluttered outside. And then Ashutosh said in an even voice, "Rudra. The mood of the moment won't endure. Trust me. Not because I am your father, but because I am older and have been young before. Can't you see it? Yesterday it was Stalin, then the denunciation came not from a bourgeois press but Moscow itself, and now it's the Chinese. I agree that the world should be a better place too but these squabbling sects can't… "

"Should? I think that the world *must* become a better place but it can't get better on its own. Can it?"

"And publishing these booklets, these little magazines, these… what are you calling it… *The Other Calcuttans*…would change the world?"

"Forgive me Baba, but if you don't believe in the power of the printed word then what are you doing in this office? Oh I agree this is not revolutionary enough. My blood is perhaps too thin for that. But let me make a beginning at least. Away from all this." Rudra swept the room with his angry, impatient hand once again.

"You don't need to pull down in order to move forward. This is the fatal mistake of the present day."

"There has to be a rubble clearing before we breathe, and think, free."

"You can not annihilate an entire tradition. Our culture, our sanskriti…"

"Culture is akin to cultivation Baba. Of the land and the mind. But when you talk of your culture, your sanskriti, all this, you don't think of agriculture do you?"

"Do you?"

"Our, our... tradition... has made the custodians of culture and cultivation strangers to each other. Let us begin now, once again, to talk of culture not as sanskriti but as krishti, as cultivation that removes the weeds, prepares the land and furrows it."

"Krishti? That's an old debate and sanskriti has survived."

"Let The Ganges Press show then that culture need not be sanskriti with its devouring fire sacrifices, presiding Brahmans and elite ways but krishti that reminds us of the sweat of labour and the peasants' – krishis' lives. And let us leave Kailash and our sanskriti behind. I have had enough of it."

Ashutosh leaned back wearily, "Why don't you give up this shadow boxing with your grandmother Rudra? She is dead and gone."

"Oh for... Let us not talk family now. Let us not reduce it to that always." Rudra's voice sounded very deep or perhaps it was just that the blood was rushing through Ashutosh's veins, warming his ears and filling his head.

"You are the one who mentioned Kailash."

"I am tired of Kailash. It stifles me," Rudra got up.

Ashutosh's heart beat an irregular rhythm again. This time it seemed to reach his throat and lodge there every now and then. He drew deep breaths to steady it as unobtrusively as possible. He must not show that it hurt. He must not let on how lonely he felt in Kailash these days despite the presence of another person there, indeed a caring and gentle presence. Uma was dutiful. She would give him company if he so wished but of late he had sensed a certain change in her. No it was not defiance or indifference. It was as though her mind was elsewhere, on another track, and she was only indulging him as the young indulge a harmless wrinkled oddity. He had carried on telling her about the past that he knew but helpless with a loneliness that slowly smothered him.

Rudra's voice floated softly from behind him, close to the window, "If truth be told Baba, I married a girl from Delhi, to escape Kailash. I thought in some foolish, foolish and unformed way, that she would help me get away from all this, that she would help me leave Kailash as she would not feel the pull of it as I do." Rudra returned to the table and smiled wryly, once again his son. "Oh yes. Kailash tugs at me still. But Uma seems to have fallen in love with Kailash. So much then for my prop."

"And isn't your politics just another prop? What do you want Rudra? I wonder if you know it yourself."

Ashutosh sat in solitude in the darkening room forcing his eyes to follow the lines of the letters that Mrs. McCluskie brought in. He longed to get up and leave his work for the day but he did not feel like going back to the yawning emptiness of Kailash either. Ashutosh bent his head and pulled another letter forward to sign. He looked tired and more than that. Mrs. McCluskie looked at him with genuine concern.

"A cup of tea for you Sir?"

Ashutosh shook his head.

So she left the room.

And then Ashutosh was by himself again. As he often was. As he often felt these days.

The Ganges Press's proud production rested just above his head, on the shelf behind. Neelkantha's *Chandimangal.*

స్తు స్తు

Uma read.

> *Ganga, Jamuna manjhere bahai naii*
> *Tahi burili matangi pauia lile paar karei....*

> The boat floats between Ganga and Jamuna
> Old Matangi helps us cross over.

The language of the doha was not entirely familiar but there was a lilt to it as it drew the contour of a goddess who was not the upper caste wife and mother grist to the mill of domestic labour or the fantastic warrior on a lion. As she read, Uma for the first time saw the goddess as a dark woman whose skin glistened with sweat as she rowed a boat with the sun dancing on the water, who worked in a green field that swayed gently in the wind or wove a basket of bamboo and twine with her legs spread out in front of her. And it was not a disguise either, taken on at will by the goddess to charm a philandering husband at a moment's play.

These are the other goddesses Uma thought who dot my country. Goddesses called Dombi, Chandali, Matangi and Shabari who have been left out of the upper caste altar:

Nagarbahiri re Dombi toheri kuriya....

Dombi your hut is outside the settlement....

Why, they are like Rudra's 'Other Calcuttans' Uma thought suddenly and then sitting in the library she felt warm and very close to her husband, as she had never felt before. She had married him and she loved him as a natural linear progression. But now came understanding, at least now she thought that she understood an important part of him. And that part was like her. Uma had never before thought of Rudra as weak or wanting. But she saw him now as mirroring her own desire for security of the familiar and felt compassion as warm as love for his efforts, however feeble, to move beyond that. The soft light of the declining day fell on the old and scratched wooden table of the library and Uma gently touched the frayed book that rested on it as though caressing Rudra's tired face.

Like one possessed Uma read through that evening and thought that meanings are inscribed variously. Songs, stories and poetry represent one way. Life yet another.

❧❧

In the room adjoining Ashutosh's at The Ganges Press, Rudra sat staring at the manuscript of the first of the series called *The Other Calcuttans*. But he thought only of his father. How he had looked and what he had said.

It grew dark.

❦

The pink walls seemed even more lurid in the dark but for Uma there was never a sight more welcome. She hurried towards it and felt the tension slowly draining out of her system with every step. Now she could see the grafitti of hammer and sickle on the wall as well. She could find Kailash now.

She had not meant to get this late. But it had happened.

Crow's nest had taken his time over the book before handing it to Uma and then Uma had been lost. The sun had lit up the big windows of the library before beginning its slow descent. Another five minutes and then another, Uma had bargained with herself as the shadows forayed into the reading hall.

Later, she could not get into one bus because of the crowd that suddenly surged forward. She missed the next one too which arrived and left just as she had hesitantly started walking towards the taxi stand a little distance away. She returned to the bus stop only to find another bus gathering speed. Its broad retreating back spewed black fumes at her with malicious glee.

"Do you need help, sister?" It was a thin oily face and the concern issuing from dark tobbacco stained lips may well have been genuine but Uma shook her head and moved closer to the swelling knot of commuters in front of the bus stop.

She looked at her watch all the while. But I have told them, I did, she reassured herself.

It did not help that the street lights came on to officially announce the dark.

The city seemed different at night when she was on her own.

Finally close to tears, Uma managed to board a bus and pushed her way through the tired and testy crowd returning home after a day's work. She got off at what seemed the familiar landscape. But it turned out to be a different bus stop. She could not bring herself to board another bus and started walking to reach Kailash.

Turning and turning about she reached an old mansion numbered 17/3 and thought she had finally reached home for

Kailash was 20/3 but 17 led inexplicably to 24 from which emanated faint strains of a familiar song by Tagore. She stood outside the house fighting down panic. Her faltering steps then took her to a busy lane with small shops of brass and copper ware that she did not even know existed so close to Kailash. The winding maze led to a narrow street whose cobbled pavement was laid out with mud stoves. Shadows moved in the damp dark and coal fires lent a charred smell to the atmosphere. Uma drew the end of her saree tight across her body to guard her modesty, and gold, in an unconscious gesture, and hurried past the knots of bare-chested men, loud-voiced women and mud-coloured children. It was then that she saw an old rickshaw-wallah resting where the shadows gathered suggesting yet another narrow curve. Or rather she heard him first and drifted forward towards the song:

> *Ooncha ooncha pavat tanhi basai sabari vali*
> *Morangi piccha parahin sabari gibat gunjari mali*
> *Nana tarubar maulil re gaanat lageli dali*
> *Ekeli savai eban hindaee karnakundalavajradhari …*

> The mountains are high and Savari resides there
> Gunja garland around her neck and peacock
>   feathers she wears,
> The branches bear flowers and shoot up in the
>   sky where
> Alone, Savari roams the forest, rings in her ears
>   and the thunder bolt she bears …

The rickshaw-wallah gently struck his bell on the bars of his rickshaw to measure the rhythm of his song. Sweat gleamed on his face and his singlet was wet, sticking to his body. But his eyes were closed and he appeared impervious to all but his song of the goddess in whose search Uma had spent the day.

Uma stood still. Her skin felt cold and then warm. She is here, thought, Uma, she is here in the streets. She has been here all the while. And I never heard it. Slowly she walked towards the rickshaw.

"Are you lost?" The rickshaw-wallah opened his eyes and then slowly sat up.

"Yes. No. Your song baba?"

"Song?"

"What were you singing just now?"

"Just a fragment. A broken song. The rest has been left behind in the village." He smiled and stood up, lifting the bars of the rickshaw with both hands. "You want a ride didi?"

"No, I mean …." She mentioned Kailash.

"You are so close to home but lost." He smiled again, shook his head and then showed her the way and she walked into the recess of the narrow lane leaving the vast darkness behind which swallowed the old man and his song.

A dim street light shone over the graffiti of hammer and sickle. The pink boundary wall had white flowers hanging over it. As she gained the footpath Uma realised that Khagen was pacing the street, his shadow swayed agitatedly in the dim light to lengthen over the pavement. Uma hurried forward too, warmed by his familiar sight.

"Babu's back," was all that Khagen said.

Khagen repeated again, "Babu came back a long time ago," as though that was all that mattered.

Kailash stood cold and foreboding.

Uma walked in slowly through the gates of Kailash, pushed opened the front doors and stepped in. Khagen vanished silently into the dark. He would enter the house from the back as always.

* *

Ashutosh's face looked foreboding. His eyes were shut. His tired body reclined in an easy chair. Pishi came into the parlour slowly but looking at the face in repose, paused before speaking. She knew that look. It was used to hold off pity. She knew the sadness hidden in shadows.

Only one lamp was on leaving much of the parlour in desolate darkness. It was dark outside too and cold as well though only

September. Or perhaps it was just she who felt it so. Pishi shivered slightly but even to draw the saree around her body seemed too much of an effort. She felt tired all the time these days. Tired and sleepy. The grandfather clock downstairs struck nine. Uma would be home soon, Pishi knew that. How nice it would have been to have the gangly form of Shivani curled over there in the corner waiting with Ashutosh for Uma. Pishi smiled at the shadows. Your daughter-in-law is fine, she is a very fine girl Shivani, you would have enjoyed knowing her, Pishi muttered and then blinked. There was a shadowy form in that dark corner, wasn't there? Her vision glazed over. Her eyes seemed to water quite often too these days. She glanced at the darkened corner again and thought maybe she could go down to her room and lie down for a while. She would hear Uma come up the stairs. She would get up then for the finishing touch to dinner. Pishi looked at Ashutosh again and her face slowly grew soft. Shivani should have been here with you, Ashu, she thought with compassion.

Shivani. Shivani. Ashutosh kept time with his erratic heart beat. You left me alone to bring up your son. I did what I could. I always tried to make everyone happy and retain peace in Kailash. But evidently it was not enough. Didn't you hear what Rudra had to say today? He got married to get away from Kailash. And his wife has left home, gone out on her own, this one day when I could not send the car, without even bothering to inform me. Slowly Ashutosh withdrew into a duskier melancholy. I don't matter anymore in Kailash, Shivani. I don't matter. Shivani you were the lucky one to have escaped Kailash when you did.

The soft cough tickled past Pishi's throat as though with a will of its own.

"Who is it?" Ashutosh sat up and caught the green gaze on his face from up close, "You? What are you doing here?"

"Khema said that you had not touched your tea. It must be cold. Do you want some more?" Pishi's voice was gentle.

"No. Let it be." Ashutosh shut his eyes.

Still she hovered. "Don't worry. She will be back soon."

Slowly the slackness went out of Ashutosh's body, "So you too know where she has gone."

"She is a good girl too. Like her..." Pishi smiled at the dark where reality loses its hold.

The green eyes stared fixedly at something, or someone, behind him. Almost involuntarily Ashutosh turned too but saw nothing but his bedroom in shadows beyond the door. A bedroom shaded in solitude, emptied of everything it seemed to him tonight; a room, cold and silent but with a repraoch that had gnawed at him. It was too late to do anything by the time I returned to Kailash, he would often say to the shadows in his mind, and the room. And gradually they settled down, so too his disquiet and guilt. So very like peace. Or so it had seemed or so he had wanted it to be.

"Shivani would have liked Uma, Shivani would have enjoyed having her here," Pishi took the name for the first time in front of Ashutosh, of the girl who had won both their hearts.

Shivani. Shivani.

The sound fluttered in Kailash. It seemed to Ashutosh that someone was outside on the staircase, walking.

Shivani. Shivani.

She fell down the stairs. We were in her room that afternoon. Young Rudra's voice whispered into his ears, merging with the chant.

Shivani, Shivani.

But there was no one who heard his cry.

Pishi moved slowly towards the door, Ashutosh stirred by an unfamiliar rage, called out in a firm voice, "Listen, are you up to your old tricks again?"

Pishi turned, "Tricks?"

"Telling tales."

"Tales?"

"I am warning you."

"You are warning me?"

"Stop repeating my words. Yes. I am warning you. You don't wish to be turned out of Kailash in your old age do you?"

With soft steps Pishi came back into the room. Her face puckered as though in concentration. "Turned out of Kailash? By you Ashu? Like a hired hand?"

"You heard what I said. I don't wish to get into an argument with you. Don't forget who you are."

"And who do you think I am? You don't think that I have a right to be in Kailash? You don't think that the Chattos owe me something?"

Uma turned from the stairs. Khema had come out of the kitchen at the sound of Uma's return perhaps. Khema's head was covered and there was a bruise close to her eye, touching her temple. It was red and raw against that smooth brown skin as though some one had caught her by that big knot of hair and banged the head against something hard with an edge. The bruise was not there that morning. Uma's eyes widened. Khema caught her gaze and seemed to draw herself up as she asked, "You are late Boudi, what happened, did you lose the way?"

Uma nodded, "You…."

"I told my….husband and my father-in-law that you had gone out on work and….and when on work one can get late. A woman as well as a man. They did not like it."

"I found it."

Khema sighed suddenly, "What if you had not found it Boudi? What if it was not written in a book? Would all our words been reduced to lies then? Would it mean then that what we know is nothing? What we are doing is…is only a …a game?"

Uma reached out and gripped Khema's hand, "Not for us, surely not for us? And don't we count?"

They looked at each other but both knew that this was not their moment.

Khema asked, "Do you want tea upstairs or shall I start getting dinner ready?"

"I will just let you know." But then Uma added, indeed could not help adding, "We will talk later. Where is Pishi?"

"Upstairs I think. Later. Yes."

They smiled a little nervously sealing the promise and parted ways.

Uma caught the murmur of voices in the parlour from the landing. But the sounds though soft, seemed to have an abrasive edge. She stood hesitating with her hand on the door jamb. A car turned into the drive.

"Owe you?" Ashutosh's voice was deep, "What nonsense are you talking. You are mad. But for my father you would have been scrabbling in the mud or scrounging in the woods for food."

"But for his father my life may have been different."

Ashutosh's heart started beating erratically again. It did not seem to be a good day for fathers.

"His father?"

"Yes. Your grandfather. Neelkantha. The worshipper of the goddess and the false ..."

"You have said enough, you may leave this room now."

But Pishi shook her head as though to shake off the interruption, "The worshipper of the goddess and..."

"Be quiet."

"And what Pishi?" Rudra pushed past a startled Uma inside the room. "Tell us Pishi, 'And', what?' Tell us."

Uma stepped forward too and stood for a moment, Rudra and Uma, side by side by the door.

Pishi turned slightly to glance at Rudra's haggard face and then turned her head away.

Rudra crossed the room to stand by his father. He prompted again, "And what Pishi?"

Pishi stood staring intensely at the dark beyond Ashutosh. She seemed to be seeking someone, or something in the gloom behind them and shook her head slowly.

"Pishi?" Rudra asked again but very gently this time.

But then Pishi turned her back to them as though she had lost her memory. Or courage. Or dignity. Everything. She shuffled with slow uncertain steps towards the door that would lead her out of the parlour.

Uma could not bear to see her broken thus. "Tell us," she said. It came out as a weak uncertain whisper, dying even before it could reach anyone. She swallowed and said again, "Tell us Pishi, whatever you have to say, whatever you want to say."

The white clad form stood still. The room was quiet.

"Didn't you wish to say something Pishi? Say it Pishi. Speak," and then Uma added though she knew not why, "Speak Pishi, for us."

Us?

Pishi lifted her head in a sudden jerky movement.

The word seemed to ring loudly in the sepulchral silence of Kailash.

Pishi nodded and nodded again and then she spoke.

※ ※

The room seemed to have grown darker.

Uma asked aghast, "But why?"

"Chittagong was a seaport. Many ships used to anchor there. A woman was taken by one of them from Portugal. They said that such… visitations were common. She was only one amongst many. Her family took her back but when her child came, she had green eyes."

"You?", whispered Uma.

Pishi smiled. "No I am only the residue. This was a long time ago. Nobody knows when. But periodically a pair of green eyes would show up the family for what it was – no longer pure Brahman but fallen from its kulin status. But they had the arrogance of wealth. Some say it was made through trade with the same Portuguese who had sullied their daughter. But they left their coastal village of the ancestors to acquire a small zamindari inland where it would not be known that their blood was tainted. Generations later, a foolish father of two daughters thought that he could hide the fact.

He married one of his daughters to a young man who sang of the goddess and said that he was a kulin Brahman."

"Neelkantha," said Rudra in a tired voice.

"Yes. Your great grandfather. But the tale of green eyes must have carried and he killed his bride, the girl who was only seven. He squeezed the life out of her. And she only seven."

Uma saw the hands, fair and shapely gathering around a tender neck. The hands seemed oddly familiar, hands that had gathered her own as instructed by the priest a life time ago in the month of May. A transluscent white hand that now revealed the glistening of blood. She shook her head to dispel the image.

"All ravings," said Ashutosh.

"Parul and Bokul. Two sisters. One seven and the other five. Bokul, my grandmother, saw it. She saw her sister Parul being smothered to death. She saw her father bend before the murderer, only grateful that the secret was safe. She did not see her mother leave the house in the dead of the night to plunge in the pond but she knew that the mother could not bear to have the man ensconced in the goddess's temple as the priest when she knew him to be the murderer of her daughter. The mother did not speak. She chose death instead. Bokul spoke, to any one who cared to listen. But... they called it the ravings of a mad mind. She tried to speak of it all her life," Pishi paused, breathless.

The others in the room fought their own demons in the turgid silence.

Uma remembered how she had drawn out Neelkantha's *Chandimangal* from Ashutosh's bed, how she had touched it reverentially and how they had gathered around it in the kitchen in Kailash hoping that it would lighten their days. How could they not see the blood on it?

"Kailash," said Rudra.

But Ashutosh interrupted him, "You cannot judge your ancestors by the standards of your contemporary society."

"But he killed her. He killed a child. And all because..." Uma spoke without thinking.

"Print and potatoes," said Rudra, "Can you imagine Kailash without either? I believe the same Portuguese brought both here. What sin then did a pair of green eyes commit?" And he looked at Uma.

Uma shook her head though she meant to nod. This was not the moment for private apologies. The night of the storm had been left behind.

But not for Rudra though.

"My great grandfather...the great dvija...the nation's poet... murdered...his wife. A helpless child. Does it make a difference to us, or not? Should it make a difference to us or not?

Ashutosh spoke but now as though to himself, "In those days....He was a great poet. Let us remember that at least." A great poet. The words gradually grew in the dark silence of Kailash thick with the press of unseen forms, threatening to banish its shadows and sighs.

"Ancestors. What do we know about all our ancestors? And who did what to whom? We can't measure life like that. We must not. And the dvija was also a great poet. A humanitarian poet. You have said so too, Uma." The baritone seemed to be gathering strength.

Uma bit her lips and looked at Pishi. And then she said though in soft tones, "His, Neelkantha's poetry too. His song, the *Chandimangal*, smothered so many too, the goddesses of women and lower castes. I heard it in the streets but in Kailash...."

"Sanskriti," said Rudra.

Pishi stared with lost eyes into the dark.

A shadow moved.

All but Pishi turned and saw Khema near the door.

"Shall I get dinner ready?"

Pishi stood still.

Then Khema who had never before been in the parlour in the presence of the men of Kailash took a few steps inside and touched Pishi gently on the arm only to cry out, "But you are burning."

"Pishi," said Uma and reached out to hold that frail body and realised that it was flushed with fever. Yet Pishi stood still as though in communion with another world.

"Do you wish to say something? Will you say something?" Rudra asked his father.

"What do you want me to say now?" asked Ashutosh in a broken baritone.

And behind him was the dark recess of the bedroom in which was a bedside table with three drawers and in the last of those drawers was a letter sent on Rudra's fifth birthday.

❊ ❊

Pishi was but a tiny bundle in white on the big bed in the room once occupied by Shashishekhar and Haimanti.

Rudra sat still by her.

The broken images wavered fathoms deep in him. A room with a red floor. A book. Pishi in green and gold. Laughing with, with his mother?

Rudra groped, fumbling, uncertain.

A book.

Did he clutch it to his chest and hide it in the depths of Kailash?

It was so difficult to remember. It had been so easy to forget.

"Forgive me, forgive me, Pishi," said Rudra, "I forgot. It was so easy to forget. Forgive me." He repeated it again and again, like an anguished mantra.

A hand reached up and rested on Rudra's briefly, "We all forget sooner or later." And then Pishi added with a soft sigh, "She reads like your mother." Her eyes shut.

Call the GP, said Ashutosh hovering by the door.

The night deepened.

The grandfather clock downstairs went on measuring the hours.

Pishi stirred.

Her restless eyes roamed the room sliding over the windows and the wall with the portraits of Shashishekhar and Haimanti on it, seeking someone. "Read to me, read …. Did no one speak of her?"

Khema, who had insisted on keeping vigil with Uma, took the wet compress and held it to Pishi's brow. "She wants you to read," Khema urged though her voice was low.

"My grandmother. Loony. Loony…." Pishi rambled, "But she had a lot to say…", the words came hoarse and low and were soon lost. The green gaze clouded. "She did not own a printing press." Pishi drew in her legs as though cold, sighed and grew quiet once more.

Uma, pulling down Pishi's saree to cover the small feet, saw the wound. The small toe was swollen, coloured in hues of ugly yellow and green. Pishi must have stubbed her toe recently, it must have hurt and she told no one. And really no one cared. Maybe Pishi too treated it as a migrant pain in order to hold herself straight. As always. Such pain, such grief and such a small frame. Uma wiped her eye. Kailash did not approve of display of base emotions.

Khema's eyes seemed to be glowing too. But her posture was awkward as she leant over the bed to hold the wet cloth over Pishi's forehead.

"Sit Khema," said Uma without thinking.

Khema shook her head.

"Just sit. Sit on the bed, close to Pishi."

But Khema stayed where she was.

Surprising the two young women, the frail white hand reached out to touch Khema, attempting to draw her forward but clearly lacking the strength. And after a moment's hesitation Khema allowed herself to be drawn.

Pishi turned her head slightly and seemed to pat the bed, gesturing Khema to come a little closer still. The familiar puckish smile grazed her lips as briefly her gaze seemed to take in the portraits on the wall. But in a moment the body was slack again.

Uma leaned forward, "Pishi?"

Uma's voice betrayed her, restricting her words, lumping them in a knot in her throat. The small bony chest rose and fell.

Khema looked at the white hand lying listless on the bed that had drawn her a moment ago and remembered it at work, stirring, stoking, shaping, sorting… Gently she gathered the frail hand and pressed it between her own, "Get well Pishi, get well soon."

Pishi opened her eyes.

Khema looked into the green eyes that seemed so tired and she bent forward, freed her hand and smoothened gently Pishi's sparse white hair from the forehead. "You are so fair Pishi, of a gentle breed but you always reminded me of my mother. She was also… tough… she had to be. A woman alone…"

Uma felt a soft stealthy breath upon her nape.

But perhaps it was only the wind touching her hair.

Khema continued to whisper to Pishi, "There is no one to match your berry pickle Pishi. I have always loved berries. When you gave me some to taste the other day I thought of the…."

Pishi raised her head slightly. "Tell me," came the whispered words from Pishi. "Tell me what you thought that day…?"

"You gave some pickled berries to taste the other day remember? It brought to my mind the old Berry Tree. You see there is this Berry Tree near the pond in our village. My mother always said that our deity resided in it. I have heard that years ago a woman of the village was betrayed. Her spirit…"

A tremor seemed to run through Pishi's body, "It is easy to forget. Simpler. Sometimes to love and sometimes to live. But remember her, remember," she said.

Her. Her?

The night breeze ruffled the curtains.

Shadows stirred in the dimly lit room. Darkening the portraits on the wall.

The ghosts gathered in the shadows.

Uma touched and held Pishi's saree.

Pishi's breath came in short rasping rattles. Flecks of foam appeared at the corner of her lips.

Kailash waited. Uncertain.

❋ Afterword ❋

The slaying of the demons by the goddess is narrated in the Devi Mahatmya, the 13th chapter of the Markandeya Purana, the text that most influenced the Saktas in Bengal. The Devi Mahatmya does not depict the militant goddess as wife but in the Pauranic narration that brackets the section she is a generic deity identified as the consort of Siva. Thus the militant goddess is inscribed within marriage. The Charjyapad, arguably the earliest literary composition in Bengal, repeatedly mentions female deities called Chandali or Dombi. The Chandimangals represent the idealisation of the mother goddess in medieval Bengal and remain till the 18th century one of the most popular tales in circulation in Bengal. Male poets, overwhelmingly upper-caste, composed the Chandimangals and gave shape to the mother goddess by sifting and selecting matter from the religious canon as well as folk material. Another group of texts, also in praise of the goddess, proliferates from the latter half of the 18th century though a couple of manuscripts have been found that date back to the 17th century. In literary reference catalogued as Durgamangal, these more or less follow the Markandeya Purana.

The Chandimangal of the Chattopadhyays, Kynsa mati or Kailash do not exist. But it seemed to me that Neelkantha, his song and his family may well have existed given the historical and social matrices. Thus grew the rest of the cast and their local habitations. Books that were invaluable in creating this world are acknowledged below.

For the Goddess and her Stories

Bharatchandra-Granthabali, Brajendranath Bandpoadhyaya & Sajanikanta Das(ed.) (1943, Calcutta: Bangiya Saahitya Parishat1962)

Bhattacharya, Ashutosh. *Bangla Mangalkabyer Itihas* (Calcutta : Modern Book Agency, 1942).

Bhattacharya, N. N. *History of the Shakta Religion* (1996, New Delhi: Munshiram Manoharlal Publishers Pvt. Ltd., 1974).

—— *The Indian Mother Goddess* (1970, New Delhi: Manohar, 1999).

Dasgupta, Shashibhushan, *Bangla Mangalkabye Debi*, Sahitya Parisat Patrika, 65th Yr., Vol. I, 1958.

Dvija Madhav Racita Mangalchandir Geet. Sudhibushan Bhattacharya (ed.) (Calcutta University: Calcutta,1965).

Dvija Ramdev Biracit Abhayamangal. Ashutosh Das (ed.) (Calcutta: Calcutta University,1957)

Kabikankan biracit Chandimangal. Sukumar Sen (ed.) (1975, New Delhi: Sahitya Akademi,1993).

Markandeya Purana, F. Eden Pargiter (Trans. with notes), Bibliotheca Indica: A Collection of Oriental Works (Calcutta: The Asiatic Society of Bengal, 1904).

Mukhopadhyaya, Tarapada, *Charjyagiti* (Calcutta: Viswabharati Granthanbibhag, 1972).

Ramananda Jati biracit Chandimangal, Anilbaran Gangopadhyay (ed.) (Calcutta: Calcutta University, 1969).

Sardamangal ba Astamangalar Chatusprahari Pachali. Abdul Karim ed. (Calcutta: Bangiya Sahitya Parishat, 1917).

Hajar Bacharer Purana Bangla Bhashaye Baudha Gaan O Doha. Sastri, Haraprasad (ed.) (1916, Kolkata: Bangiya Sahitya Parisat,1959).

Shri Shri Brhmavaivarta Purana, Subodh Chandra Mukhopadhyay (trans.) (Calcutta: n.d. National Library entry date 1933).

Vrhaddharma Purana. Haraprasad Sastri ed. Bibliotheca Indica: A Collection of Oriental Works. New Series, No 668 (Calcutta: Asiatic Society of Bengal, 1888).

For Kolkata and its Stories

Bandopadhyay, Chittaranjan (ed.) *Dui Shataker Bangla Mudran O Prakashan* (Calcutta: Ananda Publishers Pvt. Ltd, 1981).

Bandopadhyay, Sekhar. *Caste, Protest and Identity in Colonial India: The Namasudras of Bengal, 1872–1947* (Surrey: Curzon, 1977).

Banerjee, P. *Calcutta and its Hinterland – A Study in Economic History of India, 1833–1900* (Calcutta: Progressive Publishers, 1975).

Campos, J.J.A. *History of the Portuguese in Bengal* (Patna: Janaki Prakashan, 1979).

Chaudhuri, K.N. *Trade and Civilization in the Indian Ocean: An Economic History from the Rise of Islam to 1750* (New Delhi: Munshiram Manoharlal, 1985).

Chaudhuri, Sukanta (ed.), *Calcutta: The Living City* (New Delhi: Oxford University Press, 1990)

Chaudhury, Sushil and Morineau, Michel. *Merchants, Companies and Trade: Europe and Asia in the Early Modern Era* (Cambridge: Cambridge university Press, 1999).

Dasgupta, Ashin. *Merchants of Maritime India* (Hampshire: Variorum, 1994).

Dasgupta, Ashin & Pearson, M.N. (ed.), *India and the Indian Ocean 1500-1800* (Calcutta: Oxford University Press, 1987).

Das, Jibanananda, *Dhushar Pandulipi*, 1936 and *Mahaprithibi*, 1944

—— *Prakashita-aprakashita Kobitasamagra*. Jibanananda Das, Abdul Mannan Syed. compiled and ed. (Dhaka: Abasar, 1994)

Dutta, Kalyani. *Pinjare Bashia* (Calcutta :Stree, 1996).

Gangyopadhyay, Sunil. *Shei Samay* (Calcutta: Ananda Publishers, 1388 B.S)

Ray, Niharranjan, *History of the Bengali People*, John Wood (trans.) (1949, Calcutta: Orient Longman, 1994).

—— *Krsti, Culture, Samskrti* (Calcutta: Jigyasa, 1979).

Ray, Rajat Kanta. *Social Conflict and Political Unrest in Bengal, 1875–1927* (Delhi: Oxford University Press, 1984).

Sanyal, Hitesranjan, *Social Mobility in Bengal* (Calcutta: Papyrus, 1981).

Sarkar, Sumit. *The Swadeshi Movement in Bengal, 1903–1908* (1973, New Delhi: People's Publishing House, 1994).

Sen, Samita. *Women and Labour in Late Colonial India: The Bengal Jute Industry* (Cambridge: Cambridge University Press, 1996).

Sen, Sukumar. *Battalar Chapa O Chabi* (Calcutta : Ananda, 1984).

Sripantha, *Battala* (Calcutta:Ananda Publishers Private Limited, 1997).

Subrahmanyam, Sanjay. *Improvising Empire: Portuguese Trade and Settlement in the Bay of Bengal 1500–1700* (Delhi: Oxford University Press, 1990).

Tagore, Rabindranath. *Sancaita* (Santiniketan: Viswabharati, 1931).

—— *Gitabitan* (1339 B.S. Santiniketan: Viswabharati, 1407 B.S.)

❊ Acknowledgments ❊

Debasish Chatterji was the first to whom I confessed my desire to tell this story. He believed that I could do it. And Sabyasachi (Zap) Sengupta said that I should.

Shampa Roy, Partha Sengupta, P.K. Datta, Indira Prasad and Manju Kapur Dalmia gave time and suggestions that helped shape the story.

Afreen Sen Chatterji, Binata Sengupta and Aparna Yadav infected the project with enthusiasm.

Sundari Shrikant, Kumkum Roy, Ira Singh, Deepika Tandon and Sudha Tandon encouraged it on its way.

Urvashi Butalia helped unfold it.

I thank all of you for your generous and critical considerations.

❊ ❊

My biggest debt however is to Sharmila Purkayastha, Bharati Jagannathan and Bishakha De Sarkar.

Truly but for them this book could not have been.

To you three I owe more than words.